The Regulars

The Regulars

Georgia Clark

SIMON & SCHUSTER

London · New York · Sydney · Toronto · New Delhi

A CBS COMPANY

First published in the USA by Emily Bestler Books / Atria Books,
an imprint of Simon & Schuster, Inc., 2016
First published in Great Britain by Simon & Schuster UK Ltd, 2016
A CBS COMPANY

This paperback edition, 2017

1 3 5 7 9 10 8 6 4 2

Simon & Schuster UK Ltd
1st Floor
222 Gray's Inn Road
London WC1X 8HB

Simon & Schuster Australia, Sydney
Simon & Schuster India, New Delhi

www.simonandschuster.co.uk
www.simonandschuster.com.au
www.simonandschuster.co.in

A CIP catalogue record for this book
is available from the British Library

Paperback ISBN: 978-1-4711-5324-2
eBook ISBN: 978-1-4711-5325-9

Printed and bound by CPI Group (UK) Ltd, Croydon, CR0 4YY

Simon & Schuster UK Ltd are committed to sourcing paper
that is made from wood grown in sustainable forests and support the Forest
Stewardship Council, the leading international forest certification organisation.
Our books displaying the FSC logo are printed on FSC certified paper.

FOR LINDSAY,
MY EVERYTHING

Part One:

Foundation

1.

Despite her mother's impassioned insistence to the contrary, Evie Selby had never thought of herself as beautiful. There were moments when she felt cute: some high-angle, low-light selfies that made her dyed black hair and small, intent face look pixieish, even sweet. There were moments when she felt cool: the day she started wearing the thickest black-rimmed glasses she could find, the night a line of poetry was inked into her pale forearm. But beautiful? No. That was the domain of women with evenly placed, oversized features, with hair like horses' manes and bodies like foreign sports cars: angular, flashy, quietly powerful. Women like the smirking, self-satisfied model who was emblazoned on one of the glossy page proofs that were tucked under her arm. If only she had a quarter, a fifth, an eighth of that woman's allure, Evie might feel more confident about tonight's date.

Stop it, she instructed herself. She pushed her glasses up her nose and drew in a breath of summer-thick city air. *You are a goddess. You are a catch. You are, like, the outcome of every self-help book ever written. And*, she realized on checking the time, *you are also late.* She was supposed to be at the Wythe Gallery three and a half minutes ago.

Despite what those on the happily coupled sidelines might think, 99 percent of online dates weren't exciting enough to be fun or nerve-racking enough to be adventurous. They were just . . . awkward. Boring. An hour of small talk with someone you'd think twice about saving from a burning building. Online dating was like Russian roulette. Mostly misses. But sometimes, *people Evie knew* had met that all-too-rare bullet: a smart, aesthetically pleasing New Yorker who was still single. *Maybe tonight*, Evie thought, *is the night I blow my brains out.*

The gallery was only half full. Even though it was a Monday, she'd been expecting a bigger crowd, if only from the cachet of Willow's last name. A mere smattering of Brooklynites clad in sheer skirts and vintage bow ties stood chatting in front of her friend's pocket-sized experimental photographs. And they all seemed paired off. Everyone except one girl on the other side of the room. About Evie's height, but thinner, smaller. Dark hair fell to her shoulders. She was dressed simply in a T-shirt and skinny jeans. When she turned to look at a photograph, Evie's jaw loosened.

Totally cute.

Totally Ellen Page–y.

Impossibly, Quinn was even more attractive in person.

Panic coursed through Evie's veins. *I should have worn an A-game dress.*

She needed booze. A small bar offered wine and beer. Willow's boyfriend, Mark, was playing barkeep.

"Hey." She dumped the proofs onto the folding table. "Can I leave these here? Is my makeup okay? What white wine do you have?" She shot another look at Quinn, not yet ready for eye contact.

"Evie, hey." The tall, bespectacled boy gathered his replies quickly. "Yes, yes, and sauvignon blanc. Rough day at the office?"

Evie shook her head. "Date." She nodded at Quinn.

"Ah." Mark handed her a cup. "Fun."

"Nervous."

"Unnecessary."

"Lying."

"Untrue!"

Evie cracked a smile.

Mark grinned. "Go get 'em, tiger."

Evie grabbed another cup for Quinn and began walking over, trying to quell the irritating kick of nerves. "Quinn?"

At the sound of her name, the girl turned, revealing a moon-shaped face, and eyes that seemed more round than oval. Clear skin. Sweet smile. "Evie?"

"In the flesh," Evie said, trying not to think about her own less-than-clear skin, her own less-than-sweet smile. "Hi."

"Hi."

"Hi," Evie said again, inwardly kicking herself for sounding like a robot. She offered Quinn the cup. "Thirsty?"

"Actually, I don't drink. I don't need to drug myself to enjoy life."

Evie blinked. *Fucking online dating—*

"I'm kidding." Quinn grinned and plucked the wine from her hand. "Thanks."

"Oh." Evie breathed laughter. Online, Quinn was acerbic and difficult to pin down, qualities Evie found as attractive as the warmer, less artfully constructed person standing in front of her.

Quinn glanced around. "This is your friend's opening?"

"Yeah. Willow Hendriksen." Only now did she spot Willow pressed into one corner, walled in by some intense arty types. Her formless green silk shift and light ash-blond hair colored with a hint of pastel pink gave the twenty-two-year-old the look of being slightly untethered. There was something distinctly ethereal about Willow Hendriksen, like she might transform into a flock of birds if you snapped your fingers. "That's her."

Quinn looked at Willow as if she was nervous to get caught doing so. "That's Matteo Hendriksen's daughter, right? The filmmaker?"

Evie nodded. "Mm-hmm."

"Wow. Cool. Have you met him?"

"Yeah." Evie nodded again, warming to the fact Quinn seemed impressed by this. "Sure. He's not in the States much these days. But Willow still lives at home, so when he's around, we hang. We chill. We're chill buddies." Evie winced. *Did I really just say chill buddies?*

"God, I can't imagine what that must be like," Quinn said. "Having created so much great art that people like and respect."

What Evie couldn't imagine was how she was in Quinn's league. "So, you're a musician?"

Quinn shrugged. "Trying."

"You sound like you'd have a great singing voice. And you have a great look."

Quinn smiled in pleased surprise. "Thanks." She moved to the next photo. Evie trailed her. "Someone just told me what you spend most of your time doing is actually what you do. Like, if you say you're an actor, but you just go to one audition a week and spend most of your time working as a server, then you're a server. I did the math, and hey, turns out I am a musician." Quinn smiled up at Evie, almost shyly. "And your profile tells me you're a writer. What do you write about?"

Evie didn't think of herself as a writer in the way Quinn was a musician. She had a blog called *Something Snarky*, but it was anonymous, and it wasn't what she spent *most* of her time doing. That was being a lowly copyeditor for a women's magazine called *Salty*, fixing typos in stories called "How to Blow His Mind Using the Contents of Your Refrigerator." That wouldn't impress somebody like Quinn. "I write for the *New York Times*." The words fell out of her mouth, as unplanned as a sneeze.

"Whoa!" Quinn laughed a little. "Wow. That's amazing."

"I think they're trying to even out their gender ratio, you know?" Evie improvised, recalling the fact the *Times* had the biggest gender gap in the industry when it came to writers. "It has its ups and downs. Like everything."

"You're a staff writer?" Quinn's eyes stayed wide.

"Yep," Evie said. "I interned there during college, and just started a few months ago."

"Wow. I know I said it before, but that is really impressive." Quinn's eyes stayed glued on Evie's a beat longer than they should have before she slid them away. Warm, liquid desire unspooled slowly in Evie's stomach, like a cat waking up from a long afternoon nap.

"Have you eaten?" Quinn asked.

Evie shook her head.

"Oh good, I'm starving. There's a Moroccan place around the corner. Any interest?"

"Sure." Definitely. Three thousand percent.

"Great. I'll just use the restroom."

Evie slung her purse over her shoulder to go linger at the gallery's entrance. She sipped her wine, actively containing the sheer exhilaration that Quinn's suggestion—more specifically, Quinn's acceptance—had inspired. It had been six months since she'd had sex. The most action she'd gotten all summer was a Pap smear. And while (when done properly) sex could be a whole lot of messy, sticky fun, what she really missed was being kissed. The nervous, enthusiastic, almost-always-botched first kiss, memorable in its imperfection, passionately inelegant. This narrative was leading to that kiss. The meal, the drink after the meal, the amble to someone's subway, the kiss.

Of course, her lie was stupid. But she could always back out of it later. Or hell, maybe she *could* get something published in the *Times*. Sure, she was only twenty-three, but the way Quinn had been looking at her made her feel like she could climb Mount Kilimanjaro without breaking a sweat.

"Evie."

The low, almost musical murmur could only be the lady of the hour. "Willow, hey!" Evie gave her a one-armed hug, pressing her free hand into Willow's sharp shoulder blade. "Congratulations."

Willow smiled wistfully and let her gaze wander around the half-empty room. "I never wanted to be famous because of my name, but this is sort of depressing."

"No, it's not! This is amazing."

"Which is why you're leaving after . . . five minutes?"

"I'm not leaving! I'm just . . . going to a different place—"

Willow waved the excuse off and gave Evie a knowing smile. "Am I witnessing a rare Evie flirt?"

"Indeed you are." Evie couldn't help but grin. "We're getting food."

"That's great. You look really pretty."

"Oh please." Evie rubbed at the dark circles she was sure her glasses accentuated. "I look like someone just punched me in the face."

"Stop it." Willow tugged a lock of Evie's dark hair affectionately.

Quinn's voice sounded behind them. "Your friend behind the bar gave these to me. Wanted to make sure you didn't forget them."

Evie spun around.

Quinn was carrying the *Salty* proofs. The story on top was about va-jazzling. "'*Add some ooh-ah to your hoo-ha.*'" Quinn read Evie's subhead aloud, before fixing her with an odd frown. "Wowsers."

"God, are you still taking work home, Evie? I thought you said you weren't doing that anymore." Willow smiled at Quinn. "I'm Willow."

"Quinn," Quinn replied, but she was looking at Evie. "Work?"

"I've been trying to get her to quit all year," Willow said. "Maybe you can help me stage an intervention."

Evie darted her gaze from Willow, to Quinn, to the pages. Her throat had tightened. "They're not actually *for* me."

"But your name's there." Quinn pointed to the white ticket stapled to the top, reading, "'*Copyeditor: Evie Selby.*'"

"Right." Evie's cheeks were warming. Her breathing had become shallow. "Right."

"Call me later." Willow melted away.

"So you're a copyeditor as well as being a journalist," Quinn said, sounding as if she didn't believe herself.

Shit. *Shit.* "No." Evie's voice was pint-sized. "I mean, I'm just the first part."

Quinn's mouth was ajar, set into a look of bewildered confusion. "You straight-up lied about writing for the *Times.*"

"Actually, I was positively visualizing my perfect future." Evie licked her lips. "It's a very powerful technique."

"Lying?"

"Visualizing."

Quinn's expression became incredulous. All warmth, all interest had been sucked away.

"Please don't go," Evie said. "You're—fuck—you're really cute, and nice, and I am too, nice, I mean. Jury's still out on cute." She was babbling. "I fucked up, I'm sorry."

Quinn backed up a step, slowly, as if not wanting to alarm an angry dog. "Sorry, Evie. This just feels wrong."

Her date exited the gallery, leaving Evie with a plastic cup of wine and a guide on how to accessorize a vagina.

2.

It was after ten by the time Evie finished marking up the proofs. Krista's light spilled from underneath her door. Evie rapped on it quietly.

"Dude, you don't have to knock."

"That's your policy," Evie told her. "Not mine."

Krista Kumar, Evie's diminutive roommate, was burrowed in a mess of blankets and pillows, watching something noisy on her laptop. Balanced precariously on a cushion in front of her were the remnants of a pink-frosted cake. Evie frowned at it. "What's that?"

Krista hit the space bar. "The bakery down the street was chucking it out. I think the box was dented."

"You're eating trash cake."

"I'm eating *cake* cake. It's really good. Want some?"

"No." Evie sank down on the other end of the bed. "Yes."

Krista handed her the fork.

"Was this dinner?" Evie asked.

Krista shook her head, jerking her chin at the half-eaten takeout containers from Sing-Sing Palace, the Southeast Asian joint across the street. On more than one occasion, Krista had described herself as more delicious than their $6.99 lunch special, given the fact her mom was half Malaysian, half Indian, and her dad was Sri Lankan. "How was your date?"

"I got caught in a bald-faced lie and then she left."

"You lied to her? Why?"

Evie mumbled through a mouthful of icing, which she had to admit was pretty good. "Because I'm crazy."

"You're not crazy. You're awesome. Have some more trash cake."

Evie pinched her thigh and Krista yelped like a puppy. Krista *was* like a puppy. No attention span, big on cuddling, and she whined when you left her alone. Which probably made Evie more like a cat: temperamental and snobby.

"Hey, Evie?"

"Yeah?"

"What do you think Amy Poehler is doing right now?"

Evie smiled, settling back into the blankets. "Right now, Amy Poehler is drinking White Russians that she made herself, and she's giving an inspirational speech that everyone's really into. In a hot tub. In Japan."

Krista sighed, happy and envious. "Amy is so cool."

"I know," agreed Evie. "She has the best life ever. Do you have my blue tank top?"

"It might be . . . over there." Krista waved vaguely at one of many piles of clothes on the floor.

"Kris." Evie sighed, finding the now-crumpled top. "Seriously."

"Sorry. I meant to wash it. I'll wash it. Leave it here—"

"It's okay," Evie muttered. "Are you excited for your callback tomorrow?"

"So excited." Krista's gaze drifted back to her computer. "Barely containing the excitement."

Evie eyed Krista warily. It had been seven months since her college roommate had dropped out of law school in Boston and taken the Peter Pan bus to New York to try her hand at "acting and stuff." Evie was still trying to work out if this was to piss off her too-strict, too-controlling dad, because she actually wanted to be an actress, or if Krista just really liked sleeping in. "Have you set your alarm?"

"It's not till the afternoon."

"Do you have money for the Trader Joe's groceries?"

"How much was it?" Krista asked.

"Thirty-five dollars each."

"No."

"You don't have thirty-five dollars?"

"Not on me," Krista said.

"What about Venmo?"

"Evie," Krista groaned. "I'm watching a *movie*—"

"Okay."

Krista rolled her eyes. "I know, Evie. I know rent is due."

Evie balled her blue top into her fist, telling herself the irritation she felt was probably just exhaustion. She slid off Krista's bed. "I didn't say anything."

"You didn't have to," Krista said. "I can see it in your face."

"No face," Evie called, on her way out. "I'm one of those sex people from *Eyes Wide Shut*. No face!"

She heard Krista giggling as she shut her bedroom door. The argument about rent would be forgotten in less than a minute. Whether consciously or not, Krista didn't hold a grudge. And she wasn't judgmental. She didn't see someone's job as a meaningful microcosm of their entire existence.

But Evie did. She sagged onto her bed, letting herself come apart at the seams. There were times when sinking into the familiar contours of depression felt indulgent, even oddly enjoyable. Now it just felt lonely. And sad.

If only she could have a do-over for her date. She could have told Quinn about her blog, or even just the truth about *Salty*, see where that got her. Probably to the same place. If she didn't respect her job, how could she expect someone she was dating to?

She undressed, flicked off the light, and pulled the covers over her head.

Quinn was right. You were what you spent most of your time doing. Which meant she was a junior copyeditor. The lowest notch on the publishing totem pole.

In that deep, dark part of herself that she thought of as her Shame Cave, she knew that meant she was an underachiever.

A failure.

3.

Krista Indrani Kumar had never gotten ready quickly in her life.

The more pressing the deadline, the longer it took—a fashion-related stress response. She had, quite literally, missed her great-uncle's funeral, trying to make all black "work." But she could not under any circumstances miss today's appointment. Today was the day Krista Kumar was booking a national commercial, throttling the hernia of a debt that was haunting her like a fiscally aware ghost. A national network spot would run for twenty-one months, earning her in the vicinity of thirty thousand dollars. Plus it was for Bongo, the multibillion-dollar soft drink that everyone on the planet had heard of, which could only mean more bookings, more work. But somehow, despite having woken relatively early (9:30 a.m.), she was running late for her 1 p.m. audition.

It all started with a run. The thought of a long, healthy jog first thing in the morning seemed like such an in-control-of-her-life move it simply had to be done. She'd woven joyfully around the hipsters and dog walkers and hipsters who were dog walkers, popping by one of the better cafés on the loop back home for a double-shot soy latte with her last five dollars. Her happiness only vanished when she realized she'd forgotten her key. She buzzed Ben, their downstairs neighbor: no answer. Evie was already at work in Midtown. Then she remembered the fire escape. The kitchen window was always unlocked.

She had to drag the black plastic trash can under the bottom of the ladder and hop up onto the trash inside to reach; unbelievably disgusting. The ladder was rusted into place, but after a few tugs, she got it down. Climbing up onto the fire escape was a certifiable victory, and warranted a brief victory dance.

The kitchen window was locked. Krista tugged uselessly, mild panic becoming very fucking real panic. She needed to get in. The only other thing on the fire escape was a dead plant.

In a heavy ceramic pot.

Her first attempt spidered the glass. The second attempt broke through. Her heart snapped at the sight of the familiar little kitchen, as if she'd been gone for years, not minutes. The third, fourth, and fifth attempts managed to clear the glass.

She was out of the shower by noon, but outfit selection was a different story. Everything was stained or crumpled or silly or too sexy or not sexy enough. And then came makeup, which was just like cocaine: you always need a little bit more. But somehow, miracle of miracles, she was finally done: 12:40. It was half an hour on the subway into Midtown, maybe a pinch more. She'd only be a few minutes late. She grabbed her tote, slammed the door, and took the stairs two at a time, barreling straight into the two policemen at the bottom of the stairs. They'd received a report from a neighbor about someone breaking in.

It took Krista *forty minutes* to convince the cops she had broken into her own apartment. Forty minutes of nervous babble and bills with proof of address and three forms of ID and in the end, straight-out begging.

By the time she was at the subway it was 1:20. She was supposed to be there twenty minutes ago. Lightning bolt: she'd get an Uber. Four interminably long minutes passed before the black town car rolled up. Once inside, she called Dale, her agent. He picked up on the second ring. "Where the hell are—"

"I'm in a car." She lit a cigarette. "Five minutes."

"You're meant to be here now!"

"No smoking!" called the driver.

Krista swore and threw her cigarette out the window. "Can you bump me down the list? Tell them I just had surgery. Something elective."

"No." She could practically see him rolling his eyes. "Just get here."

Dale hung up. The car swung onto the Williamsburg Bridge. And stopped. Ahead of them, a sea of cars. All motionless.

"No!" Krista thumped the window.

"No hitting!" the driver yelled.

It took *forever* to get across the bridge. She screened two back-to-back calls from her dad, both times suffering an ax wound of anxiety: she'd pay for that exponentially. To say her parents were disappointed with her decision to ditch law school was like referring to the Incredible Hulk as peeved. Dale texted three times. She could only bring herself to reply to the last: **coming!! don't let them leave** 🍦 🍩 😭 🙌

Dale's office was on Seventh at Forty-Fourth Street, but by the time they just missed a green light at Thirty-Fifth, she couldn't take it anymore. After jumping out of the town car, she was off, racing up Seventh Avenue like an action hero en route to stopping a bomb. "It's okay," she panted to herself. "I'm only an hour late, they have plenty of people to see, Dale'll fix this, these things always run late—"

She burst into the foyer of Dale's building and jabbed the up button viciously. Clever Casting was on the twenty-fifth floor. She was basically there. She'd made it.

A handful of high-energy girls in heels jostled into the elevator with her, and hit the button for the twentieth floor.

"I can't believe you scored an invite to this," bubbled one girl.

"I know, right?" gushed another. "VIP!"

Krista's ears instinctively pricked. What was VIP?

The elevator doors slid open onto the twentieth floor. It was open-plan, like Clever Casting. But it wasn't an office. The entire floor was filled with mismatched racks of clothes and shoes and buckets of bags and belts. Taped to the open glass doors leading inside was an A4 sheet of paper with the words VIP Gilt City Sample Sale.

Krista's mouth went dry. Sweet baby Jeebus. This was not happening.

The girls squealed, exiting the elevator en masse. A woman with a clipboard was checking their IDs, asking, "You're all together?"

The girls chorused, "Yes."

Krista was behind them. Holy shit, she didn't even remember following them out of the elevator.

The woman with the clipboard wandered off. The girls began snatching at clothes, gasping in delight.

No. What the hell was she doing here? She had to get to her audition. It didn't matter that Gilt City curated designer bargains, and that a sample sale would be cheaper still, that was not *relevant* right now. Krista spun on her heel, determined to leave. And that's when she saw it. A red silk dress with a flirty flared skirt hitting right above the knee and a scoop neck she could already tell would reveal just the right amount of boob. A Zac Posen. The original price on the tag was $2,590. This was crossed out. The dress was forty dollars. *Forty fucking dollars!*

Her credit card debt flashed in her mind's eye: a gargantuan number that kept increasing with frightening speed. Desire and regret and an uncontrollable naked need collided hard in her chest. She had absolutely no money, so of course she shouldn't get the dress, and she was already so late.

Well, exactly. She was already late. And there was no difference between being an hour late and an hour and ten minutes late; none at all. And this was literally a once-in-a-lifetime opportunity. Literally. From $2,590 down to $40 was a savings of—Krista quickly did the math in her head—98 percent. She was basically *making* money by buying it. And most important of all, it would be perfect for the audition. Absolutely *perfect*.

Fuck it. This would take five minutes, tops. Krista snatched the dress off the rack, head whipping around for a changing room—ooh, shoes!

Forty-five minutes later, she skidded into Clever Casting, simultaneously ecstatic with her purchases, terrified at facing Dale, and nervous about the audition itself. She was breathless addressing the receptionist. "Hi, I'm here to see—"

"Krista Kumar." Dale strode toward her, eyebrows drawn. His shoulder-length hair was slicked back into a ponytail and he had an animal on a leash. Something wiggling and furry and gross.

"What the hell is that?" Krista backed up a step.

"This is Willis." Dale scooped the furry thing up. Its body was distressingly long and overly flexible. "He's a ferret."

"Why do you have a ferret?"

"My therapist told me to get a dog, but I really identified with a ferret. Didn't I, Willis?" Dale slipped into baby talk. "Didn't I identify with you?"

Krista suppressed the urge to gag. "Where are the Bongo people?"

Dale made a kissy face at the ferret, which squiggled wildly, tiny claws pawing at the air. "The Bongo people are gone, Krista. The Bongo people are gone."

"What?"

"You're two hours late. They cast someone else."

"But . . . But . . . I was locked out of my apartment. And the car was stuck in traffic. And—"

"I don't think this agency is a good fit for you, Krista."

"What? What do you mean?"

"Take Willis. If he wants something, he goes after it. He's focused. Determined." He fixed her with a disapproving gaze. "Everything that you're not. Don't bother calling me again."

Dale and the ferret ambled off, leaving her alone.

Alone.

Broke.

And . . . fired.

A phone rang, the receptionist answered, and someone rushed past her with a stack of DVDs.

Krista dropped her tote on the floor and started to cry.

Even though it was a brilliant late-summer afternoon, the inside of McHale's Ales was so dark and dingy you'd be forgiven for thinking it was the dead of winter. Krista dragged her sorry ass onto a stool and ordered a whiskey.

Her head was throbbing. Her nose was stuffy from crying. She'd fucked the commercial. How was she going to explain it to Evie? Evie. She dropped her face into her hands and groaned as she remembered breaking the kitchen window. Oh god, and she'd gotten an Uber across the bridge. An Uber! She couldn't even afford toilet paper. And then the shopping . . . And getting fired . . . Her overwhelming stupidity pressed her facedown on the bar. The red dress she was wearing suddenly seemed like a massive red flag. She was a fuckup, no doubt about it. A total and complete—

"Krista?"

That'd be right. You never run into anyone you know in Manhattan unless you've been crying. Krista squinted wearily in the direction of the voice. An elegant blonde in a low-cut black silk jumpsuit was sitting at the other end of the bar. Full, pink lips were turned up in a smile of recognition. Krista had never met anyone who owned a low-cut black silk jumpsuit, let alone someone who looked like a goddamn supermodel in it. "Yeah?"

"Krista!" The woman beamed at her. "You don't remember me." She slid off her stool, picking up a leather traveling bag that looked as expensive as the jumpsuit. Her smile was generous and forgiving. "Penelope. We took an improv class together at UCB, earlier this year. Oh, you were so funny."

"Thanks?" Krista tipped the whiskey that had appeared before her to her lips.

Penelope alighted next to her. "Do you still do it?"

"Do what?"

"Improv. Oh, you were such a scream."

"Sometimes." Krista rubbed her eyes. "I can't really afford classes right now."

Penelope cocked her head. "What's wrong?"

"I . . . Oh man, I am having the worst day. If there is a God, she's taking a big ol' dump on Krista Kumar."

"Do you want to talk? I'm a good listener." Penelope's voice sounded like torn silk.

Without planning to, Krista unleashed. She started with being late to the commercial, but in no time, it became about everything: the lack of auditions, the crappy temp jobs, the blah blah sex life, the crippling debt that not even her best friend knew about—everything. It felt so good to just *talk*. Penelope kept listening, making sympathetic little noises that were actually really comforting. "I could've seriously banked today," Krista moaned. "But I blew it. I ruined it, like I ruin everything. I'm such a fucking *idiot*—"

"You're not an idiot." Penelope squeezed Krista's shoulder. "You're not. You're really sweet. You really helped me in that class, made me feel more confident onstage." Then, almost as an afterthought, she added, "Not everyone was so nice to me back then."

"What class?" Krista peered at the woman, buzzing a little from the whiskey, but feeling certain when she said, "I've never taken a class with you. I'd remember."

Penelope ran her tongue over her top lip. She was thinking, but it looked sexy. But then again, she'd probably look sexy cleaning a toilet. "I've changed since then," she said finally. "Let me buy you another drink."

Krista sat up, now certain she had never met this kind, pretty woman before in her life. "Who the fuck are you?"

Penelope leaned toward Krista, eyes wide and empathetic. She smelled like roses and champagne. "Someone who's doing you a favor."

4.

Greetings Snarksters,

Riddle me this: Why is spending a weekend eating cheese puffs and casually masturbating while binge-watching *OITNB* considered "depressing" when you're single, and "romantic" when it's with another person? And why can't I find someone to do it with?

Not that I haven't been looking. Like half the US population, Madame Snark is contributing to the trillion-dollar industry that is online dating. But TBH, I'm not sure how I feel about it. Sure, dot-com dating has increased our choices and availability, but aren't choice and availability the central tenets of capitalism, the siren song of the rich white assholes ruining our planet? And if there are so many people out there to potentially choose me, *why aren't I getting chosen*?

The central paradox of online dating in your twenties is the need to sell yourself while working out who, exactly, you are. No one has any idea who they are, which results in dating profiles that are a confusing mix of projections, sleight of hand, and straight-out lies. But of course, that isn't necessary if you're a vanilla blonde with milk-jug tits and a mouth like a raspberry popsicle. You could list your ideal vacay destination as Alcatraz and you'd still fill your, ahem, inbox. The selves we spend so much time cultivating are reduced to the sum total of a profile pic. It's meritocracy as imagined by Disney. Think I'm exaggerating? In a recent study, 49 percent of online daters said physical characteristics were the most important factor when it came to a potential mate. Which means my lack of pen pals distinctly relates to my visage.

But a marshmallow stomach and Mole Man eyesight isn't who I am.

Evie considered the words on her screen. The tip of her tongue touched her top lip in concentration. Then she added, *Or is it?*

Around her, the open-plan *Salty* offices hummed with afternoon activity. Phones trilled. Hushed conversations were punctuated with occasional squeals. The new Rihanna album played low on the stereo, sexy and threatening.

Evie's coworkers were a sleek testament to blowouts and the art of accessorizing. Why the staff of a magazine needed to look as good as the airbrushed models in it, Evie did not know. Nevertheless, today was the monthly features meeting, so she'd made a special effort with a vintage black blouse and her most flattering pencil skirt. Plus the mandatory mask of makeup. When she first started, Evie rarely wore makeup to work. Around week three, the beauty editor, Bethany, dropped off a small pot of concealer and a pink lipstick.

"Are these for a spread?" Evie asked, blinking behind her thick-rimmed glasses.

"No," Bethany replied, smiling indulgently. "For you. From me."

"Oh. Thanks. But—"

"But what?"

"I don't wear a ton of makeup." This was delivered in the tone of someone confessing to a small domestic crime: *I was the one who ate your ice cream.*

"I know." Bethany picked up the concealer matter-of-factly. "This is for your dark circles, and it'll also tone down the redness on your chin. It's amazing, it's really expensive. And this"—she tapped the lipstick—"will give you some color. You know, liven your face up a little bit."

Evie picked up the products, trying to will away a flush of humiliation. She had a nonlivened face. A dead face.

"You can take anything you want from the red beauty cupboard," Bethany added, pointing at it. "That's where I put things after I'm done. Seriously," she added. "Anything. Mascara, blush, eyeshadow . . ." She studied Evie's face with the shamelessness of a plastic surgeon. "Lip liner. Definitely lip liner."

"Okay," Evie said. "I guess I'll check it out."

"You're more than welcome." Bethany gave Evie's arm a squeeze. "We girls have got to look out for each other, right?"

"Right," echoed Evie, thoroughly unsure if that was what had just happened.

Now Evie sat at her computer with semiexpertly applied foundation, concealer, blush, eyeshadow, mascara, and lip gloss, toeing the line of *Salty*'s professional femininity. The click-clack of heels sounded behind her. Evie switched her screen from her blog to an InDesign file seconds before the deputy editor, Ella-Mae Morris, appeared by her desk. "Hey, Evie."

"Hey, Ella-Mae." Evie smiled uneasily. There was something a little unhinged about Ella-Mae, which Evie put down to perfectionism manifested as a mild eating disorder. Above her computer, the twenty-eight-year-old had a little printed card that read "I can have it if I want it, but do I really want it?" which meant all she wanted was baby carrots.

"Did you finish those beauty proofs?" Ella-Mae's voice was high, oddly childish.

"Yup, finished them last night." Evie handed her the corrected proofs. "And for the title for the guide to Skype sex, I thought of 'Girls on Film,' 'Lights, Camera, Bedroom Action,' and 'Ready for Your Close-Up?' "

"Mmm." Ella-Mae took the stack delicately. "I can't remember," she continued. "Who was going to transcribe the Real Girl story about the woman who had plastic surgery to look like Blue Ivy?"

"You told me to do it," Evie said. "But technically it isn't actually my job to transcribe things, so—"

"Oh great," Ella-Mae said, handing Evie a silver dictaphone. "Losing my mind."

"Maybe you should eat more," Evie murmured.

"Huh?"

"Nothing." Evie smiled brightly. "Hey, did you know 'huh' is one of the only words that's the same in every language?"

"Huh?"

"Exactly. It's basically the same meaning and sound in Mandarin and indigenous Australian languages and a bunch of others. Which makes it an argument for language being a social interaction as opposed to, you know, anything biologically inherent."

Ella-Mae regarded Evie curiously, as if she were a baby carrot she wasn't sure she wanted or not. "That's interesting," she said in a way that meant, *You are so strange.*

"I'll email you the Blue Ivy transcript," Evie said.

"Thanks," Ella-Mae said. "I'm going to freshen up before the features meeting."

"See you there." Evie slapped a smile on her face, letting it drop as soon as her deputy editor turned her back. She didn't want to dislike Ella-Mae. She wasn't a bad person. Evie just had nothing in common with her, and everything she said and did was irritating. Despite putting hundreds of miles between her sur-blah-ban Chi-Town high school and her current place of employment, somehow the *Salty* office found Evie back on the playground: invisible and irrelevant.

Evie pinched the skin between her eyes. She could not get last night's date out of her head. Quinn's words circled, obsessively, dementedly on repeat. *"What you spend most of your time doing is actually what you do."* If this was true, and Evie was pretty sure it was, then she really was nothing more than an overworked underling who made second-rate sexual puns.

Maybe it was time to raise the bar.

. . . .

The monthly features meeting for what would be the November issue took place in a glass-walled conference room. *Salty*'s various section editors, the art team, and the other copyeditors were seated around a large oval table. Evie hovered next to the fashion editors, Gemma and Rose, breakable china dolls who lived on cigarettes and green tea. "Can I squeeze in next to you? I need to be close to the door in case of a snack-related emergency." They both gave Evie a smile that didn't reach their teeth or eyes, and wordlessly slid their chairs over to make room. A bone-deep feeling of being the odd one out—the last one picked for dodgeball, the first one to volunteer to be the designated driver in order to score an invite—resurfaced. Evie took a seat, reminding herself to stop making jokes with her coworkers.

The empty seat at the head of the table was reserved for Jan Stilton, their editor-in-chief. The table tensed as she stalked in, a bone-thin, no-bullshit fortysomething wearing lightweight camel cashmere and a dark, chilly lipstick. In her editor's letter, Jan came across as bubbly and celebratory as champagne. In reality, she was coolly impressive and generally terrifying, like a high-end meat cleaver. She was also extremely British. "Beauty." Jan indicated Bethany. "Let's start with you."

Bethany clacked ten tangerine-colored fingernails together in breathy excitement. " 'Law of the Jungle.' 'Survival of the Fabbest.' How to do a perfect smoky cat eye. How to get hair as thick as a lion's mane."

Ella-Mae thought out loud. "Something on Amazonian clay mud masks?"

"There's a new range of henna hair color that's inspired by that lost tribe they just found," Bethany added. "The ones who didn't have language. I thought that could work."

"Speak to Carmen in Marketing," Jan said. "Might get a spend with Revlon's winter campaign."

One by one the section editors pitched Jan their ideas, to which she mostly nodded, firing off suggestions and only occasionally screwing up her face into a *no way* expression. (Jan waged a war on wrinkles, so these were far and few between.)

Of all the section editors, Evie thought Entertainment had the best gig. *Salty*'s name got them into every event in town. Next week, they were going to the launch of *Milk Teeth*, the fifth novel by Velma Wolff, Evie's favorite writer. Evie wasn't that surprised when Jan approved running a few photos from the launch. Not because Velma's books won awards, because she dated Victoria's Secret models. Every semifamous lesbian on the East Coast would be there. This fit *Salty*'s idea of diversity. Famous, gorgeous queer women whom straight women would tweet about turning gay for.

The only section editor not to have any of her pitches rejected was the sex and love editor, Crystal. She'd been at the magazine for ten years and read her notes with the vaguely bored air of someone discussing a weekly shopping list. " '*The Secret Sex Move Even Your Best Friend Won't Admit She's Doing*,' and that's getting fucked up the ass wearing a blindfold." A nod from Jan. " '*Rethinking Oral Sex*,' subhead '*Hint: You're Doing It Wrong*,' and that'll be something about suction." Another nod. "And '*What He'll Never Admit He Wants You to Do*.' And that's sexify his favorite childhood cartoon, so he can fuck you dressed as Wilma Flintstone or April from the *Teenage Mutant Ninja Turtles*."

"Very nice," said Jan, and everyone nodded in thoughtful approval.

After going through the freelance pitches that had come in to fill the ten feature spots, Jan announced they still needed one more story. "Any ideas?"

This was the cue for open discussion. Anyone at the table could make a suggestion. Evie had never had the courage to speak up. She cleared her throat. "Uh, I have a couple ideas."

A table of startled meerkats. En masse, every head swiveled in her direction.

"Evie." Jan sounded as surprised as everyone else looked. "Yes?"

Evie held up a color printout. The table collectively *eewwed* in perverse delight. It was the most recent picture of former child star Lucy De La Mar, whose obsession with plastic surgery had resulted in a lopsided Frankenface. The candid snapshot Evie was holding had recently made the media rounds, with every commentator taking the chance to bemoan how she'd taken her "upkeep" too far.

"What's the angle?" Ella-Mae wondered. "Good nose jobs gone bad?"

"We defend her," Evie said. "The media had a field day with this. But what's interesting is the double standard. Women are told that being beautiful gives us value. But if the pursuit of this compulsory beauty backfires, as it must do because it's an impossible ideal, the media attacks."

"But she's so vain, look at how much work she's had done," sniffed Rose.

"But don't you think that's social pressure? It's unfair. It's like when you let your roots get too long, and everyone calls you Stripey."

"Who calls me Stripey?" Rose looked shocked.

"No one," hissed Ella-Mae, glaring at Evie.

"Next." Jan's voice was ice.

Evie swallowed. "I have one more. It's a feature on how women use social media in protest movements."

Jan arched an eyebrow. "Okay," she said carefully.

Evie warmed with the borderline encouragement. "We start with female Saudi activists who post videos of themselves driving on You-Tube. Maybe 'Driving Miss Dhuka' or 'In the Driver's Seat.' Then we move on to the Arab Spring—"

"Ooh!" Bethany perked up. "A spa feature? Like something that rates the top five day spas?"

"No," Evie said. "The Arab Spring uprising. The protests in the Arab world that started in 2010."

The table morphed into a circle of frowning, doubtful faces.

"Women faced pretty intense backlash, even from their fellow fighters," Evie said. "But they were vital participants, especially online. There's some really awesome bloggers we could reach out to."

Gemma fluttered her eyelashes, voice whispery-soft. "That sounds . . . kind of depressing."

"It's important," Evie said. "It's something that matters to women."

"Right," said Bethany. "But so do day spas."

"Yeah, I think we all liked the day spa idea," added Ella-Mae, scribbling a note.

"That wasn't one of my ideas!" Evie caught herself, tried to reestablish calm. "Guys, this issue is looking great, and I cannot wait to tell some guy he can fuck me while dressed as Smurfette, but maybe we can have a mix of ideas."

"A mix of ideas?" Jan asked.

"Yeah!" Evie exclaimed. "Maybe we can have an opinion on current events and all the sexist shit that's happening in the world. Maybe it's time to raise the bar."

Crickets.

Pissed-off crickets.

Ella-Mae sat back in her chair with a squeaky little huff while Gemma and Rose exchanged incredulous glances.

"Raise the bar—" Bethany began repeating caustically before Jan interrupted her.

"Evie, let's see a one-page on America's best day spas," she said. "Big cities only. Great work today, everyone." She stood, gathering her phone and notebook. Evie sat without moving. Fingers of unease dug under her collar. "And Evie." Jan addressed her from the doorway, face unreadable. "Pop by my office on your way out today."

That had been a mistake.

A huge fucking mistake.

5.

The view from Jan's office rendered New York picturesque and harmless; the city you wanted it to be as opposed to the city it was. As Jan finished up a phone call, Evie wondered if this was the last time she could hold Manhattan at such an arm's length. Krista was chronically unemployed; she was practically allergic to work. And Willow had never worked a day in her life, beyond short-lived waitress stints to try to prove she could make it on her own. Evie couldn't lose this job. It was an adult job, with adult benefits and adult prospects. Having grown up with a single mom, she saw how important each and every shift was to make ends meet. She'd been unemployed for four stressful months in New York before getting the offer to come in for the copyeditor interview, her previous summer interning stint thankfully paying off. The anonymity of being just another arts graduate in a city that was choked with them hadn't just been depressing—it'd been frightening.

Salty had been a life raft. And sure, the magazine was mostly dumb, and yes, it was copyediting, not actually writing. But it was for a magazine even her granddad had heard of, owned by one of the biggest media companies in the world. And now she might have gotten herself fired.

Evie fidgeted, fighting growing panic. How desperate did you have to be before sex work was an option? Evie had tried phone sex last winter: one of Krista's Craigslist temp jobs. When the guy on the other end asked what she liked, Evie blurted out, "*Star Wars!*" and hung up.

Jan ended her call. "Sorry about that—"

"Am I fired?" Evie all but yelled the question. "Because, uh, that would be denying me natural justice." Her memory flapped about, trying to piece together Krista's various just-got-sacked rants. "I don't believe my behavior qualified as 'gross misconduct,' and if you take a look at the terms of my employment—"

"I'm not firing you, Evie." Jan tented her fingertips, the shadow of a smile on her mouth. "I just want to talk. Are you happy here?"

"Yes," Evie said. "Of course."

"I don't mean, are you happy getting a paycheck," Jan qualified. "I mean, are you happy here? Do you like it? Do you like the magazine?"

Evie was expecting Jan to be her usual terrifying self. She twisted a little. "Can I be honest?"

Jan gestured in front of her, as if to say, *be my guest.*

"*Salty* has, what, three million readers?"

"Three and a half."

"That's an amazing platform. That's so many people! It just feels to me like we could really make a difference for girls. Women. Women girls. If it was a bit more . . ."

"A bit more what?"

Evie squirmed. Her face had gone hot. "Well, feminist, I guess."

"You don't think *Salty* is feminist?"

"No," Evie said. "I think it's the opposite. *Salty* is just sex and shopping."

Jan regarded her thoughtfully. "What does feminism mean to you? What does it do for girls? For women?"

Evie answered with the ease of someone who had attended approximately six million Women's Action Collective meetings during her four years at Sarah Lawrence. "Empowers them."

"Makes them feel good about themselves," Jan said. "Liberated. Independent."

"Sure."

Jan scooped up a copy of the current issue. Lauren Conrad simpered at them both from the glossy front cover, one cherry-red fingernail hooked into the plunge of a V-neck T-shirt to reveal a surprising amount of cleavage (Photoshop). For a magazine that generally shunned lesbianism, the cover shots were always confusingly erotic. Readers were supposed to emulate Lauren, never—despite her come-hither pout, her touch-me-now parted lips—feel anything other than friendly affection or requisite jealousy.

Weird.

Jan said, "Tell me what you see here."

Cover lines screamed in neon orange: fashion crazed, hysterically horny. Evie read them aloud with a heavy dollop of infomercial enthusiasm. "*'Eight MUST-HAVE Boots for Fall!' 'How to Make Him BEG FOR IT.'*"

Jan tapped at one of the largest ones: "*'Good Vibes: How to Buy YOUR FIRST VIBRATOR!'*" She cocked a neatly plucked eyebrow at Evie.

Evie had to stop herself from rolling her eyes. "I don't think owning a dildo will start the revolution."

"I don't think most girls want a revolution," Jan said, sounding amused. "I think they want a publication where a healthy sexual appetite is celebrated. I think they want a magazine that teaches them to give and receive sexual pleasure the way sex should be: fun. Adventurous. Nonjudgmental. Where else do you go for that? The internet's a pervy shitshow. You're not going to ask Mum about it. And your friends are probably as clueless as you are, with a collective sexual history of getting fingerbanged at a frat party." This almost sounded like a fond recollection. "I think they want a publication that celebrates the fact that girls love shopping. Fuck what the boys think. Fuck what their parents think. Our magazine says you can spend the money you earned yourself any damn way you like, and here's some options we think are pretty fab. Because that's what feminism did for women. It made us sexually liberated and financially independent. I think," Jan finished, "sex and shopping *are* empowering for our readers."

Evie was speechless. Instinctively, she didn't agree with Jan. But she couldn't work out why not. Somehow, what her editor was saying made sense.

Jan continued, "If you want to work for *Jezebel,* go work for *Jezebel.* But if you want to stay here, I need you on my side." Jan leaned forward across the desk. Her voice was soft and proper. "Our brand is sex and shopping. If you want to work for *Salty*, you need to embrace that. Can you do that, Evie?"

Evie willed herself to say no. *No.* That if Jan wasn't interested in broadening the conversation, in writing about things that mattered—in yes, raising the bar—she was out of there. Because there comes a time in every girl's—in every *woman's*—life when you have to stand up for what you believe in. When you side with morals over money, when you put your foot down and say, "Goddammit. I am *not* going to take it anymore."

This, unfortunately, was not one of those times.

"Yes," Evie said. "Of course."

"Good. Look, you're a great copyeditor and I want you to be happy. I know the spa special isn't exactly what you had in mind. But there might be something coming up you could help with. Have you heard about *Extra Salt*?"

Evie had, vaguely. It was something the digital team was doing: short biweekly webisodes.

"We might need some help researching the stories," Jan said. "Depending on who we cast as a host. Some of the girls have a background in journalism. And some are just . . ." She made a twirly motion with her hand.

"Pretty faces," Evie finished.

"Less experienced."

"So if you cast a pretty face without experience, there might be a job in it for me."

"Exactly," Jan said. "Just short term—don't go burning any more bridges yet."

Evie smiled grimly at her feet.

"We're casting tomorrow and Thursday, up on thirty-nine," Jan continued. "Pop by when you get in."

Evie tried hard to feel excited about this. A new opportunity, a new challenge. But for some reason, she could summon no such spark. How could this be anything other than more of the same? "Okay. I will."

Jan's eyes slid back to her computer screen. "Thank you." The lyrical dismissal signaled Evie's departure. "And Evie?"

She paused in the doorway. "Yes?"

For a second, her editor was just a tiny slip of a woman with incredible bone structure. Hardly threatening at all. "We are doing good work here. You know that, right?"

6.

"Turn your face toward the light a little."

Mark obeyed and moved his head a quarter inch.

"Mmm. Yep. Good."

Willow's camera shutter clicked languidly, the sound of a long exposure.

Mark tried not to move his mouth. "Are you getting the full glory of my Jew nose?"

"It'd be hard not to," Willow murmured.

Mark grinned and took a swipe at her with his foot, managing to hook her into him, pulling her between his legs. He was sitting on a stool in front of a bedsheet Willow had hung up, creating the makeshift studio. A layer of incense smoke wafted close to the ceiling, visible in the afternoon light. Even though Willow's bedroom overlooked Central Park, she'd covered all the windows in swaths of material.

The photographs weren't working. Why not? Willow tried to lull her mind, to have it find whatever it was that directed her hand when she decorated her space. The velvet-covered bed, junky old lamps, and collection of pinned butterflies looked less like a girl's bedroom and more like the studio of a 1920s poet. Creating it hadn't been deliberate: it just came into being. But the room's unearthly aura was eluding her now, refusing to present its essence in Mark's expressions. Maybe it was the fact he was here. Watching her.

The palpable sensation of failure rose in her throat. She swallowed to tamp it down. The thought of Mark offering encouragement right now would only make everything worse. There wasn't a new series idea here. Why did inspiration keep eluding her? Why couldn't she see a way forward?

Mark pressed his face between Willow's small breasts, glasses pushing back against his cheeks. He inhaled deeply and let his breath out with a muted groan. She could tell he was getting turned on. He spoke into her chest. "Tell me something I don't know about you."

Her phone chimed. She stepped out of Mark's arms to reach for it. A text, from Evie. **Just got off subway by you. Krista didn't get commercial and is in weird mood: only wine can save us now!** Willow looked back at Mark. His gaze was too intense for her to sink into it like she knew he wanted her to. Instead, Willow let her eyes drift over his thick eyebrows, down his jaw, and up over the tiny, star-shaped chicken pox scar on his temple. "I got my period today."

"I don't care." Mark's response was immediate. "I really don't."

Willow shifted the heavy camera from one hand to the other awkwardly. "I do."

Mark dropped his hands. "Okay," he acquiesced. "Can I stand up for a second?"

Willow nodded. "I'll import these."

Mark wandered over to her bed and spread out flat on his back. "Prunik asked us over for dinner next Thursday. He and his wife really want to meet you."

Prunik was Mark's business partner. Willow looked over her shoulder at him, half smiling. "Why?"

"To prove you exist. I think Prunik's exact wording in the email was *'You and your imaginary girlfriend are invited for an Indian feast.'*"

Willow froze. There it was. Girlfriend. And even though Mark had been casual, joking, when he said it, Willow still felt it sock her in the stomach.

Mark pulled himself to a sitting position. "I don't want to pressure you or anything. But . . . it's been eight months."

"Seven and a half," she corrected.

He grinned. "You've been keeping count? I thought you said that was stupid."

She blushed and ducked her head. "It is."

Mark got to his feet and crossed the room to crouch next to her. "I'm fine if you're not ready. I really am. But . . ."

"But what?"

"I don't want to sound like a cliché here, but . . . I guess I want to know where this is going. Because if you never want to be my girlfriend, I guess, maybe . . ."

"Maybe what? You'll break up with me?"

"Yes. No. I don't know." He got to his feet, suddenly frustrated. "It's been seven and a half months. I'm here half the week, you're at my place half the week, and everyone at work is always asking about you, how my girlfriend is doing, and I feel like I'm lying when I don't correct them, you know, and I kind of feel like an idiot."

Willow got to her feet and wrapped her small hands around his.

Mark. Solid, reliable, trustworthy Mark. The boy who never cheated on his taxes, let alone a girlfriend—at least, as far as she knew. If she could trust anyone, it would be Mark. But still, something whispered dark and low in her ear that trusting Mark—trusting any man—was foolish. "So ask me."

Realization flickered behind his eyes. He smiled down at her broadly. Then he coughed and cleared his throat, adopting a mock-serious voice. "Willow Alice Hendriksen."

"Yes?"

"Will you be my girlfriend?"

Fear clung to her ribs. She ignored it. "Yes."

Mark kissed her softly. She moved her hands up to his head to tangle them in his hair, and soon they were making out hungrily, like they did when they first started dating. He slid his hands to her ass, which was flat, almost like a boy's. His lips moved down to her neck. She could feel his erection through his pants. He started moving them toward the bed. She resisted. "My period . . ."

He cupped her face in his hands. "So what?"

Willow swallowed. "The girls will be here soon—"

But it was only half a protest. Without warning, Mark moved one arm across her back, one behind her knees, scooping her off her feet. The surprise of it made her squeal, a rare noise, and the two of them stumbled, tumbled onto her bed. Mark's mouth felt like a hungry live thing. An insatiable creature.

"Wait." She extracted herself from underneath him, picking her way past clothes and records to the nearest lamp.

"Leave it on," Mark panted, unbuttoning his fly.

She didn't answer, switching it off, sending the room into early night.

"I want to see you," he complained, horniness making him whiny. He tried pulling her slip off, but she resisted. He kissed her, pushing his tongue into her mouth as if to swallow her whole.

Willow closed her eyes, starting the well-worn mental porn that she both hated and couldn't come without. In her mind's eye, her breasts were freakishly huge, hideously oversized, like two bulbous watermelons strapped to her chest . . .

"Babe."

Above her, Mark's face was open and raw.

"Where are you?" he asked.

"Here." She kissed him, he kissed her back. "I'm here."

"Let's go in front of the mirror."

"What? No."

Before she knew what was happening, he was moving them both off the end of her bed to stand in front of her full-length mirror. Willow was so stunned she couldn't protest when he pulled her slip up, off over her head, his fingers clumsy with excitement. He kissed her neck, rubbing the tip of his cock over her clit. She couldn't feel it. All she could see was her body, splayed like one of the pinned butterflies on her wall.

Mark eased himself inside her. "Look at you," he moaned. "Look how fucking hot you are."

Willow stood inert, staring in horror. Nonexistent breasts that weren't even a handful, that were more male than female. Disproportionately large thighs that quivered like jelly with each thrust. Giant forehead the size of a serving platter. Why did she grow her bangs out?

Mark moaned again, picking up rhythm. "You're so fucking hot."

This was it? This was what he found so erotic—this unspecial collection of limbs and flesh? Not possible. This was *grotesque*. "No." She wriggled.

"Baby." Mark pumped. "Baby, oh shit, I'm going to come—"

"No!" In a panic, she pulled herself from him, stumbling forward and knocking over the mirror.

Mark's eyes rolled in his head before he snapped back, reaching for her, erection enormous, panting, "What? What's wrong?"

Willow ran across the room to a chest of drawers.

"Willow?" He was behind her, but not touching her. "What's wrong?"

"I didn't like that." She found a pair of sweats and pulled them on.

"What?"

She whirled to face him. Every emotion sharpened into anger. "I didn't like that!"

"Fuck, I'm sorry." Mark ran a hand through his hair, bewildered. "Baby, I'm so sorry."

The buzzer sounded from the foyer.

"That's Evie and Krista." Willow rubbed her face, distressed. She didn't want Mark to see her like this; so shaken, so undone. "You should go."

"Can we talk about this?"

"Not now."

The buzzer sounded again, long and insistent. Krista, for sure.

"Can I shower?"

"Of course. I have to buzz them up." Willow paused at her bedroom door. For a moment, she thought she might look back at him, to meet the gaze that she knew was on her back.

She didn't.

7.

They'd met in New York, the summer of 2014. Matteo Hendriksen's twenty-year-old daughter was getting a small write-up in a big It Girl feature in *Salty*, and was in the office to get her photo taken. Evie had only been interning for a few weeks when she'd been tasked with helping the girl pick an outfit. Evie still remembered the look on Willow's face when she knocked on the Fashion Room door, startling her as she whirled around. A pair of bloodred heels dangled from her fingers.

"Sorry, didn't mean to scare you. I'm Evie." Evie nodded at the shoes. "You find something you like?"

"Oh no! Not these. I just wanted a closer look. They're so . . . vicious."

"Jesus." Evie took one of the shoes out of Willow's hand. "You could take someone's eye out with this thing. Death by stiletto." Evie mimed stabbing with the heel.

Willow giggled. "I know, right? I think high heels are kind of masochistic."

"Definitely. Shhh," Evie added, a finger to her lips. "You can be shot for saying something like that around here. Treason of the highest order."

Willow giggled again. When she did her whole face blossomed.

While Willow was trying on outfits, Evie found her website, and was surprised to discover that the shy, pretty blond girl was actually a good photographer. Her work was understated and moody, with flashes of macabre humor. Evie liked the series on a run-down taxidermy shop with signs like 60% Off All Rodents and Shell Animals! while the taxidermist himself bizarrely resembled his stuffed, stiff animal preserves. A few magazines—ones infinitely cooler than *Salty*—had already profiled Willow and published some of her pictures. Evie figured the decision to make Willow an It Girl was a result of this existing approval, Willow's famous father, and her otherworldly attractiveness. When Evie successfully convinced Features to change Willow's profile label from Boho Babe to Aspiring Artist, Willow suggested they meet up for a drink. Without blinking, Willow ordered a Johnnie Walker Black. Evie, unnerved that a sort-of-famous girl was sitting across from her, ordered the same. Over the course of the night, they had two more rounds. When the bill came, Evie was horrified to see it was $108. But Willow didn't even check the total when she handed over a gold credit card. *That*, Evie thought, *is what it's like to have money.*

They spent that summer defying sunshine for dark bars and important conversations about books and art. Willow made Evie feel well-read and insightful. She suspected that was how she was making Willow feel too. She'd secretly Google Willow's name, scrolling through pictures of her at her father's film premieres; an awkward teenager in dresses that probably cost more than Evie's entire wardrobe, wincing at the camera. It seemed so incongruous with the unassuming girl and her curtain of pale blond hair sitting across from her in a divey bar, asking if she'd read *The Handmaid's Tale.*

After Evie returned to Sarah Lawrence for her final year of college, they lost touch. Evie assumed she'd never see Willow again. The only contact she received during this time was a late-night voicemail. Willow's voice sounded wispy in her brief "just wanted to say hey" message. But the most curious part was the background noise. Evie could've sworn it was a hospital.

When Evie moved to Brooklyn after graduating in 2015, she didn't expect Willow to return an email. She did. When they met up for a drink, it was like no time had passed at all. And naturally, Evie didn't bring up the voicemail. Somehow, it all just added to Willow's allure.

Krista hurricaned onto Evie's doorstep at the end of that year, trading law for acting and Boston for New York. Willow invited them both over to the Upper East Side. A foreign land. Evie felt like she'd gone through the Looking Glass and onto a rerun of *Gossip Girl*. While Evie perched nervously on the edge of a cream leather sofa the size of a sailboat, Krista bounced from room to room like a kid on Christmas morning. "Fuck me, this view is amazing! Look how big that TV is! Fuck *off*, you have an indoor pool? Dude, what the *fuck*?"

After some initial awkwardness, Willow got them all wasted on three bottles of Moët, which resulted in a late-night frolic in said pool. That's how she'd first met Matteo Hendriksen. The intimidating Dutch/American director had made the seminal prisoner-of-war epic, *No Time for Tomorrow*, starring Clint Eastwood and Burt Reynolds, which won the Oscar for best director in 1978, and directed Barbra Streisand and Robert Redford in her mom's favorite love story, *Only the Sparrows Know*. He was widely accepted as being a cinematic legend. Evie met him while drunkenly attempting a synchronized swimming routine. But he didn't seem to mind. Later Evie thought he actually seemed pleased Willow had friends.

Now the newness of Willow's digs had worn off, and Evie barely glanced twice at the Warhol in the foyer. It was simply the place Willow lived with her father and his surprisingly cool girlfriend, Claire. Evie grinned at Willow and asked pointedly, "Is Mark here?" Willow's just-fucked vibe was obvious: her hair was a mess and she looked a little dazed. Evie glanced at Krista, expecting her to tease Willow too. But her roommate was already on her way to the living room. Odd.

"My day was pretty weird." Evie followed Krista, slipping off her shoes to stretch out on the sailboat sofa. "I had a recalcitrant moment in our features meeting, which may or may not have led to a new job."

"Oh really?" Willow curled up at the other end of the sofa, pulling a cushion in front of her.

Evie began summarizing her meeting with Jan, stopping only when a wet-haired Mark appeared from Willow's bedroom, messenger bag slung over his shoulder.

"Hey, Markie," Evie sang out.

"Hey, guys." He dropped a kiss on Willow's forehead and murmured something in her ear, to which she nodded.

Willow's so lucky to be dating a guy like Mark, Evie thought idly, rifling through a glass bowl of nuts on the coffee table. Someone interesting and smart, a good guy in a sea of store-brand mediocrity. Plus, he had the whole hot-nerd thing going on. She'd give anything to have afternoon sex be a normal part of her life.

"Have a fun night." Mark waved as he headed for the elevator.

"Bye, Markie." Evie was the only one to wave after him.

The apartment seemed oddly quiet. Willow was staring off into space and Krista, who had usually flipped the cable on by now, was glued to her phone, expression intent. "Whatcha doing?" Evie asked her.

Krista replied without looking up. "Looking for someone."

Evie threw a pecan at her. "Who?"

"Someone I took an improv class with . . . Oh, check it out." Krista glanced up. "Someone added a photo of us from that party in Bushwick."

"I don't remember posing for a photo." Evie scooted down the sofa toward her roommate. That was the night they'd all drunk a bit too much tequila, before Krista made out with a guy wearing a sombrero. "But then again, I don't remember getting home."

"We're not posing," Krista replied. She held up the screen.

In the picture, Krista and Willow were both laughing at something Evie had evidently just said. Evie had a dry smirk on her face, while Willow and Krista's mouths were both open, eyes squinty.

Willow grimaced and looked away, muttering something about needing to get a haircut.

"I am not wearing that dress ever again," Evie said, blanching at the picture. "It's too tight in the stomach, I look like friggin' E.T."

"At least you don't have man arms." Krista tapped at the screen.

"If you have man arms, I have gorilla arms!" Evie exclaimed. "Two meat curtains protruding from my shoulders. And I hate my smile. Me and my handfuls of baked-bean teeth."

Krista and Willow both chuckled, but Evie felt a tiny stab of guilt. They shouldn't be doing this. Dissecting themselves. But the picture was just extraordinarily unflattering. So when Krista announced she was untagging herself, Evie found herself joining Willow in saying she'd do the same.

"How hungry are you guys?" Evie glanced around for the TV remote. "Willing to wait for the good Chinese that takes forever, or is it a bad-Chinese-that's-here-suspiciously-fast night?"

"Holy shit," whispered Krista, staring at her phone. "That's her."

"Who her?" Willow asked.

"Penny," Krista replied, her voice oddly soft. "I knew her as Penny. Penny Baker."

"Huh?" Evie scooted back down to look at Krista's phone. It was a photo of about twenty people, all young-looking and grinning. Krista's hair was long; it must've been from the beginning of the year. A vague memory of an improv class her roommate had taken surfaced.

Krista pointed at a pale, slightly chubby girl who looked more embarrassed than pleased to be posing. "That means . . ." Krista shook her head, confused. "That means . . . she was telling the truth."

"What truth? Kris, what are you talking about?"

Krista looked up at both girls, eyes comically wide. She hopped to her feet and came to stand self-consciously in front of them. "Something happened to me today. Something kind of weird."

"Oh shit." Evie froze. "Are you okay?"

"Yeah, yeah, yeah, nothing like that. I met someone. Penelope— Penny—the girl in the photo. She gave me something. Something . . . big."

"Big?" Evie repeated. "What, like, money?"

"Maybe." Krista bit her lip. "Okay, I'm just going to say it. She gave me this." Krista pulled a small glass bottle from her pocket. It was a few inches tall and filled with purple liquid. "It's called Pretty. It makes you . . . pretty."

Krista seemed so intense and serious that Evie tempered a knee-jerk reaction to make fun of her. After exchanging a quick *what the fuck?* glance with Willow, Evie hedged, "Like . . . like an herbal thing?"

Krista shook her head. "No, like a real thing. This girl Penny used to be—well, you saw her picture. And I met her again today and, dude, she was fucking *beautiful*. And it's all because of this." Krista held the little bottle aloft again. "One drop lasts for one week. It changes you."

"I've heard of this," Evie announced. "It's animal placenta. From Asia. Totally illegal."

"*No.*" Krista stamped her foot. "Not animal placenta. It changes you. Into a different person. A totally different person, that's what happened to Penny!"

"You saw this happen," Willow clarified. "You saw this woman change into someone else?"

"No, she just told me about it."

"She just told you about it?" Evie's frown softened into a smile. She loved Krista, she really, really did. But oh man, sometimes the girl was so mind-blowingly *stupid*. "Babe, I think someone was playing a joke on you." Then, "You didn't give her any money, did you?"

"No! It was a gift. Because I was nice to her. And," Krista added, "I want to try it."

"Don't be dumb, it's probably poison," Evie said. "Can we order? I'm friggin' starving."

"Eve, don't you get it? This makes you pretty. Seriously fucking hot."

"You're asking me to believe in magic?" There was a sharp edge to Evie's tone. Willow slid to her feet to go pluck the little bottle from Krista's hands curiously.

"We don't know how everything in the universe works!" exclaimed Krista. "What about ghosts? Or twins that have ESP? The Phoenix Lights, Evie, what about the Phoenix Lights?"

"Oh my god." Evie laughed without humor. "You're such an idiot."

"Hey." Willow looked up from the bottle to frown at Evie in reproach.

"Well, she is." Evie felt her face start to flush. "Magic is for kids, and besides, you're already beautiful. It wouldn't work, anyway."

"Oh please, spare me the Oprah Winfrey special." Krista rolled her eyes. "Fucking man arms, remember? If this works—"

"What?" Evie challenged. "You'd what? Be happy? Get laid? You're already having more sex than the two of us combined and she's dating someone."

"Evie." Willow's warning was gentle, but her tone just pissed Evie off even more.

Krista stared at Evie. "Why are you getting so angry?"

"I'm not getting angry!"

"If this is true—" Krista continued.

"Which it can't possibly be," Evie interjected.

"We could be freakin' *supermodels*," Krista said. "Like the girls in magazines."

"The girls in magazines are airbrushed," Evie said.

"Not Penny," Krista said. "The difference between her and *her*"— she held up the photo on her phone—"would be like airbrushing Seth Rogen and making him into James Franco."

"Jesus, Krista!" Evie spat the words. "I can't believe you actually think this is real! What's wrong with you?"

"Evie!" Krista thumped the sofa. "Don't you get it? This could change everything for me!"

"Oh, does the magic potion make you get to auditions on time?"

"No, it'd help me actually *get* them." With a jab of surprise, Evie realized Krista was fighting back tears. "I'm so sick of being so fucking anonymous. Casting calls with a million girls all hotter than me."

"I'll try it," Willow said.

"And if I do manage to get something, I'm expected to break out an Indian accent, mid–Bollywood dance. I'm always too Asian or not Asian enough, and when I explain I don't speak any fucking dialect, they just want me to 'make it up.' Do you realize how insulting that is? Like I'm a goddamn *sideshow*—"

"Guys." Willow raised her voice. "I want to try it."

Silence. Evie stared at Willow, horrified. "Are you joking?"

"No."

"But you're—" Evie swallowed her words, but she was sure both girls knew what she was going to say. *But you're the prettiest of us all.*

Willow shrugged. "I want to try it."

Evie shot her eyes from Willow to Krista, then back to Willow. She couldn't tell Willow what to do in the same way she did Krista, and Willow knew it. "But why?"

Willow shrugged, deliberately petulant. "One drop?"

"Yeah, there's a dropper," Krista said before being silenced by a death glare from Evie.

"What, here? Now?" Evie asked.

Willow's voice was cool. "According to you, it won't work anyway."

"It will." Krista scurried to sit right next to Willow, tears forgotten, face suddenly alight.

Willow unscrewed the bottle, then lifted it to her nose and sniffed. "No smell," she told Evie before offering it to Krista. Her eyes were fastened on Evie. "One drop?" she repeated softly to Krista, who nodded with the sort of happy excitement usually invoked by open bars or surprise snacks.

They watched in silence as Willow depressed the dropper carefully, sucking up a line of purple into the clear glass tube. She stuck out her tongue and positioned the dropper over it. Her eyes never left Evie's, as if daring her friend to stop her.

If Willow thinks she should be prettier, then, fuck, what must she think of me? Evie thought.

Evie said, "What are you waiting for?"

Willow squeezed the dropper. As if in slow motion, the girls watched a single brilliant purple drop of liquid fall toward Willow's outstretched tongue. It landed without a sound, instantly disappearing.

Willow winced, swallowing. "Sour." She passed the little bottle back to Krista, who obediently screwed the top shut, staring at Willow expectantly.

A moment passed.

Then another.

Evie realized that, ludicrously, she was actually waiting for something to happen. She almost started to ask if it was supposed to work straightaway or not, but caught herself: that would imply she actually believed Krista. The only noise came from the kitchen, the very faint whir of a dishwasher. Evie felt her shoulders relax. She exhaled. "See? It didn't work."

Krista's face fell. It looked like she might cry. "Yeah," she muttered. "That woman must've been batshit. Let's order—"

Willow let out an enormous, barking burp. The girls stared at her. Willow clamped her hand over her mouth.

"Dude." Krista giggled, before it happened again. A man's burp; long and deep.

Evie slid closer to her. "Are you okay?"

Willow's hands moved to her stomach. She squeezed her eyes shut. "I don't feel well."

"Oh shit," Evie said. "Krista, what the fuck was that?"

"It just says Pretty, that's all it says." Krista held up the bottle. A white sticker with smeared, handwritten black lettering.

"Evie, I think I'm going to be sick," Willow whimpered.

"Let's get her to a bathroom." Evie grabbed Willow's arm. It was clammy. "Fuck. Should I call a doctor?"

"No! No." Willow got to her feet unsteadily. "I'll be okay—" There was a loose, ripping sound. Willow's eyes went wide. The smell of shit filled the room. Willow's voice was pale. "Oh my god."

Krista's jaw dropped. "Did you just shit yourself?"

It only took a second to confirm that she had. Poop was dribbling down the backs of both ankles and onto the white carpet. Willow moaned, sounding more in pain than embarrassed.

"Bathroom!" Evie shouted, and the two girls began half carrying, half dragging their friend in the direction of a small guest bathroom. They were only one or two steps inside before Willow began retching. She stumbled toward the toilet, but was unable to contain a Technicolor wave of puke that arrived seconds too early. Vomit splashed over the bowl, the wall behind, soaking a white basket stacked neatly with toilet paper rolls.

"It's on my hands, Willow's shit is on my hands." Krista thrust them out in front of her in alarm.

"Fuck that, call 911!" Evie yelled. She was panicking. *Manslaughter!* Evie's brain shrieked, *manslaughter!*

Willow was sick again, coughing a bucketload of vomit into the once-pristine bowl. The smell was unbearable; the ripe, pungent odor of feces mixed with the sickly sweet smell of vomit.

"Where's your phone?" Evie yelled at Krista.

"I don't know, I don't know, oh god, Willow, what's happening, I'm sorry—"

"Find it! Call 911!"

Krista zoomed for the sink, switched on both faucets, and shoved her hands under them.

"Leave it!" Evie screamed hysterically. "Call 911!"

"Don't yell at me!" screamed Krista.

"I'm sorry," Evie screamed back. "I'm freaking out!"

Willow sat back on her haunches, panting. She moaned; a strange, high-pitched sigh. Evie and Krista snapped their heads in her direction . . . and froze.

Everything stopped. Evie was no longer conscious of the smell, the sickness, the panic.

It wasn't Willow in front of the toilet.

It was someone else.

The girl in front of the toilet wiped her mouth with the back of her hand and groaned, turning to gaze at Evie mournfully.

Evie stared back at a stranger.

Her brain snatched for meaning, for order, but came up empty-handed. Oddly, she flashed back to last spring, where a bad date had taken her to a surprisingly good magic show in the East Village. A guy with a thin mustache and red suspenders turned a cigarette into a Sharpie, right in front of her. She knew logically that it was sleight of hand, but the effect was extraordinary. It really looked like magic, a rip in reality. This felt like that, but a million times more pronounced. *I'm going mad*, Evie thought faintly. *I have a brain tumor and I'm going mad.*

Both faucets were still running, hissing loudly. Evie switched them off. The bathroom was silent.

Confused, the girl shifted her gaze from Evie to Krista and back to Evie. The movement was enough to cause Krista to draw behind Evie. Evie took a step back, hands outstretched, instinctively protective.

"Oh my god," Krista whispered, peeking behind Evie's shoulder. "It worked."

The girl said, "What?"

Her *eyes*. Evie couldn't stop staring at the girl's *eyes*. So wide-set they were almost unnatural. And that *color*. A brilliant, intoxicating sea-green, made even more shocking by a rim of thick, dark lashes.

"Willow?" Evie croaked.

The girl looked back at the toilet. "Maria's going to kill me. Oh god, I'm so embarrassed."

"Willow?" Evie repeated.

The girl looked back up at Evie and it was that second turn of her head, revealing a face so lovely, a neck so long, that a fresh wave of adrenaline burst through Evie's system. Without thinking, Evie lunged for her, cupping her by the shoulders and pulling her upright.

"Hey," protested the girl weakly. Evie shoved her in front of the bathroom mirror, panting.

The girl met her reflection. A jolt of fear visibly ricocheted through her and she bolted back a few steps. Krista came to hover on one side, and it was only then Evie saw the girl was at least two inches taller than Willow; slender and graceful, like a ballerina or a wisp of smoke.

Krista was grinning, crazed and victorious. "Dude, it worked, it fucking worked. It. Fucking. *Worked*."

The girl—and Evie realized she'd have to stop thinking of her that way because impossibly, *impossibly*, the girl was Willow—was standing stock-still, locked into her own reflection's gaze. Evie couldn't stop staring either, noticing now her rose-blond hair, warmer and thicker than Willow's thin, ash-blond locks. The even tan of her skin, the round end of a cute snub nose. The full, Cupid-bow lips that were parting slowly in astonishment. Her hands found her face, and she began pressing her cheeks, her forehead, tugging at vomit-flecked hair. She opened and shut her mouth a few times before turning to Evie, eyes wide, pupils dilated. "Evie? Is this really happening?"

Evie stared back at the new creature, birthed from her friend, covered in shit and sticky fluids, standing on unsteady legs. "Are you okay? How do you feel? Should I call someone?" It felt like asking questions in a dream: silly, pointless.

"Hello?" A woman's voice rang out. "Oh my god . . ."

Willow's eyes bounced from Krista to Evie. "It's Claire."

Before Evie could begin to formulate anything close to a plan, Claire Horowitz, Matteo's thirty-nine-year-old girlfriend, appeared in the doorway to the guest bathroom. She was wearing a gray T-shirt with an NPR logo and baggy jeans. Her dark hair was swept back into a damp ponytail and she had a gym bag slung over one shoulder. Her expression landed somewhere between concern, confusion, and disgust. She covered her nose with her hand, instantly reminding them all of the godawful smell.

"Evie," Claire said, then, recognizing her, "Krista. What's going on?"

Evie stared blankly at Claire. Her brain, usually a reliable and well-oiled machine, had collapsed, shattered, temporarily malfunctioned. There was still a distinct possibility that none of this was real—brain tumor—but somehow, Evie knew that it was. Claire's eyes moved to take in the vomit, the smears of shit, and the stranger in her home.

"Evie?" Claire's voice dropped an octave. "Have you guys . . . taken something?"

"No!" Evie exclaimed, too loud, too panicky. "No." She forced herself to start talking. "This is my . . . cousin."

"Oh." Claire glanced at Willow in surprise.

"She . . . is . . . sick," Evie continued, each word an effort.

"Food poisoning," piped in Krista, glancing at Evie for approval.

"Yes. Yes!" Evie exclaimed. "Food poisoning. She just flew in from . . . Idaho. Plane food. Bad plane food."

"American Airlines," Krista added, nodding then shaking her head.

Claire's expression softened. "Oh, you poor thing," she said to Willow, who still hadn't moved a muscle. "That is the worst. Do you think you're well enough for a shower?"

Willow glanced at Evie before looking back at Claire in confusion and saying, "Yes?"

"Okay, why don't you do that," Claire said. "You can borrow some clothes off Willow." Then, glancing around behind her: "Is she here?"

The girls exchanged a series of alarmed glances.

"Um . . ." started Evie, but thankfully, Claire was already pulling out her phone.

"I'm going to call our housekeeper, see if she can help clean up."

"I'm sorry," Willow whispered, but Claire waved off the apology.

"Don't worry," Claire said. "Honestly. I had food poisoning in Thailand. Worst night of my life. It was like every orifice in my body was a faucet switched on high." Then, into the phone, "*¿Hola, Maria? Es Claire. Perdón por llamarte en tu día libre—*"

Evie ran to shut the bathroom door. All three started shout-whispering at once.

"Dude, I told you it'd work. I told you!"

"How are you feeling? I can still call 911."

"A bit nauseous. But I think I'm fine."

"This is so fucking cool, I can't believe it worked!"

"How is this happening? That's not my face."

"I don't know . . . Some kind of . . . I don't know, Will."

"Who cares?" Krista spun Willow's shoulders so she was facing the mirror. "You look like a supermodel."

Evie watched Willow absorbing her doll-face reflection, her expression blasted apart and wondering, familiar and alien, all at once. Nothing about it was comforting, but Evie couldn't look away.

Krista was right.

The Pretty had worked.

Ten minutes later, Willow was showering in her own room while Evie shoved clothes from Willow's floor into a tote.

"What's that for?" Krista was perched on the end of Willow's unmade bed, clutching the bottle of Pretty she'd found under the coffee table, contents still intact.

"She'll have to stay with us."

"What? Why?"

"She's not Willow Hendriksen anymore, is she?"

There was a knock at the door.

Evie straightened, pushing her glasses up her nose nervously. "Yeah?"

Claire stuck her head in. "She okay?"

"Showering." Evie nodded at the bathroom door. "Soon as she's done, we'll get out of your hair."

Claire nodded, as if to say, *no rush*. "Where's Willow?"

Fuck. Evie'd meant to think of some clever explanation, but once again her brain had experienced a critical error. She glanced at Krista, who was staring back, wide-eyed; no help. "She's not here," Evie began. "She's . . . going to stay with Mark for the week."

"Brilliant," whispered Krista, which Evie ignored.

Claire looked unwilling to leave the boundary of the doorway. "For a week? Why?"

"Why? Why?" Evie repeated. "Good question. The truth is . . . The actual truth is . . ."

"She resents you," Krista announced.

"What?" Claire and Evie chorused.

"She resents you for moving in," Krista said.

"But I moved in a year ago." Claire's hand moved to her throat. "We talked about it. She said she was fine."

"Dude," Krista said. "No offense, but you're, what, more than twenty years younger than her dad? That's pretty messed up."

"Krista," hissed Evie, but Claire wasn't listening.

"I knew it," Claire was muttering to herself. "I knew it was too much."

The bathroom door opened.

Willow wore a pale yellow dress, low-cut enough to reveal two full breasts straining against the material. Her hair was combed and damp, falling just above her shoulders. She was grinning. The effect was momentarily breathtaking, like seeing a full rainbow or a wild horse. All three women gazed at her, each experiencing a mash of mixed emotions: giddy excitement, sour insecurity, expansive wonderment.

Willow started giggling manically, which knocked Evie back into gear. "Right, we'll go. Sorry again about all the shit. And I'm sure Willow will be fine, she just needs time."

"Huh?" Willow's ears pricked, but Evie was already guiding the precious bird girl toward the door, tote bag of clothes over one shoulder.

"I hope so." Claire stepped aside to make way. "I hope you feel better. And I'm sorry, I never got your name. I'm Claire."

Willow stopped midstep. "I'm . . . Caroline."

"Caroline?" repeated Krista, but Claire was shaking Willow's outstretched hand and didn't notice.

Evie led the charge to the elevator, trying to ignore the pungent odor of sick that now permeated the entire apartment. Once inside, Willow swung to face the mirror, to admire herself and whisper reverently, "My boobs. Jesus, look at my boobs."

The thick silver doors slid gracefully shut, cutting off the view of the gleaming foyer.

Krista glanced up at Evie expectantly. "What do we do now?"

Evie clutched the bag of clothes grimly, and said, "I have absolutely no idea."

8.

The night sky was inviting the light gray of dawn before Evie finally fell asleep. Her previously nonfunctioning brain had been working overtime to answer the endlessly cycling question: *how, how, how?* By the time exhaustion finally won, the answer lay somewhere between military-grade nanotechnology and magic beans. No time seemed to pass before something pulled her from sleep. First thought: *too light; late.* Second thought: *someone next to me.* She jerked back with a shout, hands splayed. A girl giggled, kittenish. "Morning."

Evie fumbled for her glasses. The girl who used to be Willow came into complete focus. As blond and beautiful as a cliché. Krista leaned against the doorframe, eating handfuls of Lucky Charms in her PJs and grinning. Evie groaned. "What time is it?"

"After ten."

"What?" Evie threw back her covers. "I'm late!"

There wasn't time for a shower. Evie pulled on some clothes while trying to brush her hair, issuing orders. "Get her to a doctor today. For all we know her insides are turning into radioactive goo. But don't go to your usual one."

Willow yawned. Somehow even that was impossibly cute. "I don't really have a usual one."

"Good. Get a checkup. Also, get the kitchen window fixed; it's a miracle someone didn't try and break in already. Deodorant, where's my deodorant . . . And you'll have to think of something to tell Mark."

"Like what?"

"I don't know . . . You're going to see your mom. Shoes, shoes, shoes . . ."

"Ugh. Why would I want to do that?"

"I don't know! Your stepdad broke his leg and she needs help around the house."

"How did he break his leg?" Krista sounded intrigued.

"Guys!" Evie threw up her hands. "Make some decisions on your own, okay, I have to get to work." Evie snatched her purse. "Don't tell anyone what happened. Don't do anything stupid. Got it?"

"Aye-aye," Krista said, saluting. Willow giggled.

Evie narrowed her eyes. "Just . . . don't, okay? That is our new family motto. What is it?"

"Don't," chorused the girls. They were grinning like Cheshire cats.

It was after eleven by the time Evie got to the Heimert Schwartz building. She skidded across the faux polished marble, shooting her arm into a set of already closing doors, Terminator style.

"Sorry," she puffed, as the doors reopened. "Late."

"No problem," a woman's voice replied.

Evie looked into the eyes of Velma Wolff.

For a second, Evie just stood there, stunned into stasis. Velma stood in the left corner, swiping casually through her phone. In a pair of black pants and silky white shirt, she looked effortlessly cool and relaxed, at odds with the sticky New York morning. Dark blond hair fell down one shoulder in a loose fishtail braid. The smell of lavender hung in the air.

Evie stepped inside the elevator. Why today of all days? She mentally catalogued her various failings: hair a disaster, frumpy skirt, no scrap of makeup to be seen. She was almost sure she'd forgotten deodorant.

It was only after the elevator doors closed that Evie remembered to push a button. They began moving up. Evie snuck another look at Velma. There was a boldness to her beauty: it was unconventional, unapologetic. The gap-toothed smile and the Roman nose could almost be seen as ugly, but somehow Velma made them iconic. She looked like the kind of woman who knew how to order wine, who never wore anything stained, who was always reading something better and more interesting than you were.

Say something, Evie commanded herself. *She's your favorite author, this won't happen again, you'll regret it if you don't.* Her mind moved feverishly through possible puns or witty openings, grabbing for a way to make a connection. "I just want to say I'm a really big fan," Evie blurted.

Velma started at the sound.

Evie smiled in a way she hoped wasn't creepy but almost certainly was. "I've read all your books."

Velma's voice was lukewarm. "Thank you so much." She returned her attention to her phone.

"I'm in publishing too," Evie added. "You know, so I get it. I *get* it. I do, I really just . . . I get it."

"You're a writer?"

The question was such an unexpected engagement that Evie almost yelled her reply. "Yes! Well, I have a blog. I actually work for *Salty.* I'm a, ah, copyeditor."

She watched Velma's minuscule amount of interest deflate, air escaping from the world's tiniest balloon. Telling Velma Wolff the truth proved to be as successful as lying to Quinn. For the first time in her life, Evie prayed for catastrophic elevator failure.

The doors pinged open to the twenty-eighth floor. Home of the highbrow arts monthly *Sheaf,* the sort of publication that ran ten-page features that started with, "The overall feel of a dégustation with Damien Hirst is Germanic, satanic, and the opposite of the fashions of the *Titanic.*"

Velma looked at Evie as if to say, *Well, Odd Face, our time is thankfully up.*

Evie nodded once, twice, too many times. "I'm actually not going into *Salty* today, because, well—"

Velma exited the elevator, leaving Evie's words to dissipate pathetically in her wake.

"Today . . . everything's different."

. . . . .

Evie got out on the thirty-ninth floor, where a handwritten sign read
Extra Salt Casting. *Awesome first impression*, she scolded herself. *Super
keen to work on the show, Jan, as long as it doesn't interrupt my demanding
sleep schedule. And if I do manage to rise before noon, I like to embarrass
myself in front of my literary idols.*

She barreled around the corner. Thirty girls about her age sat in a
large foyer. They all glanced up, then just as quickly looked away, carefully ignoring each other.

Evie was instantly intimidated, then annoyed at herself for being intimidated. *You're not here to audition. You're here to help them look smart.*

She picked her way through the sea of cheekbones as sharp as pocket-
knives. Was it bronzer? Or was it . . . magic? Were all the supermodels
on Pretty? Were supermodels even a real thing? What about—

"Hi." A boy with rimless glasses appeared at her side.

"Hi." Evie jumped, refocusing. "I'm—"

He handed her some forms. "Fill these out, then give them back to
me—"

"I'm not here to audition." Evie handed the forms back. "Jan Stilton
told me to come. I'm Evie, I work for *Salty*. Might be helping out with
the show?"

"Oh. She must want you in the room. I'm Lukas," he added. "Follow
me."

Lukas stopped outside a closed door, listened, then pushed it open.
Half a dozen people sat behind a long white desk. Jan caught Evie's
eye and motioned for her to come in. "Everyone," Jan said, "this is Evie
Selby, *Salty*'s copyeditor extraordinaire. She might be joining us as a
researcher. Evie, this is our director, Rich, and our producer, Kelly."

Rich, also in his early twenties, sat slouching, engrossed in his phone.
White as they come, no muscles to speak of, wearing black-rimmed
glasses and a T-shirt that said Hello Newman with a picture of Paul
Newman. He reminded Evie of the comedy nerds Krista used to do

improv with: able to quote Louis C.K., unable to talk to women. Which made Kelly the guy in his late thirties/early forties, sitting with his legs spread, radiating an urban cowboy vibe. Thick blond hair was slicked off a tanned face. Entirely unsubtle sky-blue eyes. The kind of guy who'd get drunk in an airport, then hit on the flight attendant. "G'day," he said to Evie, giving himself away as Australian.

The elegant woman in her mid- to late forties who exuded a distinct I'm-a-big-shot vibe was Laurel Flynn, the casting agent. Next to her was a smartly dressed Latina wearing lots of makeup, who Evie could tell was a "people person." Carmen Lopez from Sales and Marketing. Carmen was the only panel member to beam at Evie, revealing bleached white teeth. Evie tried to beam back without showing her teeth, which she thought of as tea-colored pebbles.

"Hi." Evie waved awkwardly at everyone with both hands, like a crab. She took an empty seat behind them.

"Let's bring our next girl in." Laurel nodded at Lukas. A glossy-haired brunette was ushered into the single chair facing them. Everything about her had been evened out, smoothed into symmetry. A bell curve in heels. Lukas handed the girl's head shot to Kelly.

Laurel led a brief round of introductions and checked that the girl had the right script, which Evie noted she called "sides."

Kelly pressed a red button on the side of the camera.

"Go ahead and state your name and agency," Laurel instructed.

The girl flashed a big smile down the lens. "Brittany Bilsen, Tony Yuro Agency." Her voice was a looping southern drawl.

"Great." Laurel nodded. "When you're ready."

Brittany tossed her hair back. "Lovely lips are a must all year-round, but which lipstick provides the longest-lasting coverage?" Her voice sounded as warm and inviting as caramel sauce. "We road-test your favorite brands to find out. Watch out—we do kiss and tell."

"Great," Rich said. His voice was sort of nasally. "Can you do it again, but try hitting the last line with a bit more sex?"

Brittany did the lines again, but this time she gave the camera a cheeky little smile for the last line, adding the slightest wiggle to her shoulders.

Jan's arms and legs were both crossed. Evie could tell her editor was underwhelmed. "Did you have any ideas for stories you'd do?"

"I sure do." Brittany recrossed her legs. "Online dating."

Jan looked unmoved. "What about online dating?"

"Oh, you know." Brittany shrugged. "How it's not just for losers anymore. My best friend's online and she's a doll."

Evie wondered if Brittany was being literal, and if the doll was getting better messages than she was.

"Right," Jan said. "But what's the angle?"

Evie knew why Jan sounded testy. Just like "30 Things to Do Before You Turn 30" and the word *netiquette,* online dating was tired, done. All the section eds knew not to pitch it, unless there was something new to say about it—a look at a popular new app or a good Real Girl horror story.

Brittany looked thrown. "Well . . . maybe I could go on an online date. I have a boyfriend," she was quick to add. "But maybe I go on one and something happens."

"Like what?" Rich asked.

"I don't know. Something funny?"

"Like what?" Rich repeated, glancing down at his phone.

Brittany cocked her head, thinking. She brightened. "Like, maybe he shows up and he's in a wheelchair! And I'm like, 'Uh-uh! No way!'" She screwed her face into a look of mock horror. Evie had to look at her shoes to hide her look of incredulity.

Kelly gave her a wink. "Thanks for coming in, Brittany."

Brittany thanked everyone and trotted out. The people at the table exchanged tired smiles.

"She had a great look," offered Carmen. "I know the sponsors would love her."

"It was the same problem as the last girl." Jan sighed. "I can't understand why it's so hard to find someone with the right look who has a bloody personality."

"We will," Laurel said.

"What about stand-ups?" Jan looked at Kelly. "Could we send some scouts out to the clubs?"

Kelly shook his head. "We don't have time. We need to find someone today, tomorrow at the latest. We start shooting Monday."

"And we need to be online by next Wednesday," Carmen reminded everyone. "The contracts are done."

"We need someone with an edge." Jan's eyebrows hinted they might be frowning. "Someone with an accent. Or a hot lesbian—"

"Hot bisexual," Carmen corrected. "We'd lose too many sponsors with a lesbian."

"Evie." Jan twisted around to face Evie fully. "Can you think of anyone we should get in?"

Evie could.

Herself.

She was bisexual. Maybe not a hot bisexual, but she'd definitely had her tongue in other girls' mouths. She knew the brand, and she was used to coming up with interesting angles for stories, albeit for *Something Snarky*. She'd never been on camera before, but wasn't it just elocution and confidence?

But she was sitting right there. And no one in the room had suggested her. She could imagine what would happen if she did. The awkward pause, the shuffling of notes, the collective chickening out of having to say, "Sorry, Evie. You don't have the *Extra Salt* look . . . You're just not pretty enough."

"My roommate, Krista," Evie said. "You could audition my roommate."

The room perked up. Evie's insides wilted.

If altruism was supposed to feel good, why did she feel so damn shitty?

9.

After three more equally disheartening auditions, Evie told Jan she needed to get back to the office. Jan confirmed the likelihood of "continuing the conversation" about working on *Extra Salt* for the first episode was high. Evie told her, "Great!" but her heart wasn't in it. Willow and Krista weren't returning her texts. She was worried.

Her afternoon's work was a write-off. She couldn't stop Googling *neuroscience, cellular regeneration,* and *military experiments about beauty.* She resolved to finish her pages after confirming Willow was still alive. At exactly 6 p.m., she bolted for the elevator. Two subways and one mad dash through Williamsburg later, and she was heaving for breath by the time she got home. It wasn't until she thrust open the front door that she registered the sound.

Beyoncé.

Two lithe bodies shimmied like snakes in the middle of the living room. Sexy snakes; snakes on spring break. The coffee table was crowded with bottles of wine. The air smelled a little like bleach.

She recognized the first snake: Pretty Willow—Caroline—wearing the napkin Krista passed off as a dress last New Year's. She didn't recognize the second, a brunette who bounded over to turn down the music. She was wearing Krista's favorite leopard-print hot pants. "Evie! Don't be mad. But . . . I did it!"

Evie closed her eyes. Maybe when she opened them the brain tumor would transport her to Hawaii or outer space or a quiet white hospital bed with tightly tucked-in sheets. When she opened them, Krista—because, of course, *of course*, the second girl was Krista post-Pretty—was still in front of her, bouncing eagerly.

"I'm Pretty!" the girl screamed. "Look at me! Look at my ass!" She spun around to shake a rump as round as a beach ball.

Evie stepped back. "Did you take Willow to the doctor?"

The girl groaned. "Stop being so boring, *Mom*. Can't you just have fun for once?"

Evie opened her mouth but was lost for a comeback. She had fun. She had fun all the time.

Didn't she?

"Evie, we went." Willow flopped down on the couch. She grabbed the wine and took a slug. "I'm fine." She grinned sweetly. "Perfectly healthy."

"Seriously, dude. This stuff is the bomb." The girl—Krista—presented herself proudly to Evie for inspection. "Check me out."

Like Willow, Krista was taller, but while Willow had only shot up a couple of inches, Krista had gained almost a foot. Her short choppy bob had been replaced with lustrous dark tresses that fell halfway down her back. Her features were sharper. Krista's nose—which she hated, describing it as too big and too flat—was now straight. Her cheekbones were high, her lips graceful sweeps of dark pink. Her sleekly oval-shaped eyes were a vibrant emerald green, just as arresting as Willow's. But the biggest difference was her skin. Krista's real skin was chocolate colored. This girl's skin resembled milky coffee. It twisted Evie's stomach into a mess of nerves. "Your skin," Evie said.

"I know." Krista whipped her eyes to the mirror above the couch. "Totally Eurasian." She struck a pose.

"The Pretty made you whiter," Evie said faintly.

"Yeah." Krista laughed. "Awesome, right?"

"No," Evie said. "Not awesome. It's such a dumb Western ideal."

"What is?" Willow asked.

"White skin being pretty," Evie said.

Krista didn't look away from the mirror, but Evie saw a tiny flare of anger ignite behind her eyes. "You don't get it, dude." She spun around, her tone walking the line between joking and defensive. "I'm a hot ethnic cliché. I can get any commercial I want."

Evie backed up a step. "That is so wrong."

Krista huffed air, quick and hard. "Don't even think about lecturing me about race stuff. You're white, you'll never get it."

Evie blinked at the two girls staring back at her—gangly, unfamiliar renderings of her two closest friends. Anxiety drummed into her chest. "This is getting too weird. We should call someone. *Tell* someone—"

"No, no, no." The girls rushed forward.

"We're fine," Willow cooed.

"Totally cool," Krista agreed, pulling Evie toward the couch.

"And we cleaned everything up—"

"So gross, but holy shit, the bathroom has never been cleaner—"

The girls deposited Evie on the couch.

"And we got you something." Willow widened her eyes at Krista, who dashed into the kitchen.

Evie slipped her shoes off. "I'm just not sure what this all means."

"Maybe it doesn't have to mean anything," Krista called from the kitchen. "Maybe it's just fun."

"Fun is a feminist issue," Evie replied. "No wait, that's fat. Fat is a feminist issue."

"Ta-da!" Krista appeared in the kitchen doorway. She was holding a bottle of Dom Pérignon, two mismatched wineglasses, and an I ❤ NY coffee mug. "We've only got two glasses," she said, nodding at the mug. "But still, ta-fucking-da."

Evie sat up. "How'd you afford that?"

Krista nodded at Willow, who smiled blithely and shrugged. Krista set the glasses down and handed the bottle to Evie. "It's your favorite, right?"

They were two puppies, dying for Evie to let them off the leash so they could cause chaos in the most adorable way. And while she was worried, Evie resented being cast as the boring one. The least she could do was pretend to have fun. Plus, if ever there was a time to get drunk on really, really, really expensive champagne, this was definitely it.

"Sure." Evie accepted the bottle and the girls both squealed.

"I knew it!" Krista beamed, so proud of herself.

Evie eased out the cork and the girls whooped. She filled up her mug and slurped it. Yum. Krista put Beyoncé back on, and suddenly it was a party again. Evie settled into the couch, drinking steadily, watching the women her best friends had become dance like everyone was watching.

It was easy to understand Krista's motivations. Nothing made the girl happier than a new pair of pumps, so naturally a new pair of legs would send her into overdrive. Evie knew her roommate was under pressure to get some real acting work, and Krista tended to approach challenges with a "by any means necessary" mentality.

But Willow? Why had *she* taken it? Didn't she think she was attractive? Willow, who rarely bought new clothes or wore makeup. Willow, who preferred cameras to cocktails, who longed to be a better artist, who already had the perfect boyfriend. In a way, Willow did strike her as the most vulnerable of their trio—and the poor turnout at her opening on Monday probably hurt more than she let on—but she wasn't insecure about her appearance. Was she?

The whole thing was turning into a Sofia Coppola film: pretty to look at, but what did it really mean? Everything? Or nothing?

The girls pouted, posing for a nonexistent photo shoot. Krista slinked toward Evie, stopped in front of her, finger to an open mouth, one hand jutted onto her hip. She looked once, twice around the room, before spinning unsteadily and stalking back to Willow, picking her feet off the floor with comic exaggeration. When she reached Willow, she slapped her hand, passing a baton. Evie expected Willow to giggle and shrink away. But to her surprise, Willow drew herself up and relaxed her face. Each foot swung effortlessly around the other, face as blank and beautiful as a Greek sculpture. She stopped in front of Evie and moved easily into two poses, only shifting her body slightly to find new contortions to show off her perfect proportions.

That looked real, Evie thought. And then, drunkenly, *this* is *real.*

"Evie!" the girls chorused. "Your turn!"

"No!" Evie shook her head, but the girls rushed forward.

"You have to!" Willow's cheeks were flushed, eyes bright as stars.

"C'mon," Krista insisted, hauling her up. "Cat the walk!"

"Okay, okay!" Evie squared her shoulders and began catwalking toward the empty couch. She pulled a model pose, hands on hips, pouting. The mirror above the couch reflected Willow and Krista beaming behind her: a blond goddess who glowed, and a bewitching brunette who simpered. By comparison, Evie looked almost sickly. Pudgy. And her model pose wasn't funny, like Krista's. Or classy, like Willow's.

It was tragic.

It was embarrassing.

Someone pounded on the front door. The girls all jumped. *Ben*, thought Evie, darting to turn off the music that had no doubt pissed off their downstairs neighbor. She rushed to the door, ready to apologize, hoping she wouldn't sound too drunk. But it wasn't Ben. It was a man. Late forties, tough-looking, wearing a bright orange vest that said Con Ed. He barely glanced at Evie before asking, "Krista Kumar?"

Evie pushed her glasses up her nose. "That's my roommate."

The man handed her a piece of paper, glancing past her into the apartment. "I'm here to shut your electricity off."

"What?" Evie peered at the paper in her hand. The words *unpaid account* and *New York State law* swam in front of her. As did the figure $612.34 in bold, red, underlined type.

"Your account's been unpaid for seven months," the man said, stepping inside. His speech sounded rehearsed. "Multiple attempts to contact you by mail and telephone have been unsuccessful."

"Multiple attempts?" Evie repeated. "No, this is a mistake. Krista's been paying Con Ed." Evie had been giving her roommate money every month.

"Are you Krista?" the man asked Krista.

"Um—" Krista's gaze switched frantically between Evie and the Con Ed guy.

"Are you Krista Kumar?" he repeated testily.

"Y-yes."

He handed her the same form he'd given Evie. "Where's your fuse box?"

Krista stared at the paper in her hand, eyes round. "Fucking fuck fuck fuck."

"Krista." Evie stepped toward the pair. "Tell him there's been a mistake."

"There hasn't been a mistake." Krista's brilliant green eyes began filling with tears. "I'm sorry, I just . . . At first it was one bill. I needed to make rent. And then it was another, and I guess another, and I just lost track of how long I hadn't been paying."

"Seven months," the man said. "Where's your fuse box?"

Evie gaped at Krista, jaw loose. Evie didn't have any savings; she was living paycheck to paycheck. She couldn't pay the electricity even if she wanted to. Which she definitely did not fucking want to.

"I'm trying to fix it!" Krista pleaded, twitching her gaze at Con Ed. "That's why I took the . . . stuff, to make money—"

"Jesus Christ, Krista!" Evie exploded. "You've basically been *stealing* from me!"

"I'm sorry—"

"What about the other bills?"

"Huh?" Krista licked her lips, panicky.

"The other bills. The ones in your name. I'm on the lease, you handle the bills?" As soon as the words were out of her mouth, Evie could hear what a monumentally stupid decision that had been.

"Um . . . I needed money for rent."

"Oh my god." How long would it be before they lost water? Gas? The internet? Oh god, not the internet. Evie stared at Krista with open incredulity. How was it possible that this girl, the captain of the debate team, the one who could calculate the tip without using her phone, could be so staggeringly irresponsible? "How much debt are you in?"

"Including student loans?"

Evie's voice was ice. "Including everything."

"A hundred and thirty grand." Krista wiped a tear away. "Give or take."

"A hundred and thirty grand?" Evie gasped. "A hundred and thirty fucking grand, Jesus, *Krista*—"

"I said I'm sorry—"

"Ladies." Con Ed raised both hands. "Look, I like a reality show as much as the next guy, but you are legally obligated to show me to your fuse box or else I'll be forced to contact your local authorities."

"Excuse me, sir?" Willow trained her gaze on Con Ed, eyes smoldering, lips parted. Evie could almost see licks of spitfire leaping off her skin.

When Con Ed spoke, his voice was a little higher than usual. "Yes?"

"I know you're just doing your job, but maybe you can cut my friends some slack." Willow came even closer to the man. Evie instinctively took a step back, away from the strange, seductive Willow.

"No," he said. "That's not possible."

"Oh, sure it is." Willow floated one hand to the man's arm. It looked like a butterfly landing on a log. "Maybe there was no one home. Maybe you'll have to come back next week to cut off the power."

"And maybe by then the bill'll be paid." Krista snatched his other arm, offering a *please please please?* expression.

The man switched his gaze between the two girls flanking him like selkies. He cleared his throat uneasily. "Maybe I could."

"Thank you." Krista sagged with relief. "Dude, for real, thanks a million."

Evie stared at Willow. Where had that come from? She couldn't have been more surprised than if Willow had declared herself an Egyptian goddess. But Willow wasn't looking at Evie. Her gaze had turned inward, pale green eyes flashing with victory. Her exquisite features had curled into an unfamiliar look: oddly determined. Almost grim.

Krista was right behind Evie when she pulled the front door closed. "Evie, I am so sorry about all this, but I swear to god, I am going to fix it."

"You don't believe in God." Evie sank into the couch and reached for her mug of champagne.

Krista dropped next to Evie, eyes locked on her best friend's. "Then I swear to Amy and to J. Law and Michelle freakin' Obama that first thing tomorrow I am going to march into CPU, land a superhot agent, book a commercial, and *bank*. I'm going to use this"—she swished her hands to indicate her face and body—"to pay you back. Every penny. I swear. On all that is good. Including you. *Especially* you."

"Sure thing." Evie drained the last of the champagne. Anger and disappointment—at herself, at Krista, at *Salty*, at everything—flattened her out, making her feel worthless. All she wanted to do was go to bed and never wake up.

"No, seriously, Eve. Eve, listen to me." Krista plucked the mug out of her hands, forcing her roommate to look at her. "I need you to believe me. I need you to believe *in* me."

"Why?"

"Because you're the only one who does."

Evie looked up at the girl who used to be Krista, surprised. Krista stared back at her, eyes steady and serious and heartbreakingly hopeful. She wanted to believe her, Evie realized. And then, more astonishingly, she did believe her. Whether it was the booze or her perfect face or the five years of friendship, she did.

"Of course I believe you, dummy. You're my best friend."

10.

"Are you sure you won't come?" Krista wheedled with the persistence of a toddler who just wanted to be *picked up*. "It's my first night as a Pretty. We have to celebrate!"

Evie shook her head. "I have work to do."

While she had brought the day's pages home, this wasn't the whole truth. The thought that was buried in her Shame Cave was this: she was worried about how it'd look.

Two Pretties and a Regular.

Evie Selby: the ugly friend.

There's no such thing as ugly, she scolded herself crossly. She was annoyed at the fact she was annoyed. It was a mini meta meltdown, and it made her brain hurt.

"It's like driving a Lamborghini." Krista gave her boobs a squeeze. "You should see me naked, dude. *I* turn me on. I can't wait to have sex in this thing."

"That *thing* is your body, and—" began Evie, but she couldn't finish, remembering Krista's comment about sounding like a mom. A pang of regret, or remorse, or maybe just sadness swelled through her, and she had to look back down at her pages. "Have fun."

It was only after the two girls left in a swirl of clicking heels and honeyed perfume that Evie remembered the *Extra Salt* audition she'd nabbed for Krista. Her thumbs hovered over her phone's keyboard, about to text her the details. But then she put her phone down. The prospect of rewarding Krista after finding out she'd been lying to her for the past seven months made her feel like a chump. *I need*, Evie thought, *to start looking out for number one.*

The top story on her pile of work was called "Five Friends to Ditch ASAP." The story began: *Number one: The boring friend. While your boring friend can always be counted on to help clean up after parties, let's face it: you didn't want her at that party to start with—*

Evie tossed the pages aside and flopped onto her bed, emitting a stage groan of unhappiness. Always such a hard worker. Always so reliable. Was she the boring one? She couldn't remember the last time Willow and Krista went out without her. Maybe that was dangerous— letting them see how much fun they'd have when she wasn't around . . .

No. She banished the wicked thought before it could land.

She stalked into the living room, found a half-empty bottle of warm white wine, and defiantly filled her I ♥ NY mug. She yanked the freezer open to knock out a few ice cubes. The tray was empty. Never, in all the time they'd lived together, had Krista ever refilled the ice cube tray. It was deeply and intensely annoying. One time, Evie had actually caught her placing an empty one back in the freezer. "Oh," she'd said, looking at it as if it had magically appeared in her hand. "I didn't notice."

With gritted teeth, Evie diligently refilled the tray, slammed the freezer door shut, then took her *warm wine* back to her bedroom.

Searching for distraction, she scrolled through Twitter. A few of her Twitter friends were retweeting a quote from Velma Wolff's new book, *Milk Teeth.*

"If you want to be the king of the jungle, wear the skin of a lion."

Her brain helpfully played back her mortifying encounter with the writer earlier that day. *"I get it. I do, I really just . . . I get it."*

The way Velma casually, even politely, dismissed her entire existence.

She shuddered and took another slug of wine. Then she Googled *Velma Wolff girlfriend* and clicked to Images.

The top three sections listed "Velma Wolff and Emiko Aki," "Velma Wolff and Drew Barrymore," and "Velma Wolff New Girlfriend."

Emiko Aki, the Japanese-American model-slash-actress, had been Velma's live-in girlfriend for almost four years. The relationship had ended six months ago, bookended by passionless statements from both their publicists stating they still cared for each deeply, yadda yadda yadda. They made a striking pair: Velma with her tumble of dark blond hair, Emiko with her scythe of glossy black. The pictures were combinations of paparazzi shots and photos taken at red-carpet events. The paparazzi shots captured oddly compelling domesticity: the pair walking down the street, eating lunch, simply having conversations. A few blurry shots of Emiko yelling, face stormy, hands flung in the air. Velma was purportedly a womanizer, but Evie figured this could easily be the fantasy of a hyperactive, hysterical media. Mostly, though, they were celebrity event photos. Evie liked these the best. Emiko was grinning like a jungle cat, one hand curled possessively around Velma's arm. Velma looked somewhere between smug and bored. She was mostly dressed in her trademark Dior pantsuits, looking like Marlene Dietrich, sometimes so cocky as to have a thin cigarette hanging from her lips. With her heavy-lidded eyes, gap-toothed smile, and hair twisted back and messy, Velma was undeniably stunning: a replica of nothing.

There were no posed couple photos of her with Drew Barrymore. Their relationship had never been confirmed. The only digital evidence was a cover they did for *Out* magazine, a series of them watching a Sleater-Kinney concert, and photos from feministy-type charity events. There were even a few of them kissing, closemouthed, deliberately provocative. As much as Evie wanted to believe they'd had an affair, they probably were just friends.

The photos of "Velma Wolff New Girlfriend" were the newest and most diverse. The witchy, tattooed Chess Hudsen, who'd won the prestigious Kaikou F. Lozzi Prize a year before Velma had with her second novel, *fghwncbuwo*. Jemima Westley, the Victoria's Secret model with a face like a kitten and body like a fifties pinup. And a series of young actresses and famous daughters and professional party girls who were bi or gay or experimenting or fame-hungry. Even though Velma had been photographed (and thus Googleable) for the past ten years, her expression remained the same. There was something unreachable about her. A distance. Velma didn't seem to care what people thought of her. It was almost as if the whole world was waiting for her cue. She acted like she was hot shit and it didn't come off as arrogant, at least not to Evie, because, well, she was. Velma was just being honest.

Evie swallowed a mouthful of wine and traced the line of Velma's cheek with the back of her fingernail.

Velma endeared herself to book snobs by railing against literary trends. For years, her favorite target was vampire novels. Then she wrote one. *Milk Teeth* was about bloodsuckers, succubi, the undead. Velma seemed to get off on being adored for one point of view, then completely reversing her position. *Milk Teeth* was Evie's favorite Wolff so far.

A tickle of desire wiggled between her thighs.

Evie opened her online dating account. Three new messages. All from guys. Nothing from Quinn. Disappointing. The first, from curry_heaven: **UR pretty. Can I take you on date lol?** The second, from WineNot: **If I told you u had a beautiful body, would u hold it against me? What about if I told u I came looking at your butt in those jeans?** And the third, from Fun2BeAround: **You look like a man in this picture.**

Evie deleted all three methodically, trying hard not to give in to the acidic disappointment that threatened to suck her under.

It wasn't as if Evie wanted to be with someone who was particularly good-looking. She'd always told herself that looks didn't matter. But deep down, she knew she thought that because they *couldn't* matter.

Because she wasn't good-looking.

One of the fears buried in her Shame Cave was this: her looks were holding her back. From being powerful; being someone people listened to, someone people responded to automatically. From finding a spectacular partner who lit up a room, from having sex with tens. From getting ahead in her career. Because of course, *of course*, she had the friggin' personality to audition for *Extra Salt*. And although she'd shoved it out of her mind, it fucking hurt for Jan not to consider it, not even for a second.

But Evie hated these thoughts.

She rolled off her bed, telling herself she was getting a snack. She could almost fool herself into thinking picking up the Pretty from the living room table was not premeditated. The lavender liquid rested in her open palm: Shakespearian folly in a bottle.

Intellectually, she knew how flawed a society was that made beauty a value, *the* value, for women.

But could the Pretty make her life better?

11.

Willow was expecting Krista to take them somewhere loud and shiny, the sort of place that had a dance floor and twenty-dollar cocktails. She was wrong. Signed black-and-white photos of old men Willow didn't recognize crowded the bar's smoke-stained walls. Guys in jeans nursed damp glasses of beer. It smelled like sweat and french fries. Krista informed her it was a big comedian hangout, and that she used to come here after improv class. The ratio of men to women was five to one, and the girls were just wearing T-shirts and jeans. Willow prickled, feeling out of place in Krista's barely-there dress. Krista ordered two glasses of white wine and a cheeseburger, bloody as hell, with a side of tater tots. When the wine appeared, Krista took a sip, darted her eyes around the room, then started playing with her hair. *She's always moving*, Willow thought. Like a child or someone on speed. But then Krista froze. "Holy shit, check it out."

Three guys had just entered the bar. The one in the middle was vaguely familiar, with a nice face and dark skin. Willow guessed he was an actor. They always had fancier watches and shoes than everyone else in the room. This guy had a Rolex and leather wing tips poking out from the bottom of his jeans. "That's Ravi fucking Harlow," hissed Krista.

"Who?"

"He's a totally famous stand-up. He's one of the chefs on that Comedy Central show *Too Many Chefs*. He was on *Fallon* last week. He's hilarious, I love him," Krista said, watching the three guys take a table.

One of the guys glanced up at the girls and nudged Ravi.

Krista swung her eyes in front of her. "Shit, did he see me?"

"Um, yeah." Willow smiled. "You were staring at him."

"It's just, he's fucking famous, like legit famous," Krista stage-whispered. "He has a million followers on Instagram. I follow him, and last week he put up a photo of him with Bill Murray, who by the way is seriously old now, but I think I'm still attracted to him—"

"Hi," a masculine voice said.

Ravi was standing behind them. "Hi," Willow replied.

Krista didn't say anything. Willow nudged her with her foot. "Hey," Krista managed, flitting her eyes to him nervously.

Ravi gestured to his table. "Would you like to join us?"

Krista practically threw him aside. "Sure!" She could not get off her stool fast enough.

Moments later, Krista and Willow were sitting with Ravi, Colin (glasses), and Dan (tall), who Ravi introduced as friends from LA.

Willow fingered the stem of her wineglass and said her name was Caroline. The guys all smiled at her encouragingly, then shifted their gaze to Krista.

"And you are?" asked Colin.

"What?" She was quivering with excitement. Her eyes were glued on Ravi. "I'm sorry, but I am *such* a big fan. You are so funny."

"Thank you."

"That episode of *Too Many Chefs* where the customer sent the food back and you ended up getting him to cook for you." Krista shook her head, giggling. "Hilarious."

"Yeah, that was fun." Ravi nodded. "Dan actually cowrote that episode."

"Amazing," Krista said. Her eyes didn't leave Ravi's. "Amazing. This is so cool," Krista announced to the whole table. "This is awesome."

Even though Krista was acting in a way Willow thought was flat-out crazy, the guys all looked thrilled, even starstruck, as if Krista were the famous one, gracing them with her presence.

"Are you an actor?" Ravi asked.

"Me? Oh, kind of. I mean, yes, I guess."

"That's how I feel." Ravi dropped his voice. "Don't tell anyone, but I'm faking my way through all this. When I first got started, my 'agent' was just me doing a different voice."

Dan and Colin both laughed in a way Willow took to mean this was actually true. Krista caught Willow's eye and grinned. Willow smiled back, feeling papery.

Ravi addressed Krista. "So, what's next in the pipeline for you?"

"What do you mean?"

"What are you working on right now?"

Krista's smile became unsure. "I'm trying to get an agent."

Ravi cocked his head. "*Get* an agent?"

"Change agents. My last guy wasn't getting me jack." Krista took a nervous sip of wine.

"Who were you with?" Ravi looked interested.

Krista flicked her eyes to Willow, panicky. Willow stared back at her. Krista could say anything—CAA, William Morris; these guys wouldn't know. Or would they? Who were their agents? They should have gotten more of their stories straight before they left.

"Cheeseburger?" A chubby-cheeked waitress set a towering plate of food in front of Krista. The burger was the size of her head. The smell of fresh-cooked meat instantly made Willow's mouth water.

"Fucking awesome, I am *starving*." Krista maneuvered both hands under the burger and took the biggest bite she could muster. Her eyes rolled back in her head. "Uh. *So good.*" It was only after she'd mown through half the burger that she realized the entire table was silently watching her.

"You want some?" she offered Ravi.

"No. Thanks." He regarded her as if she were an exotic animal that'd wandered into his room. "I've just never seen anyone eat like that."

Krista jammed a fistful of tater tots into her mouth. "Like what?"

Willow excused herself and went in search of the bathroom.

It turned out to be small and sort of grubby. She papered the toilet seat lid with the entire box of toilet seat covers, sat down gingerly, took out her phone. Two missed calls. One from her dad and one from Mark. Mark had also sent a text. **Are you home? I'd like to see you.** She typed back. can't . . . with krista cat . . . soon. He immediately messaged back. **I'd like to. At Lenny's if you feel like coming by.**

Willow switched her phone off. Lenny's was Mark's favorite neighborhood bar, down the block from his apartment in the East Village. She pictured him eating peanuts and watching baseball. Her stomach squeezed.

Their spots of tension would usually be resolved by Mark wooing her back, his attention comfortingly consistent. She secretly enjoyed this part of a squabble: making herself invisible for a day or two, then tiptoeing back in his direction, cautious and shy. But right now, she wanted to see him and avoid him in exactly equal measure. Which probably wasn't how you were supposed to feel about a boyfriend. Not that Willow had anything to go off. None of her past—what would you call them? Situations?—were ever official. Because if you weren't ever official, you could never get officially hurt. Or officially hurt someone else. There was something very unsettling about the fact you could commit to someone, commit a crime, and be committed. *Commitment*, that hard, bladed phrase, seemed to draw blood, even as she felt it wasn't in hers.

She twisted some toilet paper around her little finger, stalling on rejoining Krista, who was surely well into a boisterous flirt session.

The sex-in-front-of-the-mirror freak-out hovered at the edge of her thoughts like a tipsy frat boy: insisting on attention despite blatant *get lost* signals. Willow definitely wasn't the instigator when it came to sex. Sometimes she even kept a tally, relieved when they'd already done it the night before. That sort of freak-out hadn't happened before. But maybe it had been inevitable. Maybe this was part of why commitment tasted so bad to her: the unavoidable intimacy, the private, humiliating showing of scars. Or was it just that Willow knew what so many others tried to deny, that everyone loses their appeal, their special shine, after a certain amount of time . . .

The bathroom door banged open. Two girls came in. Willow was only half listening as they chatted about an audition they'd both been at, whether or not to get another drink. She only tuned back in when one of the girls said, "Did you see how fast she went to his table?"

"I know, so gross," the other one groaned. "Chuckle fuckers give us all a bad name."

Were they talking about her and Krista?

"And what about that blond one? It really shits me that that's what guys find attractive. She looked like she had the personality of a pencil."

"I know! But at least a pencil can write." A stall door banged open, and Willow jumped. Her phone slid off her lap, clattering to the floor.

"Was that mine?" The girl's sneakers outside her stall swiveled. Willow drew her heels up off the floor, heart pounding. Whispers, too low to make out. One girl murmured, "Oh shit." For a horrible moment, she was afraid they were going to attempt to apologize. But instead the bathroom door whined back open and the girls scurried out.

She knew she couldn't take their comments personally—this wasn't her skin, this was a mask. A costume. A stranger she was inhabiting, borrowing for . . . why? Somewhere, in the deep recesses of her mind, she was sure there was a drive, a reason hiding, but she couldn't catch it. It kept slipping from her fingers, sliding through the cracks of what was knowable.

She waited for a few long, silent minutes before pushing the toilet door open. Strangely, she was almost afraid to lift her eyes to the girl in the mirror. Something dark was crawling in her belly, up, inside her throat. She looked at herself.

There was someone behind her.

She whirled around, too scared to cry out.

But there was no one there. What she thought was a face was a poster, an advertisement for a stand-up comic. She was alone in the bathroom.

She switched on the faucet and bent to splash water on her face. *I'm drunk*, she thought. *I'm seeing things that aren't there.*

She could hear Krista before she could see her. Her friend was holding court like a queen. The guys were all leaning toward her. Willow imagined invisible leashes curled around Krista's fingers. There was a fresh round of drinks on the table—they'd switched to what looked like whiskey.

Willow slid onto an empty barstool. She didn't want to move any farther into the bar in case she saw the two girls from the bathroom. She ordered a white wine and pondered her next move. Home, probably. Evie would be worried.

"Can I get you a drink?"

Dan, the tall one, the writer, was standing next to her, smiling amiably.

"I just ordered one."

"Mind if I join you?" Willow shrugged, and Dan signaled the bartender. "What she's having." He took the stool next to her. "Caroline, wasn't it?"

She nodded.

"Dan," he said, touching his chest.

She nodded again. "I remember."

He seemed pleased. "So, can I ask you the world's worst question?"

"What's that?"

"What do you do?"

She exhaled a little laughter. "That is the world's worst question."

The bartender placed two glasses of pale yellow wine in front of them. Dan reached into his wallet and withdrew a twenty-dollar bill. "Allow me." She could feel his interest as palpably as if he were covering her in plaster.

She swung to face him on the stool. "I'm a model," she said. "That's what I do."

He smiled boyishly. "I thought you must be."

"Why?"

He shrugged, his smile turning skittish. "Because you're so beautiful."

Willow played the words again in her head. *"Because you're so beautiful."* Mark said things like that to her, but they were dating. No man had ever said something like that, not in a way that felt genuine, like it was an observation, not a pickup line. Interest in something, not him, but something about the situation, woke up inside her. "You think I'm beautiful?"

"C'mon," he said with a small laugh. "You know you are."

She let her eyes amble around his face. He was turning red. "Do you want to have sex with me?"

He blinked, once, twice. "I'm sorry," he said. "I must be hallucinating, because it sounded like—"

Willow spoke over him. "Do you want to go somewhere and take our clothes off and put our mouths on each other's bodies and make each other come?" Her insides were mercury: liquid, dangerous. "Do you want to have sex with me?"

He looked down at his hands, wrapped around his wineglass, then up at her. His voice was soft. "Of course I want to have sex with you, Caroline."

Willow was not going to sleep with this terrified young writer. She'd never do that to Mark. But this game was fun. She was playing a character, someone from the past, someone inevitable, and lustful, and *in* her in a way she couldn't define but couldn't deny. As dangerously thrilling as the whole situation was, there was also something oddly comforting about it, something known. Something familiar. "Where?"

"I, ah . . ." He swallowed. As if it were the most important revelation in the history of time, he said, "I have a hotel room."

Her pulse was racing. "You don't have a girlfriend?" she asked playfully.

He stared at her. A spray of sweat coated his forehead. "Fuck."

It was her turn to blink. She'd been kidding. "You . . . have a girlfriend?"

He exhaled more air, looking pained. "I have a fiancée."

Anger surged inside Willow, hot and unexpected. Her voice slashed like a knife. "Well, that's really fucked."

"What?"

"You fucking jerk! You'd fuck me? You'd cheat on your future wife?" She had the urge to throw the wine in his face. Glass and all. "Fuck you."

"Caroline, wait."

She snatched her purse. "Oh, fuck off."

Outside, the city was roiling. Willow stumbled into a clump of drunk boys. They laughed and grabbed her arms, breath stinking of hot dogs and beer. A boy with a face like a cinder block slurred, "Hey, sexy. You wanna party?"

She elbowed him in the stomach. He swore and called her a bitch. His friends laughed. The street was a mess of cars, crawling over the concrete skin of the city; everything was crawling, everything was abject. She hailed a cab, and when the driver asked her where to, she replied, "East Village."

12.

"Of course they should have a movie made about them!" Krista slammed her fist onto the table, not feeling it. "Ben and Jerry are *American heroes*."

"A piobic." Ravi hiccuped. "Bio. Pic."

Krista tipped a glass to her lips, surprised to find it already empty. "So. Who should be in it? I'm really fucking good at this: Ben . . . Stiller obviously."

"Obviously." Ravi's head drooped into a nod.

"Yeah, he's a safe bet, he's usually—Ben Stiller and . . . Ugh, what's his dad's name, he's so fucking funny—"

At the exact same time, Krista and Ravi widened their eyes at each other. Their hands slapped the table in excitement, jittering the glasses.

"Jerry!"

"Ben and Jerry!"

"Whoa!" Krista couldn't handle this. "Whoa!"

"Did he, like, name his kid that on purpose?"

"Whoa! Ben and Jerry! Ben and Jerry!"

They stared at each other, slack-jawed with wonder.

A second later, Krista launched herself at Ravi Harlow.

The storeroom was musty and smelled like ketchup, but Krista didn't notice that because her tongue was in Ravi's mouth. "Jesus." His voice was muffled. "You are . . . excitable."

"Uh-huh." Krista hooked one leg around the back of his thigh, propelling herself forward.

He stumbled, almost losing his balance.

"Whoops." Krista paused, midmaul, and wiped her mouth. "I'm not used to being so big."

"What?"

She pushed him back, grinning. "Doesn't matter."

Tongues, arms, legs entwined, the couple teetered past boxes of napkins and pallets of beer. Opening her eyes, Krista caught movement. There was another couple in here. And the guy looked just like . . .

"Shit, it's a mirror." In it, her hair was wild and loose, legs long, butt perfect . . . "I'm so fucking hot," she moaned, turning a quarter inch to leer at herself.

Ravi's mouth found her neck. "And a rock-solid ego to boot."

Krista didn't hear him. Her head was swirling. Her skin was itching. Sex needed to happen. Now.

She dragged Ravi toward a low freezer in the corner. Hopping up onto it, she could still see herself in the cracked mirror. Perfect.

She pulled Ravi's mouth to hers. He reeked of whiskey. "Do you wanna eat my pussy?"

"That's not . . . that's not a question, is it?" His eyes were a little glassy. "More like . . . more like a demand."

She ran her tongue around the outside of his ear. In the mirror, an Axe commercial reflected back at her. "You want to."

He nodded, swaying. "I do." He pressed his fingertips between her legs, sending a jolt throughout her body.

She groaned, and then laughed. "Fucking hell." This was going to be memorable.

Underwear was removed, already sticky. Fingers grasped the inside of her thighs. Every nerve ending was poised to jump out of a plane; eager, boiling with adrenaline. And then . . . bliss. Hot, sharp, intense bliss. Pleasure rocketed from her clit up her spine. She gasped, then groaned noisily. This was *insane*. Between the dude between her legs and the hottie in the mirror, it was almost like she was having a threesome. Or watching porn. Or being *in* porn, but, like, really good porn, the kind you pay for. "Yeah, baby," she half moaned, half grunted. "That's right. Eat my pussy." Her words were gasps. "You sexy little bitch, yes."

Usually, Krista didn't talk either. But as it turned out, the girl in the mirror was . . . chatty. "You sexy little man. You sexy little man eating my pussy, my wet, wet pussy—"

Ravi paused. Krista glanced down to see two eyebrows furrowed. "Dude. I didn't say stop."

Ravi resumed his rhythm, and she responded by rocking faster against his mouth. "That's right. That's right. Yeah, you're hungry. You haven't eaten in days, have you, you sexy, hungry little man."

This body, this boy, it was *better* than the fantasy.

The mouth between her thighs started pumping, and a wave was coming, a tsunami, she could feel it. "Eat it! Go for seconds! Go for thirds! Yes! Yes!"

Taking the Pretty was the best decision she'd *ever made*.

"Fuck. Fuck, I'm gonna come . . ."

And then . . . the free fall. The moment where orgasm is inevitable, the point where you're sailing, sliding, skiing down the mountain, into the abyss, the void, the great beyond.

"Don't stop, don't stop, don't stop . . ." Eyes now shut, legs out straight.

Bingo. Blammo. Bull's-eye. Her orgasm jerked through her with all the subtlety of a marching band. Ravi, still working like a champ, eased up on the pressure but kept his tongue moving. Whip-sharp flashes of heat ricocheted around her body, making her muscles twitch like a puppet on a string. "Yes! Fuck! Yes! Fuck!"

Eventually, sensation began to subside. Ravi stood up, bowlegged, hair mussed. "Damn, girl. You got a mouth on you."

Krista let her head fall back, and she laughed. Everything was good with the world. Everything was right.

Everything was going to work out *perfectly*.

13

Watching Mark felt illegal. Everything about the situation was counter-intuitive. Wrong, like a convicted felon loitering outside a police station. But she couldn't move. And she hadn't moved for the last twenty minutes. Instead, Willow sat at the other end of the bar from her boyfriend, watching him watch the Red Sox.

Watching him sip a dark beer.

Watching him snap open peanuts from a wooden bowl.

Watching him check his phone.

Just watching.

He looked comfortable sitting alone. He didn't seem self-aware, like he wanted anyone to think he was waiting for someone. This was a new Mark; the Mark he was when she wasn't around.

Actually, she had seen him like this before. The night they met. It was Evie's book club friend's Christmas party in Park Slope. By the time Willow and Evie arrived, it was already half-full: shouty, sweaty, with cheese platters that had been worked over by wolves. Willow and Evie had started hanging out pretty constantly, but house parties in tiny walk-ups without doormen that were full of people talking about PhDs instead of club nights were still somewhat of a novelty. Willow ended up in a corner in the kitchen, sipping Prosecco and listening to Evie monologue about white privilege to an Asian boy who kept nodding and stealing glances at her boobs. Her mind drifted into thoughts for a new photo project that had something to do with Saturn's rings and Dante's *Inferno* and newborn kittens with their eyes still squeezed shut, when she noticed Mark. He stood in front of an enormous bookcase in the living room, talking to a short girl with cat-eye glasses. There was something about him that was so instantly . . . agreeable. His eye contact was steady without being invasive, he smiled when he talked, he laughed when it looked like she'd made a joke. Willow, who at that time was sleeping with an NYU film major who was more in love with cocaine than with her, found herself staring at him sadly, thinking that was the kind of guy she should be with. At that exact moment, apropos of nothing, he looked up, right at her. When he smiled, it felt like an embrace.

She was staring at him now. But he wasn't looking over.

"*Sweetheart?*"

She jerked her head up guiltily. The bartender—an older guy, not one she recognized—was giving her a look. "Sorry, what?"

"Do you want another wine?"

"Um. No. Thanks."

The bartender cast a weary gaze at Mark. "Sometimes you have to make the first move."

"What?"

But he'd already turned his back to start putting away clean beer glasses.

"*Sometimes you have to make the first move.*"

How many girls had the bartender told that to? How many girls had hit on Mark when she wasn't there? How many had he let? How many had—

Mark swiveled around. She stiffened. His eyes raked around the handful of other patrons. Landed on her. A thrum of energy shot through her. Then his gaze moved on, to the bartender. He signaled for another beer and resumed watching the game.

Willow's heart was racing. She felt relieved, of course, that Mark didn't try to catch her eye. But at the same time . . . disappointed.

She slid off her stool. When she was a few feet away, Mark sensed her, glancing up. She was searching his gaze, anticipating a sense of expectation met. But there was nothing. Just polite curiosity, morphing quickly into confusion, as she stood there awkwardly. "Could I . . . borrow your phone?"

"Oh. Sure." Mark slid his iPhone across the bar toward her and smiled. A helpful, friendly smile, complete with helpful, friendly boundaries.

She picked up his phone gingerly, not sure what to do. Her fingers entered his code automatically, 9891. The year he was born, backward.

Mark's head snapped up. "How did you know my code?"

"That . . . that's your code too?"

"What?"

"I . . ." She exhaled nervous laughter. "Oh, that's so weird. I just entered my code, on instinct—"

"It's the same as mine?"

"Guess so."

They stared at each other. Mark's face broke into a smile. "That's crazy. The odds of that are . . . That's really crazy."

Willow glanced down at his home screen. What now? Who could she possibly call? "I'm locked out of my apartment."

"That sucks."

She handed the phone back. "I don't know my roommate's number."

He gave her a look: *Then why did you ask for my phone?*

"Sorry." She shrugged, laughing at herself weakly. "I'm a bit out of it."

"Why don't you email them?" Mark suggested. "Or tweet them? Are they on Twitter?"

Typical Mark. He could even solve nonexistent problems. "No, that's okay. I left a note. She'll be here soon, I think."

"Okay."

The two regarded each other. *This is it,* Willow thought. *This is the test.* Would he offer to buy the hopelessly pretty blonde with the perfect pink mouth a drink? Was he imagining kissing her?

Fucking her?

"Good luck," Mark said. "Hope you're not waiting too long."

He turned his attention back to the Red Sox.

"Can I sit with you?" Willow took a step forward, moving through the doorway before it closed. "While I'm waiting?"

Something flickered around Mark's face. There was a pause, but before it became uncomfortable, he said, "Sure."

Willow took a seat, careful and triumphant. She was a vampire who'd been invited inside. A killer let in for tea. It was Krista's hot pink purse she put down on the bar, but it was unlikely Mark would recognize it.

"You live around here?" Mark asked. Friendly. Helpful.

"Uh, yeah. Eighth Street."

"I'm on Tenth, between A and B."

Willow nodded. *I know.* "Nice area."

He cocked his head, considering the sentiment. "It's okay. My girlfriend and I are moving to Brooklyn later this year."

This caught her by surprise. The word *girlfriend* was deliberate, she knew that instantly. Good, reliable Mark was telling the helpless blonde who'd locked herself out that he had a girlfriend. But they'd never discussed moving in together. It had been hinted at, the joking *When we move in together, we'll have this or that.* Was he just setting the blonde straight? Or was this Mark's plan, something she—his actual girlfriend—didn't even know about?

"I've never lived with anyone," Willow said truthfully. Neither had Mark. Moving in together would be a first for both of them.

Mark blithely cracked open a peanut. "I have."

Willow hid her surprise behind a bland expression. "Really?"

"Year after college."

The year after college, Mark was dating . . . Michelle? Marissa? Some *M* name. Willow's memory scraped for the details. The relationship was shitty; she drank a lot of cheap gin that turned her quick wit nasty so he was only half in it, emotionally. They fought a lot. They *lived* together? Willow tried to recall if she'd ever asked Mark outright about living with someone or if it had just never come up, if she'd just assumed he hadn't. She couldn't remember.

"How many roommates do you have?" Mark asked.

"What? Oh, one." Willow grasped for words, floundering. "Just one."

"Cool." Mark took a long swallow of beer. "I live alone."

Silence settled. Mark gulped more beer. His gaze flitted from her, to the game, to his phone. Was he nervous? Or just bored? She was reminded again of the Christmas party in Park Slope. By the time he'd managed to casually bump into her, hands knocking as they angled tortilla chips to an open jar of black bean dip, it was past midnight. Neither of them could remember what was said in those first few moments of awkward small talk, but Willow remembered worrying that he was bored. He watched her talk, head cocked to one side, a strange half smile on his face. She asked, "What?" wondering if she was slurring or had dip on her face. He said, "You remind me of someone." Weeks later, in a moment of shared breath and punch-drunk love, he'd confessed she'd reminded him of his future girlfriend.

"Are you looking forward to moving in with your girlfriend?" The question pulled Mark's attention from the game. "That's a big step," she added. "Living together."

Mark nodded slowly. His face looked complicated. "Yeah. I am. I mean, it's the next step, isn't it?"

Willow shrugged. "Is it?"

He chuckled a little. "Yeah. Date, move in, marriage, babies. All that good stuff."

"Do you want to marry her? Your girlfriend?"

And even though Willow had tried to ask lightly, playfully even, Mark still stared at her in surprise before fumbling out, "I don't know if . . . that's something—"

"Oh, sorry. Just making conversation." Willow drummed her palms lightly on the bar. "It's just—you're so young." She leaned toward him, arching an eyebrow, faux lascivious. "Don't you want to spread your seed before you settle down?"

Mark raised his glass to his lips. "I didn't think anyone actually said that."

"Said what?"

He swallowed before answering. "Spread your seed."

"I guess it's something I say." She made a face at herself—*dummy! You can't even flirt with your own boyfriend!*

Mark chuckled, and when she looked up, he was studying her.

"What?" she asked, suddenly self-conscious.

Mark shook his head and drained his beer. He set the glass back on the bar and leaned forward a half inch. His eyes were warm liquid brown. "You remind me of someone."

Willow's heart stopped. Sound sucked into a vacuum.

You remind me of someone.

A phone started ringing. It took her a full five seconds to realize it was hers, bleating from inside Krista's purse. Insistent. Incriminating. She snatched at it, but it was too late. Mark's eyes widened in surprise.

"I'm sorry," she muttered. She slid off her stool. "I shouldn't have come."

"Wait a second—"

"No, really." She stepped back from his outstretched hand. Shame burned behind her eyes. "You don't deserve me."

14

Krista's hangover was a vicious, circling thing: giant birds of prey *pick-pick-picking* over a rotten carcass in some far-off desert. Rogue eyeliner turned her into a sexy zombie. She yanked feebly at the bathroom door. It opened. A stranger stood in the doorway.

Krista screamed.

The stranger screamed.

Willow jerked upright from the couch.

"Kris, it's me. It's"—the stranger gulped—"Evie." The girl was wearing Evie's bathrobe and a stunned, guilty expression. From beneath damp brown bangs peeked eyes as round as planets and so brilliantly blue they were almost purple.

Krista choked in a gasp, her hangover momentarily forgotten. "Dude." She swiped away sleep to take in the girl's porcelain skin, raspberry-red lips, and extra few inches of height. "You look like Zooey fucking Deschanel. What do your tits look like?" She tugged at Evie's robe.

"Kris!" Evie slapped Krista's hand away. "Prison rules: no touching."

Willow padded over sleepily, stretching limbs as long as evergreens. "But you said you wouldn't do it."

"It's just for a week," Evie insisted, tightening her robe. "And I have a plan." She drew herself up, affecting bravado. "I'm going to become the new host of *Extra Salt*."

"Awesome." Krista grinned knowingly, nodding. "Right on." Then she frowned. "Wait, what is that?"

. . . .

Evie put on the kettle and opened a tin of coffee, explaining that today was the last day of the web series' auditions. She'd already emailed Ella-Mae, claiming her grandmother had passed away and she had to fly to Florida for the funeral. That would buy her a week.

"Cool." Krista yawned. The last time she'd been up before 8 a.m. was never. She sat slumped into one of three mismatched wooden chairs, all street finds, circling a matchbox-sized kitchen table. Willow was showering in the bathroom, which had just been thoroughly cleaned for the second time in the last twenty-four hours. "And . . . then what?"

"Then I Trojan horse it. The host can write her own stories." Evie spooned out three tablespoons of coffee into the French press, took note of Krista's appearance, and added a fourth. "I'm using beauty to subvert the system. Like *Glamorama*. Except for all the terrorism." Evie glanced at her reflection defiantly in the microwave door. The outline of a stranger's face stared back at her. The world tipped and wavered, dreamlike and wholly unreal. But as she held her reflection's gaze, it steadied again. Even with damp hair, even while still feeling vaguely nauseous, the girl in the microwave was so . . . pretty. More than pretty. Beautiful. Flustered, she averted her eyes, flushing with embarrassment.

She had a plan. She was subverting the system. And that did not involve mindlessly ogling oneself in a microwave.

"Awesome." Krista rubbed her face blearily. "So, is it an open-call thing?"

Evie busied herself with pouring boiling water over the grounds. "Hm?"

"An open call. You said it was a web series?" The subtext was clear— *can I audition?*

Evie willed her voice to sound flat, reasonable. "No. Invite only. They had me managing the list. Someone called in sick, so I'm going to take her place."

"Sneaky. That's not like you."

"Isn't it?" Evie asked, but she knew Krista was right. It wasn't like her to pull something so brazen. But it also wasn't like her to steal her best friend's audition spot, the spot Evie herself had gotten for her. Did the Pretty affect behavior as well as looks? Or was that just the effects of being pretty: an ingrained sense of entitlement or a survival-of-the-fittest-type cunning?

"No. It's not." Krista cocked her head at Evie, searching her new face. She was frighteningly good at detecting Evie's lies—a skill that had made her a pretty good lawyer-to-be—but right now she looked unsure rather than suspicious.

Evie ducked her eyes, pretending to busy herself with the French press. "You're up early. Don't tell me this is the start of a whole new Krista."

Krista nodded emphatically, pulling herself up straight. "Today is the first day of my real—" She winced, and crumpled forward. "I feel like dogs' balls."

"You should be careful. Maybe it'll wear off faster if you're hungover."

Krista shook her head. "Penny said it'd last a week. Plus, she was in a bar when I saw her. She was drinking. We can trust her."

"Neither of us really knows her," Evie said. "Or what this stuff is. What the side effects are. Or the long-term effects."

Krista opened her mouth, immediately defensive. But then she paused. There was no denying what Evie said. Evie handed her a cup of coffee uneasily. This could have been a mistake. But it was too late for regrets now.

Krista whimpered and rubbed her eyes.

Evie regarded her doubtfully. "Still going in to see your superfancy agent?"

"Yes," Krista shot back. "*Yes.*"

"Okay. Don't get defensive."

"I'm not getting defensive." Krista pouted. "It's just, I could totally use your support here. Can't you come with me?"

"Sorry, babe. I have an audition to nail." Evie paused in the doorway. "Huh."

"What?"

Evie sipped her coffee, trying to morph unease into excitement. "That's usually your line."

"Yeah," Krista said. She stared at Evie long enough for it to send a surge of guilt through her. "Guess you're playing my part today."

Evie almost choked.

Getting into the Heimert Schwartz building was an exercise in playing dumb. *Can't use my security pass. Can't say hi to anyone. Can't remember Lukas' name.* After signing in as a guest, Evie caught sight of herself in the elevator mirror. It took her a long moment to realize the pretty, timid face staring back at her was her own. She could swear the other two guys in the elevator were checking her out. It was such an unfamiliar sensation she was completely at a loss about how to react. Did this new girl like that sort of thing? Or was it passé, too familiar to even be exciting or annoying?

At least she knew what to expect at the casting. A foyer full of primped girls, all exuding a carefully constructed nonchalance. It had taken a blowout and four outfit changes to join their ranks. She'd settled on a vintage floral-print dress with a Peter Pan collar that had never actually fit her—one of her "when I get a stomach virus and lose fifteen pounds" outfits—and a pair of Krista's red peep-toe pumps. The most unusual inclusions were two subtractions: first, she no longer needed glasses. Evie had been wearing them since middle school. There was a lightness to her face, a distinct absence she was still getting used to. And second, her tattoo was gone. This struck her as odd: she was fond of her tat, but the ink had spread over the years and was sun-faded. By comparison, the space where it used to be on her forearm resembled pristine carved marble.

Like yesterday, the waiting actresses looked up en masse when she rounded the corner. But unlike yesterday, they didn't immediately glance away. Their eyes lingered for a second longer, taking in the dark-haired girl with the heart-shaped face: her ballerina shoulders and anime eyes. And when the girl closest to her looked back down, Evie could have sworn her shoulders sagged a little.

Yesterday, she had been dismissed. Today, she was competition.

"Hi." Lukas appeared at her shoulder, *Groundhog Day* style. "If you can fill these out, you'll be called in the order you arrived."

Evie took the forms, too nervous to say anything in case she somehow blew her cover: *Thank you and I'm Evie Selby, and this morning I took a magic potion and now I'm different!*

She sat down. The girl next to her, a very tan platinum blonde who smelled like peppermint candy, shifted over soundlessly. Time trickled by. Every few minutes she reaffirmed she was still a different person by pretending to check her makeup; a seesaw of anxiety, relief, anxiety, relief.

Finally, she heard her name. Her new name. "Chloe Fontaine?"

Evie had been mentally psyching herself up for this moment ever since the tiny drop of purple splashed down onto her tongue and released her bowels in a truly spectacular fashion. The moment when her boss, a casting agent, and the rest of the team would smile their hellos to someone hiding behind an impossible mask. It was a time loop, a bucking of reality, and she held the reins. Her heart felt like a hummingbird in her chest. When Lukas let her into the room, she was so disoriented that she began making her way to the seat she was in yesterday.

"No." Lukas stopped her. "Over here." He moved her in the direction of the empty chair in front of the camera. "Unless you want to cast yourself," he added kindly.

"That'd be great." Evie took her seat. "Then I'd get the job."

Rich, Kelly, Laurel, and Carmen all laughed. Even the corners of Jan's mouth tugged up into a smile. Evie chuckled along thinking, *Jesus. That wasn't even that funny*. Her coworkers never laughed at her jokes.

Laurel introduced herself, then ran down the panel; the college-aged Rich, Kelly with his steel-capped boots and slicked blond hair. The neatly presented Carmen in a definitely-from-Zara blazer. And, of course, Jan, wearing a thin cashmere sweaterdress and a curiously engaged expression.

Evie smiled at everyone individually. Her lips stretched over her teeth, feeling fuller and wider than usual. Chloe Fontaine had a no-doubt-about-it killer smile.

Lukas checked Evie's form. "And this is Chloe."

"With a C," Evie added.

"That's important, huh?" Kelly's tone walked the line between joking and judgmental.

"I assume you're not Kelly-with-an-I," she responded.

She was expecting a titter. The collective reaction was closer to a guffaw. Kelly shrugged, grinning, like, *I walked into that.* "Do you have a head shot, Chloe-with-a-C?"

Evie shook her head. Her hair felt long and heavy as it brushed against her cheeks. "I just changed my hair and haven't had the chance to get new ones done yet."

"Oh. Okay." Kelly pressed record on the camera.

"Go ahead and state your name and agency," Laurel said.

Evie looked down into the bulbous black eye of the camera lens. It felt like it was sucking her in. "Chloe Fontaine. Unrepresented."

Kelly pressed pause, frowning. "How'd you find out about this?"

Evie addressed Jan, praying this would be a good move. "I'm Evie Selby's roommate."

"Oh." Surprise flashed across Jan's face. "Yes, she mentioned you. I thought your name was Chrissie—"

"Krista," Laurel corrected.

"She must've misspoken," Evie said. "We've only been living together for a few weeks. I just moved here last month." She was acutely aware of how much the panel was paying attention to her. Even Rich's phone sat in front of him, untouched. She could feel them thinking about her.

"Welcome to New York." Carmen beamed, all bleached teeth and shiny lipstick. "Do you like it?"

"Yeah." Evie made herself smile. "Apart from the giant rats. I swear, the one this morning was the size of a football. I was worried it was going to mug me."

The table burst into laughter. And even though they seemed more relieved than genuinely entertained, a warm glow of acceptance flooded Evie's system. They liked her. And it felt *good*.

"Oh, and you have the cutest dimples." Carmen's face crumpled in delight. The sponsors evidently loved dimples.

"Let's get started," Kelly said. "Do you have the sides?"

Evie nodded. Kelly pressed record again, and Evie began. "Lovely lips are a must all year-round, but which lipstick provides the longest-lasting coverage? We road-test your favorite brands to find out." She dropped her voice a little, aiming for seductive. "Watch out—we do kiss and tell." And even though it felt sort of silly, she added a wink at the end.

Rich nodded, looking pleased. "Can you do it again, but try to make the beginning more of a question?"

Krista had told her directors would often ask for a different take, to make sure you could take direction. Evie obediently repeated the script, emphasizing the word *which* and trying to look more puzzled at the beginning.

"Very nice," Laurel said when she finished. The casting agent looked particularly polished today, in a structured black blouse and a string of pearls Evie assumed were real.

"Do you have any story ideas?" Jan sounded the closest to hopeful Evie had ever heard.

"I do." Evie extracted a manila folder from her bag and handed a printout to each panel member. "I listed out ten ideas, including the hook, suggestions of graphics, and who we might interview. Plus some additional reading I might do on the topic."

Kelly read out loud. "'*Rise of the Feminist Action Hero*.'"

Evie nodded eagerly. "I thought we could kick it off with heroines in young adult literature, which is a really interesting space for female-created heroines, but then dig a bit deeper into how many female action heroes have true agency, and how many are just, you know, submissive sexy sideshows."

The panel nodded, looking somewhere between taken aback and intrigued.

"I see why you moved in with Evie," Jan murmured, her eyes moving quickly over the printout. "You must have a lot to talk about."

Evie nodded, smiling a tight-lipped smile.

"This looks cool: '*Who Makes a Better Date?*' " Rich looked up at her. "Can we see some of that?"

Evie repositioned herself, channeling her inner Krista: bubbly, vibrant, flirtatious. It wasn't hard. She could feel the energy of the panel expanding and solidifying, breathing fire underneath her. They were ready for her to nail this. "Last week, I went on two first dates. One of these dates bought me dinner and peonies, the other ended with me faking a family tragedy in order to get the hell out of there. So far, so standard. But in my case, one was a woman, and the other was a man. After five years of dating both genders, it got me wondering: Who's a better date, men or women?" Evie paused and looked over at the panel. "So then I have five categories: confidence, manners, sex, enthusiasm, and follow-up. We could have a score count and some cool graphics. And we could interview people on the street about their best and worst dates, or who they think makes a better date."

The panel's faces seemed to be frozen, twisted into strange grimaces. Then as one, they all exhaled at once, laughing with what sounded like a combination of shock and relief.

"Wow," Carmen said. "That was *fantastic*. I just think she's *fantastic*."

Kelly leaned back in his chair and offered Rich a high five. "Boom."

Evie felt as if the Death Star had just exploded inside her. Her heartbeat was rushing, racing, pounding. The acceptance. The enthusiasm. She could practically *taste* it.

Laurel looked at Jan and nodded confidently. Jan's eyes didn't leave Evie's. She nodded too. "I'm glad Evie . . . suggested you."

Evie's excitement stopped short. Why did she pause before *suggested*? Did Jan look skeptical? No, Evie decided. She probably just assumed Evie coached Chloe, told her exactly what the panel was looking for, and there was nothing wrong with that.

No one suspected a thing.

15.

"Hello? Claire?" Willow's voice sounded as cautious and experimental as a kitten. "Maria?"

Nothing. Which was what she expected. Claire was teaching summer school at Columbia, her father was in Europe until next week, and Maria didn't come on Thursdays. Willow stood in the foyer, listening. It was strange being back here. It felt like she was breaking in. Nothing looked that different, except for a new flower arrangement on the side table where the elevator opened. Yellow lilies. Willow had a vague memory that yellow lilies signify falsehood. Lies.

She moved through the empty rooms like a ghost. The kitchen looked alien: too big and aggressively clean, silent except for the hum of the water filter. As always, the fridge was full, neatly arranged with Claire's kale and blueberries and almond milk: she was annoyingly healthy. Willow grabbed a half-open bottle of white wine.

Claire's bathroom cabinet was just as organized, just as healthy. Vitamin D, Tiger Balm, organic sunscreen. Her father's cabinet was more helpful. Klonopin, Ambien, and yes, Valium. Willow had been on a low dosage of Paxil a couple of years ago, but the effect flattened her out more than she liked, numbing her creativity along with her social anxiety. But these days, the occasional Valium didn't hurt. She liked the way they made her feel like she was behind glass, watching the world like a stage show. She slipped a handful into her pocket.

Willow was half expecting her bedroom to be clean, even though Maria was under strict instructions never to touch a thing. She imagined

Claire, in some passive-aggressive move, deciding to clean up the dirty coffee cups, splayed novels, and dried flowers crushed into the carpet. But a dim, familiar mess greeted her. A pang of disappointment. She almost wanted an excuse to work herself into a meltdown.

Underwear, tops, flats. Sleeping mask, phone charger, vaporizer. It was still strange to see these new fingers, slimmer and longer than her real hands, pick at the things she wanted. What was even stranger was how fast she was getting used to them.

A mouthful of wine tumbled down her throat, and then another.

She powered up her Mac and opened Photoshop. The last images she'd imported popped open. Mark. The portraits she'd taken, the night she'd turned Pretty. His mouth open, midquestion. A goofy expression, to make her laugh. The serious expression she'd been asking for. In her mind, these portraits had been moody and dark; containing something about the inherent sadness of masculinity. But there was nothing in these pictures. Nothing sad or secret or newly exposed. And certainly nothing worthy of a show.

A well of sadness, of inevitable failure, rose inside her like a thin mist.

She wasn't just a bad artist.

She wasn't even an artist.

She dragged the files to the trash.

Her phone rang, making her jump. Mark. Her stomach kicked hard. "Hello?"

"Willow?" Mark sounded shocked.

"Yeah."

"Hi! Hey."

She tipped more wine into her mouth and swallowed. "Hi."

"Hang on a sec, I'm just going to . . ." She heard muffled, indistinct noise, then footsteps. Chatter and music burbled in the background. She assumed he was at work. Then the chatter dropped away. Mark's voice reappeared, clearer now. "I didn't think you'd pick up."

"Sorry about that." Willow slid onto the stool she'd had Mark sit on, back curved like the letter *C*. "I've been sick."

"Yeah, your voice sounds strange. Look, I really want to talk about the other night."

Willow froze before she realized he was talking about the freak-out in front of the mirror. That all seemed like it happened to a different girl, one she'd only ever heard about, never actually met. "Don't worry about it. I was . . . don't worry about it."

"I am worried about it," Mark said. "I—" And for a second she was afraid he was going to say "I love you," but then he paused and just said, "Of course I'm worried about it. You haven't been returning my calls."

"I know. I'm sorry." Willow rubbed her face, hair curtaining around her. "I should've gone to see you at Lenny's."

A pause, and then, "I didn't go."

Willow felt a hot snap of alertness, like an animal sensing a hunter. "What?"

Mark blew some air out. "I ended up working late. It's nuts in here right now."

Willow tried to keep her voice calm. "No Lenny's? You must've been bummed to miss the game."

"Yeah, look, why don't we do dinner? At that Japanese place you like, Noshi Sushi Sumi whatever. Tonight? I can be out of here by seven."

"I have to go." Willow ended the call, dropped her phone to the carpet. The room swooped, dipping like a roller coaster.

Mark lied to her.

She couldn't believe it. Mark, who never tipped less than 20 percent and called his mother every Sunday. Why would he have done that?

Because of Caroline. Because he wanted to keep meeting the blond, beautiful Caroline to himself. What did he see? Who was that girl?

Willow's camera was still set up, aimed at the stool. She switched it to automatic and sat back down, holding the wireless remote like a grenade. All she could see was Mark, smiling nervously, sitting next to her at Lenny's.

A single hot tear trailed down her cheek.

The flash went off, blinding her.

16.

Krista almost didn't make it to CPU because she had the address on her phone, but then her phone died, and she thought it was Fifth and Twentieth (nope) or maybe Sixth and Twentieth (nope again), but then she asked a bunch of people and eventually one of them knew.

Creative Professionals United, Fifth Avenue and Thirtieth Street.

The foyer was much fancier than Clever Casting. The couches alone were nicer than anything in her apartment: bright red and firm, with no armrests and no throw pillows. The only artwork on the wall was a painting of a man in a suit with a green apple in front of his face. This was obviously meant to be a metaphor, but Krista was too hungover to work out what for. She was also highly, excessively caffeinated. In an effort to thwart said hangover, she'd drunk the entire pot of coffee that Evie had left. She hadn't had that much caffeine in years. Her heart was beating alarmingly fast. Her underarms prickled with sweat.

"Can I help you?" A girl with neatly combed dark hair smiled at Krista from behind an imposing front desk.

"I hope so. I mean, yeah, totally. I'm here to see Cameron Mitchell?" She had Googled the young agent-to-the-stars before she left.

"Your name?"

"Lenka."

"Last name?"

What had she decided on? She'd whittled down hundreds of odd, curling names to something as cool and arty as Lenka. Mishra,

Prajapati, Dwivedi . . . The short list swam before her, refusing to settle into a solid, believable name.

"Your surname?"

Krista stared back at the receptionist. In front of her was a stack of Post-it notes and a felt-tip pen. "Pen . . . ka."

"Lenka Penka."

"Yeah."

She could have kicked herself. That was the stupidest name in the whole entire world.

The receptionist gave Krista an almost imperceptible once-over. Then she picked up a phone and punched in an extension. "I have Lenka Penka here for Cameron?" She listened for a second, then hung up. "Cameron's out of the office right now, but if you take a seat, he'll be back in about ten minutes."

"Awesome, dude," Krista said. "Sweet."

She tottered over to one of the couches. The skirt she was wearing was so freakin' short she couldn't cross her legs without treating the guy waiting across from her to a full view of her punani. She dug through her tote for a stick of gum, wishing her phone wasn't dead, but also glad it meant she could stop screening her dad. She couldn't bring herself to listen to the voicemails: long-winded speeches about why she needed to reenroll at law school, no doubt. With a wince, Krista realized she couldn't even use any of Lenka Penka's potential acting achievements as argument fodder: her dad wouldn't even recognize his own daughter right now. He better not show up at the apartment, uninvited . . .

"Nice boots."

The guy opposite was smiling at her. Soft wavy hair, soft easy face. Faded jeans, flannel shirt. The kind of guy who'd cry at a Disney movie and listen to folk music. First thought: *not interested*. Second thought: *I would murder this guy for a cigarette*. "Oh, thanks." Krista glanced down at them. "I guess I went for the more-is-more vibe today." Every time she moved, she jangled.

"I can see that." The guy smiled again, nodding at Krista's furry waistcoat, feathered ear-cuff, and seven million rings.

"Yeah, but to be honest, I'm feeling less 'it girl' and more 'stoop sale.'"

The guy chuckled. "You look great. I'd definitely shop at that stoop sale."

Somehow, he didn't sound sleazy when he said it. Krista found the gum and popped it into her mouth, relieved to have something to do.

"I'm Greg."

"Kris—Lenka. I'm Lenka."

"Were your parents hippies or foreigners?"

"Um, both?"

He laughed again. A pleasant, inviting laugh. "And what brings you to these hallowed halls, Lenka?"

"I'm an actress. I mean, actor. I act."

Greg cocked his head at her. "Did you do *True Blood* a few years ago?"

"No. Mostly indies. And theater. A lot of theater."

"Like what?"

The only play Krista had scored a role in so far had been a trippy one-act at the New York Fringe Festival, about a suburban family who turned into potted plants. She'd played a fern. She cast her mind back to high school, groping past memories of beer bongs and groping. "Um, *Hamlet.*"

"Fantastic."

"*Our Town.*"

"Wow."

"I'm working on something with The Wooster Group," she added, recalling a recent *New Yorker* article.

Greg nodded, eyes alert with low-key awe. "You're part of the current company?"

Krista nodded, barely, as if the tiny movement diminished her duplicity.

"What are you guys developing?"

Her eyes flicked to the painting on the wall. "'Apple . . . Face . . . Man.' What do you do?"

"I direct feature films." He announced this rather proudly, as if it was still somewhat new.

The fact Greg was a director was definitely cool. But Krista got the impression that beautiful, cool thespians like Lenka Penka met feature film directors every single day. She nodded, laid-back, channeling her inner heiress. "Neat."

Greg snapped his fingers. "That's where I recognize you from." He pulled out his phone. "Ravi Harlow!"

Krista stopped breathing. "What?"

Greg scrolled through his phone. "What a small world." He lifted up the screen. "That's you, right?"

It was Ravi's Instagram. And yes, it was her in the picture. Ravi was on all fours and she was riding him like a horse around the bar she'd taken Willow to last night. Fully clothed, but fully drunk. "Oh my god," she whispered, before fighting a giggle. The picture was hilarious.

"You must've been pretty hammered to let him talk you into that," Greg said.

"Dude. That was one hundred percent my idea."

"Really?" Greg looked impressed. "Lenka, who are you here to see?"

"Cameron Mitchell."

"Cameron's your agent?" Greg lifted both hands, as if to say, *What a coincidence*. "Fantastic." He glanced over Krista's shoulder. "Ah! Speak of the devil."

A squared-jawed man in a navy suit, pink shirt, and patterned pocket square was striding through the heavy glass doors. Cameron Mitchell. He was on his phone, but when he saw Greg, he spread out both arms. "G-man!"

The two men embraced, pounding each other on the back.

"Do *not* freak out," Cameron began. "I already have five girls perfect for the part lined up. You are going to want to eat tapioca pudding out of my ass when you see them. Seriously: you'll need seconds—"

But Greg was waving his hands, saying, "Don't worry, it's cool." He gestured to Krista. "I found her. Lenka."

Cameron trained sharky eyes on Krista. "Lenka?"

Krista knew she was out of her league, but no one was treating her that way. She was one of them. She could feel it. So she rolled with it. "Hey." She stepped forward to shake Cameron's hand. "What's up?"

"Lenka." Cameron nodded in approval. "Where have you been hiding, young lady? If you say CAA, I'll fucking kill you." He laughed. He had veneers.

"Wait," Greg said, "you guys don't know each other?" He shook his head. "Doesn't matter."

Cameron let his eyes trail up and down Krista's body. He started nodding intently. "A little exotic, a little different. Fuck white bread. Yeah. I'm in!"

Greg smiled at Krista fondly. "Lenka, I'd like to offer you a part in my next film."

"What?" Krista's mouth fell open. "Are you serious?"

Greg nodded. "I am."

"Let's do it!" Cameron began pumping his hips in Krista's direction. "Let's put you in a fucking movie!"

Krista's face split into a smile. She'd done it. She'd gotten a part, in a movie, in the goddamn *foyer*. Finally, someone had unhooked the velvet rope and was ushering her inside.

To Hollywood.

To motherfucking stardom.

17.

She felt him noticing her.

Amid the slipshod energy of peak hour in Soho, she could sense him recognizing her: Caroline, the tall, willowy blonde who'd claimed to be locked out of her apartment. She swung her eyes up to meet his.

Mark started. He'd been letting his eyes linger. Not just look.

For a moment, neither said a word: two players unsure how to begin a game. Then Mark cleared his throat. "You found your phone." He nodded at it in her hand.

She blushed and ducked her head. "I'm sorry about that," she said softly.

A wave of commuters started threading between them, compelling Mark to come closer. "Were you even locked out?"

Willow shook her head. "I . . . I'm shy." She shrugged helplessly and laughed. "Pretty lame, right?"

He smiled at her. "Points for invention. And bravery. Next time—keep your phone on silent."

Willow made a face at herself and tucked a lock of hair behind one ear. "Look, I'm sorry if I—"

"No need to apologize. Seriously."

"Okay." Once again she felt his gaze start to linger, to slide into softness, before he caught himself.

"Have a good night." Mark gave her a quick nod, and turned away.

"I'm Caroline," she called after him. "By the way."

He turned back. His face contorted for a moment, as if he'd forgotten his own name. Or was considering telling a lie. "Mark."

"You look like a Mark." The breeze from a passing cab whipped her dress and hair around, reckless and warm. She could feel the effects of her eyes on him, those wide-set eyes the color of the Mediterranean. Hypnotizing. Like a drug.

"Bye." He started striding off again. The wrong way. His subway stop was in the other direction.

Willow watched her boyfriend join the bobbing sea of commuters and shoppers and tourists filling the cobbled streets of Soho. She watched until he was swallowed up by the city.

Now she knew.

She knew what the beginning of betrayal felt like. A strange mix of sweet and sour. Of success and failure.

She started walking in the other direction, longing to be lost in the crowds.

18.

By the time Evie got home, she was overflowing with fizzy, prickly excitement. Despite her efforts to keep her emotions stitched inside Chloe's smooth skin, they were pouring out, filling up the living room like a fish tank. She gave a little scream. She laughed out loud.

I got it!

I cheated Krista.

. . . I got it!

She snatched the Pretty from the coffee table, head spinning, wondering why Penny had given it to Krista, where they should keep it, and what exactly was in this tiny bottle, this tiny bottle that had already changed so much . . .

The front door burst open. Krista blew inside. "Dude, you're never going to believe what happened to me today! I'm going to be in a movie!"

"What? That's amazing!" Evie swallowed. "I have news too—"

Krista started running on the spot, shaking her hands in front of her. "You'll never guess who with. *Tristan McKell!*"

Evie gaped. "Tristan McKell?"

"Tristan McKell! Tristan McKell! Tristan McKell!"

"Okay." Evie ran her fingers through Chloe's long hair, trying to catch her breath. "Here's what we're going to do. We are going to go to the roof—"

"Amazing."

"We are going to watch the sunset—"

"Love it."

"—and we are going to get. Fucking. High."

Krista squealed and pumped her fist in the air.

The girls didn't often use their apartment building's rooftop. While it did have views of South Williamsburg and even a sliver of the East River, it was derelict and dirty and only accessible via a six-foot skeletal iron ladder Evie referred to as a death trap. But now, the victories of the day gave them the courage to climb. They left a note for Willow that simply said *ROOF*.

Soon they were reclining on plastic folding chairs in faded bikinis and cheap sunglasses. Below them, Brooklyn rumbled softly, glowing in late-afternoon light the color of mandarins. The air was warm and smelled faintly like melting tar and sunscreen: the summer breath of the city. Chloe's body felt long and lean, like a sword. In the past, Evie found beachwear decisions to be complex affairs of trying to feel as confident as she was acting, equally uncomfortable in a bikini (too much pudge) and a one-piece (too much kowtowing to societal expectations). But Chloe made this dilemma a moot point.

Evie didn't have to fake excitement at the news that Krista had gotten a part in a feature film. This rendered the *Extra Salt* audition switch completely irrelevant. There was no way she'd ever find out Evie had taken her spot. And even if someone, implausibly, ever told her, Evie would simply deny it. People believed whatever Chloe Fontaine told them.

Krista explained the film was called *Funderland*. It was about two best friends who discover the owner of their favorite childhood amusement park, Funderland, has died and left it to them, so they move from New York back to their hometown to run it. It was being filmed at an actual amusement park in Connecticut, starting Monday. "They're sending a car to come get me. A car! Do you think it'll be a limo?"

Evie wet the cigarette paper with her tongue. "What character are you playing?"

"Get this: Dream Girl."

"Dream Girl? What does that mean?"

"I'm not totally sure. I kind of blacked out after they told me how much I'd be making." She shot Evie a sly sideways look.

"How much are you—"

"Fifty thousand dollars!"

"No way!"

"I know! We got the studio up from thirty-five thousand. And I negotiated being able to keep my wardrobe." Krista smiled proudly. "It was actually really fun to work on the contract. Cameron said I was a natural."

"You are," Evie said. She no longer played Monopoly with Krista because of the incessant negotiation and backdoor bargaining that always left Evie bankrupt.

"I gave them my social. Do you think that'll work? Like, to get paid?"

Evie shrugged, twisting the top of the joint. "I guess so. I mean, you can always say the name you gave is your stage name. What is it?"

"Don't laugh—Lenka."

Evie lit the joint. "Pretty."

"Penka." Krista pulled a face. "Lenka Penka."

"Lenka Penka?" Evie coughed laughter. "You sound like a Russian porn star."

"Shut up." Krista plucked the joint out of Evie's fingers. "Let's get back to Tristan McKell."

"Ah, ex-Disney kids. You are the most interesting breed of all." The mental image Evie conjured was dated, she knew that. Perfect wave of hair, full bottom lip, and perpetual sad eyes that sent tween girls into overdrive: Tristan McKell, at the height of Boyz Unbridled fame, the ultimate boy band of the aughts, now relegated to being spun ironically at about 3 a.m., any club, anywhere. He was, what, fifteen then? Sixteen? Evie guessed he must be at least ten years older than that now. After Boyz Unbridled disbanded (the ultimate use of the verb), he'd reportedly had a spiritual moment, and then, bizarrely, popped up in a PT Anderson film a few years ago. He played a morose security guard at a strip mall, a supporting role as part of a big ensemble cast, something he actually picked up a few awards for. Maybe he'd done another movie after that, Evie couldn't remember. And now Krista was going to be in a film with him. Krista. Her roommate. With Tristan. The former pop star.

"You're not actually into him, are you?" Evie asked. "Isn't he too pretty for you?"

"He was my first crush," Krista said. "Ever. He awoke my libido. I have to do the sex with him." Krista exhaled with a sigh. "That's just karma."

"You know the rumor about him, right?" Evie grinned at Krista. "Apparently . . . he's the king of cunnilingus."

Krista thumped Evie's arm. "No!"

"Ow! And yes."

"How do you know that?"

Evie shrugged. "It's the sort of useful information you pick up working for a glossy."

"Oh my *god*." Krista thrashed her legs around. "Now I *have* to do the sex. He is number one on my vagenda. Ravi Harlow went down on me last night."

"The guy from *Too Many Chefs*?"

"Yep." Krista lowered her sunglasses. "There weren't too many chefs between *my* legs."

Evie took another hit of the joint. "How is it these guys never break your heart?"

"They have! Remember Edward Cullen?"

"Yeah, but he's fictional." Evie exhaled.

"What about you?" Krista ripped open a bag of jalapeño cheese puffs. "You said you had news?"

Evie closed her eyes, starting to feel swimmy and soft, like she was made of nougat. "I got it. I got the hosting part."

"Dude, that's amazing! Congrats! You're gonna nail it, I know it. When's the first episode online?"

"Next Wednesday."

"Cool. But what about episode two?"

Evie's muscles relaxed into the plastic chair. "I only need one." She was going to write stories. Smart stories, good stories. Like a real journalist. People were going to listen to her. The Trojan horse plan had worked. Just like she knew it would. The image of the little purple bottle swirled into her mind's eye, tempting and mysterious. "Why do you think Penny gave it to you?"

Krista sighed, turning her face to the sun. "Because I was nice to her."

"But don't you think it's weird? That she gave you it for free?"

"Maybe she has more than she needs. Maybe, I don't know, she was feeling generous."

"It's just . . . so weird. We don't know . . . anything about it." But even as Evie said the words, they floated away from her, like smoke clearing.

Krista munched cheese puffs, happy and high. "Hey, Evie?"

"Yeah?"

"What do you think Amy Poehler is doing right now?"

Evie smiled dreamily. "Something amazing. Something brave. Something cool." She tipped her head to gaze at Krista. Her best friend licked cheese dust off her fingers, looking long and lustrous and absolutely beautiful. They'd done it. They'd twisted the reins of the Pretty through their fingers. They were the ones in charge. "Just like we are."

Part Two:
Shadow

19.

The Pretty was a potion that opened doors.

Literally and metaphorically.

The metaphor openings included the free cookie the acne-sprayed barista gave Evie with her latte, the enthusiasm a complete stranger showed when offering to hail her a cab. The way her landlord, the very grumpy, highly suspicious Mr. Gorbul, was entirely unfazed by the fact he'd caught Evie's "sister" using her own key, despite the fact this was *strictly* forbidden. "Stay as long as you like!" he'd insisted, one damp hand clamped on her shoulder, breath pickle-sour. "Really. *As long as you like.*"

She told him she'd only be visiting for a week.

One drop. One week.

Over the weekend, the girls had decided the Pretty would be kept in the bathroom cabinet and they weren't to tell anyone else about it, no exceptions. Krista promised she'd try to find Penny Baker to get more answers about what it was, and where she'd gotten it in the first place. They taped a timetable to the bathroom mirror. Evie marked she'd taken the Pretty on Thursday morning, one day after Krista, two days after Willow. She'd only have enough time to film one episode of *Extra Salt*. Of course, if she could be Chloe Fontaine for a month, or maybe two, then . . . No. She stopped the thought in its tracks. That would be far too dangerous: physically and emotionally. What if someone found out? What if she started to lose all her hair or grow a few extra limbs? Surely the Pretty was some form of poison, given how horrific the transformation had been.

One week was an adventure. Anything more was dangerous. Anything more might seriously mess with her head.

After all, Evie Selby didn't fail to notice how much better people treated Chloe Fontaine. And that was definitely weird.

It was almost as if she were a lovely, slightly vulnerable wild animal—a fawn, perhaps—that people were quietly thrilled to be around. Their gazes lingered on her face, and when she caught people looking, they'd glance away, not wanting to frighten her into fleeing. Of course, some people—men—wanted to shoot the fawn. The construction workers opposite the Heimert Schwartz building hollered at her as she waited to cross the road.

"Hey! Hey, sexy!" one called.

"Sexy! Sexy girl!" another followed, demonstrating the mental faculties of a toddler.

Evie narrowed her eyes, inwardly bristling. Exactly what reaction did they want here? *Oh, hello! Yes, I am interested in you sexually. Why don't you take me out, and I can talk about postmodernism and you can talk about pouring concrete?*

And the Pretty opened literal doors too. Studio doors, with red-and-white On Air signs.

On Monday morning, Evie rode the elevator to the twelfth floor, an as-yet-unseen part of the enormous Heimert Schwartz complex. The elevator doors opened onto a wide corridor, with ceilings twice the height of those at the *Salty* office, and gray concrete underfoot instead of polished floorboards. Kelly was waiting, arms folded. His jeans were hitched in place with an enormous silver belt buckle of a hissing serpent. "Chloe-with-a-C," he announced. "Thanks for being on time."

They headed through a set of double glass doors, around a corner into a large square space. Here, people with multicolored rolls of duct tape attached to their pants were wheeling in cameras or carrying lights. "Studios are all here." Kelly pointed to four separate doors, each with an On Air sign. "We'll always be in Studio B." Kelly checked his watch. "They'll be out in a minute."

Evie peeked through the narrow strip of glass set into the door to Studio B. A mess of lights and cameras pointed at three men sitting behind a brightly lit desk in front of a green painted wall—a green screen, she assumed. The men were wearing suits and had necks like tree stumps. "What's their story?" Evie asked.

Kelly glanced in. "*Sports Weekly*, I think."

Evie watched the men's muted discussion. Soon she would be the one in front of the green wall. Today they were shooting all the intros and outros to the other reporters' stories, plus the promos. Kelly had sent the script to her new (fake) email over the weekend, pages of "Need more goss and glamour? Subscribe to *Extra Salt*!" and "From liners to lashes. Jeepers creepers, we show you how to get the peepers of the stars." Evie's eyes had rolled so hard they almost fell out of her head.

The studio door opened. "Okay, guys!" a voice boomed. "That's a wrap." Evie stepped out of the way as their crew began exiting.

"We'll bump our gear in as soon as they're all out," Kelly told her. "For now we'll get you into hair and makeup." Kelly waved at someone over Evie's shoulder. A striking-looking black guy was weaving his way toward them, pulling a small, wheeled suitcase behind him. A white fedora was angled on his head. His black shirt, complete with red buttons, was rolled up at the sleeves to reveal toned arms. As he got closer, Evie saw his lower lip and both pinkie fingernails were also bright red.

"Marcello," Kelly greeted him.

"Australia." Marcello sniffed at his hair. "Mmm, you smell *good*. What is that: eau de nicotine?"

Kelly socked his shoulder. "Fuck off, you know I quit. I did!"

"Mm-hmm." Marcello gave him a doubtful look. "And I'm the queen of England."

"You're the queen of something."

Marcello arched a well-groomed eyebrow. "Don't I know it."

Kelly snorted. "Mate, this is Chloe Fontaine, our host."

"Slash journalist," Evie added.

"Right." Kelly nodded, without skipping a beat. "Host slash journalist."

Marcello regarded her politely. His top eyelashes had a light coat of mascara. "Hello, Chloe."

For the first time since she arrived, Evie felt a creeping sense of intimidation. Not just because of Marcello's style. Because he carried himself with the air of someone it'd be impossible to impress. "Yo," she replied, and instantly regretted it.

She followed Marcello to a small door marked Dressing Room 4. A padded leather chair was positioned in front of a bench set into the wall under a long mirror bordered by light globes the size of oranges. There was a black washbasin in one corner. Marcello tossed his fedora on the bench and swung his suitcase up next to it. He popped it open, revealing a neat array of lipsticks, powders, mascaras, and more. He began unpacking everything with practiced efficiency. Evie paused in the doorway, unsure. He waved a blush brush at her. "Take a seat at the basin, beautiful, we don't got all day."

Say it. Trojan. Horse. Remember?

"You need to use the restroom?" Marcello sounded wary. "It's down the hall, second on the left, but, sweetheart, I can tell if you be using that for a quick-fix *diet*." He mimed sticking a finger down his throat. "And I *will* tell Australia, because I will *not* be working with females who think throwing their guts up is—"

"What? Oh god, no," Evie cut him off. "It's just . . ." She took a deep breath and tried to mimic Marcello's look of haughty defiance. "I won't be needing hair and makeup."

Marcello frowned. "Australia didn't say anything about y'all bringing your own people."

Evie shook her head. "I don't have my own people. I just don't want any hair or makeup done."

Marcello considered her, not quite intrigued, but certainly not bored. "Why not?"

Evie drew herself up until Chloe was towering. "Because it sets an unrealistic beauty standard for women and girls. Because it encourages women to perceive their value to be linked to their appearance. Because we need role models who look like *real girls*."

Marcello stood stock-still, completely stunned. Then he tipped his head back and burst into laughter. "That's good!" he said, giggling appreciatively. "You're good, Chloe." He pulled a white lace handkerchief from his pocket to dab at the corners of his eyes. "Ooh, you got me smudging. Go ahead and sit down at the basin, beautiful."

Evie's cheeks were warm. Nerves were starting to be replaced with irritation. "I'm not kidding. I don't want to wear makeup for the shoot."

Marcello smiled at her quizzically. "You don't want me to do your hair?"

"No."

"And you don't want any makeup."

Evie shook her head.

He opened his mouth, closed it, then opened it again. "'Cause you want to apply it yourself?"

Evie shook her head.

"'Cause you . . . brought your own product?"

Now Evie was smiling when she shook her head. She was literally blowing this man's mind.

Marcello glanced at the closed door. "Does Australia know about this?"

"No. But I'm not asking his permission," Evie added. "This is the choice I'm making."

"And this is because you think makeup is"—Marcello waved a hairbrush around—"bad for females."

"Because it sets an unrealistic—"

"Okay, okay," Marcello spoke over her. "Settle down, this ain't *Oprah*." He leaned back on the bench in front of the mirror and stared at her thoughtfully. Evie could see a million thoughts rushing behind his cat-shaped eyes. Was he going to bribe her? Beg her? Knock her out with hairspray and make her up while unconscious?

He shrugged. "All right."

Evie blinked, surprised. "All right?"

He began packing up his kit. "You gotta do you, girl. If you don't want my help, that is fine and dandy by me."

Evie nodded, reminding herself not to act too grateful. "I'm sorry we won't be working together."

Marcello swung his kit back onto the floor. "Oh, we'll be working together. You can trust me on that." He paused, assessing her with a cool, curious eye. When he spoke it was almost more to himself. "I've dealt with my fair share of newbies, but I've never had this."

Kelly hadn't said anything to Marcello about this being her first gig. But it didn't sound like that was what the makeup artist meant. He was looking at her in the same way Jan had in the audition: as if Evie was hiding something. As if he *knew*. She tried to mask her alarm. "How do you know I'm a newbie?"

"Oh, honey. It's written all over your *newbie* face." He gave her a long, meaningful look, then sailed out of the room.

20.

Gemma and Rose, *Salty*'s fashion editors, were waiting outside the dressing room with four racks of frocks. The sharp pinch of insecurity Marcello's comment had inspired promptly worsened. Just like the popular girls at her high school, Gemma and Rose had never been mean to her, not directly. They just treated her like she was irrelevant: young and uncool. Instinctively, she braced herself for the effortless way the pair normally looked right though her.

"Chloe, hi! I'm Rose—"

"And I'm Gemma." She fluttered her false eyelashes at Chloe's waist approvingly. "Oh, I'm so glad you're really a two—"

"So many girls lie," Rose whispered.

"But you'll fit everything we have. Is there anything that catches your eye?"

Evie stared at the duo in front of her: obedient chipmunks in couture. Their heads were cocked, eyebrows raised, waiting—impossibly— to *follow her lead*. Evie felt a little surge of anger before trying to focus on the clothes. Everything looked too bright, too shiny. She tugged at the first thing her fingers landed on. "Um, this?"

"Definitely!"

"Love that!"

Evie frowned, moving her fingers at random. "Or this?"

"Even better!"

"So cute!"

They were performing monkeys, dancing on command. But before she could work out just what to do with this, Rose extracted a green snakeskin catsuit. "If you like those, you'll *love* this."

"It's a Luksus," Gemma added, stroking it lovingly. "Ferosh, right?"

Evie read the price tag: $3,150. That was more money than she made in a month. And she had a full-time job in Manhattan. She tried to make her voice sound gushy. "Totally ferosh. But, actually, I have an even better idea. What if I just wear this?" She indicated the soft gray T-shirt she was wearing.

The chipmunks blinked, trying hard to follow along. "What do you mean?" Gemma asked.

"I mean, I wear this. It was made in Brooklyn, and some of the company's profits fund microloans in South America. Isn't that . . . like, fresh?" Evie said, trying hard to remember the lingo the girls used. "Conscious consumerism is really my jam."

Rose stared at the shirt as if it were a dirty dish towel. "But it's just a *T-shirt*."

"You can't just wear a T-shirt," Gemma said. "You can't. You just can't."

"Yes, I can," Evie said, smiling. "I think it's so cool. I love this shirt, it's totally my favorite."

The girls stared at Evie unhappily. They couldn't defy her, Evie realized. Talent was in charge. She was talent.

Gemma held up a delicate purple scarf. "What about if we just add this?"

"Yes!" Rose gasped, expertly tying it around Evie's neck.

It felt luxuriously soft against Evie's skin. "It's beautiful," Evie admitted.

Gemma jumped on her interest eagerly. "It's organic silk."

"Please?" Rose's eyes were puddles of naked need. "It looks so pretty on you."

"All right," Evie said. "I'll wear the scarf, but only if I wear the T-shirt." Rose winced and nodded.

Gemma pulled a brave face. "Yay?"

. . . . .

Evie came back into the studio feeling triumphant. While Evie Selby could be assertive, even downright vicious, online, she was not like this in person. Chloe Fontaine was. Chloe didn't seem to care as much about what other people thought. She was like a Russian spy who drank vodka during the day and wore fur, even though that was politically dicey. Now all Chloe had to do was stick around for a few more days, and not suddenly disappear on camera. Imagine that, turning back into Evie Selby, in front of all these people. And what if it was just as abject, just as painful? The thought gripped Evie with such a quick, hot horror that she had to force herself to deep-breathe until it went away.

One drop. One week.

She hoped.

The *Sports Weekly* desk and chairs were gone. In their place was a bright red chair tucked into a hot pink desk, which was decorated with a glass bowl of sweets and a vase of white tulips. The Girl Fairy had paid the studio a visit.

Kelly appeared beside her. "Is there a problem with your style team?"

Evie shook her head. "No."

One of the crew members called, "Camera up. Ready when you are, Kell."

Kelly cursed softly under his breath. "We saw a hundred girls, you know. I pushed for you."

"And I'm still going to do a really good job," Evie said. "I'm the same person you saw last week."

Rich wandered over, rubbing his jaw. "She doesn't look that bad," he said, looking Evie up and down as if she were a mannequin.

Kelly checked his watch. "We don't have time to piss-fart around. Let's just shoot her as is. Chloe, take a seat."

Evie obeyed. From her vantage point overlooking the studio floor, she saw various crew members frown at her, perplexed. An older man with silvery hair approached Kelly, but Kelly just waved him away, hissing, "I know, I know."

Evie looked down at her hands, pretending not to notice. *Stay strong. You're in charge.*

"Okay, Chloe." Rich addressed her from next to the huge camera aiming at her. "You'll just be reading off the teleprompter. Ready?"

Evie nodded. "Yep."

"Then let's roll sound." A flurry of crew calls, then they were recording.

For the next thirty minutes Evie read and reread the script. Rich had her say things like, "All the goss and glam you've been craving" and "Want a little extra? Subscribe to *Extra Salt*" a bajillion times, each time emphasizing a different word or adding a wink. Her cheeks hurt from smiling. But she was determined to prove to Kelly and the crew that she was a professional. A professional who didn't need five inches of makeup and fuck-me cleavage to do her job.

Eventually, it was time to take a break. Before Evie had the chance to stand up, Kelly approached her with a white plastic box. He emptied the contents onto the desk. A dozen different dildos tumbled out merrily.

"Ah, okay." Evie chuckled cautiously. "You have some fun hobbies you're not afraid to share."

"Jan wants to feature one as Dildo of the Week," Kelly announced.

"Dildo of the Week? Isn't that a little crude?"

"Mate, it's playful and fun," Kelly said. "Pick whichever one you want. And don't worry," he added as Evie opened her mouth to protest. "We're saying it was a viewers' pick, not your own preference."

Kelly strode off, leaving Evie alone with the dildos. What a ridiculous task: picking the Dildo of the Week. Once Chloe had proved and asserted her authority, they certainly wouldn't be doing silly stories like this. Evie picked up the closest dildo warily: an enormous black thing the size of a child's arm. *I shall call you Morgan Freeman.* She waved Morgan Freeman around a little, trying to get the magic-pencil thing going. Huh, it was working. Stiff old Morgan Freeman was going all squiggly . . .

A new thought popped into her head. A deliciously exciting and absolutely perfect thought that eclipsed the desk full of dildos. "Kelly?" she called, squinting out into the blackness of the studio floor.

Kelly reappeared a few feet in front of her. "What's up?"

Evie tapped Morgan Freeman against her cheek, trying to appear thoughtful and not insanely eager. "We should cover Velma Wolff's book launch tonight."

"The lesbo?"

Evie was too excited to be annoyed by this. "For *Milk Teeth*, it's her new one. It's about—"

"I've heard of it." Kelly hitched up his jeans. "You sure it's tonight?"

"At the Pembly. *Salty* is covering it for the magazine, so I know Jan would be into it."

"How do you know that?"

Evie swallowed, regaining her composure quickly. "Evie told me. My roommate, Evie. She was in the features meeting."

Kelly glanced at his watch doubtfully.

"I can prep the questions," Evie added. "I've read every single one of her books. She's a *New York Times* bestseller," she added. "And stacks of celebrities will be there. Literally. There'll be so many celebrities they'll be putting them in stacks—"

"Okay, okay, hold your horses. I'll get Jan on the blower."

Evie assumed this was Australian for *on the phone*. "Amazing!"

"Only if she says yes," Kelly warned. "And we'd need an actual interview with her."

"Of course."

"And you'll need to"—Kelly pursed his lips together—"dress up. That's not negotiable. I don't even know if these fucking promos will be usable—"

"I'll dress up," Evie promised. Her cheeks were hot. She felt a bit giddy. Velma Wolff. Beautiful, classy Chloe Fontaine was going to interview Velma Wolff. Her excruciating elevator encounter with the writer was the only time she'd even met a celebrity, if you didn't count seeing James Franco making out with someone he should probably have been babysitting.

"Did you pick a dildo?" Kelly asked.

Evie gathered them all in her arms, grinning ecstatically. "How can I pick just one?" she gushed. "They're all my babies."

21

Krista was in the middle of a really good sex dream about Tristan McKell and something to do with midgets when her phone started ringing. Her room was impossibly dark as she fumbled for the offensive noise, eventually finding it and croaking out, "Hello?"

She heard a man's voice, tinny and with an accent. "Mes Penka? Your car is here."

"My car?"

"Supernew Pictures? Lenka Penka?"

Her car. The film. Her car to the film. Krista mashed her eyes with her palm. "Yeah. Shit. I'll be right down."

It was 5 a.m. The call sheet she'd been emailed over the weekend did state a 5 a.m. pickup, but Krista assumed that was a mistake. But when she emerged from her apartment building twenty-five minutes later and saw the relief in her driver's eyes, she realized that yes, she was supposed to be ready at 5 a.m. In the morning. Just like . . . a baker.

In her mind's eye, she had imagined watching the city streets flow past her, from her position as Famous Important Actor in the backseat of her very own chauffeured car. In reality, she fell straight back asleep. Hungover. Again. The weekend had been, well, *epic* was an understatement. She'd gotten home at four in the afternoon on Sunday. Her left shin was sporting a bruise she didn't remember getting, she could not get "Copacabana" out of her head, and for some reason the phrase "Now *that's* what I call a burger!" struck her as very funny but she couldn't remember why. Her nose was running. She hadn't paid for a single drink all weekend. Amazing.

She was woken sometime later by a gentle, "Mes? Hello, mes?"

Dirty gray dawn had given way to raw pink morning. They were pulling into a lot full of trucks. Krista pulled a hand mirror from her pocket, checking quickly that it was still Lenka Penka in the backseat. It was. "All good," she told her reflection. "You got this."

A young guy wearing a headset opened her door. He had very curly pale blond hair that looked like pubes. "Lenka, hi, good morning."

"Hi. Hey," Krista replied, emerging from the car somewhat ungracefully.

"I'm Damian. We're a little behind so I'm going to get you straight into hair and makeup."

Damian strode off. Krista followed him, her sleepiness gone. The buzz in the air was palpable. She couldn't believe that this many people were up *so early*. There were crew members everywhere: carrying equipment, walking briskly with clipboards, wheeling racks of clothes. After they cleared the parking lot, Krista realized they were on the grounds of an actual amusement park, albeit one that appeared abandoned. The tall gates they walked through were covered with peeling red paint. The rides and game booths were faded and ghostly still. "Is this part of the set?" Krista asked.

"No, this is all base camp," Damian replied. "We're only shooting on about a quarter of the actual park itself, which is up ahead. Okay, here we are."

They stopped in front of a large silver trailer. The sound of hair dryers and the smell of nail polish remover wafted from inside it. "See you later," Damian said.

Krista watched him walk away, just as efficiently as he'd arrived. Then she flagged down the nearest crew member and asked where she could find Greg.

She was directed to the part of the amusement park that had been turned into the set. Lights were being set up around a games booth that, unlike the other ones, was freshly painted and looked brand-new. Greg was examining some storyboard sketches on an iPad when Krista approached. Again, he was dressed in soft flannel and washed-out denim: just as ready to milk some cows as direct a feature film.

"Lenka!" he exclaimed. "Hi!"

They embraced warmly.

"This is so exciting." Krista beamed. "I just wanted to have a quick word with you about my character."

"Absolutely. What's up?"

"I read the script over the weekend—so funny, by the way, big congratulations—"

"Thank you." Greg smiled.

"But Dream Girl doesn't really have a lot of lines." Krista cocked her head at him.

"Right," Greg said. "Like I said, it is a small role, but a very important one."

"I get that. I do. But the way it's coming across now is that Dream Girl is just—and no offense or anything—a pair of tits in a skirt. But obviously even superhot girls have depth. Hot girls like me," she was quick to add.

Greg's eyebrows drew together slightly. "Obviously."

"So, I was thinking, what if Dream Girl isn't just hot, she's also funny? What if she had a few quirks or a running gag?"

"Like what?"

Krista consulted the list of ideas she'd compiled on her phone. "What if she has a really big vagina?"

Greg flinched. "A what?"

"A hilarious *Mary Poppins*–style vag that she keeps tons of stuff in."

"A big . . . vagina," Greg repeated slowly. "I'm not exactly sure how that would work."

"Name something."

"What?"

"Name something. Something one of the characters needs."

Greg folded his arms, looking concerned. "A . . . hat."

Krista mimed pulling one out from between her legs. "A hat, you say? I have one right here!" She mimed putting the hat on, smiling. "Obviously in the film it'd be a real hat. Name something else."

"I don't think a really big vagina strikes the right . . . tone," Greg said.

"No worries." Krista glanced back at her phone, determined to keep the ideas coming. "Oh, this is a good one: What if Dream Girl secretly wants to be a singer? So whenever she's talking with anyone, it starts normal." And now Krista started singing enthusiastically, arms flung wide. "*And then she breaks into soooonnng! She sings every word, like I'm singing them right noooowww!*"

Greg gave her a weird look. For the first time, Krista sensed a lost connection. A niggle of anxiety picked at her optimism. Her ideas were funny, weren't they? She wasn't making a fool of herself, was she?

Greg waved at someone over her shoulder, looking relieved. "Yo!" he called. "My man!"

Ravi Harlow was sauntering over. On seeing Krista, the grin on his face faltered. But it was too late. Greg had already stepped past Krista to engulf the actor in a hug.

"Hey," Ravi greeted Greg, but his eyes were glued on Krista. "What . . . uh . . . what's up?"

"Surprise!" Greg said with a laugh in his voice. "We found your Dream Girl!"

"Ta-da!" Krista turned her palms upward, grinning, unsure why Ravi wasn't.

"Whoa . . . What?" Ravi's frozen smile was fraying around the edges.

"Yeah, your buddy, Lenka," Greg said. "You guys know each other, right?"

"Yup," said Krista at the same time Ravi said, "Nope."

Krista cocked her head at Ravi, confused. Someone called Greg away. He slipped off, seeming happy for the distraction.

"How's it going, dude?" Krista asked. "Hey, you don't have a cig, do you?"

Ravi looked at Krista as if she'd just asked him for his home address. "Uh, no."

"Hey." Krista stepped forward toward him, lowering her voice. "Look, it doesn't have to be weird. If you just want to be buds, that's totally cool."

"I never said I'd call," Ravi said, backing up a step.

Krista felt a flash of annoyance. "Neither did I."

"Whatever." Ravi turned around and began walking away.

Krista stared at his retreating form, jaw loose with surprise. In the past, she'd assumed some guys didn't want to see her again because they weren't into tiny brown girls. But now, it was becoming apparent some guys were just jerks.

22.

Willow woke up to a full body assault: sharp stabs of stomach cramps. She doubled over, moaning, the pain spotting her vision. Her period? No, that was only last week. Food poisoning? She noticed her fingers: bony, pale. Willow's fingers. She pulled herself into a sitting position, wincing. The mirror above the sofa revealed stringy ash-blond hair with a memory of pale pink dye and skin the color of skim milk.

She was Regular again.

The morning was muggy and overcast. The sky was a dull sweep of off-white, as if nature or God or whatever had simply forgotten to make weather today. Her sickness subsided more quickly than the first transformation. Evidently, it was easier turning Regular than it was turning Pretty. Willow took the subway from Williamsburg back to the Upper East Side. This was where she belonged now, squashed next to disinterested businessmen with their gray hair and skin and hearts. The streets seemed dirty and lackluster. Her doorman looked tired, barely managing a wave. Even the elevator opened into the apartment with what sounded like a bored sigh.

There was a leather duffel bag by the side table. A pair of scuffed men's shoes. Her heart tightened.

Her father was home.

She could hear them in the kitchen. Claire's measured, unflappable tone. Matteo's booming voice, loud even in his own home. Despite having lived in the US since he was a teen, his looping, blunt Dutch accent was still strong. Sometimes, Willow wondered if he'd kept it deliberately, somehow. To charm people. Or intimidate them.

Matteo and Claire had met when Claire had been writing her PhD dissertation on him, *Lost Boys, Macho Men, and Wanton Women: The Cinema of Matteo Hendriksen*. What was most interesting about their relationship was its longevity. In his day, Matteo had been a notorious womanizer. A Google search brought up images of a grinning young man, surrounded by near-nude women with Farrah Fawcett blowouts. Claire was (roughly) girlfriend number six, the tail end of a string that followed Willow's parents' divorce when she was ten.

There was a sizzling noise and the smell of cooking onions. Willow paused by the entryway and took three deep breaths. She made her face blank. Then she walked in.

The pair stopped talking. Claire was by the oven, her hand on the handle of a frying pan. Her father was leaning against the large kitchen island. A newspaper was open in front of him. Two fingers had frozen, about to turn a page.

Claire was the first to speak. "Willow!"

Her father didn't say anything.

Neither did Willow.

Claire glanced between the two. She crossed the clean tiles to give Willow a quick, hard hug. "Hey. We, um . . ." She glanced at Matteo. "We didn't know when you'd be home."

Willow gave a noncommittal shrug.

Matteo turned the page of his newspaper, but he was looking only at Willow.

Claire moved back to the onions. They were starting to smoke. "Would you like to stay for lunch? I'm making a stir-fry."

An equally blasé shrug.

"She'll stay," Matteo said. Even when speaking quietly, his voice seemed to make the glassware on the shelves shiver.

"Will I?" Willow shot back. How typical of her father. Telling her what to do.

"She'll stay," Matteo continued evenly. "Or she won't get the present I bought for her." He lifted his eyes. Now his expression was playful. Mischievous.

Willow tried to scowl. But she couldn't. Her father, for all his many, many flaws, always brought back frustratingly wonderful presents from his trips abroad. The Venezuelan death mask. The taxidermy Moroccan spider. The silver pipe from Joni Mitchell's Parisian pied-à-terre. In spite of herself, she felt intrigued.

Claire glanced between her partner and his daughter, relief softening her stance. "Fifteen minutes," she told Willow.

They ate in the dining room, three people circling the edge of a table that easily fit twenty. Claire's stir-fry was delicious—seared tofu and julienned carrots and yellow bell peppers over brown rice—but Willow ate with deliberate slowness so as not to convey how good she found it. (Had her sense of taste become more acute after changing back or was she looking for comparisons that weren't actually there? Too hard to tell.) She drank the glass of sauvignon blanc she'd poured for herself considerably quicker. Her father talked nonstop about potential locations he'd scouted on this trip; the wonderful old church in Prague, the tiny inn with the secret courtyard in Rome, the zoo that time forgot in Madrid. "In fact, it was in that zoo," Matteo concluded, "that I found this." He lifted a gold paper bag from between his feet and slid it across the polished tabletop. It was light. Willow reached inside and pulled out something wrapped in purple tissue. She could feel both Claire and her father watching her as she unwrapped it.

It was a wooden figurine of a lion. Three inches tall, painstakingly carved from honey-colored wood. Willow turned it over, eyes traveling over her lion's flowing mane, whipping tail, and bared teeth. It was wild and delicate at the same time. Violent and precious. It was wonderful.

She smiled. "Thank you."

Her father grunted with pleasure and pushed his empty plate away. "So," he announced to the room. "You've been staying with Mark."

It was a statement. Not a question. Willow pushed her plate away too. "Yes."

"Have you moved in there? Finally flown the coop?"

This question surprised her. "No," she said. "I just—" She glanced at Claire. "Needed a break from living here."

Her father snorted sarcastically. "Yes," he said. "I can see how all this"—he raised his hand to indicate the dining room, the apartment in general—"must be so tiresome for you."

"Matty," Claire said. "That's not what she means." Claire leveled her gaze at Willow. "Is it?"

Willow shrank down into herself, feeling the weight of their respective gazes drill into her. She couldn't tell if she felt exactly fourteen years old because her father was treating her like a teenager, or she'd started acting like one. After all, she had no rational-sounding explanation of her absence, so in a way it was like being a teenager again: feelings she couldn't explain and memories of regrettable acts. She didn't know what to say, so she said nothing.

Matteo touched a napkin to his lips. "Why haven't you moved out yet?"

Willow's voice sounded louder than she wanted it to. "You want me to move out?"

"That's not what I said, is it?" Matteo replied.

Willow shrugged and lifted her wineglass again. "I don't have any money." And then, before her father could protest, "Any of my own."

"What about your photographs?" Matteo asked.

Willow bristled.

"Your exhibition," he pressed. "Haven't you sold—"

"I sold one, Dad, okay? I sold one fucking photograph." Willow reached for the bottle of wine and sloshed her glass full.

Claire looked sympathetic and uneasy. "Oh, honey. I'm sure you'll sell more. I can put some postcards up for you in the student lounge if you like."

"Don't bother," Willow said. "They all suck. Everything I do is stupid."

She swallowed some wine, bracing herself for her father's inevitable words of encouragement. Matteo picked at his teeth. "Make some more work."

"What?"

"Make some more work. You're right. Your photographs lack . . ." His eyes wandered, searching for the right word. "Life. They are flat. Like . . . an advertisement."

Willow blinked rapidly. "You haven't even seen them—"

"I went this morning. As soon as I got back."

Embarrassed anger built in Willow's chest, spreading to her cheeks as a hot flush. "You don't like them?"

"I've seen you do better." Matteo leaned forward, hand raised for emphasis. "Do what scares you, my pet. *Be unsafe.*"

Willow found herself looking to Claire—Claire!—for support. "I . . ." she stuttered. "I . . . Fuck you!"

Matteo leaned back in his chair, with something like amusement in his eyes. "The eternal words of the scorned artist. 'Fuck you.' Sweetheart, you'll have to learn to take criticism. No one's any good when they start. Look at *Smoke and Summer,*" he added, referencing his first film, which had been enthusiastically panned worldwide. He glanced at Claire, who squirmed in her seat and chuckled weakly.

Willow turned on her. "Thanks a lot. Real nice."

"No," Claire protested. "Willow, I was just—"

Willow pushed back her chair so fast it screeched. The idea that her father wouldn't be supportive, thrilled, proud beyond belief of her first solo show hadn't even crossed her mind. She was so stupid. Of course he'd be a bastard about it. *Of course he would*. "Why is it so fucking hard for you to act like my dad?"

"I'm being honest, Willow. To help you grow."

"Oh, honest? You want honest?" Breathing hard, she turned back on Claire, whose face was raw with alarm. "He'll leave you for someone my age."

Claire made a small strangled sound. Matteo's face turned a fierce, muddy red.

Head whirring loudly, Willow ran for the elevator, collapsing inside it only after the doors slid shut.

23.

Krista called Evie from outside the large white tent that was set up for lunch. The phone rang so long Krista was worried it'd go to voicemail, before Evie finally picked up, breathless. "Lenka Penka, star of stage and screen. How's it going?"

"Disaster is a massive fucking understatement." Krista lit a cigarette, inhaled deeply.

"What? What's wrong?"

As various crew members drifted by with plates of steaming food, Krista relayed the morning's respective failings: the fact she had no good lines whatsoever, how Ravi Harlow was not only treating her like a stalker but was *in* the fucking film too, and how because she was basically just an extra, she'd been assigned a junior makeup artist who was about as experienced as an Amish schoolgirl. "What should I do?" she whined into the phone. "Should I call Cameron? Should I leave? Evie? Fuck, are you even there?"

There was a pause before Evie said, "Sorry. Trying to find an outfit for tonight. You'll never guess who I'm going to interview—"

"Evie!" Krista stamped her foot. "Can we focus on me for five fucking seconds? *What should I do?*"

"Nothing!" Evie exclaimed. "You shouldn't do anything. You're there to make money as quickly and quietly as possible. Who cares if you don't have any lines? *You're* not in the movie, Lenka Penka is. And she's not even real!"

"But it's so unfair! And how should I handle Ravi? I can't believe he's being such a douche—"

"I don't know. I have to go, I'm sorry—"

"Wait, I'm not finished workshopping this—"

"Babe, I'm sorry, we'll talk tonight. Or tomorrow. I might be home late. Bye!"

Evie hung up. Krista stared at her phone incredulously. That phone call didn't solve any of her problems at all. In fact, Evie sounded positively uninterested in what was undoubtedly the biggest life drama she'd ever experienced. Krista exhaled angrily and ground her cigarette butt into the earth.

Everyone. And. Everything. Was. Fucked.

At least it was lunchtime.

She stalked into the tent and saw the spread. "Jesus titty fucking Christ." The buffet looked as if it had been attacked by wild dogs. All the good stuff was gone. The large metal trays of chicken cordon bleu and steak and potatoes were scraped clean. All that was left was fruit, bagels, and plastic bowls of limp-dick salad. Fuck it, Krista decided. Dessert for lunch would have to do.

Not much was left in that department either—a bowl of gluggy fruit salad, a pile of plain, dry cookies, and—*a cupcake.*

One single, perfect cupcake.

Moist chocolate base. Thick cream frosting. Mini Reese's Pieces delicately covering a generous domed top. Cue white light and heavenly music. Krista's anger ebbed and was replaced with the single thought of *cupcake.* Cupcake would make all this go away. Her feet moved toward it, hand outstretched—

Someone grabbed it.

Krista flinched. Her head whipped to the cupcake kidnapper . . . Ravi Harlow.

They stared at each other.

What should she say? Hello? Fuck off? Give me the cupcake and we're even?

But before she could command her mouth to say anything at all, Ravi put the cupcake on his plate and started walking toward a group of guys sitting in the corner of the tent.

Just like that. Without a word. Without a *hint* of acknowledgment that just a few days ago, the mouth he'd be using to eat that precious cupcake had been eating her precious pussy. Evie was right: guys like Ravi treated women as if they were as disposable as goddamn razors.

And that's when Krista got mad.

"Hey," she called. He didn't turn around, but she knew he heard her. "Hey!" She strode after him, grabbed his shoulder, swung him around. Shock was written all over his face.

"You don't want to be my friend?" she exclaimed. "Fine—I have, like, a million friends. But we had sex, jerk face. You know it, and I know it." Ravi was frozen, mouth hanging open, allowing Krista to steamroll on. "We. Had. Sex. So the least you can do is *acknowledge my existence*. Because that's what grown-ups do." She plucked the cupcake off his plate and took an enormous bite. Her last three words were muffled through frosting. "Common. Fucking. Courtesy."

24

"Willow! Darling! I'm so glad you came by!"

And with that, Willow was unceremoniously wrenched from the reverie she'd been in for the last hour. After leaving her home, she'd numbly stumbled in the direction of the 6 train, desperate to get off the Upper East Side and back to Williamsburg. Once there, she'd just been walking. Walking without seeing, trying to escape her father's cruelty, Claire's face, and the things she'd said. Which was why she was so shocked to hear her name. And then even more shocked to realize it was Meredith, the curator of Wythe Gallery. *Her* gallery. With her horrible photographs. That she was standing in front of. Without realizing it, her mindless ramble had brought her back to the scene of the crime. Drawn inevitably to her own failings.

Meredith dropped the cigarette she was smoking and raised a hand in greeting. Her bun was held in place with bright red chopsticks, and her fashionably oversized black-rimmed glasses gave her an artsy, intimidating air.

Willow drew her arms across her chest. "Hi, Meredith."

Meredith kissed an inch above both of Willow's cheeks loudly. "Come in, come in," she warbled in her vaguely pretentious, swallowed sort of voice. "Let's have a chat."

Willow tried to avoid looking at her photographs as the pair crossed the gallery—completely empty, Willow noted—on their way to Meredith's cramped little office in the back. Meredith made oolong tea, prattling on about some *amaaaazing* group exhibition she'd been at last night, all artists Willow had never heard of. "You should've come with me, sweetie," Meredith insisted. "You need to get out there, meet your fellow artists. It's such a small world, everyone knows everyone."

Willow accepted the teacup Meredith offered with just a nod.

"Have you been working on anything new?"

"Um . . ." Willow let her gaze trail around Meredith's busy office space, over art books and cardboard tubes and rolls of bubble wrap.

"Because I really think you have so much potential," Meredith continued. "And look, I know this exhibition has been . . . underperforming. What would help is if you were more active online. You're the brand, Willow. You need to build a fan base. Instagram, Twitter, Facebook." Then, with a deliberate kind of caution, "What about your father?"

The question sliced at Willow. "What about my father?"

"Something from him would really help. Maybe, a tweet? Or a quote—"

Willow's voice was brassy. "Actually, I have been working on something new."

Meredith's eyes lit up. "Wonderful!"

"I've been working with a new model," Willow said. "Caroline. She's . . . really different. Really . . . unpredictable."

"What sort of themes are you exploring?"

"Doppelgängers. Shadow selves. The idea that you can be your own worst enemy."

Meredith looked as if she was deciding whether this was genius or bullshit. "Show me what you've done so far."

Willow slouched in her chair. "We haven't really started yet. They're only tests."

"Show me." Meredith waved her hand at Willow. "I'm your curator. I can help."

Willow drew out her phone reluctantly. The self-portraits she had taken, the day Mark lied to her, had been pushed to her iCloud. Caroline, beautifully mournful, heartbreakingly tear streaked, stared back at her: a former life, a ghost. Her hand was trembling when she gave Meredith the phone.

Meredith swished through the series. Her face was unreadable. Then she pressed her hand into her chest. When she looked up, Willow was surprised to see her eyes were glassy. "These are fantastic."

"Really?"

"Such raw emotion," Meredith breathed. "Pain. Suffering. I can feel it. And your model is exquisite. What did you say her name was?"

"Caroline," Willow answered, before adding, "but she's not a professional model." *So don't go looking for her.*

"Even better!" Meredith exclaimed. "*You* discovered her. This is why I signed you up. I knew you had depth. I could feel it. When can I see more?"

"You really think these are good?"

"I don't think. I know. Because I feel. These make me feel." Meredith leaned forward to hand Willow's phone back. As she did, the shadows around her face shifted, pooling under her eyes. The effect was disconcerting: oddly ominous, even minacious. Then Meredith settled back in her chair, and the moment passed. "When can I see a proper shoot?"

"Soon," Willow replied. "Soon."

25.

Krista sat slumped in a corner of the extras' tent, feeling invisible. When could she go home? She didn't even have a trailer; another cruel joke from the universe. She was sitting on a milk crate, for chrissake. *A milk crate.*

She scrolled through her phone. Krista Kumar's unexpected absence was taking its toll: texts from her gym buddy after she was a no-show this morning, a planning thread for a surprise birthday party she'd miss, a message from an improv friend wanting to plan seeing a show together. Her FOMO made her feel anxious and depressed in equal measure, and it was this rare moment of vulnerability that led to impulsively picking up a call from her dad. "Hey, Papa."

"Krishnakali!" Krista winced. Her Indian name always preceded a lecture. "Why haven't you been taking my calls?"

Krista mumbled that she'd been busy.

"With acting? Krista, that is not a good use for your brain. You must reenroll at Boston. You must complete your studies."

"Krista?" It was her mom, picking up on the other line.

"Hi, Mama—"

"Sweetheart, why don't you just get a job, like Evie?" her mother began. "She is such a good girl. Except for that tattoo." Her mom tutted disapproval.

"Why don't you want to become a lawyer?" her father asked. "All these years, you tell me you want to become a lawyer, and then you change your mind?"

"Well—" Krista tried to interject but her mother spoke over her.

"She can change her mind! She just needs to get a job."

"No, she *must* finish her studies."

Krista listened numbly as her parents began to bicker. Maybe they'd just wear her down. Maybe it'd be easier to capitulate to at least one of their demands. She wished she'd hidden her smarts from them more effectively—who knew all those glowing middle school report cards about the "highly intelligent if easily distracted" Krista Kumar were going to lead to her parents taking on the role of career counselors long after she graduated high school? Why wasn't there so much pressure on her brothers? Maybe because none of them had defied her parents as much as their youngest child had, the child whose GPA was also the family's highest. She knew her parents loved her. She just wished they didn't have to be so first generation about it.

Her phone chirruped. Evie was calling. She tapped to pick up. "Hey, I'm on the other line to my parents, not that they'd even notice I wasn't there—"

"Krista." Evie's voice was hushed and insistent. "You're on the internet."

"We all are, genius. It's 2016."

"No, I just texted you a link. Shit, Krista." Evie exhaled. "You were supposed to *keep a low profile*."

Krista whipped the phone from her ear and saw the text from Evie. A link. To a gaudy gossip website. She tapped it open. A splashy headline around a video burst onto her screen. The title: *Cupcake Girl Serves Ravi Harlow!* The video started playing.

It was her.

And Ravi.

In the food tent.

She heard Lenka's voice. Tinny. But perfectly distinct. "You don't want to be my friend? Fine—I have, like, a million friends. But we had sex, jerk face—"

Krista closed the web page. She couldn't breathe. How? Who?

Someone filmed that? Shakily, she pressed the phone back to her ear. "How did you get that?"

"How *didn't* I get it?" Evie snapped. "It's all over Facebook. There's a GIF of you biting the cupcake. You're a hashtag, Krista!"

"I'm a hashtag?"

"Yes!" exploded Evie. "Hashtag cupcakeoftruth! Kelly just called me, he wants to do something about it on the show tomorrow, instead of Dildo of the Week. It took me ten minutes to talk him out of it!"

"What's the Dildo of the Week?" Krista asked, because quite frankly none of the ones she had were very good when it came to—

"Krista!" Evie shouted. "Focus! You. Are. Viral. Everyone on that film set is going to find out any second!"

Krista looked up. Greg and Ravi were marching toward her, expressions apoplectic. "I think they already know."

Greg kept it together long enough for the three of them to make it to his trailer. As soon as the metal door swung shut, he turned on Ravi and Krista.

"Who?" Greg sounded like he was trying very hard to keep his voice even. "Who the hell filmed that?"

Ravi mumbled something at his shoes.

"What?" Greg asked him.

"My brother. My little brother, he was hanging out in craft services."

Greg's hands clenched into fists. "There's *Funderland* chairs in the background! Everyone's going to know this is from *my* film set."

"What about me?" Ravi jabbed his finger at Krista. "That crazy bitch made me look like a total douchebag!"

Krista lunged at him. Ravi shrieked, scrambling back. Greg grabbed her shoulders and yelled, "Stop, stop, stop!"

The trailer door swung open. A woman breezed inside without knocking. Early fifties, attractive in a severe way, with silver hair cut into a bob. "Everyone stop yelling." She addressed Krista brusquely. "Lana Lockhart, *Funderland*'s publicist."

Panting a little, Krista shook her hand. "Lenka Penka," she said. "Resident harlot."

"Fuck!" Greg wailed. "It was hard enough convincing the studio I could direct *Funderland*, and now this! I look like I can't keep control of my—"

"Calm down," Lana ordered. "It's all fixable."

Greg raked both hands through his hair. "How?"

"We say it was a rehearsal," Lana replied. "For a scene in the film."

"But she's barely in the movie!" Greg cried. "And there's no scenes like that!"

Lana shrugged. "So it was a scene we cut. All you have to do is bump up the size of her part, and it all goes away." Lana put one hand on Greg's shoulder and squeezed it. "Honey, we can use this. Cupcake Girl is trending on Facebook. We need to step in, claim it, and turn it into a story about *Funderland*. Cupcake Girl is *our girl*."

Ravi was nodding. "Yeah. Yeah. A rehearsal. Not real, yeah."

Lana directed her gaze at Ravi and Krista, speaking in the same soothing voice a parent might use on a crying child. "You two are friends. You've never had a sexual relationship."

"Yeah." Ravi nodded. "Friends."

"See?" Lana said. "Everyone wins."

"And I . . . get a bigger part in the film?" The corners of Krista's mouth twitched upward. "Do you want to use some of my ideas?"

Greg gave Krista a weak smile, shoulders slumping. "Sure. Why not?"

26.

A coiffed crowd billowed out from the entrance to the Pembly. Women with shaggy haircuts under pork-pie hats lit cigarettes for men in colorful bow ties and stripey shorts. Evie tugged down the hem of Krista's gold sequined dress an inch. She hoped she wasn't overdoing it. But it was Velma Wolff. She wanted to make an impression.

She maneuvered her way through the crowd, trying to keep her balance in three-inch heels, a decision she was already regretting. How did human women walk in these things, seriously? Her two-person crew was faithfully in tow: Adrian, a heavyset guy shouldering the camera, and a boom operator, Lo, a Korean chick wearing a Comic-Con shirt. At the hotel's entryway, Evie told a severe-looking woman with a clipboard who they were, and they were ushered inside.

You know you've made it, Evie thought, *when there's a door list for your book launch.*

When the Pembly first opened its doors in 1921, it served the city's best bathtub gin to Hollywood's most fawned over: John Gilbert, Charlie Chaplin, Alla Nazimova, Pepper Rose. It was one of those hotels that hosted artists, musicians, and writers as both long-term residents and short-term troublemakers. Elizabeth Taylor was rumored to have had an affair with John F. Kennedy in room 42 while married to Richard Burton. Debbie Harry overdosed here twice. Ernest Hemingway fought here regularly.

And now, history would once again be made. Evie Selby was going to her very first celebrity book launch, in the skin of another girl.

Gold-lettered signs affixed to dark wooden walls indicated where the party was, but they were unnecessary. Music, chatter, and just the fizzle in the air led the way to the hotel's ballroom. Once inside, Evie couldn't help but gasp. The room was royally, even ridiculously, sumptuous. An enormous chandelier hung from the ceiling, like an alien spaceship decked out for Christmas. A gleaming white piano dominated a raised stage at the front of the room, where a woman in a white tuxedo was playing "All of Me" under a huge *Milk Teeth* banner. The walls were adorned with bold modernist paintings: bright, violent slashes of color. A table was piled with cheesecake and berries.

"Champagne?" A silver tray of flutes was being offered to her. There was something about the way the waitress was smiling—suggestive, inviting—that seemed unmistakably dykey. Evie felt a surge of interest and promptly blushed. "Thanks," she said, taking two. The waitress grinned and walked away.

Someone passed her, murmuring, "Great dress."

The compliment came from a woman in a floaty pea-green frock who looked a lot like Julianne Moore. No, wait. That *was* Julianne Moore. "Th-thanks," Evie stuttered, wholly flustered.

Her eyes raked the room. More pings of celeb identification: Neil Patrick Harris chatting with Samira Wiley and Ingrid Nilsen, Ellen and Portia giggling with Rachel Maddow. Alison Bechdel having her photo taken with the cast of *Girls*. Ruby Rose and Jane Lynch were splitting a slice of cheesecake. It was weird and exciting and wholly unreal, like seeing zoo animals gallop up Madison Avenue.

"Excuse me." Someone was sliding past her.

Evie felt a jolt of recognition. "Quinn!"

The Ellen Page look-alike from the Wythe Gallery, her failed date. Evie could see the petite brunette's mind working, trying to place the statuesque Chloe. "Um, hi."

Quinn's coolness inspired a wash of loneliness. For a moment, Evie felt marooned in Chloe's body, trapped in a stranger's skin that Quinn didn't even recognize. The pause lengthened into awkwardness, and Evie rushed an explanation. "I saw you at a show last month. You were great."

"Oh. Thanks. That's really sweet."

"So, how are you?" Evie inched closer. "Are you working on anything new?"

"Yeah. Always." Quinn backed up a little. "I'm going to grab a drink. Nice to meet you." She turned away, heading for the bar.

Evie watched her in surprise. Most people jumped at the chance to speak with Chloe Fontaine. Maybe she'd come across as too stalkery, too familiar. Or maybe Chloe just wasn't Quinn's type. This was oddly flattering.

"Where's Velma?" Adrian's question brought Evie back to reality.

"I'm guessing over there." Evie pointed to the far corner of the ballroom with her glass. Dozens of people stood knotted in front of a huge reproduction of the *Milk Teeth* cover. As they began pushing their way toward it, the crowd grew thicker. Evie spotted a wall of books, hundreds of copies of the hardcover. White camera flashes burst over a clutch of people standing nearby. Evie's breath caught in her throat.

Velma.

Velma Wolff, in the flesh, looking beautiful and insouciant and 100 percent really right there. She was wearing her trademark Dior suit: a fitted white shirt, open at the neck, and tailored black pants. Her hair was pulled back into a sleek low ponytail that curled around one shoulder. Evie knew she was staring, but she couldn't help it. Even from across the crowded room, Velma exuded sex. It was in her eyes, hooded and almost lazy; it was in her stance, shoulders straight and confident. And of course, it was in her smile, which teased everyone around her.

"I'm guessing that's her," murmured Lo, plucking the second glass of champagne out of Evie's hand.

Evie didn't even notice. She felt dopey, like she'd just woken up.

"Yo," Adrian prompted. "Are we going to do this?"

Evie's heart rate began to rise. "Do this" was interview Velma Wolff.

Velma Wolff the celebrity. Velma Wolff the author. Velma Wolff the sex goddess. Who was she to get a second chance with Velma Wolff? She was the girl who cried—hysterically—when she didn't make Student Council and was too scared to use tampons until she was seventeen. She couldn't. She couldn't!

"Chloe?" Adrian nudged her. "I don't want to be a dick, but I really need to work on my fantasy baseball team tonight and—"

Adrian's monologue faded, eclipsed by a single word. Chloe. *Chloe*. She wasn't Evie anymore; she of uneven teeth and secret fat. She was Chloe, a beautiful swan who could rock a dress even Joan Rivers would've approved of. Evie downed the rest of her champagne. "I'll go get her."

Kelly had confirmed that Velma's publicist knew they were coming, so this shouldn't be a surprise. She was a professional, Evie reminded herself, who (for all Velma knew) met famous people every single day. She practiced the words in her head: *Hi, Velma, I'm Chloe from* Extra Salt. *Would you mind if we shot a quick interview with you after the reading?*

Finally, she was just a few feet away. Velma was shaking the hand of a gushing young fan who was telling her *she* was the reason why she came out in the first place and she loved all her books and she could not wait to read *Milk Teeth*, she just *could not wait*.

"Thank you," Velma was saying. "Thank you so much."

Velma's eyes rose languidly. They settled on Evie. The corners of her mouth lifted into a slow, gap-toothed smile. "Hi."

Evie forgot what words were. She failed to recall how her mouth worked.

Velma moved toward her. Evie could smell her: the heavy scent of lavender. "I'm Velma," she said, offering her hand.

Evie stared at the hand hovering a few inches from her belly button. The world seemed to warp around her. All she could think was *that's Velma Wolff's hand, that's Velma Wolff's hand, that's Velma Wolff's hand*. As if in a dream, she took it. As soon as she felt Velma's soft but certain palm enclose hers, a full-body shudder quivered over her skin. Evie opened her mouth to say the only thing she could say, the only thing she had ever been sure about in her entire life. "I love you."

Velma looked amused. "I love you too."

"No!" Evie shook her head. "I mean, hi. I'm Ev—Chloe." The link between her brain and her mouth was as stable as a bubble bath. "Chloe Fontaine."

"I'm Velma Wolff."

"Yeah, I know. There's a really big picture of you above the stage."

Velma grimaced at it, taking a half step closer to Evie as she did. "Hideous. Publicists, you know. Not my idea."

It sounded as if she actually cared that Evie believed that. "I'm here to interview you. For *Extra Salt*. A web series. Can I meet you after the reading?"

"Sure." Velma glanced around. "Where do you want to . . . do it?"

Evie blushed. She couldn't help it.

Velma's eyebrows pincered, surprised. Then, pleased.

Evie couldn't meet Velma's gaze. "Over by the chocolate fountain. I'll be the one swimming in it."

Velma laughed. A genuine, unexpected laugh. "Okay."

A woman wearing a headset tapped Velma on the shoulder. "Babe. You're up."

Velma nodded. "See you after," she said to Evie. "Chocolate fountain."

"Swimming." Evie continued to speak even after Velma had turned away. "Really looking to . . ." And now her voice dropped as she stared, starstruck, at Velma's retreating behind. "Work on my form."

27.

She'd been at Lenny's for over an hour before Mark came in. When they locked eyes, he froze. After a second, he spun around, but there was a group of people behind him, and in the few seconds he got caught up in the which-way-are-you-going dance, he looked back at her. She smiled at him, laughingly. He shook his head and smiled back.

"Hello again," Willow said.

"Hello, Caroline." Mark nodded at the bartender and ordered a Brooklyn Lager. He glanced at the empty stool next to her. "Is anyone . . ."

"No. Please." She liked the way Caroline's voice sounded airy and expansive, like a house made of glass. She hadn't even been sure that Caroline would reappear a second time: Krista hadn't specified whether the Pretty worked the same way with every dose. But the single drop of purple that hit her tongue after Evie was safely out of the apartment heralded the encore of her simpering blond alter ego. Briefly, she'd considered discussing the decision with Evie, the friend whose moral barometer she could always trust. But Evie had been more interested in getting her opinion on shoes, and hairstyles, and to-cat-eye-or-not-to-cat-eye, and in the end, she'd made the choice on her own. And so Caroline was back.

Mark took his seat as if he couldn't remember the normal way to sit on a bar stool. "What are you reading?"

She showed him the cover of a tattered paperback that looked straight out of the 1970s; *Lacan and the Shadow Self* by Dr. Thomas F. Pfiefferson, MD. "Heavy stuff."

Willow shrugged, fingering the pages. "There's a lot in here I relate to."

"Really? What are you, like, a philosophy student?"

She dropped her gaze down to the book shyly. When she looked up at him again, her eyes were dancing. "Yes. Exactly."

"Really? Wow. That's so cool."

"Is it?"

"This is going to sound dumb, but that's something I always wish I'd done. Studied philosophy."

I know. "I bet you studied something like industrial design."

Mark gaped at her. "You must be a mind reader. That's exactly what I studied!"

"What do you do now?"

"I design glasses."

She held up her wineglass in a question.

He shook his head, smiling, and tapped the side of the glasses he was wearing. "Eyeglasses. I founded a start-up with a friend from college. We create sustainable eyewear right here in New York using locally sourced materials."

The first time Mark had told her this, sometime after midnight at the party in Park Slope, Willow fumbled for a response. "I didn't realize people actually designed glasses," was what she'd said, and he'd frowned at her, as if she'd just asked him what kind of cheese the moon was made of. She'd replayed this moment repeatedly for the next week, scratching the itch of intellectual humiliation over and over again. Mark was smarter than she was. He knew it, and so did she. She suspected he liked this: if Willow had money, and connections, then at least he was smarter.

But Mark wasn't necessarily smarter than Caroline.

"Isn't the optical industry a perfectly integrated monopoly?" she asked. "I bet you've had some success being able to offer a lower price point."

"Exactly!" Mark's face lifted in surprised delight. "That's exactly right!"

Mark's entire beer was drained by the time they stopped talking about the social impact of affordable eyewear. While he was in the bathroom, she checked her phone: 9:45. She—Willow—was supposed to be meeting him for a late dinner at 10. His idea. She sent him a text. **sry somethin came up. see u later this wk?**

A strange feeling enveloped her when she pressed send. A blinding, joyful recklessness shot through with an undercurrent of sadness, of pain. She didn't want Mark to leave the bar; she was having fun with him. She wanted to hurt him; he was flirting with someone else. It felt like shoplifting: the excitement and the fear combining for a full-body rush. Or, more specifically, it felt like being an artist: accessing something beyond the ordinary, something dangerous and deep and true.

Be unsafe.

Mark slid next to her and gestured to her empty glass. "Another?" He sounded defiant.

Willow propped her head up with one hand, her cheek pressing into her palm. "You don't have to see your girlfriend?"

He flinched badly.

Willow giggled. "Relax. I have a boyfriend."

"You do?"

She nodded, tucking wisps of blond hair behind her ear self-consciously. "Of course I do."

Mark let out a breath. "Right. Of course you do."

"We're not doing anything wrong."

Mark nodded, unsure. He signaled the bartender and ordered another round.

"What's she like?" She didn't need to clarify who.

Mark shifted. "She's great. What's your boyfriend like? Is he a student too, or—"

But Willow swatted his words away. "You didn't answer my question." She cocked her head, words low, almost dangerous. "I bet she's gorgeous."

Mark laughed nervously. "Sure. Of course."

"You don't sound that convinced."

He took a sip of beer. "I don't know if I'd call her gorgeous."

She looked at him sharply. "No?"

"It's too pedestrian a phrase." He frowned. "Willow is more . . . unusual. More of an acquired taste."

Something began spreading inside her, something thick and wet and hot. She swiveled to face him fully. "Do you love her?"

He shifted his weight, his unease clear. "I don't know. Do you love your boyfriend?"

"I don't know either." She laughed suddenly. "I have no idea."

He smiled at this, stuck somewhere between fascination and terror. "At least you're honest."

Willow stretched both arms out in front of her. "If I'm honest," she said, "then I'd say I don't think my boyfriend is trustworthy." She turned her arms over. Blue veins traced all but invisible lines under the skin at her wrist. *This body is a map. Where is it taking me?* "Or maybe that's me." She looked up at Mark. He stared back, captivated. Captured. "I can't tell."

28.

Although the ballroom was completely full, Evie felt like she was the only one there, listening to Velma read in a tone as lazy as Sunday morning.

" '*You have never tasted anything. You think you have tasted lemonade. You think you have tasted salted french fries. You think you have tasted apple cake, and hamburgers, and delicate Swiss chocolates. But you have never tasted any of these things. Because you have never tasted blood.*' " Velma turned a page. The room was utterly silent. " '*After three days, the boy stopped trying to escape. Three days was usually how long it took. For someone to give up hope. For someone to stop screaming. For someone to simply stop. After three days of being locked in the old ski lodge's basement, the boy stopped thumping, crashing about like a bird who'd flown in through a window. Silence feathered into the dimness. It settled into the sturdy wooden rafters. It stretched out, languid, on the piebald velvet sofa where Lita sat, lost in a yellowed paperback. The basement was silent. She raised her head. It was time.*' " Another page turn. Evie's skin pimpled with goose bumps. " '*Blood is not metallic,*' " Velma continued. " '*It is not wet, or red, or messy. Blood, you see, is this: laughter that has begun to hurt. The whoosh of warmth from a firelit room when the night has turned nasty. A generous, sympathetic smile.*' "

Velma looked up, laconic and sheepish. She closed her novel. The room exploded with applause.

. . . .

Evie was on her third chocolate-covered strawberry when Adrian nudged her. "Here she comes."

A full hour had passed since Evie had confessed her undying love to Velma Wolff, but that didn't mean her nerves weren't still on high alert. Velma cut through the room like a shark. Evie subtly wiped her chocolatey fingers on the tablecloth and tried not to look terrified.

Velma nodded a hello to Adrian and Lo before addressing the girl in the gold sequined dress. "So. Evidently I'm not your only love."

Evie froze. "Wh-what?"

Velma wet the back of her thumb and smudged the corner of Evie's lips. Evie almost lost equilibrium, as if she'd been tossed into a dryer, put on full spin. Then she realized Velma was wiping away chocolate. As if she were a child.

"Oh god." Evie pawed at her mouth. "Is it gone?"

"Sadly, yes." Velma slipped both hands into her pants pockets and took a step back.

Lo hitched a boom mic. Velma flicked her gaze to Adrian, who was shouldering the camera in front of them. "All set?"

The light on the camera turned red. "Rolling."

The interview had started so unexpectedly that Evie completely blanked on the first question. "Hi," she blurted.

"Hi," Velma replied.

"I'm Chloe. From *Extra Salt*."

"Yes, I know."

Evie heard someone snicker. She willed herself to ignore the camera and sets of eyes behind it. "Velma Wolff. Your novels are known for their unreliable narrators. You delight in reversing your positions and confounding reader expectation. What's your stance on truth in fiction?"

Now it was Velma's turn to fumble, just for a second, before finding an answer. "I guess I don't really believe fiction can create truth, because each reader creates truth for her- or himself."

"How do you think your characters create truth for themselves?"

"I think most of my characters are completely delusional," Velma drawled, prompting titters of laughter.

Evie raised her eyebrows. "More or less so than actual people?"

"Equally."

"So you don't think people have great self-awareness."

Velma's voice hitched up in what sounded like surprise. "No."

Evie's voice became more confident. "Lita claims she resents being a vampire, but she gives in to her bloodlust continually and joyfully. Why is that?"

"She's a hypocrite."

"Why?"

"Because the body will always win over the mind."

"Is that your view on humanity in general?"

Velma shot a quick glance at someone watching. "Don't you want to ask me about what I'm wearing?"

"I couldn't care less what you're wearing." *Unless you're taking it off.*

As if she'd heard the thought, Velma held her gaze. For one second. Two. Three. Her eyes: gunmetal gray, the color of rain. Evie's chest constricted.

Velma blinked, looking like she was consciously pulling herself from a moment she hadn't planned on. "I think that's a wrap." She nodded at Evie, and her gaze bounced away.

Adrian switched off the camera light, Lo dropped the boom mic, and suddenly it was all over. Evie exhaled harshly, not sure if she was angry, excited, or disappointed. Maybe all three. It was that look that had thrown her off. That knowing, intimate look, as if they were already lovers and Velma had just proposed something scandalous—a quick fuck in the bathroom. Velma was the conductor; Evie was the orchestra, performing on command, almost beyond her own will . . .

"Chloe."

It was her. One hand on her arm, squeezing it slightly. Voice as discreet as a spy's. "A few of my friends are getting together in one of the suites upstairs. Would you like to join us?"

29.

It had taken Evie longer than it should have to realize the question was a direct invitation, but by then, Velma had already been absorbed by the clutch of literary hipster types who'd been trailing her all night. The friends, presumably. She had no idea if she was supposed to follow them, so she busied herself with thanking Adrian and Lo and seeing them off. She lingered at the entrance. From here, she was equidistant from the huge stairway that swept upstairs to the hotel's suites, and the cobbled Soho streets outside. But she couldn't wait around like a crazy fan forever. She had just decided to leave when Velma breezed out of the ballroom.

"Chloe. I'm so glad you're still here." Velma offered her an arm.

Together, they ascended the stairs, Evie caught up in Velma's followers like debris in a tornado.

The suite was already crowded by the time they arrived, brimming with music and laughter and the smell of weed. Like the ballroom, the interior design was Renaissance-meets-modern. Velvet rubbed shoulders with chevron. Bold black-and-white artworks hung on the bright red walls. Balcony doors were flung open, inviting the low roar of New York City into the room. Velma disappeared, swallowed up in a scattered round of applause. Evie hung in the doorway and tried not to be intimidated by the fact the suite was bigger than her entire apartment and probably cost a month's rent per night.

"Great dress." A woman with a long black braid and a short green dress appeared at Evie's side. She flicked salt off the rim of a margarita glass with her tongue and smiled approvingly. "How do you know Velma?"

"I don't, really. I just interviewed her."

"Oh!" The woman twisted to face Evie in full. "Are you a journalist?"

Evie puffed out her chest. "Yes."

"Maybe you can interview me." The woman batted her eyelids coquettishly. "I'm a designer. My name's Luksus."

"I've heard of you!" Evie exclaimed. "I mean, I've seen one of your designs. Green snakeskin catsuit?"

"Yes!" Luksus batted her arm. "Clever girl!"

"My style team showed me it. As an option for one of our shoots." It felt pretty cool to say *style team*. And *shoots*.

"You're on camera? Oh, you have to wear it! It'd look so beautiful on you!" Luksus purred. "Promise me, promise me you will!"

Evie laughed, overwhelmed and excited. "Okay, maybe! But only if I can do a quick interview with you." She wasn't sure where this might go, but the opportunity seemed too good to pass up.

"Of course! Let's get you a drink first." Luksus slipped her arm through Evie's. She smelled like tequila and vanilla perfume. "What's your name, gorgeous?"

"Chloe."

"Out of the way! Chloe needs a drink!" Luksus tugged Evie off the wall and into the writhing mass of the after-party.

One hour later, Evie had met Velma's agent, Velma's agent's boyfriend, Velma's agent's boyfriend's best friend, and basically everyone short of a partridge in a pear tree. She'd been expecting wall-to-wall celebs, but so far, the selection seemed far more random. Hannah Hart was in a deep conversation with either Carrie Brownstein or someone who looked exactly like Carrie Brownstein, and she thought she saw Cara Delevingne in the line for the bathroom, but apart from that, all the famous people were gone.

But that didn't matter, because after she interviewed Luksus, the designer started introducing her as "the next Alexa Chung" or "the hottest thing on the net right now." The guests all nodded, wide-eyed, immediately believing her. After a while, Evie almost believed it herself. Even though Velma was nowhere to be seen, she was having a blast. The more margaritas she downed, the easier it became to meet people. And people wanted to talk to her. Often she found herself talking to three or four people at once, the center of attention without even trying. After a while, Evie had her own entourage: Imogen and Ivy, two impeccably dressed style bloggers ("actually, we think of ourselves as 'curators'"), and two sarcastic, handsome gay guys who were both called Declan. They refilled her glass, laughed at her jokes, and whispered bitchy gossip in her ear. To them, she was "fabulous" and "essential" and "totally adorbs." Whenever they asked her something, they listened to her answer as attentively as if she were doling out the secret of eternal youth.

Actually, she had that. It was in a little purple bottle in her bathroom cabinet.

"Excuse me," she said to the Declans. "I need some fresh air."

"Baby," one of them cooed. "You *are* fresh air."

On the balcony, New York City spread out before her, bright and insistent. She slipped off her heels and leaned against the railing, breathing in the city air. She couldn't stop smiling. She felt like a rock star, like she was radiating light, like she was really and truly *alive*.

When someone came to stand next to her, she wasn't surprised to see who it was.

Velma said, "You're in trouble."

Evie addressed the city, not the woman next to her. "Oh really?"

"You're more popular than I am. And it's my party."

Evie glowed. Velma had been watching her. "You should try wearing a gold sequined dress."

Velma laughed quietly. "I don't think it's that."

"No?"

Velma inched closer. "It's your charisma. Your spirit. It's practically blinding."

Evie couldn't help glancing at her. The sight of her, so close, in that suit, made her feel itchy. Her next words were a husky purr, femme fatale movie dialogue that was entirely un-Evie. "Maybe you should put on sunglasses."

Velma grinned. "Maybe." She held Evie's gaze for a beat, long enough for Evie to feel it racing up her spine. Then Velma turned her attention to the view. "How long have you been a journalist?" She asked it in the tone you'd ask a stranger what the time was.

Evie swallowed. "That's a hard question to answer."

"Is it?"

"How long have you been a writer?"

Velma snorted. "Touché." In the same casual tone, she asked, "Do you have a boyfriend?"

Evie's voice sounded squeakier than she wanted it to. "No."

"A girlfriend?"

So bold. So brazen. When Evie replied this time, she left more of a door open. "No . . ."

Velma moved one, two steps closer to Evie. Her voice tickled directly in Evie's ear. "I have a driver waiting downstairs."

Desire pounced into Evie's chest like a jaguar. She wanted Velma's mouth on hers. She wanted to feel her skin pressing, rubbing, sweating, sticky, writhing, explosive—

But Evie stepped back. "You'll have to try harder than that."

She scooped up her heels and began padding back to the party. The glass doors of the suite reflected a tall, delicious brunette in a glittering dress who looked powerful and in control. Not someone who came as soon as their master called.

"Chloe. Wait a second."

"Sorry, Velma," Evie called breezily over her shoulder. "I think that's a wrap."

30.

Being Cupcake Girl was unequivocally awesome. An entire tray of cupcakes was delivered to her trailer (yes, she had one now), with a note: *For Cupcake Girl, From your fans at Magnolia Bakery.* Krista screamed with delight. But best of all, *she had good lines now.* Greg had gone with the Dream-Girl-as-secret-singer idea, letting her help pen a short musical number toward the film's finale. Krista scribbled ideas gleefully from her position under a hair dryer. The head makeup artist, Ora, was working on her now, not the terrified junior assistant.

The first scene she was shooting was outside, in the part of the park that had been brought back to life with fresh paint and props. Dream Girl ran one of the game booths.

"Lenka." Greg looked like he hadn't had much sleep, but he still gave her a hug hello. "Your first day of shooting. You psyched?"

"*So* psyched," Krista gushed. "Cupcake Girl is all over the internet, I'm totally famous in a totally legit way—"

"Great," Greg interrupted. "So, in this scene, you're doing your thing here in the booth, and Tristan's gonna come in from over there—"

"Hold up a sec." Krista's eyes widened. "This scene's with Tristan McKell?"

Greg gave her a weird look. "You have read the new script, right?"

"I wasn't sure who was playing who."

"Zach is Tristan's character."

Krista found it hard to form the words. "Tristan McKell is going to be my love—"

And that's when she saw him. In her mind's eye, she'd been imagining someone much younger, closer to the Tristan of ten years ago. But he wasn't a kid anymore. Tristan was a young man. Krista sucked in a throaty breath. He still looked like the heartthrob in every teen makeover movie, the one who played lacrosse but was surprisingly deep and resented being from the right side of the tracks. Jaw: chiseled. Hair: perfect. Cock: obviously it had to be the size of a dachshund. Krista felt straight-up drunk as Tristan, god among men, strolled on set. Spotted Greg. And began *heading her way*.

"McKell." Greg hugged Tristan and slapped him on the back. "I'd like you to meet Lenka. Your brand-new Dream Girl."

Tristan smiled at her, extending his hand. "Hi, I'm Tristan."

None of this was real. Maybe Evie was right. Maybe it really was a brain tumor. "Hi. I'm Tristan. Krista!" She corrected herself. "No. I mean, Lenka. My name's Lenka."

"Looks like we're making a movie together." Tristan gave her a wink. "Very groovy."

Krista tried to nod. "Groovy. Groovy blueberry. Eat those groovy blueberries." What?

Greg glanced between Krista and Tristan. "Hey, Trist, can you check in with Jen? She was asking for you."

Tristan nodded, and after one more smile, he headed back in the direction of the crew.

"Look, he's just another actor, Lenka," Greg said. "Don't treat him any differently."

"Hm?" Krista toyed with a lock of hair, staring after him.

"Lenka!" Greg summoned a strained smile. "This scene is very simple. Tristan's going to come in from right over there. He's going to notice you, give you a little smile. You're not giving him anything back. Uninterested. Okay?"

"But why would my character be uninterested in Tristan McKell? I mean . . . look at that butt." Krista chewed a pinkie. "You could tenderize a steak on that thing."

Krista heard someone nearby chuckle, but Greg huffed out some air, refusing to be amused. "You're just not. Okay?"

Min, the tiny but terrifying Chinese American woman Krista knew to be the first assistant director, clapped her hands together. "Last looks, please!"

A makeup artist dusted some powder on Krista's cheeks. People began clearing the set, quieting down. The camera, which was set up on what looked like train tracks, was pulled into a starting position.

"Quiet on set!" Min called. "And, roll sound."

Someone called, "Sound is speeding."

"Roll camera," Min called.

Another voice. "Rolling."

Someone popped in front of Krista with a clapboard. "Scene 14A, take one. Mark." They clapped the slate.

"Everybody settle," Min called. The set became preternaturally silent. "Camera set?"

"Set."

Now it was Greg who called out, from his position behind a monitor. "And action!"

Tristan emerged from behind the edge of one of the other booths, walking confidently. The camera swooped to follow him. A tinny blast of music pierced the silence. Boyz Unbridled. Krista snorted. Some idiotic Tristan worshipper hadn't turned off their phone. The camera stopped swooping. Heads turned in her direction. A hot slap of realization: it was *her* phone. She'd changed the ringtone as a joke. She fumbled it free from her pocket, but before she could see who was calling, it was plucked from her hand. "Hey!" She spun to see a stormy-faced Damian holding it. "I was trying!"

In a few minutes, they were all set to start again. "And . . . action!"

Once again, Tristan strode around the corner and this time, there was no stopping him as he crossed the grass on his way past Krista's booth. He caught Krista's eye. And smiled.

Krista sighed. And smiled back.

"Cut!" Greg called. He stood up from behind the monitor, pulling off a pair of headphones. "Lenka! Uninterested!"

"Sorry, sorry!" Krista yelled back. "Sorry," she called after Tristan, who was making his way back to his starting point. She shook her head, trying to clear it out and get into the zone, like she used to before an improv show. *Stay focused*, she told herself. *You got this.*

Everything began again. Greg called action. Tristan appeared. The sight of Tristan's perfect face made her involuntarily happy, so the safest thing was obviously not to see his face at all. Krista ducked her eyes.

"Cut!" Greg called. "Lenka! What are you doing? You need to *look at him*."

"Oh, okay!" Krista called back. Oof. Filming a movie was harder than it looked.

They set up again.

It took twenty-five takes to get it right.

31.

Evie dragged herself into Studio B feeling a notch above completely dead. The fact she'd forgotten to eat anything more than chocolate-covered strawberries for dinner combined with her own body weight in both champagne and margaritas had produced a hangover that required sunglasses. Indoors. She was praying it wouldn't affect the Pretty in any way: her capacity to troubleshoot right now was less than zero. Kelly, Rich, and a few other crew members were crowded around a laptop. She was only able to manage, "What . . . doing?" before needing to sit down.

"Adrian sent in the stuff you shot last night." Kelly spun the screen around to show her. It was paused on a shot of Velma and Chloe. Both women were grinning at each other like prizewinners. In Krista's slinky gold dress, all made up and flushed from the attention, Chloe looked . . .

"Gorgeous," Kelly said. "You scrub up well, Fontaine."

Evie couldn't reply. It was almost impossible to believe that was her with Velma. Of course, it wasn't really her . . . but in some way . . . in some way it kind of was. Evie couldn't drag her gaze from Chloe's huge eyes made enormous by eyeliner, the white slash of teeth, the creamy, clear skin.

"We've also got the rushes for the promos and intros," Rich said. He was wearing a T-shirt that read Harvard Law and underneath it Just Kidding. He punched a few keys, and the footage changed. As did Evie's enthusiasm.

The girl sitting at the hot pink desk looked pale. And not in a sexy vampire way. In an English consumption way. She wasn't ugly—it was still Chloe Fontaine. It was just compared to airbrushed meeting-Velma-Wolff Chloe Fontaine, the girl on screen was . . . faded. Like a gold coin that'd lost its luster.

She didn't want Velma to see her like that.

Kelly snapped the laptop shut. "We'll be ready to shoot your 'Better Date' story in thirty, Chloe." He addressed the men setting up the lights. "Can I get a first look in five, please, fellas?"

Okay, Evie told herself. *Let's get some perspective here. That's not you. You only think Chloe looks bad because we've been trained to think women wearing tons of makeup is normal when it's not. Chloe doesn't look that bad. I mean, she doesn't look good, but she doesn't look that bad.*

Marcello strolled into the studio. He was dressed in a lilac summer suit and was wheeling his makeup case behind him. He leaned against the back wall. When he caught Evie staring, he tipped his Fedora at her in a way that somehow seemed . . . significant. A brush of apprehension tightened Evie's muscles. Did Marcello really suspect something? Or was she just being paranoid? Or—new concern—was paranoia a side effect of the Pretty itself?

"Why is Marcello here?" Evie hissed at Rich.

"He's on a four-week contract. He gets paid whether he works or not."

"Oh." Evie pursed her lips. "How did you think I looked in the promos?"

"Like someone who wasn't wearing any makeup," Rich replied.

Evie rubbed her forehead with her fingertips, trying to think. She just looked so . . . blah in that footage. Plus, today's hangover wasn't doing her any favors. She could keep Marcello at arm's length. Besides, even if he did suspect something, what could he possibly say? Evie addressed Rich. "Maybe I should get some of the natural look going."

Rich nodded. "I think that can only help." He flagged down a passing PA. "Can I get a diet Bongo, but only if there's lemon slices and if there's not, I'll get a regular Bongo on ice."

"Okay." The PA nodded.

"The ice is very important," Rich said.

"Got it."

Rich looked back at Evie. "Definitely start with the natural look."

In Dressing Room 4, Evie let Marcello set her up at the washbasin. His fingers dug gently into her scalp, flushing her follicles with warm water. In spite of her desire to endure rather than enjoy this, she felt herself melt. The lemony-smelling shampoo soothed her hangover, and by the time Marcello was squeezing the water out, it had downgraded from unspeakably hideous to almost tolerable.

When he took aim with a hair dryer, she issued a warning: "No bouncy hair."

"Bouncy hair?"

"Yeah, that cookie-cutter look actresses always have. The big loose curls," Evie tried to explain, spinning her fingers around her face. "I just want normal hair."

Marcello nodded coolly. "Coming right up."

That's another ridiculous beauty standard, Evie thought as Marcello began blasting her hair dry. *In the movies, women with straight hair have it done in curls, and women with curly hair have it straightened . . . and then done in curls. If all that time was spent instead on, say, getting their input on the script or teaching them how to set up lights, surely Hollywood would be a better place.* Evie had so many good ideas on how the world should be run, it honestly just seemed weird that it had taken until now for people to start listening to her.

After he finished her completely normal, could-barely-tell-it-was-a-blowout blowout, Marcello clipped her hair away from her face. His fingernail color had changed: today it was a pretty rose pink, except for his ring fingers, which were jet black. He addressed her via the mirror, hands resting lightly on her shoulders.

"So," he said. "The natural look."

Evie glanced at the pale, unglamorous face reflected back at her in the mirror, and tried not to grimace. "Exactly."

Marcello emptied some cleanser onto a cotton wipe and began swabbing her face. Dark smudges stained the wipe. "I see you were wearing makeup last night," he murmured.

"Yeah," Evie said, shifting a little. And even though she had decided not to bond with Marcello, in case he really was on to her, she found herself explaining, "I was at an event. And sort of . . . on a date. Sort of."

Marcello hooked an eyebrow. "Who was the lucky gentleman?"

Evie hooked an eyebrow back at him. "Actually, it was a woman."

Marcello paused, midwipe. His face shifted, a sun coming out from behind clouds. "Really? I had no idea you were part of the rainbow family."

"Card-carrying queer." She fixed him with a wide-eyed stare, deliberately dumb. "You're not telling me you're gay too?"

He burst into laughter. "You are funny," he said. He ran his fingertips over the foundation bottles set up on the bench, a dozen variations of tan. When he spoke again, his tone was warmer. "So how was your date with the lucky *lady*?"

Evie recounted the night in brief, culminating in her hard-to-get move at the end, which Marcello congratulated her on. "That's how I landed my man," he said, smudging dots of foundation onto her cheeks and temples. "He asked me out every weekend for a year, and I said no every time. Drove him crazy. Crazy in love," he added.

"Why'd you keep saying no?"

Marcello began blending the thick liquid into her skin. "He was a player. I didn't want to get played. So I made him work. That's what he wanted. Someone to say no to him."

"Quite the student of human nature."

Marcello made a sound of agreement. "Or maybe I was just scared. I don't know."

"Scared of what?"

Marcello shrugged, turning back to his kit. "Being in love, maybe. Going after something I wanted. Damn, girl." He twisted back to shoot her a look. "You got me all taxicab confessing."

"Sorry." Evie bit back a smile.

Marcello touched the blush brush lightly to her cheekbones. "Don't apologize. That's part of your job, right? Interviewing people."

"Yeah," Evie said. "Yeah, I guess so."

"Then it looks like they chose the right girl."

"I'll at least pass as her," Evie said, admiring her rosy cheeks. "Thanks to you."

Marcello smiled. A small, private smile. "Oh yes, Chloe Fontaine. You're definitely passing as the right girl."

When Marcello finished, Evie felt considerably better. Marcello's natural look, which only took twenty minutes, brought her back to square one. And that didn't really count as wearing makeup.

Kelly's eyes darted briefly around Evie's face, to the lilac blouse she was wearing. Evie had stood her ground with Gemma and Rose. Nothing designer or expensive, they had assured her, just a simple V-neck top from a local designer who used organic cotton. But she was willing to go from gray to lilac, and from loose to fitted. It was just a bit more flattering. Velma would be watching.

She took her seat in the hot pink host's chair. She could make out the beginning of a script on a teleprompter next to the giant camera pointed at her. Rich was standing next to it, arms folded. Frothy excitement bubbled in her chest. Her first on-air piece. And it was a story that normalized bisexuality. While that was a no-brainer in her friendship circle, where everyone was gay or bi or somewhere on the spectrum, or knew a million people who were gay or bi or somewhere on the spectrum, she was oh so aware this was not the case in Middle America. That was all about to change. She was going to spearhead a sexual revolution. Somewhere, someday, someone would probably make a statue of her.

Rich called action.

Evie smiled brightly and began. "It's a question as old as time itself, a question that we here at *Extra Salt* are determined to answer: Who's better in bed? Do guys have the best moves? Or are girls the ones who should take home gold? We take to the streets to find out—wait, wait, stop." Evie squinted for Kelly. "This isn't right."

Kelly appeared in front of the desk. "What's wrong?"

"It says there '*who's better in bed?*'" Evie pointed at the offending words. "It should be '*who's a better date?*'"

"We had to make a few changes," Kelly said. "It's basically the same story." He addressed the studio floor. "Okay, starting again—"

"No, wait, *wait*." Evie grabbed Kelly's arm. "It's not the same! My story was about who's a better date, for me, a girl. This is just cheap battle-of-the-sexes shit."

"No," Kelly countered. "It's a playful, risqué story that equalizes male and female sexual power."

Evie gave him a withering look. "Don't patronize me. It's meant to be about bisexuality. I thought you guys liked that. I thought you wanted someone different. What about all that stuff about needing a host with a 'bloody personality'?"

Kelly frowned.

Too late Evie realized that was what Evie had heard, not Chloe. "Evie may have mentioned that. My roommate."

"We do want the bisexual stuff," Kelly said. "It's just . . . not in the first episode."

"So this *is* a different story," Evie said. "More heteronormative bullshit."

Kelly crouched down next to her. "I'm on your side, Chloe. But if we come out of the gates with that sort of story, we'll turn people off. We become niche, when we want to be broad." His tone of voice suggested he was letting her in on a very important secret. "This way, we get the viewers in, establish trust, build an audience. Then we can push boundaries. I promise."

Evie regarded her producer doubtfully. "Are you at least going to interview queer people for the on-the-street footage?"

"Sure." Kelly nodded. "Absolutely. If we find them, definitely."

"*If* you find them? This is New York—"

"Mate, any more holdups chew into the 'Feminist Action Hero' shoot this arvo," Kelly said.

"Kelly?" Rich called. "Can we keep moving?"

Kelly looked back at Evie. "Are we good?"

This was shitty, and she couldn't tell if Kelly was lying to her or not. "I don't know."

"C'mon, mate." Kelly squeezed Evie's shoulder. "Let's not let Marcello's hard work go to waste. You look gorgeous."

A smile crept to Evie's lips. She shook it away. "No, I don't."

"Are you kidding me?" Kelly leaned toward her ear. His breath smelled like coffee and cigarettes. "I can see what she sees in you." He nodded at the studio entrance. Sitting on a small desk was a huge bouquet of flowers. "They just came for you. Looks like you really made an impression on Velma Wolff, Chloe."

Kelly drifted back behind the camera. Evie didn't even see him leave. The bouquet was *enormous*, a gorgeous garden of lilies and roses and hydrangeas. And it was from *Velma Wolff*. It was all she could do to keep from bolting across the studio floor to see if there was a card. Every nerve ending prickled and pulsed. Velma Wolff had sent her *flowers*.

"Ready to go again?" Rich called.

Evie looked back at the teleprompter. An enormous grin plastered her face, summoning the dimples she knew looked absolutely adorable. "Ready."

32.

After finally nailing the Dream-Girl-Ignoring-the-Hotness-That-Is-Tristan moment, it was lunchtime. Krista had loitered around Tristan's enormous silver trailer for ten full minutes before she screwed up the courage to knock. She coughed a little from the woodsy-smelling smoke, blinking into the semidarkness. "Hello?"

Tristan sat cross-legged on a white leather couch, hands placed serenely on his knees. He opened his eyes. "Lenka."

"Sorry." Krista hovered in the darkened doorway. "Didn't mean to interrupt."

"That's okay." Tristan stood and stretched. "Come on in."

A burst of adrenaline whizzed through her veins. She. Was. In. Tristan's. Trailer. And it was all because of the Pretty. Krista Kumar had no business being in a former-pop-slash-current-movie-star's inner sanctum. But Lenka Penka? She did.

"I just got back from a meditation retreat in Phuket." Tristan opened a kitchen cabinet, fished out a glass, and switched on the faucet. "It's incredible how noisy our minds can be, without us even noticing."

"Totally, I hate that." Krista's eyes raked over everything, trying to absorb as many details at once. Kitchenette, with a sink, two-burner stove, minifridge, and microwave. The white couch sat flush against one wall. A Formica-topped table jutted out next to it, with a couple of chairs under it. On the other side of where she was standing was a narrow door, open to reveal the corner of a toilet and shower stall.

Beyond that, another door. Presumably, the bedroom. She'd be able to get a good look at that later.

Something was nestled in bubble wrap on the kitchen bench. A gold statue of a little man with a bald head. A trophy. *Tween King! Lifetime Achievement Award* was etched across the base. She'd seen him accept it live on MTV. "Oh my god," she said, and reached for it.

"Hey!" He grabbed her wrist, her fingertips inches from the tiny bald man.

Krista flinched, yanking her hand back.

"Lenka." Tristan gathered himself. "Sorry. I didn't mean to yell. It's just—" He made his lips into a circle, like he was searching for the right way to phrase something. "That's not a trophy. Anymore. It's more like a talisman. It's something that Umsa blessed for me." In response to Krista's look of confusion, he added, "Umsa is my spiritual adviser."

"Your . . . what?"

"My guru. Mentor. No, like a . . . guide, I guess." Tristan sighed. "It's complicated. Maybe one day, I'll explain it to you. But for now . . . please don't touch it."

"Oh." Krista pouted. "All right."

Tristan positioned himself between her and the statue. "So, Lenka. What can I do for you?"

"I thought we could go over some of our scenes. Maybe then I won't suck so badly," she added, with a rueful yet sexy smile.

Tristan took a deep breath though his nose and half closed his eyes, evidently deaf to Krista's self-deprecation. "I'm feeling that. Sure, why not?" He picked up a script that was lying on the table.

Krista took a seat in the middle of the sofa. Tristan sat at the far end of it. "Okay, so the carnival scene," he said, flipping his script open. "I'm really feeling this is when Zach is starting to see Dream Girl in a different light. What do you think?"

What Krista thought was that Tristan was not acting like someone digging her neon-bright Open for Business vibes. "Hey, let's free ourselves from these." Krista plucked Tristan's script from his hands and tossed it aside. "I find them way too prescriptive. I use a method that's much more . . . primal."

Her costar shook his head. "What do you mean?"

"I work from—" Krista's gaze landed on her sandals. Her leopard-print sandals. "Animal metaphors." The idea came lightning quick, energizing her further still. Performing Lenka for Tristan was a thousand times easier than performing Dream Girl for Greg. "Like in this scene, I'm a lioness and you're the lion."

Tristan nodded, eyes alive with interest. "Yeah. Yeah, I like it. Primal. Intense. Should we give it a go?"

"Yes!" Krista jumped to her feet. "Okay, I'll start here. You go over there." She pointed to the far end of the trailer.

"Awesome!" Tristan bounded over. "Hands and knees? On the ground?"

"Yep." Krista nodded. That'd be better for her cleavage. "You have to commit, okay?"

He nodded, face serious. "Absolutely, Lenka."

Tristan closed his eyes. Krista suppressed a grin. Then she drew herself inward. *I am lioness,* she told herself, *queen of the Serengeti. Tristan is my mate: my strong lion-y mate.* She arched her back and wiggled her butt. When she refocused, Tristan was staring at her, forehead lowered, eyes blazing. An electric thrill zipped through her.

Tristan let out a low *rawr.*

Krista responded in turn.

He crawled one step toward her.

She stayed where she was.

He crawled a little more. His eyes didn't leave her. She could almost hear a hollow, rhythmic drumbeat as he approached her, building in intensity. Their eyes were locked. The air was charged.

And in that moment, she was a lioness and he was a lion, their fur golden and coarse, rippling over their muscular bodies, paws enormous, teeth sharp, eyes a brilliant tawny gold.

He came closer. She felt a pull toward him, immediate and elemental. It was basic instinct, it was an indecent proposal.

He snarled.

She snarled.

He sat back on his haunches, ready to strike, ready to take her, and she wanted him to, she needed him to. He roared, about to kiss her, about to devour her—

Krista's head dove forward, expecting to find Tristan's mouth, but instead: air. Tristan had popped to his feet. "Whoa," he breathed. "I *really* felt that."

Disappointment sliced through her, quick as a paper cut. But surprisingly, what she felt more powerfully was . . . satisfaction. Creative clarity. The flush of success that washed through her was as warm, as vindicating, as applause. "Me too," Krista admitted. "I really felt like a lion just then."

"If we can tap into that on camera, that'll give Dream Girl and Zach serious chemistry." He grinned at her, amazed. "Awesome technique, Lenka."

"Thanks." Krista grinned back.

Tristan checked the time on his phone. "Okay, I have to get to set, but when I get back, let's try the hot dog scene. Maybe we can be monkeys."

Krista nodded. "Totally! Yes!"

Tristan put one hand on her shoulder and squeezed. For one wild second, she thought he was going to pull her toward him, plant his mouth on hers. But instead Tristan just smiled at her and bounded out of the trailer.

Knees weak, Krista sank to the sofa, a quivering mess of happy. It was happening. They had chemistry. Just like Dream Girl and Zach did. Krista closed her eyes. She imagined Tristan's mouth on hers, kissing her softly, sweetly, hands tangled in her hair. He was in a crisp, dark tux, while she was wearing a long white dress. And it was Krista, not Lenka, kissing Tristan back . . .

Krista's eyes flew open.

That was a *wedding* fantasy. Unbidden. She thumped the side of her head with her palm. Tristan wasn't going to fall in *love* with Lenka

Penka. And he certainly wasn't going to fall in love with Krista Kumar: he wasn't even going to *meet* her.

Krista drew in a deep breath and sighed. Time to start waiting around again. Maybe there'd be more cupcakes in craft services. But when she glimpsed the ordinary, unspecial world bustling outside Tristan's trailer, she paused. The Pretty was her passport into this trailer. And it wasn't going to last forever. And part of being an engaged, forward-thinking adult was saying yes to things, to grabbing life by the coattails and hanging on. And Tristan hadn't told her to leave: not explicitly.

Quietly, Krista pulled the trailer door shut.

33.

Her key entered his lock with deceptive ease. She hadn't wanted it. "For emergencies," Mark had said, pressing the piece of metal with its bronze teeth into her palm. His breath was tangy with whiskey; liquid courage for a bold offer. "Just in case."

Willow had never used it. Until now. All things considered, it felt like it should be harder to use. But the key slid into place like a knife slicing through silk.

She stood in the doorway, absorbing the quiet. From here, the chatter of Tenth Street was muffled into an almost imperceptible soundtrack. Afternoon light snuck in through the half-open blinds.

Mark's apartment.

She knew he wasn't here, a fact she'd double-checked minutes earlier in the foyer. She'd called his work and been told Mr. Salzburg was in a meeting until 5 p.m.

So she was alone.

She closed the door behind her. The lock clicked slowly, soft as a kiss. Her heart was racing, at odds with the quiet familiarity that spread out before her: a bachelor pad in still life.

Neat. Clean. Unassuming.

Just like Mark.

Just like her boyfriend, Mark.

She drifted forward, fingertips flitting over the back of the sofa, the edge of a lamp. The contents of his fridge were predictably sparse: a six-pack of Sierra Nevada, soggy Chinese takeout, a jar of sad-looking pickles. The dishes were done, dry in the rack. A plate, a bowl, a water glass. Nothing surprising.

Do I want to be surprised?

The black bag full of camera gear was under Mark's bed. A postproduction company had sent it to her father as a gift: he'd given it to her, and she'd given it to Mark. Her real camera was at home, of course, and thus, off-limits. She was avoiding Matteo and Claire.

Unzipping the bag, she found the camera, lenses, even a little tripod. Mark wouldn't notice its absence. But that wasn't all. She was after . . . something else.

She toed a towel on the bathroom floor, still a little damp. She flushed the toilet. The sudden rush of water sounded almost musical. Back in the living room, she looked through the mail that had accumulated on the side table next to the door. A Time Warner bill, preapproved credit cards from Citibank, a flyer for Barry's Bootcamp.

And then . . . something.

Her heartbeat, which had settled, complacent, picked up again.

Underneath the pile of mail was a beer coaster. Thick, round cardboard, emblazoned with a logo, website, and street address. It was dotted with red. Like splashes of blood. Or red wine.

It was a coaster for Lenny's.

She flipped it over. On the back was a sketch. Simply done, probably with one of the mechanical pencils Mark always carried with him.

It was a girl, with impossibly large eyes, an impossibly long neck, and impossibly sweet lips.

Caroline.

Her chest was rising and falling now, the initial shock becoming something else, something infectious and terminal spreading throughout her body. When she realized it was probably from last night, when she sat with Mark drinking three glasses of shiraz, the feeling spread from her chest and into her limbs, filling her head with a dull roar, a horrible, wonderful feeling, as if she were the coaster: absorbing everything, staining, growing heavy.

Be unsafe.

And then she was moving.

Rushing to unzip the bag still on Mark's bed, fit the lenses, set up the tripod. Hurrying, so she wouldn't miss it.

She didn't.

Because when Meredith opened an email less than an hour later, the curator's chest constricted. The email contained no words, only twelve black-and-white portraits. Caroline, face a perfect lake of misery. Caroline, a single tear streaking down her cheek. Caroline, lips parted in a silent sob.

It was the agony of youth, the ecstasy of beauty, and as those words formed in Meredith's mind, she knew she had something. *Really* had something.

Meredith's email back to Willow was just a single word.

"Brilliant."

34.

The thrill of hanging out in Tristan McKell's trailer refused to dissipate. Even though it reminded her of a not-that-amazing hotel room, it had an aura. Krista could feel it. Plus, when Tristan came back they could pretend to be monkeys, animals that had a refreshingly liberal attitude toward sex.

She tucked her legs underneath her, snuggling into the sofa, letting herself relax. Her imagination sashayed to Tristan's face, his perfect, slightly stubbly face. Strong shoulders that looked good in a suit, and there he is, smiling eagerly, standing under an arch of red roses, holding out a ring with a rock the size of a golf ball . . . Krista started, jerking her eyes open. *No*, she instructed herself. *Not a wedding. Sex. Just. Sex.*

She closed her eyes again, determined to keep it dirty. She pictured Tristan, throwing her onto a king-sized bed, then ripping off his pants as smoothly as a stripper. Tristan, pulling her toward him with pro-athlete arms. A warm ripple swished through her body, its final flourish ending in her clit. She slid her fingers under the band of her underwear. She could masturbate. In Tristan's trailer. So naughty. Such a turn-on.

Tristan, glorious as a god, taking her from behind. Tristan, face enveloped by her pussy as she rode his mouth like a prizewinning jockey. Tristan, hog-tied and helpless and loving every second of it. Tristan, Tristan, *Tristan*!

She was barely conscious of reaching for the Tween King trophy. Horniness was a hot veil, culminating in a driving urge to *be penetrated by anything*.

She groaned as the smooth gold head slipped inside her. The size was perfect and Tristan was back in her fantasies, in crystal-clear focus and surround sound. Tristan, making it rain as she swung around a pole in a trashy stripper's outfit; Tristan, tying her up and spanking her like a naughty schoolgirl; Tristan, on top of her, biceps rippling as he thrust into her, again and again and again, about to come, close to climax, nearly there, yes, yes, *yes*—

"Jesus!"

A male voice—not from her fantasy. Krista's eyes flew open.

Damian and a girl PA stood in his trailer's open doorway. The duo were rooted to the spot, twin expressions summed up simply as *What the fuck?*

"Shit." Krista pulled the trophy out from between her legs, sweaty, still delirious.

The female PA gasped. Damian made a choking noise.

"I was just . . . waiting for Tristan to come back." Krista struggled to pull her underwear back up, her skirt back down.

When Damian spoke, his words were slow and disbelieving. "You fucked Tristan's Tween King trophy."

Krista glanced down at the trophy-slash-dildo in her hand, glistening gently in the overhead light. "Yeah. But it totally made the first move." She chuckled lamely.

No one else laughed. The PAs exchanged a horrified glance. In a squeaky voice, Damian said, "Lenka, why don't you come with me? We need you out of here."

"I'll wash it," Krista offered, but Damian raised his palm in immediate protest.

"Just, oh god, just give it to me."

Krista handed it over.

She followed the two PAs away from Tristan's trailer, head bowed.

Those had not been the actions of a forward-thinking adult who was saying yes to life.

They had been the actions of someone who was literally insane.

35.

Deciding what to wear for an actual date with Velma Wolff caused Evie to have a minor mental breakdown. Her bedroom floor was a sea of discarded options. Of course, nothing could happen with Velma. Like, really happen. Chloe was an impostor. A spy. A double agent with a limited life span. But that didn't mean she wasn't excited. And curious. Could she, Evie Selby, hold her own on a date with a celebrity?

She had no idea, but what she did know was she was running late. The shoot for the "Feminist Action Hero" story had run over. Kelly had been surprisingly supportive, letting her talk for ten straight minutes about how young adult fiction was a stronghold for heroines created by and for women, a far cry from the sexualized female heroes of patriarchal superhero movies, and a variety of other salient points that were slipping her mind right now because she had *absolutely nothing to wear*. Not only that, but her bangs needed straightening. They were just long enough to tickle her eyelashes. The effect was indie-rock-moody and certainly sexy, but damn, they were starting to get annoying. If Evie'd had any choice in her Pretty persona, she wouldn't have chosen bangs, from a purely practical standpoint.

Her phone rang. She assumed it was Krista, who'd been texting all afternoon about a "legitimate actor emergency." But it wasn't a number she recognized. The restaurant? Someone from *Extra Salt*? "Hello, this is—" Wait, careful . . . "—me."

"Hello, my darling. I had a feeling you'd pick up."

"Mom." Her voice looped high in surprise. Evie checked her phone again. "I didn't recognize you. What number is this?"

"The new landline. I know, a landline. Your mother is ancient."

"Oh right. Yeah, you did mention that." Evie glanced around her bedroom, feeling like she'd just misplaced something she couldn't remember putting down. "How are you? How's . . . everything?"

"Well, I don't need to see another moving box again in my life, that's for sure."

"You're settling in okay?" The journalist in her whispered that was the same question as before, but she was a bit too thrown to think clearly. She sank onto the corner of her bed and tried to remember exactly when her mother had moved.

"I am." Her mom took a deep, satisfied breath. "The air here is so fresh. I can already feel the toxins leaking out of my skin."

Her mom was being literal: for the past sixteen years she'd worked in the neighborhood's most upmarket hair salon (but at forty-five dollars for a women's cut, that wasn't saying much). "I bet." Evie heard the pleasantly tuneless sound of wind chimes. She tried to picture her mom, Tina, watching the sun set over the Adirondack Mountains, but the image was fuzzy. Was the view east or west? Was her gray hair up in a bun or loose over her shoulders? She still couldn't quite believe that her mom had actually gone through with the much-talked-about dream of ditching the suburbs and moving to a mountain town.

"You'll have to come visit. You'd love it up here. There's a farmer's market every Sunday. I'm thinking of selling my jam there."

The prospect of leaving New York brought Evie back to the present with a thud. "I'd love to. But not right now. Everything is . . . busy." Evie twisted in front of her mirror to check out her butt.

"Well, soon then. You sound a bit . . . stuffy. Do you have a cold?"

"Um, yeah, I think I'm getting one." All good on the butt front.

"Have you been taking echinacea? Do you still have that Rescue Remedy?"

The word *remedy* always made Evie wince. Remedy Dashall had been the gum-snapping, hair-flicking, queen bee of Evie's grade. Evie didn't go to prom. But Evie's mom did Remedy's and all her little worker bees' hair for the big night. Evie was sure the appointments were some dig at her. The image of her mom being bossed around by Remedy with a head full of foils was simply horrifying.

Evie made a noncommittal noise. "I can't talk right now. I have a date."

"Really? Who with?"

Of course, Evie would've loved to tell her the truth—that *the* Velma Wolff had sent her flowers and a reservation for dinner tonight at Whitewood, a fancy restaurant in Tribeca part owned by Jeff Goldblum. But that would invite too many questions. "Online date. I haven't met her yet."

"I'm so glad you're still dating women, sweetheart. Lesbianism is the ultimate expression of feminine energy that we need to heal this earth."

"That's definitely why I'm doing it," Evie deadpanned, and they both giggled. "But I'm sorry, I really can't talk right now. I'm late."

"But we haven't spoken in weeks." Her mom sounded disappointed and Evie fought a wave of guilt.

"I know, but I have to get to the restaurant. In exactly"—she checked the phone: 7:40—"twenty minutes! Shit, I haven't even started my makeup."

"Oh, darling, you don't need makeup." With perfect sincerity, her mom said, "You are so beautiful."

Evie's hand froze, midway to a hair primp. This was usually her cue to roll her eyes and mumble, "No I'm not," or, "Face only a mother could love." But after catching Chloe's eyes in the mirror—a human-sized doll in the middle of her bedroom—all she could manage was, "Thanks, Mom."

"I love you."

"Love you too. Bye."

36.

The rest of the date prep happened at hurricane speed. Evie had to finish doing her eye makeup in a cab. Marcello said the trick was blending. She tried to imitate his easy fingertip swishes, hoping the outcome was sexy and not black eye.

She was ten minutes late to Whitewood, the entrance to which was discreetly tucked away off a back alley. No name out front, just a heavy, metal door. Opening it, she walked into one of the nicest restaurants she'd ever been in. Only a dozen or so tables were scattered on a polished wood floor, draped with cream tablecloths, set with square vases of white roses. Lush green plants spilled artfully from the walls and between the tables, creating private screens. The light was low, romantic, thrown discreetly from subtle wall sconces. Everything—from the heavy silver cutlery to the large monochrome paintings on the walls—looked expensive.

She told the hostess—a swanlike black woman in a beautiful yellow dress—she had a reservation under Velma Wolff. The hostess told Evie that Ms. Wolff had not yet arrived, and please, wouldn't she take a seat at the bar?

A tall glass of water was placed in front of her by a smiling bartender in a crisp white shirt and bow tie. When he asked if she'd like to see the wine list, she nodded a little too emphatically. A little liquor to calm her nerves. A few minutes to shake off the stress of the mad dash across town.

The cheapest glass of wine was fourteen dollars. *Fourteen dollars.* That was more than she'd usually spend on a whole bottle. *Oh well,* she thought grimly. *When in Rome.* She ordered it, but when she pulled out her (embarrassingly ratty) purse, the bartender raised a hand in polite refusal. "We'll put it on the table."

"Oh. Of course." Evie tried to make it sound like this had just slipped her mind.

She sat. And sipped. And waited.

Five minutes passed.

Then ten.

The chance to relax morphed into the chance to worry. Velma had written her cell number onto the flowers' card; Evie had texted her earlier to accept the date. Velma had texted back I'll **see you there.** But there was no new message explaining her absence.

At eight thirty, she was considering leaving. She'd downed one and a half glasses of wine; if she ordered a third she'd be drunk before the appetizers. She didn't want to call or text; that seemed desperate. She had the right restaurant, right time. She'd leave. She'd foot the bill and just leave. She was Chloe Fontaine, after all, and being half an hour late was totally and completely—

"Hi."

A man's voice. Hushed and velvety.

It was Jeff Goldblum.

Her mouth went dry. There were no words.

"I'm sorry to intrude, I just wanted to say hello." His eyes were easy and warm behind elegant rimless glasses. His mouth was as soft as hotel pillows.

"To me?" Evie wished she didn't sound so terrified-slash-stunned.

Jeff Goldblum chuckled and extended a hand. "I'm Jeff."

"Ev—Chloe." She caught herself just in time. He let their hand-shake linger, and she blushed.

Jeff Goldblum nodded at her half-empty wineglass. "Can I get you another glass of rosé?"

"Sure," Evie managed. "Yes, please."

Jeff Goldblum, aka the sexiest chaos theorist in the history of monster movies, nodded at the bartender. "I couldn't help but notice you've been here for almost half an hour." He leaned against the bar next to her. There were only six inches between her and Jeff Goldblum. "Are you waiting for someone?"

"Yes. They're late."

"Half an hour is far too long to keep a beautiful woman waiting." His hand drifted down to rest an inch from hers. His fingernails were spectacular. "Can I be so bold as to ask you to dine with me?"

Jeff Goldblum was inviting her to dinner. Her head whirled like a carousel, but before she could even begin to formulate an answer, she heard someone growl, "Goldblum."

It was Velma. Standing with her hands casually in her pants pockets, glowering good-naturedly at the man next to Evie. "Are you hitting on my date?"

Jeff Goldblum glanced at Velma, then at Evie, then back at Velma, connecting the dots. He grinned. "Velma, you old slut. How are you?"

Minutes later, Evie was being seated at one of the better tables at White-wood by a deferential waiter good-looking enough to be an underwear model.

"We'll get a bottle of the Lancaster Estate cabernet sauvignon," Velma told him.

"Excellent choice." The underwear model smiled.

Red wine wasn't exactly Evie's preference and it did seem somewhat odd that Velma had ordered it before Evie had even properly settled, but the fact Velma had done it without looking at a wine list was so impressive Evie decided not to care. For a few moments, they busied themselves with placing napkins on their laps, finding the best way to sit. They smiled at each other uncomfortably, as if they were waiting for a third person who was running late. Velma gestured at Evie's dress. "You look beautiful."

Evie almost said, "So do you," but she stopped herself, not wanting to appear sycophantic. "Thank you."

There was a pause.

An awkward pause.

Evie glanced around, hoping to see their waiter on his way over with menus, or water, or something for them both to do, but he'd disappeared. *Say something!* Her brain shouted at her. *Anything, say anything!*

Evie blurted, "I did my makeup in the cab—" at the exact same time Velma said, "That's a lovely dress."

"I'm sorry, what?" Velma asked.

"Nothing." Evie shook her head quickly.

Velma laughed quietly to herself and placed both palms flat on the table. "I'm sorry," she said, looking Evie right in the eye. "I'm nervous."

Evie stared at her, stunned.

"I'm a terrible first date," Velma continued. "I don't know what it is, but I never do well on first dates."

"I changed my dress five times," Evie confessed.

It was Velma's turn to look surprised. "Really?"

Evie nodded. "I'm so nervous I think I might throw up."

"Feel free. At least we'd have something to talk about."

Evie laughed.

The waiter appeared, bearing a bottle of wine and a couple of leather-bound menus.

"Thank god," Velma announced dramatically, which made Evie giggle again.

Two glasses of dark wine appeared before them. Velma lifted hers for a toast. "To first dates. May we have as few of them as possible."

Evie smiled. She saw them as if viewed from across the room: two women, one famous, both beautiful, clinking bulbous glasses of undoubtedly expensive wine. The image made her shiver with pleasure. If only Remedy Dashall could see her now. "Cheers."

They clinked glasses. The sound rang out like a bell. The wine tasted like blackberries and dark chocolate.

"So, tell me more about *Extra Salt*." Velma sounded genuinely curious. "It's a TV show?"

"Web series. I was only cast as the host last week. You were my first interview."

Velma seemed surprised. "I think you did really well. Much better than most."

"Oh really?" Evie said. She folded her fingers together and rested her chin on them. The sweetly prim gesture felt coquettish, not entirely her own. "Pray tell."

Velma told Evie about her worst interview ever—a college newspaper in the UK whose book editor loathed Velma, describing her as "the devil incarnate but less charming." Evie giggled, breathless, not entirely present. *Velma Wolff is making me laugh. She's sitting right across from me. She's looking right at me!*

When the waiter returned to take their orders, neither had opened a menu. Velma told him they'd need a few minutes.

"Did you go to college here in New York?" Velma asked.

"New York State. Sarah Lawrence." On partial scholarship, but mentioning it seemed too braggy.

"And you majored in . . . ?"

"Being a cultural cliché." Evie smiled prettily. "Minor in journalism, major in gender, sexuality, and feminist studies."

Velma smiled, amused. "And what attracted you to that?"

The way Velma drew out the word *attracted* made Evie tingle. There was no one in the restaurant, in the city, on this earth, except for the woman sitting across from her. "I imagine a whole host of complex socio-politico-economico factors. But a pivotal one was Call-me-Charlie."

"I'm sorry?"

Evie settled farther into her chair. "Okay. It's tenth grade, and I'm mostly bored out of my brain in suburban Chicago. This is the kind of place where Olive Garden is considered fine dining and an eyebrow ring has the cultural significance of a swastika." Velma laughed, and Evie paused to take a gulp of wine. "One day I get to school and find our frozen-in-carbonite history teacher, Mr. Dillard, has inexplicably disappeared, and we have a sub."

"Call-me-Charlie?"

"Exactly. Call-me-Charlie has dyed red hair, five earrings in each ear, and Doc Marten boots. She's sitting *cross-legged* on Dillard's desk when we get to class."

"Wow."

"She was the most badass person I'm sure any of us had ever seen in real life. And lucky for me, she was subbing during Women's History Week. History of the suffragettes; first-, second-, third-wave feminism; Germaine Greer; bell hooks; Naomi Wolf: the works. I just remember her being so passionate and ballsy about it." Evie shook her head. "I remember more from that week than from a whole year of class. I think we all were either terrified or in love with her. Maybe both."

"How cool."

"Did you have anyone like that? Anyone at school who gave you a new perspective or something?"

Velma sat back in her seat. Her smile became complex, almost shy. Evie sensed she had crossed some kind of invisible barrier. "And so that's why you chose women's studies?"

Evie cocked her head, considering this. "It's probably why I joined the Women's Action Collective, once I started. I associated feminism with this very cool, badass thing that cool, badass women were into. And, at least at my college, that ended up being true. I mean, we probably did more drinking and karaoke and making out with each other than we did actual activism, but it was fun." Evie rolled the stem of her wineglass between her fingers, smiling at the memories: hazy, weed-soaked, up-till-4-a.m.-planning-the-revolution memories. "They became my social circle, and that's what everyone was majoring or minoring in, so it was kind of a no-brainer."

"And journalism?"

"Well, my uncle's a radio journalist, so I guess it's in the blood. Uncle Mike. He's also gay, so guess that runs in the family too."

Velma's lips lifted in a smile, her eyebrows pulling together. "Interesting."

Evie ducked her eyes, feeling positively incandescent. Velma Wolff found her interesting. Evie wasn't so insecure as to think she wasn't—journalism and basic self-esteem had taught her everyone had a story—it was just . . . Velma Wolff found her interesting. There was so much more she wanted to tell her—how her stint at the student newspaper made her think taking over the media was as easy as wanting to, and the crushing realization this simply wasn't true; how her summer internship at *Salty* had been purely a means to a job somewhere else in the Heimert Schwartz kingdom and how radically that had backfired; how when her uncle came out as gay at age forty her grandparents disowned him but her mom refused to stop loving her brother—but before she could, the waiter returned for a second time.

"I'm sorry," Velma said without sounding sorry at all. "We'll look now, I promise." The waiter smiled and told them to take their time.

Evie's eyes ran over the menu without reading it. Was it going well? It was. Wasn't it? Evie snuck a glance at Velma. The hint of a smile played on the writer's mouth as she skimmed the menu. Evie clicked her eyes back in front of her, still feeling luminescent.

"I think I'll go for the duck," Velma announced.

Evie closed her menu. "I was thinking the same thing."

After the waiter took their orders—two ducks and a house salad to share—the conversation resumed, but refused to relax. There was an underlying urgency to everything they said. Their banter was giddy, resembling less an ebb and flow and more the logic of lightning. They scurried down conversational rabbit holes, forgetting what started them. Evie repeated herself twice. Velma dropped her fork. They were excited and nervous in equal measure, and the cumulative effect made for laughter that was too loud, pauses that seemed terrifyingly long. Wishing desperately to cut the adrenaline that insisted on tightening her muscles, Evie kept reaching for her wineglass, which the waiter kept refilling with a magician's grace. They finished the bottle before the mains arrived, and ordered another. As the waiter uncorked it, Velma asked Evie if she had any siblings. Evie groaned, dropping her cheek into one hand. "Brothers and sisters? Oh god, have we come to that?" A small voice in the back of her head warned her this was rude; she was getting drunk. She told the voice to fuck off.

"I'm interested!" Velma protested. "I want to work out if I'm dealing with the baby of the family or the classic example of an only child."

Evie slurped a mouthful of wine. "I have a sister." It was so automatic it almost felt like the truth. "Evie."

"Evie," Velma repeated. "Pretty name." Evie felt an odd flick of jealousy—Velma hadn't complimented Chloe on *her* name—but before she could untangle the feeling, Velma leaned forward and said, "Tell me about her."

"Okay." Evie sat back, fluffing her hair with slightly numb fingers. "She's twenty-three—"

"How old are you?"

"Twenty-five," Evie said.

Velma's face twitched in either relief or concern.

"She's a copyeditor for a magazine," Evie continued. "She's very re-sponsible. She's a good girl." She rolled her eyes.

"A good girl?"

"Got a job, right out of college, at the place she interned. Said yes right away." Evie remembered this desperation, so eager for the position at the bottom of the totem pole. "She was one of those girls who pre-tended being unpopular was a rebellious choice when in reality it wasn't something she had a say in."

"Were you popular?"

Evie pretended to look demure. Of course Chloe would've been pop-ular. Popular and datable and powerful. "I did okay."

"What else?"

"She's sort of a snob."

"How so?"

"She thinks she's smarter than everyone else in the room."

"Is she?"

Evie shrugged. "I don't know. Maybe. She has a blog. *Something*

Snarky; it's not bad. She loves you," she added, lowering her voice. "You're her favorite writer."

"So she has good taste." Velma sounded like she was only half kidding.

"Oh, she has pretty good taste with stuff like that." Viewed objectively, Evie felt this was true. "Relationships, not so much. She's never been in love."

"Have you?"

"Have I what?"

Velma's gaze traced Evie's face slowly. "Been in love."

Heat rushed to Evie's cheeks with an urgency that caught her off guard. But she didn't break Velma's gaze. "No."

"Ladies." It was their waiter, bearing two plates the size of tires. Dinner was served.

Evie hadn't eaten duck in years. If she'd actually read the menu, she wouldn't have chosen it. But as she dug into the tender pink meat, she was glad she had. She was having the same sensory experience as Velma. Her vegetarianism seemed like a distant silly idea in the face of both of them groaning about just how perfectly the chef had prepared their meal. It fused them even closer.

Everything was going better than expected. Whether it was Evie's wit or Chloe's beauty, in this intimate restaurant, it felt less like she was Velma's audience and more like they were on the same footing. Velma was embarrassed when she confessed she hadn't read any of Joan Didion's essays (Evie: "But she's an icon!" Velma: "There's just so many books!"); when she mispronounced *Degas* ("Really? That's how you say it?"); and when the waiter came to clear their plates, she accidentally elbowed him in the side ("I meant to do that"). He presented them with dessert menus.

"Interested?" Velma asked.

"Yes," Evie replied. "I am." This time, she read the menu. "Ooh, what about the tiramisu?"

Velma frowned. "Might be a little rich after the duck. How about the olive oil cake?"

Even though this was the least interesting dessert on the menu, Evie nodded. "Perfect."

Velma asked for an espresso, so Evie did too. Velma excused herself to use the restroom. Even the way she walked was supremely confident, like Moses parting the Red Sea. *And*, Evie thought, *let's face it. The woman has an ass like a Georgia peach*. She picked up her dessert spoon and met her reflection in the warped silver. Her eyeliner was slightly smudged, but in a way that looked rebellious rather than wrong. Her dark hair was mussed. Her lips were wine stained, bloodred against otherwise even skin.

There was no denying it.

She looked hot.

Not cute. Not cool.

Hot.

The spoon clattered to the floor. Evie made no move to retrieve it.

Evie Selby was dead.

Long live Chloe fucking Fontaine.

37.

Mark was a good boy.

Mark paid his taxes on time, helped women carry strollers up the subway steps, and cleared away the dirty dishes without being asked. He'd had exactly two one-night stands, both of whom he gave his number to: they were the ones who never called.

Which partly explained Willow. Willow was not a good girl. Not in that way. She could tell Mark's parents didn't approve of her. They couldn't define Willow like they could define Mark, and it made them nervous. On the few occasions they'd gotten together for what always seemed like an interminably long meal, no one could say the right thing: Willow didn't respond to being mothered and Mark became overly— painfully—aware of his parents' parochial taste. Mark and Willow worked best on their own: a cozy cave of *just us*. Mark once told her she was a road trip without a map. For Mark, who never drove so much as a few blocks without GPS, she could see how that would be thrilling.

She didn't have a road map now.

As usual.

He buzzed her up without asking who it was. When he opened the door, she could tell he'd been expecting Willow.

"Caroline?" Mark threw his gaze up, then down the empty corridor, as if expecting someone to jump and yell, "Gotcha!"

Her words came in a nervous rush. "You left this. At the bar. It had your address on the inside." She held out the small Moleskine he kept tucked in the side pocket of his bag.

"Oh." He flipped the notebook open. His mathematically neat hand-writing confirmed its identity.

She was wearing the same dress she'd been wearing when she saw him outside his office in Soho: a long floaty thing covered in tiny yellow flowers, something from the back of her closet, something pre-Mark. It was hard to remember pre-Mark. Wasn't it? "You probably shouldn't write your address in things like that. Maybe some psycho could use it to track you down."

He blinked at her from behind his glasses. "Maybe one has."

Willow felt her mouth become small.

"I'm kidding," he said quickly.

"I'm not a psycho." She backed up a step.

"I know, I know, I was kissing, *kidding*. I was kidding." His face was going red. "God, please, come in, Caroline."

"You sure?"

"Yes. I was just—doing literally nothing, so I'm happy for the company. Please."

He stepped aside. As she passed, she heard him breathing in the smell of her hair and her mouth relaxed, unfurling into a smile.

"This is really nice." She dropped her bag on the couch and looked around the familiar apartment. "Great that it's south facing."

Mark masked a double take. "That's one of the reasons I took it. People don't seem to realize how important that is."

"You save so much on heating if you can rely on the winter sun, right?" Another thing Willow had embarrassed herself over: Who knew the sun could affect heating costs? She took a seat on the end of the sofa, kicked off her flip-flops, and tucked her legs under herself comfortably.

"Can I get you something to drink? I don't have any wine . . ."

"Beer's fine." She stretched her arms above her head and arched her back like a serpent. "Don't suppose you have Sierra Nevada?"

"You're not going to believe this . . ." Mark disappeared into the kitchen to return with a six-pack of, yes, Sierra Nevada. He was grinning like a lucky door-prize winner.

They sat at opposite ends of the sofa, sipping their beers and talking with a strange, easy familiarity about their respective days. Willow remembered Mark had given an important presentation that day. He seemed relieved to have someone to dissect the minutiae of it with. She told him about her day of classes: a wonderful double life full of lectures, and assignments, and professors.

They finished their beers and started on a second round without breaking stride.

Willow told Mark about Caroline's bohemian upbringing, a fiction that was as warm and comforting as it was untrue: a mother who painted, a father who cooked, both of them madly in love with each other and life itself. Houses in Tuscany and the Greek islands and an island off the coast of Australia: details plucked from travel magazines and the sort of movies where a divorcée falls for a suntanned young fisherman and learns to make pasta and love again. Nothing hard or painful or disappointing in this new life. Only warmth, and acceptance, and love, from a father devoted to his family and a mother who was as brilliant as she was unconventional. Nothing at all like Willow's real mother, who had moved to Maryland after divorcing Matteo when Willow was ten to get quietly remarried to an inoffensive-to-the-point-of-being-dull insurance salesman called Phil. Willow could only manage long weekends at their prosaic suburban home: any longer and it felt like her very soul was being turned into a fake flower arrangement.

"Where did you go to school?" Mark asked.

"Oh, everywhere," she said with a light, lyrical laugh.

Mark said that sounded wonderful.

It did. It did sound wonderful.

There was something about being Caroline that was so incredibly freeing. Caroline didn't carry herself with an invisible shield. Sometimes Willow felt like she was always conducting two conversations with the world: the one that was spoken out loud, and the one she carried with her, inside her head. Caroline wasn't like that. Caroline didn't hide her body. Caroline didn't double-check her statements to make sure they sounded smart. Caroline knew how to flirt. Caroline was liberated.

And seeking, of course.

That was why she was here.

She drained her beer and held it up. "Another?"

"Really?" Mark checked his watch. "It's a school night."

"I don't have to be at school until eleven."

"God, lucky for some." Mark groaned, getting to his feet. "All right. But I'll have to kick you out at midnight or you'll see me turn into a pumpkin."

"I'd love that," she called, and he chuckled. He popped off their bottle tops and offered a toast. "To new friends."

She smiled. "To new friends."

They clinked their bottles. She didn't look away as she took her first sip. He didn't either.

"I'm always up for new friends," she said.

"Me too. You can never have too many friends, right?"

They'd said the word *friends* so much in the last minute they'd robbed it of meaning and made it sound weird.

Maybe it was time for things to get weird.

Willow waved the tip of her bottle in a circle. "You never gave me the tour."

Mark shifted awkwardly, his eyes darting left to right.

Willow stood up. "Show me."

"There's not much to see—"

"Oh come on." She laughed, like she'd suggested a game.

"Okay." Mark got to his feet, looking around the neat apartment as if it was foreign to him. "This is the living room that we've been enjoying so much."

She smiled and tucked some strands of hair behind her ear. "Right, got it."

"Kitchen." He led the way. "Fridge. Sink. Shelves. Uh, fruit basket, with a distinct absence of fruit." He was treading water, tap-dancing. "All in all, small but functional."

"Not how you'd describe yourself, I hope." She shot him a wicked smile, and it took him a full five seconds to realize she was making a dick joke. His face froze.

She burst into giggles. "I'm kidding, I'm kidding!"

"Um, right." Mark was going red again. He crossed back quickly through the living room. "Bathroom through here. Featuring all the usual bathroom accoutrements."

"Mmm." She gave the white tiles a cursory glance.

"And then, there's just . . . Well, the bedroom is just through here." He paused in the doorway. "But it's pretty messy, so I probably wouldn't—"

"Cool." She pushed the half-closed door wide open.

Mark picked up a towel and T-shirt off the floor. "Wasn't expecting company."

Willow perched on the end of his bed and looked up at him innocently. "No late-night visit from your girlfriend planned? What was her name again?"

Mark grimaced slightly. "Willow." His eyes moved self-consciously to a framed photo of them, from a wedding in the Hamptons earlier in the year. Willow, only half smiling, in a simple silk slip and a crown of daisies. Him, grinning affably, black silk tie loosened at the neck, one arm slung around her neck possessively.

"That's right." She nodded. "Willow." Her voice was a murmur, quiet and curious. "I could never understand why you liked this picture so much."

"What do you mean?"

"It's just—it's just an odd angle of her." She hated that picture. She wished he'd never had it framed.

Mark's voice sharpened. "Why would you . . ."

But Willow leaned back on her elbows and Mark's words faded away. All the simple fun of the evening was sucked away and replaced with something white-hot and electric, as sudden as someone flicking a switch. There were only three feet between them. Three feet between his mouth and hers. He checked his watch without reading the time. "I better call it a night."

She leaned back farther, opening her body to him. One of her nipples had almost edged out of her dress. His eyes kept twitching down to it. When she spoke, it was coyly. "Are you sure?"

Mark backed away from the door, speaking to the hallway. "Yeah, I have a start. Early start."

"Okay."

She heard him take their four empty bottles to the recycling and tip what was left in the two others down the sink. She slid her feet back into her flip-flops, swung her backpack onto her back. By the time he came out, she was standing by the door. "Thanks for the beer, Mark."

"Thanks for bringing the notebook back." He unlocked the front door, subtly sweeping his gaze into the hallway. "See you later."

Willow cocked her head to one side. "Don't I at least get a hug?"

"I'm not sure if—" he began, but she was already moving toward him, circling her arms up. One hand snaked around his neck. The other found his back, and then she was pressing herself, all of herself, to him. She sensed resistance; a tensing of his muscles into a physical barrier. But she kept her arms around him, around his familiar, subtly athletic body. And then he gave in. He hugged her. Held her. Let himself melt like butter in the sun. When she moved back, so slowly, so dangerously slowly, Mark looked drugged. For a second their lips hovered inches from each other.

She could pull away.

Wrench them apart.

But he was so impossibly close. She was almost there. She could almost feel it.

Her mouth connected with his. Everything inside her collapsed and was constructed, simultaneously. It lasted one, two, three seconds before he stumbled back. "No, no, no. No. No."

"It's okay," she whispered. "*Be unsafe.*"

"Go. Please."

Willow moved into the hallway, holding the feeling close to her chest, cradling it like a baby. "Caroline." His voice was scratchy; he had to clear his throat to take control of it. "We can't see each other again."

She looked back at him now. Her cheeks were flushed. Her eyes felt as bright as stars ripped from the night sky. When she spoke, it was soft but certain. Playful, and almost a threat. "That's just not possible."

She ran lightly down the hallway. The stairwell would work. The lighting there was strangely flat, appropriately somber. Mark wouldn't be leaving anytime soon. From her backpack, the tools. Camera. Tripod. Remote control.

She faced the lens.

She summoned everything she had, everything the past few hours had created.

And she started to work.

38.

Naturally, Velma paid for dinner, sliding a silver credit card into the leather booklet. In the past, this was Evie's cue to fumble for her purse, peppering the moment with, "Wait, are you sure?" "I don't mind." "Thank you so much, that's so generous, are you sure you're sure?"

But the idea that someone might want to pay for her dinner did not fill Chloe Fontaine with such uncomfortable nervous guilt. After Velma signed the check, Evie just smiled, and said, "Thank you. That was lovely." And that was all there was to it.

When Evie suggested they split a cab, Velma admitted she only lived a few blocks away. *Oh, really* . . . She insisted on walking Velma home. They wandered down the quiet street in easy silence, hands swinging inches from each other, each passing swish as palpable as a paint stroke. Happiness coursed through her, and she was drunk, deliciously drunk: with the wine, with the night, with the city, with life, with women, with Velma. The sky looked like a Van Gogh painting, the air smelled like honeysuckle, and anything was possible, everything was probable.

Of course it wasn't a real date because she wasn't really herself, but somehow, that didn't matter. Chloe's wide smile and deep blue eyes had kept Velma transfixed. But it was Evie's jokes that made her laugh, Evie's insights that caused the author to furrow her brow in surprise. Velma made her feel clever. Bright. Fascinating. Evie was reminded of how Willow used to make her feel this way, years ago. But this was different. She didn't want Willow to kiss her.

"This is me." Velma stopped in front of a beautiful redbrick building with classic molded window edges towering down over the cobbled street. The foyer was awash in yellow light, hung with artwork.

Evie nodded, smiling, and waited for Velma to open the door for her.

"Chloe. Miss Chloe Fontaine." Velma wrinkled her brow and put both hands in her pants pockets. "I don't think you should come up."

Evie felt like an actress who'd forgotten her lines. "Oh."

"I want you to. Don't get me wrong. It's just . . ." Velma's face became complicated, as if several different emotions were jostling for front-runner: apprehension, displeasure, woe. Evie felt a cool chill, a long tickle of foreboding. Suddenly the night air didn't seem so warm. "I like you, Chloe. I really like you. I'm just not in the position where I can get involved with someone right now."

Evie swallowed. Still the script eluded her. "Oh."

Velma met Evie's gaze carefully, each word now feeling handpicked. "I got out of a relationship six months ago. We were together for . . . a while, let's just say that."

Emiko Aki, the gorgeous Japanese American model-slash-actress Velma had been with for a record four years. Last public appearance: LA premiere for *Dying Comes Easy*, the Michael Bay film Emiko starred in. Evie said, "I didn't know that." And then, emboldened by both the wine and how close they were standing, "Why did it end?"

Velma spoke with a deliberate casualness that betrayed past pain. "We didn't have a strong enough connection."

We have that connection.

The words formed instantly in Evie's mind, immediate and unsummoned.

She let them play again, slower this time, more deliberate.

We have that connection.

She could feel it, humming between them, crackling the night air. Gently, Evie took Velma's hand, spidering their fingers together in slow exploration. The sensation sent a whoosh through her entire body. They locked eyes.

"I just want to make sure," Velma said quietly. "That we're on the same page."

Evie nodded. She understood. Velma had been hurt. By someone who, however talented and beautiful, she didn't mesh with on a soul level. Velma couldn't commit to the first pretty girl she took out for dinner. And of course, she shouldn't commit either. Evie Selby would have to reappear eventually. But the potential for love—great love, earth-shattering love—was there. It was just so clearly there, and denying it was like denying the existence of the sun. Maybe naïve, self-doubting Evie Selby wouldn't be able to see this potential. But Chloe could see it in such bright, hard relief she almost winced. Desperation and sadness and lust collided inside her, forcing her to draw a step closer. Distance was not possible.

"Yes," Evie whispered. "We're on the same page."

Velma's pupils were dilated, wide, wet pools of black. "Good."

Evie tipped her mouth up, wanting, needing, for their lips to connect.

But Velma swerved her face away. Evie's lips planted on Velma's cheek. She pressed into it awkwardly.

A chuckle sounded in Velma's throat. "Baby." She stepped back, in the direction of her building. "There's no rush." She tugged her hand out of Evie's grip, smiling crookedly. "We've got all the time in the world."

39.

Krista was dreading her third day of filming.

Yesterday afternoon had been godawful. God. Awful. Damian, that snitch, must have told Tristan about the trophy incident. After an hour of flubbed lines, Greg took Tristan aside for a chat. When the pair returned to the set, no one missed the look of incredulous disgust on Greg's face, nor the strained look he shot at Krista. The knowledge seeped around the set like an invisible but odorous gas leak: Lenka Penka was responsible for Tristan dropping the ball. Needless to say, Lenka Penka was less than thrilled when she was awakened by her driver, Eduardo, with the usual, "Mes? Mes?" indicating they had arrived back at the set.

Immediately, she became aware of the pain. Cramps, as if her insides were being tortured by a thousand red-hot pokers. She must be getting her period. *Fuck*. Didn't she just finish it? She let out a moan.

The car door was pulled open. Damian's annoying cheery face was set to a smile. "Good morning, Lenka—" But then the smile dropped. "Oh, I'm sorry, I thought Lenka was in this car."

Krista hauled herself out, face contorted with pain. "Oh man. It must be fucking Shark Week in my pants right now." That was weird. Her jacket felt strangely big on her. Like it used to when—

"I'm sorry." Damian peered at her. "Who are you? Where's Lenka?"

She had changed. She had changed back to Krista Kumar. She was Lenka when she got into the car; she knew she was. But now suddenly, and completely inexplicably, she was a different person.

Shorter.

Darker.

And with two chunky man arms.

"I—I—I—" Krista grasped for a nonexistent excuse, her cramps forgotten.

The car rolled off, tires crunching slowly over the gravel. Damian glanced between it and her, confused. He can't check with Eduardo, Krista realized. Eduardo had picked Lenka Penka up. "I'm her assistant," Krista babbled. "Yeah, yeah, yeah, assistant. She's right behind me."

Damian directed his gaze at the stream of black town cars and trucks making their way into the lot. "Behind you?"

"I mean, in front of me. She's already here. Do you have a bathroom? I really need to go."

She pushed past Damian and began speed-walking in the direction of the toilet block, hunched over to protect both her sore tummy and her identity. There was only one thing that mattered, only one thing that could save her now. The Pretty. Did she remember to pack it in her tote?

Thanks to the timetable taped to the bathroom mirror, she knew she was supposed to change back this morning—she'd taken it on a Wednesday, and it was Wednesday today—but when she woke she was still Lenka. This was met with fervent relief; one more day until she'd have to radically shit herself to stay Pretty. But just to be on the safe side, she decided to chuck the Pretty in her tote anyway. Hadn't she? Or was that one of those things she'd planned to do, but didn't actually do, like go to yoga or take birth control?

Her phone started buzzing. Damian. Calling for Lenka. She stabbed at the screen to reject the call. Anxiety made her feel like she was covered in ants.

Thank god the toilet block was empty. There were two near the entrance, and evidently she hadn't been the only girl to work out that this was the grossest. Now she was thankful for the fact there were no paper towels and the whole place smelled like pee. She locked her stall door and began digging through her tote. Keys, wallet, phone, pen, lip gloss, lipstick, call sheets, copy of *Salty*, pizza cutter (what?), mascara, more lipstick. But no Pretty. Krista began dumping her shit out onto the floor, panic blooming. She'd put it in! Hadn't she? Her phone buzzed again, insistent, refusing to be ignored. With a sharp cry, she shoved her hand into her pocket and ripped out her bleating phone. As she did, the bottle of Pretty flew out of her pocket and splashed into the toilet bowl.

"*Yes!*" Krista rocketed her hand into the water, wiping the bottle dry on her shirt. Hands shaking, she unscrewed the dropper. The small sensation of wetness hit her tongue. She yanked down her underpants and positioned her butt over the bowl, waiting for the inevitable.

Ten minutes later, Krista heard someone come in. "Jesus." The girl's voice sounded disgusted. "Is anyone in here?"

Krista banged her door open. The dirty mirrors reflected a statuesque woman with mocha skin and eyes the color of the forest floor. A curtain of glossy black hair fell around her shoulders like a cape.

The PA's eyes widened, no doubt recognizing the woman before her as Lenka Penka: Cupcake Girl, Tristan's costar, general troublemaker. She shrank back a step.

"I wouldn't go in there for a while," Krista said, wiping her mouth with the back of her hand. "Someone, who isn't me, really went to town in there."

40

When Evie woke, she was relieved to find that the room was in perfect focus. She was still Pretty.

She rolled over, the dull buzz of yet another hangover greeting her. But they were worth it. Because last night—and she couldn't even conjure the phrase *last night* without breaking into a toothy grin—last night had been perfect. Her smile stretched wider as she recalled the nervous energy that had permeated dinner, a perfect dinner, in a perfect restaurant. With a perfect woman. A perfect woman she'd . . . never see again.

Today had to be her last day. A small part of her was relieved not to be constantly checking for side effects or unexpected transformations. But a larger part was disappointed. Back to being a Regular. A face in the crowd. A copyeditor. At least she'd be able to distract herself by watching *Extra Salt* go live. The memory of a date with Velma Wolff was just a souvenir. A warm, sweet souvenir that made her stomach flip-flop.

Krista called Evie just as she was about to leave. "Hey," Evie said. "How's the moviemaking biz?"

Krista's voice was a hoarse whisper. "I changed back this morning. After I got to the set."

Evie dropped her purse. "Shit—"

"It's cool, it's cool, I had the Pretty with me. But you should be careful. It's probably like your period, or something. Maybe it varies?"

"Of course." Turning back on set. Exactly what she'd been afraid of. "Where's the stuff you left for me?"

There was a pause. Krista's voice became tiny. "Um, what?"

"The Pretty." Evie's eyebrows shot up. "Tell me you didn't take the whole bottle."

"You said you were only doing it once!"

"But what if I turn back on set like you just did? What then?"

"If you're still Chloe now, it'll probably last the full day. I think it happens when you're asleep—"

"*Probably?* You *think*?"

Evie heard a muffled knock and a voice call, "Lenka?"

"I have to go," Krista whimpered. "I'm sorry. I didn't think—"

"Of course you didn't," Evie shot back. "Why should I have expected that?"

Fucking Krista and her crazy plans. They always bit her in the ass: Why would this be any different? Piercing her nose with a safety pin. Barhopping on Staten Island. 'Shrooms before a flight. All idiotic schemes that resulted in pain and/or terror.

She could skip the screening. Stay home, fake an illness. That was what Evie Selby would do. Play it safe. But this was the reason she'd taken the Pretty in the first place. This was supposed to be her day, her chance to shine. Evie met her reflection in the living room mirror. Beneath thick, blunt bangs, enormous azure eyes stared back at her, gorgeous and defiant.

Screw it.

Chloe Fontaine took risks.

Things worked out for Chloe Fontaine.

A PA directed her to a green room. When she entered, several voices said her name at once. Milling around three black leather couches all facing a flat-screen TV were the crew and four carbon copies of California blondes: the other reporters. These girls were nice enough, at least to Evie, which she suspected had something to do with being mistaken for one of them: a fellow hot girl, and one in a position they probably coveted. She felt an odd sense of protective empathy for these young women, who, like Chloe, had gotten their jobs based on their looks. Her gaze dropped to her hands. She still had Chloe's strong, clear nails, her long piano-player fingers. God, she almost expected to see Evie's hands . . .

Someone squeezed her arm. She jumped.

"Sorry, beautiful." It was Marcello. "Didn't mean to scare you."

Evie forced a chuckle. "Just stage fright, I guess." She curled her fingers into fists, willing them not to disappear.

Rich stood up to address the room. "Okay, folks, here it is: the first episode of *Extra Salt*, going live in T-minus five minutes. Featuring our very own Chloe Fontaine." A small round of applause broke out. Evie smiled and ducked her head modestly. "Can someone get the lights?"

A pink-and-red *Extra Salt* logo burst onto the screen. Gemma let out a tiny squeal. Evie exhaled. She was so full of nervous excitement it felt like two huge hands were squeezing her rib cage. Bubbly pop music started: the title sequence. Chloe Fontaine filled the screen, looking pretty if a little plain in a gray T-shirt. Choppy, quick cuts started. Chloe smiling cheesily. Chloe laughing. Chloe waving a big black dildo around.

The room broke into titters of laughter.

Evie bolted upright.

Chloe with an armful of vibrators, hugging them like they were more precious than gold.

It was footage from when Kelly was getting her to choose the Dildo of the Week. Footage she didn't know was being filmed. It was mortifying. The girl on screen grinned at the camera, the *Extra Salt* logo popped up, and the music finished with a flourish.

"Hey, I'm Chloe Fontaine." She flashed a wide grin. The footage had been blown out, overexposed so much she barely looked human. You couldn't even tell that she wasn't wearing makeup. "Welcome to *Extra Salt*, where you can find news and views on all things girl. First up: let's talk lips. Lovely lips are a must all year-round . . ." Her intro to the first story started, drowned out by the dull roar in her ears. Kelly had tricked her. The dildos were a setup. From the corner of her eye, she could sense the producer shooting her quick, cautious glances. She didn't return them, training her gaze straight ahead. One of the blond reporters was planting her lips on a guy's cheek and shaking her head at the lipstick mark it left. Evie was too mortified to even roll her eyes at this. The image of her waving Morgan Freeman around like a cock-obsessed clown was tattooed on her brain.

The "Who's Better in Bed" story ended up being street interviews of a lot of giggling, embarrassed girls and annoyingly bravado guys interviewed by clone reporter number two. Every single New Yorker interviewed was straight and white; two minutes of not-so-subtle eugenics.

A montage started: a mix of celebrities on the red carpet, smiling, twirling, blowing kisses at the camera. Suddenly Velma Wolff was on-screen with a made-up Chloe, asking her, "Don't you want to ask me about what I'm wearing?" It was footage from Velma's book launch. But before the sight of Chloe had even really registered, the images cut to a countdown of 2016's hottest red-carpet looks, hosted by clone reporter number three. Evie's mouth fell open in silent disbelief. That couldn't be it, could it? They were going to come back to the interview, weren't they? But as the episode continued and the red-carpet story was replaced by something about fall's must-have purse, Evie realized they were not. That was the edit of her Velma Wolff interview. She'd told Velma to watch this: she'd practically bragged about it. *At least I'm bringing it home with the "Feminist Action Hero" story*. Evie clung to the idea like a life raft. Kelly had promised her. It wouldn't all be cheap sex and makeup tips.

She tuned back into the screening, desperate to hear the opening words of the story she'd been working so hard on: *Feminism has a new friend in publishing's hottest genre. Feminism has a new friend in publishing's hottest genre. Feminism has a new friend in—*

"And that's all we have time for this week." Chloe flashed a shit-eating grin straight to camera. "And remember, folks: diamonds aren't a girl's best friend—" The footage cut to Chloe waving the dildo around. A female voice that wasn't hers cooed, "This is."

The screen cut to black. The room broke into laughter and applause, a chorus of "That was so good!" "You looked so pretty!" "Are you kidding, I hate my nose."

The room was pitching, listing like a ship in heavy seas. Evie's forehead prickled with sweat. With anger. With embarrassment. She remembered Luksus introducing her at Velma's after-party; a hot new journalist with her finger on the pulse. Ira Glass in a miniskirt. Turned out, she was just the skirt. Someone tugged at her arm. She jerked it away and stormed out of the room.

41.

"Absolutely not. No way." Evie planted both hands on Jan's enormous desk. "You are not using those opening credits."

"I thought they were great," Rich offered. "Super funny." He was swiping through his phone, sitting slouched next to Kelly. Infuriatingly, the young director seemed not at all intimidated to be in Jan's corner office.

"If we do them again," Rich went on, "can you pretend to fellate the dildo?"

Evie stared at him incredulously.

"You know." He mimed fellation. "Like that. Like you're—"

"I know what fellating is," Evie hissed. "No! We're reshooting them with *no dildos*. I didn't even know you were filming me! That's totally illegal, a breach of contract!"

Rich snorted. "You should read your contract more carefully."

"Is that true?" Jan asked Kelly. Her calm British accent sliced through the hysteria. "Did you film her without her consent?"

Kelly sighed. "Yes. But we needed—"

"Cut something else for the second episode," Jan said.

"The second episode?" Evie exclaimed. "No! You have to recut something now, before it goes online."

"It's already online," Rich said, holding up his phone. "We've had over a thousand views on YouTube."

"No!" Evie gasped. "You have to recut the opening credits, put my story back in—"

"Chloe," Jan interrupted.

"*And* the interview with Velma. Fuck!" Evie threw her hands up. "Everything good I did is gone!"

"Chloe!" Jan snapped. She fixed Evie with a penetrating stare. "Please. Take a seat."

After a long hesitation, Evie sank down into a chair. She took a deep breath, trying for rational. "It was made clear to me that the host— me—would have the chance to contribute to the show. Why has all of my content been cut?"

"The Velma Wolff interview was completely unusable," Kelly told Jan.

"No, it wasn't!" Evie protested.

"'*Your novels are known for their unreliable narrators*'?" Kelly looked scornful. "It's *Extra Salt,* not Comparative Literature 101. None of our viewers would've understood what the hell you were on about."

"And her action hero story?" Jan asked.

Kelly sighed, running one hand through his hair. "It was a tonal thing. It didn't mesh."

Rich looked up at Evie. "You said *feminism* thirty-five times."

"So?" exclaimed Evie.

"In two minutes." Rich met her gaze evenly. His T-shirt read T-Shirt Gag. "That's pretty insane."

"I'll tell you what's insane." Evie shot to her feet again. "Forced prostitution! Backyard abortions, date rape. Ten-year-old girls made to undergo female circumcision—"

"Jesus!" Rich exclaimed, at the same time Kelly said, "Chloe—"

"Okay, okay." Jan raised a hand. "Let's all take a breath."

Evie was panting. She'd been lied to. She'd been *had*. She had a sudden image of Kelly, sniggering under his breath as she did take after take, dismissing her as a gullible bimbo. "You were never going to run it. That's why you let me say whatever I wanted, you were never even going to fucking *run* it."

Kelly jabbed a finger at her. "You can't prove that—"

"Kelly will recut the opening credits for the second episode," Jan interrupted. "No further changes."

"What?" Evie gaped.

Jan's voice took on an edge. "Chloe, Kelly is the producer. Rich is the director. You are the host."

"Right," Evie said. "I'm the *host*. I should have some say over *what* I'm hosting."

"Chloe, love," Kelly said. "We're all professionals here. Why don't you let us do our jobs, and we'll let you do yours."

"Which is to say whatever's in front of me," Evie said. "Even if it offends every moral fiber in my being."

"Huh." Rich's nasal voice sounded amused. "It's like she's just worked out what acting is."

Evie opened her mouth to retaliate, but before she could, Jan announced, "All right, everyone, that's it." Her eyes moved to her computer screen. "Thank you."

Their cue to leave. Rich and Kelly ambled for the door. Evie was fuming as she followed.

"Oh, and Kelly?" Jan called. "I was wondering if you'd heard anything from Evie Selby."

Evie pulled up short, her own name ricocheting through her like a pinball.

"Nah, mate. Radio silence," Kelly replied. "Shame. We could use a researcher."

"I agree." Jan looked directly at Evie, her words measured and steady. "Hopefully, Evie makes an appearance very soon."

42.

Krista sat on a milk crate behind craft services, sucking on a cigarette, trying to temper her nerves. Ordinarily, Krista wasn't an anxious person. Not like Evie could be. But right now, a nonspecific feeling of foreboding was eating away at her, dissolving rational thought like acid.

Things didn't feel right. And it wasn't just her position as most hated on this stupid film set. It was the Pretty.

She yanked out a pocket mirror and studied her eyes intently. It seemed like they were different: not as brilliantly green as they had been before. But maybe she was just getting used to them. She couldn't tell. She couldn't tell and it was starting to make her feel downright paranoid.

Had Damian spoken to Eduardo about this morning? She could picture this conversation so clearly, the soft-spoken Eduardo insisting, swearing on his *life*, that he picked up Lenka Penka. What if they dug further into Lenka Penka's nonexistent past? What then?

She ground her cigarette into the grass, regretting lighting it to begin with. She couldn't shake a lingering feeling of nausea from her transformation. It was definitely harder than the first time. What if the nausea never went away? What if the Pretty was poison? What if it was eating away at her insides, slowly cooking her like a rotisserie chicken?

Evie was right to be suspicious. They didn't know enough about the Pretty. Why did Penny give it to her? She replayed their encounter in McHale's Ales, searching her memory of the beautiful blonde for a twitch of anxiety or a grimace of pain. But all she could remember was just how lovely Penny's full pink mouth was, how svelte she looked in that black silk jumpsuit.

Her phone chimed. An email. Hi Krista, This is Ella-Mae, *Salty*'s deputy editor. I have your details on file as Evie's emergency contact. I know she's been in Florida, but I'm unable to get in contact with her—she's not replying to texts and her calls are going straight to voicemail. I just need to confirm when she'll be back in. Blessings, Ella-Mae Morris. P.S. If you like, I can change her emergency contact to Chloe Fontaine: it might make more sense as she's Evie's roommate.

Krista was surprised: it wasn't like Evie to drop the ball. She forwarded it to Evie, adding a message of her own. hey dude, looks like u need to run recon on salty. how are u? what's happening with velma? when will u be home? i miss u. have u heard from willow? she's always out or passed out when i get home. assuming they're her vino bottles piling up in the kitchen: very Lilo, ha ha. are u having fun? IDK if I am anymore—

But her Olympic-speed typing was interrupted. From around the corner of the craft services tent, she heard her name, spoken in a whisper.

"—Jen walked in on Lenka Penka throwing up this morning."

"No!"

"Yep. In the toilet block by the entrance."

"No shit. That explains a lot."

"Seriously. I never see her without a cupcake in hand."

"Ugh, that makes me sick."

"I bet she wanted to get caught doing it. Like, why wasn't she doing it in her trailer?"

"Totally."

That'd be fucking right. Now the Pretty had the crew assuming she was bulimic. Screw them. She strode around the corner of the tent. Two PAs stood stock-still in horror. They were both cool-looking dark-skinned girls—one was black, the other looked Indian—and with a jolt of surprise Krista realized that under normal circumstances, she'd probably be bitching with them, part of their crew. Krista towered over the girls, anger mixing with hurt. "If you have something to say to me, say it to my face."

The PAs looked terrified. Neither moved an inch.

"Firstly, I'm not bulimic," Krista said. "I was just having a regular vomit, like a regular person. Secondly, what if I was bulimic? What if the pressure to be thin and perfect had gotten to me so much that I felt the need to make myself sick? This is your solution? To gossip about it? Not very cool, guys. In fact, it feels like weird jealous backstabbing of someone who might need your fucking help, if I was bulimic, which I'm not."

One of them finally found her voice. "We're really sorry, Ms. Penka."

"Do you know how hard I've worked to get here?" Krista continued. "How much I've sacrificed? Don't judge a book by its cover, okay? Just because I look like a very diverse Playmate doesn't mean I don't have problems. I do. I have a lot. I have a lot of problems." This line of argument was beginning to make it sound like she had mental problems, so Krista changed tack. "Don't punish me for your own insecurities."

"We're sorry," the other girl piped up. "It won't happen again."

"Okay." Krista huffed. "Cool."

The trio stood in awkward silence.

"So, like, what are you guys doing right now?" Krista asked.

The girls exchanged an odd glance. "We have to get back to set," the black girl said.

"Me too." Krista about-faced, tossing a lock of shiny dark hair over one shoulder. She made a show of stomping off, when all she really wanted to do was tell the two girls the truth about absolutely everything.

Krista was examining the contours of her face (Had it changed? Why did she still feel sick?) when someone rapped on her trailer door. "Hello? Lenka?"

She pocketed the mirror. "Yeah?"

A woman climbed into her trailer. Smart black blazer, neat pencil skirt, and rich brown hair slicked back into a perfect ponytail. She looked like the kind of person who would refer to a pop of color as "fun."

"Hi, darling. Do you mind if I come in?" The woman was already advancing toward her with an outstretched hand. "I'm Gillian."

"Hey." Krista shook Gillian's hand warily. Her palm was baby soft. Her manicure was perfect. "Do they need me on set?"

"No, not right now." Gillian pulled a chair out to sit across from Krista. Even though she had a pretentious way of speaking, like she had a mouth full of caramels, her voice oozed sympathy. "How are you?"

"Hungry."

"Oh. We could get you something . . ." Gillian twisted in her chair as if the act itself might summon a cheeseburger.

"No, that's okay." Krista sighed. "Sorry, who are you? What do you want?"

Gillian leaned forward, brow crumpling in concern. "You've been having a bit of a rough time here, haven't you?"

She reminded Krista of a psychiatrist. Maybe Greg had sent one to see her. "Yeah, I have. No one's speaking to me. Everything's . . . well, everything's kind of fucked."

"Why?" Gillian asked. "What happened?"

Krista hesitated.

"You can tell me, sweetie." Gillian patted Krista's hand. "Just between us girls."

Krista drew in a breath and began telling the probable psychiatrist everything that'd happened in the last week. Not about taking the Pretty, of course—she didn't want to get locked up in a nuthouse or, worse, for anyone to take the little glass bottle off her. But she told her about sleeping with Ravi, a video of her losing her shit at him going viral and turning into Cupcake Girl, needing twenty-five takes for her first scene, fucking Tristan's trophy, and being accused of bulimia. "And now, Greg's totally cut me from the day's filming, which he can't do because he promised I'd have a part, and no one's talking to me, and I just think doing the movie in the first place was a massive mistake in the series of massive mistakes that are my life."

Gillian sat perfectly still in her chair. Her expression reflected something between disbelief and horror.

"Ah, Gillian." Krista snapped her fingers. "Hello?"

Gillian's face reanimated. "Sorry, darling. I just don't know what to say."

"You could prescribe me some Valium?"

"What?"

"Psychiatrists can do that, right? Or maybe some Perkie Cs? Xannies? Bennies—"

"Lenka!" Gillian laughed airily. "I'm not a psychiatrist. I'm from the studio. And you're fired."

Krista felt like she'd just been shaken awake. "What?"

"You're fired. Effective immediately."

The air around her warped. She struggled to focus. "You can't fire me! On what grounds? That's—that's unfair dismissal!"

Gillian stood up and smoothed her skirt down. "Lenka. You're a disaster. Don't make me say it again."

"What about procedural fairness? I'm being denied natural justice! This is a, a breach of contract—"

"Lenka, please—"

"I went to law school, bitch!" Krista leaped to her feet. "You can't fire me, you don't have the grounds!"

"Firstly, yes I can, I'm the head of production." Gillian's voice was black ice. "I can fire Greg. I can fire you. Secondly, I won't stand for being called a bitch, by anyone, least of all you. You're. Fired."

Krista wilted. Her words became a plea. "But . . . I need the money. I mean, I seriously really need this. Can't we just . . . work something out?"

"No," Gillian said. "And if you breathe one more word to the press, and that includes social media, we'll have to sue you." She regarded Krista with a look of pity. "Thanks for being so honest, sweetie. And good luck." The look on her face said, *You're going to need it.*

43

Willow stood alone on a street corner and watched men watching women.

She watched their eyes linger, uninvited, unwanted, on women's bare shoulders, on their necks, on their asses. She watched them circle women's stomachs, skate over their thighs, plunge into their cleavage. She watched the way they'd look at each other after setting their gazes loose on a passing female: congratulatory, bombastic.

Men watch, and women watch themselves being watched.

She'd read that somewhere, or maybe Evie had told her. Men walked around like they were checking on their own factory floor. Women seemed to want to slip by, undetected. In a hurry to escape.

Escape.

The word sounded sweet and alluring in her brain. She rolled around with it, letting it wash over her, pushing it under her skin.

Escape.

With no destination in mind, she began heading downtown. The streets were tight with jostling people. The midafternoon heat made everyone tired and irritated. Willow let herself get bumped and pushed around; flotsam in the city's current. She passed two girls consoling a crying third, their faces bent into twin expressions of concern. "He doesn't *deserve* you," they implored. "You can do *so* much better."

"But I'm in *love* with him," the crying girl wailed. Her eyes were liquid with tears. "I fucking *love* him."

Street vendors hocked cheap bronze jewelry, laid out on folding tables. They fanned themselves, sweating and squinting in the sun. She passed artists selling spray-painted subway maps to tourists and stopped at a vendor hocking movie scripts to people who'd buy them with pipe dreams of writing their own. Her fingers said hello to old friends: *The Shining*, *Being John Malkovich*, *Stranger Than Paradise*, *Only the Sparrows Know*. By Matteo Hendriksen.

Her fingers stopped.

Her father.

Even here, alone on a crowded street, he found her.

"You like that one?" A red-faced man at the stall gave her a friendly smile. "Real romantic stuff, huh?"

Willow drew her hand back.

"Tell you what, pretty girl like you, I'll do you a deal. Ten dollars. They're usually fifteen, but—"

"No," Willow said. "I'm not a fan."

She pushed her way out of the street, joining the crowds on Broadway. If she kept her eyes averted, she saw nothing. But if she looked at people, if she looked at men, they stared back at her. Openly. Without shame.

Men were always hungry. And they expected to be fed.

She crossed a busy intersection, stopped to check her phone. Messages from Mark, Evie, Krista, and Meredith. Anxiety clenched her chest. For a second she considered dropping her phone into the grate at her feet, fantasizing about seeing it disappear, like krill sucked into a whale.

She looked up, wondering where she was. Leering down at her was a billboard.

In it, a woman wearing nothing but a pair of unbuttoned jeans was splayed out on a carpeted floor. A man stood over her, but only the top of his jeans, a glimpse of his back, and one arm was visible. The woman held her breasts loosely. Half a nipple was visible through her fingers. Her lips were parted. Her eyes, only half open. As if she was drunk. As if she was drugged. As if she wanted nothing more than to be fucked.

Out of nowhere a scorching darkness tore up Willow's throat and she had to clamp her hand over her mouth to keep from crying out. She wanted to set that billboard on fire, to destroy it and its photographer and the company that made it and people who pasted it up and men who went home and jerked their pathetic penises thinking about that woman up there, sprawled and naked and helpless. She wanted to destroy everyone involved in putting up a billboard in New York City that said, that basically goddamn begged: FUCK ME.

But my photographs will be different, Willow thought, turning her head away, wanting to unsee it all. *Because I have already been fucked.*

44.

When Evie got home, she was disappointed to find the apartment was dark and empty. In the kitchen, she filled a glass with water. When she went to get an ice cube, the tray was empty. Krista hadn't refilled it. Again. Evie stared at it, nostalgic rather than annoyed. She needed her best friend now more than ever. She briefly considered calling her mom, but she'd want to know how yesterday's date went. Her date with Velma.

Velma.

Velma hadn't texted. Their message thread was depressingly stunted: her first text accepting the offer for dinner, then Velma's simple response. Nothingness stretched out beneath it. Of course, Evie shouldn't text her. Tomorrow she would be plain old Evie Selby again, and Velma would be relegated to the stuff of midnight masturbation and aimless Google stalking. But Velma didn't know that. Why hadn't she texted?

Evie tossed her phone aside and whimpered. The reality was, she'd failed miserably on both fronts. Velma wasn't interested and *Extra Salt* was a shitshow.

She stood in front of the living room mirror. She stuck her hand on her hip, mimicking the model pose she'd made the night Krista turned, chin lowered, eyes blank. The girl in the mirror glowered back at her: as mysteriously moody as a perfume ad.

Chloe Fontaine could have whomever she wanted. And she'd only be around for a few more hours.

Fuck it.

She picked up her phone and typed a text to Velma. **Feeling like Dorothy, over the rainbow: you make me see in Technicolor.**

She waited for a reply.

And waited.

And waited.

Nothing.

She tried to distract herself, with Taylor Swift's Instagram, with Hangrid Tumblrs, with her readers' comments on *Something Snarky* demanding their weekly post. But the more she tried to run from her feelings, the more speed they gained.

Square one, they chanted. *Square one.*

Tomorrow she'd be back to square one.

To awkward first dates of two disappointed people trying hard to be cheerful. To surreptitiously scanning the room at parties, as if meeting someone was a job she never signed up for but couldn't quit. To the thoughts she had buried ocean-floor deep in her Shame Cave.

You are ugly.

You are unlovable.

If someone wasn't texting Chloe Fontaine back, what possible hope did she ever have of them texting regular old Evie Selby?

The front door opened. "Hey," Krista croaked.

Evie leaped to her feet, beyond grateful for the distraction. Her words came in a manic babble. "Hey! Oh god, I'm so glad you're home!"

Krista held up the Pretty bottle. "I'll put it back. Sorry again about that."

"Oh, that's okay. I have had *such* a shit day," Evie said, relieved to dig into the less upsetting drama of the web series. "Have you seen *Extra Salt*?"

"No."

"Good. Don't. It makes *Girls Gone Wild* look positively progressive. Everything of mine was cut, it's a total disaster! And now I don't know what to do. I failed." She slapped her chest in disbelief. "I, Evie Selby, am responsible for more brainless rubbish that puts the sexy in sexist.

And my Pretty will probably run out tomorrow. So it's adiós Velma Wolff, hello online dating. Or should I say 'hating.' Because it never leads to 'mating,' which is very 'frustrating.'"

Krista found an almost empty bottle of whiskey in the cupboard above the sink and poured what was left into a coffee mug.

"I should never have listened to Kelly," Evie groaned. "That stupid urban cowboy cost me my— Hey, are you okay?"

Krista's voice was a mumble. "There was sort of an incident on set today."

"What kind of incident?" Evie shook her head. "Wait, we'll get back to that when we work out what I should do—"

Krista turned to face her. Her eyes were puffy and red. "I was fired."

Evie gasped. "What?"

"I was fired. By the studio." Krista shuffled into the living room, explaining the whole tawdry tale: everything she'd just told Gillian, everything that had gotten her unceremoniously escorted off the set. "So now I won't get paid, and Tristan hates me, and everything's fucked."

"Wow," Evie said. "Oh, Kris, I'm so sorry." It had been a while since she'd had to play the role of the consoling best friend, empathetic to yet another of Krista's famous fuckups. And while Evie did feel sorry for her, she also felt annoyed: Didn't Krista promise to use the Pretty to pay back the money she'd effectively stolen from her? "What's next?"

Krista sipped from the mug. "Um. Not sure."

"No backup plan?" Evie pressed. "No next scheme?"

Krista shook her head. "Hey, have you seen Willow lately?"

Evie knew her roommate was changing the topic, instinctively dodging any talk of responsibility, but it worked. "Not since, let me think, Monday afternoon. She helped me get ready for my interview with Velma." An interaction where Evie had been more focused on her dress than on her friend. "But I saw her—Caroline—asleep on the couch this morning before I left, so I guess she turned Pretty again."

"Really?" Krista raised her eyebrows. "Huh."

"What?"

"I guess I'm surprised. I thought she just wanted to try it once, like, for the experience."

"Well, you did it a second time," Evie said.

"Yeah, but I'm doing *Funderland*. What's Willow up to?"

Evie exhaled slowly. She didn't know. And to be honest, she couldn't even really take a guess. "She's so . . . mysterious."

Krista widened her eyes, nodding. "Totally. Sometimes I think I really get what she's all about, and sometimes I'm like, 'Who are you? What is your life?'"

"Kids who grow up in New York are different," Evie said, settling back into the cushions. "They go to the opera as a field trip in middle school and are put into analysis before they can ride a bike." Briefly, Evie considered telling Krista about the voicemail she'd gotten from Willow, the one she thought might be from a hospital, but decided that'd be too gossipy—after all, that was just a theory she had. "Sometimes I'm so jealous of her—having all day to work on her art, not having to worry about a dumb job."

"I'm not," Krista said. Evie glanced at her in surprise. "Dude, if I had as much spare time on my hands as she does, I'd be locked up in the nuthouse by now. Think about it: we have to study hard at school to get into a good college, to get a good job to make sure we have a good career. Willow doesn't have to do any of that 'cause of her dad. I don't think lots of spare time is good for someone like her. Too much time up here." Krista tapped her temple.

"God, you're right," Evie said. "Fuck, I wish I knew what she's been up to. She's not returning my texts. I wonder if she realizes that's weird."

"Maybe that's just an introvert thing," Krista said. "Or, like, a famous person thing."

"I just hope . . ."

"What?"

Evie sucked in a breath. "I just hope we didn't let her take the Pretty when she shouldn't have."

"What do you mean?"

"I mean, I think Willow is kind of fragile. I don't know, sometimes I think she can be a bit self-destructive. Like, she always gets way drunker than we do. And she day-drinks. On Wednesdays."

"I never noticed that," Krista said.

"She's always so hard on herself about all the art stuff. I think Willow believes that if she doesn't become as successful as her dad then she's a complete failure."

Krista nodded somberly. "Let's organize a dinner. Get her back to the apartment. Check in."

"Great idea. Oh, speaking of checking in, I have to message Ella-Mae." Evie pulled her phone out. "Thanks for forwarding that email."

"That's okay." Krista drained the last of the whiskey. "How did you explain Chloe to *Salty*?"

Evie's eyes were on the email from Ella-Mae, on the part where Ella-Mae mentioned Chloe being Evie's roommate. "I told you: that we lived together."

"Right." Krista nodded. Then she shook her head. "No, wait a second: Didn't you take someone else's spot?"

"Hm?" Evie twisted a lock of hair around the end of her finger. "Oh yeah. That's right."

There was a slight pause. "Evie?"

Evie busied herself with her phone. Still no word from Velma.

"Evie." Krista's voice sounded odd.

"What?"

"You're hiding something. I know that look."

"What?" Evie popped her head up and tried to look offended.

"You're lying to me."

"I'm not."

"You're twisting your hair, you're visibly nervous." Krista cocked her head, more suspicious than angry.

"It's nothing." Evie jumped up. "I have to shower—"

"Tell me!" Krista advanced on Evie. "Evie, tell me!"

Evie steeled herself. "I told them you could audition, when I was

Regular. Krista Kumar, my roommate. Then when I became Chloe, I"—Evie shrugged, raised both palms—"told them I was you. That Chloe was Evie's roommate."

Krista didn't say anything. Evie's heartbeat was thudding in her ears. Krista put her whiskey down on the coffee table carefully, like she'd just discovered it'd been poisoned. "You, with the stick up your ass about the bills, you poached my spot?"

Evie spoke quickly. "You were going into CPU that day anyway, and then you got *Funderland*, so it all worked out for the best."

"I would've been great at that. And even if I didn't get it, there was a casting agent there, right?"

"Well, yeah. But—"

Krista spoke over her. She was pissed. "When I started taking acting classes, people told me it was pretty cutthroat in New York. That other actors would try to undermine you, take down audition notices, shit-talk you to casting directors. They said I'd have to watch my back." Her voice became harsh. "But I never thought the first person to fuck me over would be my best friend." Krista spun on her heel, heading for her room.

"I'm sorry." Evie grabbed Krista's shoulder. "I really need you."

Krista twisted out of Evie's grasp. "Whatever. I can't deal with this right now."

45.

In the past, Willow's desire to have sex was slow and slothlike, something that emerged blinking from a long nap, and could be just as easily convinced to go back to sleep as acted upon. But as she rounded the corner to Tenth Street, she felt the opposite of slothlike. Caroline was a hissing, whipping thing ready to sink her fangs into someone's flesh.

Mark buzzed her up without asking who it was.

She couldn't wait for the elevator. She flung the stairwell door open and took the steps two at a time.

Her heart was smashing her ribs, her breath hot against the back of her throat.

First floor. Second, third, 3A, 3B—

As soon as her hand connected with his front door, it was open. Mark's face was alive and vampire-hungry.

There was no pause for hello.

They slammed into each other.

Her mouth, a storm. His hands, hungry sharks.

She pulled Mark toward the bedroom with such force he almost tripped. Fire was surging through her, a flood of silver adrenaline that made her feel like she could pick up a train and toss it off a cliff. She shoved him onto the bed. He fell with an "Oof." She straddled him, her lips raking his, kneading herself against the bulge in his pants.

He groaned, trying to push himself up to roll her over, but she reared back, pinning him to the bed with her knees. She pulled his hands above his head and pushed them into the pillows.

"Uh-uh," she said, hot and breathless. "Don't move. No," she insisted, as his hands reached back toward her. "Don't. Move."

When he obeyed, she slid off him, moving quickly to find a black silk tie in his closet. Mark was wide-eyed as she threaded it between his wrists and the wooden slats of his headboard, tying him into place.

"Can you move?" she whispered.

He tugged at the knots. "No. I'm your prisoner."

"Good."

Without losing eye contact, she walked her fingers down his chest, unbuttoning each of his shirt buttons. He was panting as she pulled his shirt apart, his bare chest soaring and dipping and soaring again. Her fingers trailed to the top of his jeans. The top button had popped open. Slowly, agonizingly slowly, she began unzipping his fly.

Mark shifted against the restraints and emitted a whimper.

Willow darted her eyes back to his. Her words were an order. "Don't. Move."

She tugged the top of his jeans down. He was wearing boxer briefs. The dark blue ones, the newest pair, the pair, she realized, that he'd wear when he knew he was getting laid. She froze, the truth of the underwear catching her off guard.

"What?" she heard him whisper.

He knew Caroline would be coming over. For a wild second, Willow wondered if Mark and Caroline had somehow planned this without her knowledge. If Caroline truly had split from her and was a woman of her own, living a parallel life.

"Caroline?"

She slid her hand into his pants and pulled out his penis. Mark's breathing was quick and shallow. For a long moment, she considered the thing in her hand.

The thing that led Mark, her boyfriend, to her. To Caroline.

The thing that led men to make billboards with sprawling naked women. To put their private fantasies in public, unashamed, without hesitation or guilt.

The thing that broke promises. The thing that betrayed.

She watched his face as she began stroking it. Contorting, eyes squeezed shut, opening briefly to flicker to her, her face, her body, the hint of her breasts visible through her dress, before squeezing shut again. A thousand serpents wriggled under his skin.

Heat between her legs. She was getting turned on.

The rhythm, and the wrongness, combined to turn her into a wet and slippery creature made of lava and heat and light.

She moved her hand faster.

Their breath combining, twin pants and snuffles and groans.

Faster.

Toward the cliff top. Horses racing blindly, a driver who's lost control, a carriage on wheels skittering over rocks, toward the edge, almost there, almost—

Willow let go of him.

Mark cried, "Don't stop!"

Willow tugged off her underwear, sticky, soaked through, and hitched her dress over her knees. Swinging herself around, she lowered herself onto Mark's mouth, facing his feet and the full-length mirror on the opposite wall.

His tongue found her pussy, sliding clumsily over her clit. She couldn't help crying out: every movement sent off a thousand sparks, every nerve ending housed hundreds, thousands, millions of bright shooting stars.

She'd never done this, although he had asked her to, many times. It felt crude, in theory: something women did when they were being paid to.

But now, it felt different.

She felt untamed. Reckless. Powerful. She pulled her dress away from her, off her body. Her fingers found her hair, her nipples, her skin, velvet with sweat, supple and strong. The mirror reflected this truth back at her: Caroline, with her full lips and tits and muscular thighs, Caroline, an erotic, magnificent, vital creature. A snake.

A devil.

A demon in a dress.

A tidal wave was building inside her, a coming orgasm as unstoppable as she was.

Her eyes found the photograph. Taken at a wedding in the Hamptons. Mark and Willow.

Her. Not her.

Her hips rocked furiously.

Her pants came audibly.

The girl in the mirror was perfect.

The girl in the mirror was poison.

She began to come, loudly, gloriously, without restraint.

Her shouts shot through the brick walls of the apartment, into the night, across rivers and highways and skyscrapers, and into the stratosphere. She was beyond consciousness, beyond control.

She was in flight, beating broad wings to manipulate the air, soaring, inevitably, toward the brutal sun.

46.

Sleep eluded Evie, both because of her fight with Krista and because she was waiting for Velma to text back. As the hours passed, vague curiosity (*Why hasn't she texted back?*) morphed into itching, obsessive delirium (*Fucking hell,* why *hasn't she texted* back?).

Just before 10 p.m., she put a haphazard plan B into action. She'd take herself out for a nightcap, to a bar that *just happened* to be close to the Williamsburg Bridge. If Velma texted, Evie could conveniently be a stone's throw away from wherever she was. *I'll jump in a cab*, she imagined texting. *I'll be right there.*

That wasn't desperate.

That was clever.

There was a very obvious difference.

Evie sat at a dark, noisy bar by herself for three hours and fended off a series of increasingly drunken advances. At first, she was polite: "No, thanks, I'm waiting for a friend" or "I already have a drink, thank you." By the end she was rolling her eyes, groaning, "Really?" or just a flat, snapped "No."

It felt like her beauty demanded that people approach her with a strategy. That was the worst part: she could see the thought process in every potential suitor's mind so clearly it was as if their skulls were made of cellophane.

There were the pliable, vanilla types: middle management, school-teachers, yoga instructors. They were harmless and gave up easy, like cows: "Can I buy you a— No, okay, have a nice night."

There were the weird artist types with too much facial hair whose opening lines were deliberately odd: "Do you want to go to Coney Island with me, right now?" "Have you ever tasted someone else's blood?"

Evie felt the worst for the young, smart guys, the strange-looking boys who honestly would've had the best chance with her if her brain wasn't a cable channel devoted exclusively to Velma. Their fast-moving eyes belied the workings of their busy brains, and Evie could practically hear the critical inner voice that chastised them through even a banal encounter. For these guys, exquisitely crafted women like Chloe held the appeal of a good thriller: entertaining, seductive, and terrifying, all at once.

And then there were the players, suffering from what Evie termed the Little Prince syndrome; entitled without even realizing it, treating the world like their personal playground. Sexual bullies, offering insults designed as compliments: "That dress is cool but does nothing for you," "Are you friends with that girl over there? She's so hot." *Ultimately*, Evie thought, *these kind of men just don't like women.* They found female desire for emotional connection needy. Sensitivity was weakness. Enjoyment of aesthetics? Stupid. *They don't like us but they want to fuck us.* Their own hellish catch-22. Their sexual politics were a hall of mirrors: women who didn't comply with their sexual demands were frigid, and those who did were sluts. An ignored "Hey, beautiful" was inevitably followed by "Dumb bitch."

At 1 a.m., she called it quits, walking home in the humid, heavy air, defeated and alone.

She woke feeling more exhausted than when she went to bed. Her stomach felt like it was being sliced open with a switchblade. She knew why. The girls had warned her.

Evie Selby was back.

Her glasses weren't in her usual spot beside her bed. When she felt well enough to move, she found them atop her dresser. She slipped them on reluctantly and met the eyes of a beast.

So strong was her surprise at the face in the bedroom mirror that she scuttled back a few steps. A squat, pasty-faced girl with a horridly thin mouth and uneven coffee-stained teeth peered back at her. Cinderella's ugly stepsister. The "before" of a movie makeover.

Surely not. Had the Pretty somehow made her uglier; a cruel twist to trick the vain?

No. Because even as her eyes drank in the frankly foul sight before her, her memory reminded her that this was her: Evie Elizabeth Selby. This was her regular self. Nothing had changed.

Except, everything had.

It was shocking how quickly she'd gotten used to Chloe's doe eyes meeting hers in the morning, her luminescent skin as smooth as a seashell, her wide mouth full of white teeth.

Unable to face the one in mirror, she reached for her phone.

Velma had texted her.

At 1:37 a.m.

where r u?

Evie's mouth fell open.

Velma had texted. Right after she'd gone to bed. She'd missed her by minutes. *Minutes!*

Evie sank onto the side of her mattress, legs no longer a reliable ally.

If she didn't take the Pretty, she would never see Velma again. Because how could Velma, she of Dior suits and silver credit cards, be interested in plain old Evie Selby?

Distracted, she tapped open her email.

And promptly forgot all about Velma Wolff.

Evie had set a Google alert for "Chloe Fontaine" and *"Extra Salt"* the day she'd gotten the gig. So far, nothing. But today her entire inbox was full. She tapped the first one.

Salty Makes a Web Series, Internet Dies Laughing. The gang at *Salty* has taken time out from their busy schedule of having sex in the wheelbarrow

position to create a web series called *Extra Salt*. It's the usual truckload
of garbage that you'd expect from these dopey airheads, held together by
model-slash-bimbo Chloe Fontaine, who does a great job impersonating a
baby deer who just got punched in the face. Highlights include—

She couldn't read any more. Her face was burning up. That was her.
The story was about *her*.

She clicked onto the next one.

Hottie Alert! Gentlemen, meet the newest addition to your spank bank,
Chloe Fontaine. This dark-haired beauty will keep you and your johnson entertained for exactly 3.5 minutes. Hint: mute the video.

This was some sort of men's pop culture site; sidebar features alternated women in bikinis with stories about power tools. *Extra Salt* was
embedded below the text. Astonishingly, there were already forty-five
comments.

Mmmm . . . daddy likes.
what's wrong with her face?
i'd do her
This is the dumbest and stupidest thing I've ever seen. Why is she alive?
BEND OVER BITCH I'M GUNNA STICK—

Evie dropped her phone. Her skin was crawling. Her breath snagged
in her throat. The comments were so extraordinarily nasty, so incredibly
disrespectful. About Chloe! Sweet, idealistic Chloe who was just trying
her best, who was actually a really nice person. And that was just one
website, *Jesus*. How many comments would there be on YouTube? Hundreds? Thousands? How many people were laughing at her, dismissing
her, rolling their eyes at brainless Chloe Fontaine and her armful of
fucking dildos?

"I was supposed to make things *better*!" she cried to her bedroom.

And there was only one way she'd get a second go at it.

One way to erase the hideous specter in the mirror.

One way to see Velma again.

She drew in a deep breath and let it out in a calm stream of air.

Just one more time.

47.

The sound of the front door slamming jerked Krista awake. She pulled the covers over her head and whimpered.

It wasn't just that she'd gotten fired. She couldn't shake the feeling that the Pretty was . . . affecting her. It was like every audition she'd ever lost, every capitulation to her father, every depressing breakup—every failure rolled into one huge wallop of anxiety, as concentrated as the Pretty itself.

It was so unfamiliar, this untamable, gnawing unease. Usually Krista wasn't overly obsessed with her appearance. It was one of a thousand daily concerns, easily forgotten, only occasionally a drama. But now, the face that was reflected back to her in the bathroom mirror, as stunning as it was worried, was all she could think about.

There was only one person who had answers.

Penny Baker.

Penny's Facebook page had been inactive for six months. An hour of online sleuthing produced only one picture of the woman she'd met in McHale's Ales, taken at some fancy party in Abu Dhabi, on the arm of a darkly handsome man with sculptured facial hair. The captioned name read *Penelope Worthington, née Baker*. Penny might not even be in New York anymore, Krista realized. But she had nothing to lose in trying to find out.

She rode the subway with trepidation. Too many people seemed to be looking at her, watching her every move. At Union Square, she ducked out of a crowded subway car, convinced a man in a black overcoat was following her, a feeling that ballooned mild concern into a full-blown panic.

No one is after you. You're just being silly.

Wasn't she?

The brightly lit foyer of her old improv school's training center was instantly calming. Familiar, low key, domestic. Young men and women sat comfortably on beat-up couches, under posters of famous comedians and old sketch shows. Krista remembered when she'd briefly been one of them: doing bits with her classmates, gossiping about the new improv teams or which teacher they *had* to study with next. Her life was easy then, easy in a way she wasn't aware of until it wasn't.

The boy behind the desk had a pale face overshadowed by a shock of red hair. He masked a now-familiar double take, inspired by someone who recognized either Cupcake Girl or supreme hotness. "Hey, what's up?"

Krista flashed a big smile. "I took a class here at the beginning of the year with a friend of mine, Penny Baker. She's . . . dropped out . . . of the world. I'm worried. Is there any way you could give me her address?"

The boy gave her a bemused smile. "Sorry, we can't give out students' information."

"Right, I thought so, but it's an emergency. I think something might have happened to her."

"If you're her friend, why don't you have an email? Or a cell number?"

Krista leaned forward, letting her cleavage deepen. "God, you have such incredible eyes. What would you call that: cerulean?" She batted her lashes, speaking the words like she was sucking a candy cane. "Or baby blue? Are they baby blue?"

The redhead looked unimpressed. "I'm gay."

Krista huffed out a breath and yanked her top back up. "Look, I fucking need her address, okay? I'm seriously just trying to help someone I think might be in trouble. So don't be a fucking pussy and help me out. Please?"

This approach worked.

Penny had listed her address as an apartment in South Park Slope, near the Gowanus Canal. It took Krista an hour to find it, then another hour to convince the current tenant to give her the forwarding address "Penelope Worthington" had left. Which turned out to be 500 Park Avenue.

A Pretty address.

A doorman in a crisp navy suit opened the wide glass door for her at 500 Park. The interior was all marble and chandeliers and money. When Krista told the sleekly presented woman at the front desk she was here to see Penelope Worthington, she swore the woman cocked her head, just a quarter inch, as if masking surprise. "Your name?" the woman asked, one ear pressed to a phone.

"Krista Kumar." It was the first time she'd introduced Lenka as Krista.

The woman repeated this into the receiver. Then she hung up and smiled at Krista.

A careful smile. A smile that held some sort of warning.

"Penthouse."

48

"Fantastic. I can't even begin to describe your evolution, Willow. This work is just *blowing me away*."

"Thanks, Meredith." Willow pictured her curator in her office, clicking through the new portraits she'd just emailed. She was slumped by the window in a quiet café in South Williamsburg, an untouched black tea in front of her. She'd left Mark snoring gently in his bed. The memory of last night hung around her like a soft, strange vapor. She felt like she was either falling or flying, and the confusion twisted her insides in a sickly pleasurable way. "I'm glad you like them."

"Like them? Sweetie, I love them. Oh, the pain. The drama. I love it!"

The praise—so natural, so real—warmed her from the inside, burning away her hangover. She had to stop herself from grinning like an idiot. "Good."

"Okay, screw it. I'm just going to go with my gut here. I want to give you another show. In two weeks."

Willow straightened. Her first show had been booked six months in advance. "What?"

"I have something lined up, but I'm going to bump it back. I just have a very good feeling about this, Willow Hendriksen. I think this is the work that's going to make you a star!"

"Wow. Thank you. That's amazing. I just hadn't . . ."

"Hadn't what?"

Willow swallowed, drawing back into herself. "I guess I hadn't really imagined them hanging on a wall. In a gallery."

Meredith trilled laughter. "Where did you imagine them? You're an artist, Willow, and art needs an audience."

You're an artist. The words bounced around inside her, building in momentum until she almost felt giddy. "Right."

"I think we just need one more series and we have a show. Tell me Caroline's still in New York. Oh, her face." Meredith sighed. "I could just stare at it for *hours.*"

In the window next to her, she met her own wide-set eyes, ghostly in the glass. In her mind, she imagined forming the word *no.* Telling Meredith that Caroline had left town, that it was all over. After all, she was hurting Mark, through actions she didn't feel entirely in control of, obeying urges that came from a murky, almost mythical place.

But Mark had agency. He was making choices. And better she know the truth about her boyfriend now, before it was too late. After all, it was too late for her mother. Ten years of her life down the toilet after marrying a man who probably fucked a different woman every weekend.

Like Meredith said, she was an artist.

And art required risk.

"Yes," she said. "Caroline's still here."

49

As Krista raised her finger to the penthouse's small, gold doorbell, an unexpected wave of fear paused her hand midair. What if Penny was . . . different? Disfigured? Deformed? Did she really want to know? Did she really want proof of the fate they had all sealed for themselves?

She rang the doorbell.

Footfalls approached.

Krista stiffened, suddenly wanting to run but unable to command her limbs into action.

The door opened.

Krista strangled a gasp. Her hand flew to her mouth.

The girl who answered the door was Penny: chubby, ordinary Penny whom she'd taken the class with. But her eyes were bloodshot. Her skin was red and puffy. Her mouth was as downturned as a toad's.

"Krista?" the figure wheezed. "Is that you? How the hell did you find me?"

"Penny!" Krista stumbled back a step. She was right. The Pretty was a death sentence, a bad drug, a bad deed, Quasimodo, the beast—

"Come in." Penny gestured. "Usually I don't let anyone see me like this. I guess you're an exception."

Krista took an unwilling step inside, taking in the impossibly tall ceilings that Penny's voice echoed around. The immaculate designer furniture. The geometric, multipaned windows. It was so cold she almost shivered.

Penny peered at her. "What's wrong?"

Krista swallowed. "I could ask you the same question."

Penny rolled her eyes and tightened the cord of a pink satin robe. "Boys," she said with a weak smile.

It was only then that Krista understood. Penny wasn't deformed. She'd just been crying. The relief that flooded her system caused her to physically sag, and she steadied herself on the side of an enormous Chinese urn.

Penny yanked a few tissues from a gold tissue box and blew her nose. "Do you want a drink?"

It was noon. "Uh, sure." She followed Penny into an industrial-sized kitchen. "This place is incredible." It made Willow's apartment look minor league.

"You're lucky you caught me. I've only been back in New York two days this summer. Today, and the day we met."

Krista ran her hand over a polished granite countertop, admiring shelves of sparkling wineglasses. "Where have you been?"

"London. Then Monaco. Then back to London."

"Cool."

"It's exhausting." Penny opened a freezer door the size of a billboard. "Vodka okay?" She selected a hefty bottle from a freezer stacked full with booze.

Krista arched an eyebrow. "You keep the place stocked, huh?"

"Someone does. One of the . . . 'benefits.'" Penny poured two glasses, added half a splash of seltzer, then led the way to a sofa facing one of the huge, angular windows. The sofa was bright orange, extremely uncomfortable, and, like every other piece of furniture, looked brand-new. Penny handed Krista her glass. "Cheers," she said. The sound of the two glasses tapping rang out for a second before being swallowed by the space.

"Whose pad is this?" Krista asked. Even though the thought made her feel guilty, Penny seemed out of place here.

"My . . ." Penny took a moment to search for the word. "Friend. Although we're in one of our unfriendly phases right now." She waved loosely at Krista's face and body. "I like what it did for you. It's different. Are you enjoying it?"

Krista glanced down at herself, feeling an unplaced sense of shame. "What is it?"

Penny smiled and gave a half laugh. "I don't know."

"Shit. Really?"

"Sorry. My guess is as good as yours."

"Why didn't you tell me how rough it'd be, taking it?"

"Didn't I?" She sounded surprised. "Guess it slipped my mind."

Krista couldn't imagine being so used to the transformation that it could slip her mind. What a horrifying thought. "Who gave it to you?"

Penny was silent for a moment, then she waved her glass around, at the apartment the size of a football field.

"The guy who owns this place?" Krista guessed.

Penny nodded. "More or less."

"Is he on it too?"

Penny put her finger to her lips. "He'd kill you if you told anyone."

This was said in such a light, casual way it almost sounded like a joke. But somehow Krista knew it wasn't. Goose bumps pimpled her arms. Penny watched her silently, swirling vodka in her glass.

Krista asked, "Why'd you give it to me?"

"I told you. You were nice to me—"

"But we didn't even really know each other."

Penny sighed, turning to gaze silently out the window. Acne scars pockmarked her cheek. "Maybe you caught me in a weak moment." She took another long sip. "Are you unhappy I gave it to you?"

"No. Hey, I wake up every day with awesome boobs. Like a boob job I didn't pay for." Krista gave a short laugh, but even to her ears it sounded hollow. "I guess it is kind of a mind fuck. But some people don't have enough to eat, so how can I complain?"

Penny nodded. "I know."

"Were you trying to get rid of it?" Krista asked, only realizing as she said it that this was a possibility.

Penny stared at her with bloodshot eyes that were big and sad and serious. "God, it's really good to see you, Krista. Sometimes . . . Sometimes I feel like—" But she was cut off by the sound of the front door unlocking. Penny jumped, and not just at the unexpected sound. Fear, a flash of it, cut through her. A man with dark features strode through the front door. He wore a suit and carried a well-made leather briefcase. Krista recognized him as the guy with the ornate, perfect facial hair who'd been in the picture that the Google search had unearthed.

When he spotted the two women, he froze.

Even though it was already cold in the apartment, it seemed to get colder.

Penny almost tripped in her hurry to get up. Her eyes were wide, panicky. She gestured at Krista without looking at her. "I'm grooming her for Naseem. He sent her. This is Carlos," Penny told Krista, indicating the man in the suit. "The one I've been telling you about."

"Hi." Krista rose to stand next to Penny, instinctively moving closer to the girl.

But Carlos only slid his eyes over Krista for a second. Instead, he focused on Penny. His expression shifted, as if he could smell something bad.

Penny tightened her robe around herself. "I thought you were leaving for Shanghai. What happened to your meeting?"

Carlos didn't answer. Instead, he indicated her face. "What is this?" His voice was soft, but so clearly displeased.

Penny's jaw was set. She was breathing through her nose. "You weren't here. I need to see my mom."

Carlos snorted a laugh. Krista had never wanted to get out of somewhere so badly in her life. But that would mean leaving Penny alone with this man. "We have rules," Carlos said.

"You have rules!" Penny took a step toward him. "I can't do it all the time."

Even though she had tears in her voice, Carlos regarded her as if she were a child: silly and inconsequential. "I have a dinner tonight. Be ready by six."

Penny sucked in a breath. "Tonight? No. I can't."

Carlos began heading for the kitchen.

"I'll leave!" Penny raised her voice. This stopped him. "I'll go," she said. "I will."

Carlos turned, slowly, until he was facing her again. A pinched, dark smile pulled at his lips as he crossed back toward her, a cat advancing on a wounded bird. Penny was trembling. A tear, then another, rolled down her cheek.

Krista's chest had seized up, the tension in the room physically painful in her body. Scared to move, scared not to.

Carlos reached Penny and placed both hands on her shoulders. He looked down at her, almost pityingly. "Where," he asked quietly, "would you possibly go?"

In the elevator back down, Krista burst into tears. The tension and the crushing awfulness of what she'd just witnessed overwhelmed her. She hadn't wanted to leave Penny, but Penny insisted. "I have to get ready," she'd muttered. Krista told her she didn't have to, she could just leave, she could leave with her right now.

"And go where?" Penny asked. "Do what?"

"I don't know, crash on my couch for a few days. Get a job."

"A job?" Penny repeated. "In New York? I never went to college. Half the bartenders here have PhDs. This is my best option." She sighed and rubbed her eyes. She looked more than tired. She just looked done. "It's really not that bad."

Krista left 500 Park feeling like she'd just made bail, wandering into the sunlight in a daze, ending up in a mostly empty coffee shop, ordering a latte she didn't touch.

She had to make changes, she knew she did. While sometimes she was able to think of her debt as something that was fixable, something that would somehow sort itself out, the truth was she was deeply ashamed. And more than ashamed: confused. Every purchase that had snowballed into debt, every one made sense at the time. Like the Zac Posen dress at the Gilt sample sale: it wasn't just a bargain, it was a smart investment, it was saving money. It was scary to realize how unreliable her own brain could be, how easily she could be convinced of the wrong path. How did you know what was wrong and what was right?

Krista yanked out her phone and began typing a text.

hey tristan,

it's lenka penka. i'm really, really sorry about what happened the other day. i didn't respect you or what was important to you. my actions were regrettable and i never intended to cause offense.

i hope you can forgive me. good luck on the movie. i miss being there.

lenka xxx

She sent it to the cell number listed as Tristan's on the call sheet. Then she sat, barely moving, staring dully at the customers filtering in and out of the coffee shop or watching a triangle of sunlight inch slowly over the laminated tabletop. An hour passed. Then another. Her phone rang, startling her. It was a number she didn't recognize. "Hello?"

"Lenka. It's Cameron Mitchell. Your agent." A pause, possibly just for effect. "I have some surprising news."

50.

"I could work on you all morning, Madame Chloe, but ain't nothing is gonna make you pretty when you's looking so sour." Marcello pointed at Evie with a tube of liquid eyeliner accusingly. "What's happened? And no, I won't take 'nothing' for an answer."

Evie sank down even farther into her chair. The Pretty had chewed up her stomach and spat it out her butt. She'd brushed her teeth five times to get rid of the taste of vomit.

But it wasn't just that.

Kelly wasn't even fazed by the vicious internet attack *Extra Salt* had inspired. He'd told her not to pay attention to the haters, calling them "man-hating feminazis or horny pricks living in their parents' basement." Jan had called to congratulate him: everyone thought *Extra Salt* was great. Of course they did. They were all idiots. "What'd you think of it?" she asked Marcello.

" 'It' being the first episode?"

Evie nodded.

"I thought it was—" Marcello screwed up his face.

"Lame? Lamer than Tiny Tim?"

Marcello smiled. "It was exactly what I was expecting."

Evie groaned and dropped her head into her hands. "The worst part is, for some ungodly reason, I was actually excited about it. I thought I could make something good and meaningful. Something I'd be proud of!"

"Me too." Marcello pursed his lips at her. "But now I'll have to start over."

Evie caught sight of herself in the mirror. She'd just smudged mascara and eyeshadow all down her cheeks. "Shit. Sorry, Marcello. I'm such a klutz."

"No problem, beautiful." Marcello wet a sponge with some cleanser and began dabbing at the dark stains. "Let's just save the dramatics until you're off camera, okay?"

Evie sat obediently as Marcello began repairing his work. He paused to tweezer an errant eyebrow hair and Evie yelped. He smirked at her. "Be thankful you didn't live during the Renaissance," he said. "Back in the day, ladies used to pluck their hairlines to achieve the high foreheads that were so *en vogue*."

"Ugh." Evie shuddered. "Why have beauty standards always been so damn painful? Why can't we decide they're, I don't know, all about cellulite and milk mustaches?"

"Does that annoy you?" Marcello asked, dotting Evie's skin with foundation. "The fact you're not in charge of how you look?"

Evie stiffened. In one sense, he could have been talking about himself; after all, he was the one currently prepping Chloe's on-camera look. But it almost sounded as if he was asking about Pretty, and the fact it turned her into an ideal, but not necessarily her ideal. Evie had to resist the urge to drop her gaze to her forearm, to the place where her tattoo used to be. In reply, she made a noncommittal noise and redirected the conversation. "Why do you like it?"

"Like what?"

"Makeup."

"Makes me feel purdy." He smiled at her coquettishly.

"Is that why you like putting it on other people?"

"Mmm-hmm."

"Because it makes them look pretty?"

"Because it makes them *feel* pretty." Marcello pulled a chair over and sat down so he was sitting eye to eye with Evie. "My job is to make women, and some very forward-thinking gentlemen, feel like the best version of themselves. And I know you think makeup sets an unrealistic standard and yadda yadda yadda, but the way I see it, I'm just helping people bring out their inner goddess. I can't make you beautiful, Chloe. I can just help you see, with a little color here and a little color there, that you are already beautiful."

"I get that," Evie said. "I do. I felt pretty damn hot when I met Velma the other night, and I think that did have something to do with a little color here and there. But it's still not right to me."

"Why not?"

Evie bit her lip, thinking. "When I was about ten or eleven, I got super into red lipstick. I wanted to wear it all the time: to school, to the park, to watch TV, to bed. And my mom was like, 'Uh-uh. That's not for every day. That's for special days.'" Evie looked up at Marcello. "But now for any woman on TV, or in politics, or who expects to be listened to, it's become everyday. Hollywood couldn't give a shit if women feel beautiful. They only want women to look beautiful. All the time."

Marcello cocked his head, not denying this.

"If you're not born with good genes or you don't want to pile a ton of crap on your face every day, then you're not as powerful. Beauty is power," Evie said, realizing. "But it's not real power."

Marcello nodded thoughtfully. "I think what you're saying is true."

"And it's a bitch to put on!" Evie exclaimed. "It's expensive, and it takes ages, and it's bad for your skin." Evie gestured at where the mascara stains had been on her cheek. "I can't act like a fucking human being without totally messing it up. And there's something very wrong about the fact you can't make out with someone while wearing lipstick, right?"

Marcello laughed.

"I mean, isn't that the point?" Evie laughed too. "It's so dumb!"

"I hear you, Chloe Fontaine. I do. I think what you're saying makes a lot of sense. And it seems to me someone like you is in . . ."

He paused, as if carefully choosing his next word. "A *unique* situation to do something about it."

Evie met his knowing look with a blankness that didn't accept or deny the implicit accusation. "You're right," she said. "I am in a unique situation."

Marcello rocked back on his chair and arched an eyebrow at her. "So what's your next move?"

51.

Evie arrived home to find the apartment bathed in warm late-afternoon light, still and empty. She flopped onto the couch. Her body was humming like a speaker turned all the way up. She and Marcello had hatched a scheme that was a. flawless, b. wicked, and c. wonderful. Her first Trojan horse plan hadn't aimed high enough. This plan did.

Plus, she was going out with Velma tonight. Evie had texted her back a few hours ago, setting off a chain of deliciously flirtatious banter. In no time at all, Velma had suggested getting together again. Evie replied she was only free this evening, which admittedly was a lie, but a lie that worked. Velma immediately invited her to a "small get-together with friends."

Her phone chimed. Velma. **Can't decide what to wear. Does that mean I'm nervous?**

Evie's thumbs flew across her phone. **Step 1. Open wardrobe. Step 2. Select black pants, white V-neck, and black blazer. Step 3. Rinse and repeat.**

Seconds later, a reply. **That made me laugh. See you tonight.**

Evie glowed, tingling all over. She tossed her phone onto the couch and peeked at the living room mirror. The flushed face of an excited, happy girl met her eyes. Chloe's eyes. She took a moment to admire Chloe's smooth skin, graceful height, and flat stomach. She was happy to have her partner in crime back. Her sister. Her perfect disguise.

And even though Chloe was that—a disguise, a mask—Evie felt a quickening of her heart as she allowed the next thought to surface.

Could Velma like Evie?

The real her?

It was Evie's sense of humor Velma responded to, Evie's history at college, Evie's observations.

Evie exhaled noisily, pushing the thought away as quickly as it came. This was an elaborate game of fancy dress, but at the end of the day, she'd have to hang up her costume and get back to real life.

But not *right* now.

Evie shouldered her bag, intending to start date prep. Her gaze landed on the mess on the coffee table. The apartment had fallen into general disarray over the last week and a half, mostly because she hadn't been cleaning up after Krista, or Willow, or herself. But now, amid the greasy takeout containers and unread *New Yorker*s, was something new.

A large rectangular envelope, ripped open down one side. Evie recognized the sender's logo: Eden Photographics, the place Willow had her photographs printed. She picked it up, curious to see if it was new work or not. Willow wouldn't mind.

The photographs were of Caroline.

Dozens of them; silvery black-and-white images rendered on thick, glossy paper.

Evie leafed through them. Something cold and black began unspooling inside her, seeping a quiet horror into her chest.

The photographs were nightmarish.

Willow, as Caroline, crying.

Distressed.

Ruined.

Evie sifted through the photographs quicker and quicker, hoping for some explanation. Every time she met Willow's eyes—those wide-set, alien eyes—she felt a jab in her stomach; a quick, sick blow. She was reminded of an ad campaign that *Salty* was forced to pull earlier in the year. In the images, beautiful women with black eyes and rope burns clutched expensive handbags. Evie had railed against it in *Something Snarky*: her readers had been some of the most vocal opponents. And now Willow was making art like this, eroticizing suffering. Even with tears streaking down her face, Caroline was beautiful.

In pain.

And gorgeous.

Why was Willow taking pictures like this? What the fuck was going on?

A key sounded in the front door. Krista. Evie hadn't spoken to her since they'd argued last night. On seeing Evie she did a double take, looking wary. "Hey."

Evie thrust the sheaf of offending pictures at Krista. "Have you seen these?"

Krista frowned at the photograph on top of the pile: Caroline, naked, cowering in an empty bath, staring at the camera with a pleading expression. "What's with the weird selfies?"

"I don't think they're selfies." The girl in the bathtub reminded her of a pitiful dog. Her friend. That was her friend looking like that.

"They're kind of cool," Krista said. "But at the same time . . ." Krista handed the photos back to Evie abruptly. "I don't like these. Is this what Willow's been up to?"

"I guess so." Evie grimaced. "Ugh, I can't even look at these, they're too freaky." She knew the Pretty hadn't been good for Willow. In some way, she'd just felt it. Had it been warping Willow's mind? Changing it, as much as the Pretty changed their appearance? "Did you organize that dinner with her?" The question sounded more like an accusation.

Krista looked startled. "What?"

"The dinner! You said you'd organize a dinner, check in."

Krista backed up a step, darting her eyes sideways. "I thought you were doing that."

"No, you were supposed to!"

"Quit yelling at me!"

The front door opened again.

The girl in the pictures, Caroline, breezed into the apartment. Evie and Krista froze, deer in twin headlights.

"Oh, hi guys." Willow's voice sounded drifty and slightly thick. Evie assumed she'd been drinking. Her gaze fell to the photographs in Evie's hand, and she gave a small sigh. "They need so much work."

Evie and Krista exchanged a glance.

"What needs work?" Evie asked. "Will, what are these?"

"My new series," she answered. "I'm having another show in two weeks. I just found out today."

"You're having a show? With these pictures of Caroline?"

Willow nodded, a dazed smile coloring her mouth. "Pretty great, huh?"

Evie tried to slow the swirl in her head. Maybe if she didn't know the girl in the picture, she'd see them differently. But she did know the girl in the picture. "I don't know if *great* is the adjective I'm looking for right now."

Willow slid her eyes to Evie's. "What do you mean?"

"You're crying in these pictures. *Really* crying."

Willow nodded. "That's what makes them so good."

No, that's what makes them so weird. Evie curled her fingers into her palms, trying to keep her voice even. "Are you okay?"

Willow gave her an odd look. "I'm fine."

"It's just . . . I mean, you're obviously wasted, which is totally cool, except it's five in the afternoon." Evie exhaled, feeling jumbled. "Look, I know your last show was kind of a bust, and it must be hard not seeing Mark when you're 'Caroline.' So, like, maybe the whole Pretty thing has just been messing with your head a bit. Let's just talk about it."

Willow stared at Evie as if she'd been speaking in French. "Do you have any idea how patronizing you sound?"

"I just want to know if you're okay."

Willow raised her voice. "I told you I'm fine."

"Fuck!" Evie's patience was fraying. "I'm worried about you. We both are. These seem like a cry for—"

"You're *worried* about me? Really. You too, Kris?"

"Yes," Evie said. "She is."

"Now you're speaking for her?" Willow scoffed. "That was only a matter of time."

"What's that supposed to mean?" Krista said.

Willow's voice was steely. "What do you think of my photographs, Krista?"

Krista shifted between the two girls in front of her uncomfortably. "Um, I don't know."

"Yes, you do," Evie said. "You told me you didn't like them."

"That's not what I meant." Krista fiddled with her sleeve. "Look, things are really weird for all three of us right now. Maybe we shouldn't be so quick to judge."

Evie exhaled angrily. "Way to back me up." She turned back to Willow. "Will, what is going on? Did something happen with Mark?"

Willow bristled, a full shudder quaking her thin frame. She snatched the pictures from Evie, sliding them back into the envelope. Evie watched, dumbstruck. The air crackled with discomfort. Willow stormed for the front door and yanked it open. She cut her eyes back to Evie. "You like that I'm not a successful artist."

"That's insane," Evie said. "Why would I like that?"

"Because it makes you feel better about what you're not doing."

When Willow slammed the door behind her, it echoed through the apartment like a gunshot.

52

Evie showered furiously, blasting her skin with boiling hot water.

Maybe it was a little comforting that her friends were still figuring themselves out, but it didn't make her feel good that Willow was struggling. She wanted Willow to succeed, of course she did. But that didn't preclude being honest. Willow would have to learn to take criticism. Because she'd be getting it once she put those horrid photos up in a gallery. Every time she pictured them—Caroline's weak, weepy eyes—she felt like throwing up. This depiction of women as sexy, sad creatures, half nude and helpless, was everything Evie was working against. It was a veritable slap in the face for anyone who said women could be strong and independent and courageous. And it was Willow—Willow!—putting that message out there. Had she taught her nothing?

But was she supposed to be teaching Willow? Was that just self-righteous narcissism to micromanage Willow's art in order for it to better express Evie's own philosophies? Maybe she should just let Willow be Willow. But there was something wrong with Willow, not artistically wrong: *wrong* wrong. The line between meddling and concern was wavering. No option felt right and it was winding her up into a tight little ball.

But she was not going to let this ruin her date with Velma. She absolutely *would not*.

Wrapped in a towel, Evie hesitated outside Krista's door. On the verge of chickening out, she made herself knock.

"Come in."

Krista was curled in her unmade bed. On seeing Evie, she sat up. They regarded each other formally.

Evie was the first to speak. "Kris, I'm really sorry about the audition. It was absolutely the wrong thing to do. You needed that spot way more than me, and I really wish I hadn't done it. I'm sorry."

Krista nodded. "It's okay. I get why you did it." She bit her lip nervously. "I'm, ah, back in the movie."

"Really?" Evie sank down on the edge of Krista's mattress. "How?"

Krista shrugged. "I texted Tristan an apology. My agent called me a few hours ago."

"That's great."

"There's something else." Krista lowered her voice. "I found Penny Baker."

Krista recounted her afternoon: the penthouse at 500 Park, the fight with Carlos, how trapped Penny seemed. "I guess the takeaway is: we have to make sure it doesn't trap us too. You're not taking it anymore, right?"

"Right." Evie hesitated. "Well, I took it again this morning. It's my only chance to see Velma again," she added. "And fix the *Extra Salt* mess."

"Hey." Krista put her hands up. "You don't have to explain yourself to me. I took it twice too. We should just be careful."

"Totally." Evie nodded. "I'm just doing it one more week."

"Me too," Krista said. "As soon as we finish shooting *Funderland*, it's over."

The girls regarded each other. Evie was unsure who, exactly, sounded most suspicious. "Can I borrow a dress?" she asked.

Krista nodded, gesturing at her closet. "Where you going?"

"Just a lo-fi thing with Velma." Evie tried to appear nonchalant. "And her friends."

Krista's eyebrows shot up. "She's introducing you to her friends? Dude, that's huge."

"I met some of her friends already," Evie said. "At the after-party for her book launch. But that was like, 'Come to this party that I'm inviting everyone in a short dress to.' This is like, 'Welcome to my world, here's the people who know me the best.'"

Krista nodded in understanding. "It's GF territory, for sure."

"I know. And I know it can never be anything, but still." Her smile turned goofy. "She wants me to meet *her friends*. She told me to dress to impress." She held up two dresses: one red, one black.

"Red," Krista said. "For sure. It's way more, 'Look out, I'm hot as hell, bitches.'"

Ordinarily that would be Evie's cue to take the black dress. But tonight, Krista was right. If there was one thing Chloe could do well, it was dress to motherfucking impress. "Done."

Krista hunched forward, circling her knees to her chest. "About all that stuff with Willow. It's not good, right? The photos."

Evie let the dress fall to her side. "No. I don't think so. But she's an adult. She can make her own mistakes." But even as she said it, doubt niggled. Was she supposed to be doing something more for Willow? Call Mark? Certainly Evie felt Mark could get through to Willow, maybe even better than she could. But was that just another impulse to intrude?

"Hey, Evie?"

"Yeah, babe?"

Krista fixed Evie with a surprisingly earnest expression. "What do you think Amy Poehler is doing right now?"

Evie took a deep breath and sighed. "I think she's just trying her best, Kris. I think she's just taking it one day at a time."

53.

Evie slammed the cab door shut. As it rumbled off into the night, she took a few seconds to marvel at the sight across the road.

Velma Wolff, head bent to her phone.

Waiting. For her.

As her interest in women had begun to cement itself as more than just sexual fantasies, more than just thoughts she'd assumed (incorrectly) that every girl had, the accompanying relationship fantasies had begun to bloom. Evie would spend subway rides imagining extended scenes of being someone important's girlfriend, the one thanked in speeches or mentioned in interviews. Of course, in these fantasies, Evie was equally famous—a celebrated columnist like Carrie Bradshaw without the terrible relationship, or an overly accomplished twentysomething feminist icon—a Lena, a Tavi, the next four-letter-named cultural phenomenon.

Standing across the road from a cute-looking Fort Greene bar called Sweet & Lowdown, she realized that impossible dream was coming true. In a completely unbelievable and logic-defying way, it was actually becoming a reality.

Maybe her mother was right. Maybe you could manifest your own destiny.

When she was just a few feet away, Evie called to Velma, "Excuse me."

Evie sashayed the four-alarm-fire red dress toward her. Velma's eyes bugged, practically zooming three feet in front of her face like a cartoon character. It was the kind of outfit that inspired stand-up bass on a soundtrack and caused cigarettes to fall from open lips. Sure, it took two hours to create and was intensely uncomfortable, but right now, that all seemed worth it . . .

"Sorry to bother you." Evie curled her fingers around Velma's lapels. "But are you . . . Velma Wolff?"

Velma regained her cool. "I might be."

Evie hovered her lips an inch from Velma's. She could smell the sweet hint of alcohol on the writer's breath. "Can I have an autograph?"

Velma shifted forward without letting their mouths connect. "Maybe. If you're a good girl."

Evie was getting wet. "What happens if I'm a bad girl?"

Velma's hands found Evie's hips. Her voice was husky. "I think you know," she murmured, "what happens to bad girls."

For a long, electrifying second, the two women stood there. Evie wanted Velma to break.

Velma said, "Let's go in."

Abruptly, she pulled back from Evie, circling around her to pull the bar door open. Music and the loud babble of conversation spilled from inside, breaking the tension. Evie's entire body was thrumming.

This night would be wonderful.

"Thank you," she said to Velma as she strutted into the bar.

Sweet & Lowdown was nicer inside than the modest exterior suggested, all warm wood and low-hanging Edison lightbulbs. The crowd was well dressed without being preppy, and while it was noisy, you didn't have to shout to be heard. The guys behind the bar were wearing black button-downs with red suspenders and artful mustaches. It was a thirtysomething bar, Evie decided. A grown-ups' bar.

Velma steered her toward the back. In front of a set of wooden stairs leading up, a sign read: Upstairs Bar Closed for Private Event. Velma unhooked the red velvet rope. "After you."

Evie assumed Velma was checking out her butt as they went up the darkened staircase. She added a little wiggle for her benefit.

The stairs gave way to a large, private room, smaller than the bar downstairs, and less crowded. A bar ran across the back wall. One bartender mixed something in a cocktail shaker, while another circled with a silver tray of champagne and wine. Louis Armstrong's tender, guttural voice underscored the chatter from the small group of polished-looking people who were closer to Velma's age than to Evie's. But what caught Evie's attention was the sign that was strung up. Gold lettering on a black banner: Congratulations Karyn + Mitch OO!

The two Os were meant to be rings. Wedding rings.

"Is this an engagement party?" Evie asked Velma in surprise.

Velma nodded. "That's Karyn." She indicated a woman who was laughing with a gaggle of other women, the center of their focus. In her polite black dress, not too high heels, and flawless French braid, Karyn looked pretty, if on the conservative side. Someone who had a gym membership she actually used; someone who didn't swear a lot. "And Mitch is . . . over there. By the windows." Velma pointed to a man with short curly hair and a pleasant open face talking earnestly with another man who looked similar—his brother, maybe.

The waiter with the tray of drinks approached. Evie took a glass of champagne gratefully. Was it odd Velma hadn't mentioned this was an engagement party? Maybe. But what difference would it make?

Karyn's eyes met hers. Her face twitched subtly, as if detecting smoke. Then she saw Velma. A look of raw shock surged onto her face. It took her a few seconds to recover. She excused herself and began walking over, touching the side of her braid self-consciously.

Velma circled her hand around Evie's waist, casually protective.

"Velma, oh my god." Karyn's smile was wide. Almost too wide. She pressed her cheek to Velma's, air-kissing her. "I didn't think you'd actually come."

Velma shrugged. "You invited me. Congratulations, by the way."

Karyn was staring at Velma. Evie couldn't get a read on her expression: she was either thrilled or horrified. It took a long moment for Karyn to take in Velma's words. "What?" She shook her head. "Oh, thanks. Mitch'll be . . ." She smiled hard at Velma, cocking her head. "I think he'll be surprised you're here." Her face clearly said, *As am I.*

"This is Chloe," Velma said.

Evie stuck her hand out. "Hi. Congratulations."

Karyn's handshake was quick and cold. "Hi." Her eyes moved around Evie's face and she began nodding. Somehow, the visual of Chloe confirmed something. Karyn looked back at Velma. "Well, she's gorgeous!"

Evie felt a snap of surprise, of anger. "And she's right in front of you," she said, forcing herself to keep smiling.

Karyn gave a loud, odd laugh. Velma chuckled too, tightening her grip around Evie's waist. The whole thing was decidedly awkward. Did Velma bring her as a trophy date?

Karyn addressed Velma again. "Congratulations on *Milk Teeth*." Karyn's hand pressed into her chest. "I read it last weekend. Couldn't put it down. God, I love when you work with Brett. He really knows how to push you."

"Brett's my editor," Velma said to Evie. "Karyn and I . . . used to work together."

"That's diplomatic!" Karyn exclaimed. "I used to work *for* you."

Velma made a face as if she disagreed. "No, I like to think of it—"

"I used to work for you." Karyn almost snapped the words. She addressed Evie. "I was her publicist."

"Oh." Evie nodded, affecting polite interest, masking biting discomfort.

Karyn took in Evie's expression. "You didn't know that? She hasn't told you . . ." Then, under her breath, "No, of course she hasn't."

Evie glanced back in the direction of the fiancé, Mitch. He was staring at them from across the room.

"I have to mingle," Karyn announced with a hard-won sort of cheerfulness. "Lovely to meet you, Chloe, and . . . I'll . . . see you guys later."

Karyn headed back into the party.

Velma nodded in the direction of some empty leather couches. "Let's grab a seat."

As soon as they sat down, Evie turned to Velma incredulously. "Okay. So?"

Velma looked back. "So?"

Evie elbowed her lightly. "Don't play dumb, just tell me."

Velma's lips curled up teasingly. "Tell you what?"

Evie gave Velma a hard look. She wasn't going to be taken for a fool. She grabbed her purse and made a move to get up. Velma grabbed her arm. "Hey, don't go. I'm sorry, I'll stop being a bitch."

"What, did you used to date or something?"

"Yes." Velma nodded. "Actually . . . We were engaged."

"Engaged?" Evie felt the blood drain from her cheeks. "As in . . . to be married?"

"No, engaged to be astronauts."

Evie sneaked her eyes back at Karyn, who was air-kissing an older couple who'd just arrived. "When?"

Velma creased her forehead.

"If it's anything less than a year, that's seriously weird," Evie added. "Anything less than six months and I'm leaving."

"Oh god no, it was ages ago," Velma said. "Eight years. Nine?"

Karyn looked about thirty. Eight years ago she would've been twenty-two. About Evie's age. "So she was gay then," Evie said.

Velma shrugged. "She was in love with a woman."

"Why didn't you get married?"

Velma rolled her glass between her palms. "It was . . . complicated."

"Who ended it?" Evie asked.

"Hm?" Velma said, even though Evie was sure she'd heard her.

"Who ended it?"

Velma held Evie's gaze.

A male voice boomed, "Velma fucking Wolff!"

A barrel-chested man with a scruffy beard was grinning at Velma, arms flung wide.

"Theo!" Velma exclaimed. She rose in one quick, graceful motion. "I thought you were still in Tokyo!"

Theo was an extreme food writer who'd turned his blog, *Dare Me to Eat It,* into a book of the same name. He'd been kicked out of Japan for overstaying his visa, a fact cheerily relayed from his position sandwiched between Velma and Evie.

More guests arrived. Soon the half-empty room was full.

Being Velma's date was a stamp of instant cool. Evie could feel people wanting her attention, her approval, almost as much as they wanted Velma's. And it felt great. Because if a special person had chosen you to give their attention to, that made you just as special.

She also felt good about how she'd handled finding out about Karyn, particularly the instinct to get up and leave when Velma was withholding the truth. Velma liked this, she realized. She liked it when Evie was tough and witty. And while this girl—the ballsy, beautiful girl who teased Velma and didn't mind being teased herself—seemed to entice Velma, she wasn't as neat a fit for Evie. Evie wanted to be able to cuddle up to Velma, to have Velma baby her for a minute. But Velma didn't seem very interested in that. *Because you're her date,* Evie reminded herself. *Not her girlfriend.*

As the hour crept closer to midnight, Evie and Velma drifted apart. As a longtime singleton, Evie knew how to take care of herself while flying solo. But after getting stuck in a bad conversation with an investment banker, Evie realized it'd been over an hour since they'd checked in. "You have to start saving for retirement right now," the banker was saying to her. His dark hair was set like concrete with too much gel. "Are you an actress?"

Evie glanced over his shoulder, looking for Velma. "Sort of."

"I thought so." He smiled smugly. "Women like you assume you can monetize your looks forever, but you can't. You need a financial strategy to deal with what happens when you're forty."

Finally, she spotted Velma, talking with Karyn on the other side of the room, all but hidden by an enormous potted palm. Karyn had her arms crossed across her chest. The conversation looked intense.

"Do you have that?" the banker asked.

Evie willed Velma to look over. "Have what?"

The banker's eyes dropped unsubtly to Evie's cleavage before fixing on her again. "A financial strategy."

I'll tell you what my strategy for right now involves, Evie thought. *An untraceable bullet and a body bag.*

Velma's head lifted. Her eyes swept the room. They landed on Evie. Evie widened her eyes and made a *save me* face. Velma ducked her head back to Karyn and placed a hand on her shoulder, murmuring something. Karyn laughed and pushed Velma lightly, which made Velma chuckle. But she made no move to leave. Evie stiffened.

The banker inched closer. She could smell his sweat. "The thing about women like you is—"

"The thing about women like me is they know when to walk away from creeps like you." Fuck this. She was out. She pushed past him, intending to grab her purse.

"Chloe, is it?" Mitch, Karyn's fiancé, stepped into her path.

"Um, yes. Hi." Evie tried to gather herself. "Congratulations . . . Wedding."

Mitch blinked glassily. He looked equally intent and drunk. "I was wondering if you could get your girlfriend to leave now."

"My what?"

Mitch waved his hands in the air. "I know everyone's fucking so impressed that the famous Velma Wolff is here, but this is *my* engagement party." He slapped himself on the chest. "This is about *me,* and *my* wife, soon-to-be wife, and I just think showing up with a perfect fucking ten"—Mitch gestured at Evie to indicate she was the ten in question—"it's just not that classy, you know? It took Karyn a long time to get over her and all the bullshit she put her through. I would just *prefer* if she would kindly get the fuck out of here."

Evie stared at Mitch dumbly. Mitch nodded, his gaze shifting past Evie. He clamped an unsteady hand on her shoulder and lurched toward the bar.

Velma was still in the corner with Karyn. As Evie watched, Velma lifted one hand and lightly touched Karyn's cheek. Karyn's face broke into a smile.

Evie felt like she'd been socked in the stomach. Velma didn't care about her. Chloe was a pawn; a prop. She snatched at her purse and cut through the dance floor, unable to leave the whole mess fast enough.

Down on the street, she searched desperately for a cab. How stupid to assume Velma actually liked her! She was stupid, she made terrible choices all the time, and this was just one of what would surely be a lifetime of—

"Chloe!" It was Velma.

Evie ignored her. A cab with its light on appeared at the end of the street. Evie signaled for it.

"Chloe, wait!" Velma jogged toward her. "Where are you going?"

"I wanted to give you and Karyn some space," Evie replied. "That's who you were really here for, right?"

"What? No!" Velma ran a hand through her hair, frustrated. "I mean, yes, she's my friend, so—"

"She's your *ex*." Evie spat the word. "But it looks like you'd prefer her to be something else." The cab pulled to a stop. Evie opened the door. Velma placed one hand on it gently before she could get in.

"Karyn is getting married," Velma said. "To a man. End of story." She sucked in a breath. "Did I want to smooth things over between us tonight? Yes. I did. I like being friends with all of my exes."

Evie shot her a snarky look. "Must be nice, being so popular."

The cabdriver called, "You getting in?"

"You brought me here tonight to make her jealous," Evie continued hotly. "You barely said two words to me all night!"

"I know, and I'm sorry. There were a lot of people there I hadn't seen in a while. You said this was the only night you had free, and I wanted to see you. It wasn't how I wanted our second date to go."

"Miss?" The cabdriver revved the engine impatiently.

"Just a minute," Evie told him, still holding the door open. She eyed Velma uncertainly. "How did you want our second date to go?"

Velma's face softened into a smile. Cautiously, she moved her hand from the cab door to rest on Evie's shoulder. "I wanted to cook you dinner. Three courses. Open a bottle of something special. Candles. My grandmother's china. I wanted," she continued, "to woo you, Chloe Fontaine. Because you're a woman who deserves to be wooed."

Evie felt herself melting. That just sounded so . . . nice. Sophisticated. Sexy.

Velma gazed at Evie intensely. "Let me drop you home. Please. Let's not end our night like this."

Evie glanced between the open cab door and the woman in front of her. She didn't want the night to end with a solo cab ride home either. Just once, just for once, didn't she deserve to be dropped home, like a woman who deserved to be wooed?

Evie slammed the cab door shut. "Take me home," she whispered to Velma. "But first, I want you to kiss me."

As the cab sped off up the empty street, Velma pulled Evie close to her. The softness of her body, the smell of her skin, the anticipation of the kiss made Evie swoon. Her eyes drifted shut. As their lips met, an electric shiver spiked through Evie's body. What was at first tender quickly became passionate. Evie wanted Velma, every part of her. She wanted to open a door in her chest and climb inside. The feeling of kissing this sexy stallion of a woman was almost too much for her, and if Velma hadn't been holding her so securely, with such strong, gentle hands, she would probably have lost her balance.

There was only one thought that settled, as calmly as a cat finding a spot of sun to sleep in. One word that felt inevitable, as they kissed and nibbled and quietly laughed with the delirium of it.

Home.

Part Three:
Conceal

54.

Krista returned to the *Funderland* set on Friday with an entirely new game plan. This time, she'd take it seriously. This time, she'd be a professional.

There's a first time for everything.

She set her alarm so early she was downstairs waiting for Eduardo when he came to pick her up. She was polite and friendly with the crew. But her most important new rule had to do with Tristan. This time, sex was off the table. If he allowed it, this time they would just be friends.

To her surprise, this was easy. Tristan forgave the trophy incident generously and quickly. And there was an extraordinary amount of downtime on set. They spent the weekend sprawled out on Tristan's white leather sofa, sipping the green tea and kale smoothies Tristan was addicted to, just talking.

She told him what it was like being brown in rural, northern Westchester County, the far-flung suburbs of New York City, past the Bronx. Scrubbing her skin in the shower to make it white when she was a little girl. Hiding pungent school lunches that were different from everyone else's, her mom's constant overfeeding matched only by the constant criticisms of her weight, criticisms her three older brothers never faced. The impossible juggling act of being in between two cultures—being told her speech or clothes or personality were becoming "too American," but then getting in trouble for not doing well enough in her American high school, pursuing the American dream. How bringing home a 95 percent test score would mean getting asked about where the other

5 percent was, and how any complaint about that would trigger a one-hour lecture about her parents' immigration struggles—her mom made it sound like she'd walked all the way from India, while her dad battled sea monsters and border security to emigrate from Sri Lanka. How her declaration of wanting to be a lawyer was motivated only by the fact she hated working the front desk in her father's boring medical practice after school, and apart from being a doctor, becoming a lawyer was the only other acceptable (i.e., lucrative and respectable) career path.

She recalled losing her virginity three weeks before her fifteenth birthday in the back of Tim Klinchin's blue Ford, a gearshift pressed into her back, someone's elbow blasting the horn in jerky fits and starts. It was a textbook case of sweaty, awkward, but surprisingly fun rebellion. She discovered that sex wasn't something her parents could control, that it was just for her, and that she wanted to get as good at it as she was at everything else. She started to realize that while she loved her parents, she wasn't really herself around them. She wanted—craved, even—to just act how she felt, when she felt it, to indulge her desires and stop denying them all the time.

She told Tristan about meeting her best friend, Evie, at Sarah Lawrence when they were in the same dorm freshman year, how insepara-ble they were, how it felt like meeting the sister she'd always wanted. She told him how insanely proud her dad had been when she'd gotten into law school in Boston, how he'd teared up and bought her a silver Tiffany ring, and then how furious he'd been when she'd dropped out, not even six months later, after an acid-fueled revelation that *she never wanted to be a lawyer.* How she wanted to please her father, but couldn't just blindly obey him, and how hard that was to explain to him, and how now, every conversation just ended in a fight and she didn't know how to stop that. She recounted the decision to try acting, landing her first agent, getting just enough work for her plan not to be a total di-saster, but not enough for it to be a success, and about her debt, and the Con Ed guy, and how meeting Greg and landing *Funderland* changed all that, gave her hope, and well . . . here she was.

Tristan listened to all this patiently. He asked the right questions. He was genuinely interested.

In turn, he shared his life story with her. How he was always the kid goofing off in front of the camera, singing, dancing, dressing up and lip-synching to the radio, actions that weren't "manly" according to his father, a quietly angry man who worked fishing trawlers in the Bay Area. Tristan's interest in performing was so vehemently discouraged that his mother had to lie about driving him to an open-call audition for a show on the Disney Channel, the audition that saw him landing a main part at age eleven. This stuff Krista knew, although she let Tristan explain it anyway: how *Heartache High* ran for two seasons, during which time the producers discovered he could sing. How singles from the show almost went gold; modest, in the scheme of things, but still deemed a success. He was "put on" Boyz Unbridled at age thirteen—"I don't remember it being a choice. It just happened." Krista could picture this Tristan almost more clearly than she could picture him now: the youngest of the five, golden-haired and cherubic, entirely innocent. They began touring and recording, more or less constantly, for the next four years.

"At first, everything was new and fresh and exciting," he said. "Winning Best New Act at the Teen Choice Awards in 2002. Crowds that kept getting bigger. Fans that kept getting crazier. Being number one in countries I'd never heard of."

The wave broke two years later. Tristan was fifteen, and had graduated from being a sweet and grateful kid to "a resentful, egotistical maniac." He fired his mother, who'd been acting as his manager. Years later he realized how much she'd been shielding him from the bad stuff, but at the time it felt claustrophobic. What teenage boy wants his mom on the tour bus?

He started doing a ton of drugs.

"It sounds like a cliché, but they were just everywhere. And no one ever said no to me. Not ever. I never had to wait in line or pick up a check. We were always VIP, always being hustled in some back entrance.

I forgot what normal was. It was so crazy, Lenka. I remember talking to people and seeing in their eyes that this conversation—whatever it was about, usually nothing—was the most exciting thing that'd ever happened to them. And part of me wanted to shake their shoulders and scream, 'Get over it, I'm nothing, I'm just like you!' But another part of me believed I was like a god or something. A part of me believed I was better than everyone else. Every girl wanted to sleep with me: other performers, people who worked for us. Fans. Fans' *moms*. Just to say they did, you know? Just for the story."

"I bet you've slept with thousands of girls," Krista said, eyes as round as dinner plates.

"No." Tristan sat up. "I never did. I fooled around with some, sure. But I never slept with fans, not like the other guys did."

Krista gaped at him. "Why not? I mean, you were sixteen, you must've been horny as hell."

Tristan drew his lips into a straight line for a moment, then continued. He told her about the publicist who died after a blood clot from routine liposuction, the two-hundred-thousand-dollar kickbacks from wearing a Chinese company's diamond cuff links, the stalker who broke into his hotel room in Seoul with a screwdriver and stabbed him in the thigh. How one tweet would kick-start a friend's career, and how tiring that got, and how sick he was of constantly being needed, by everyone, all the time. The implosion of Boyz Unbridled, a messy, hot, drug-fueled end, fights that were circular and bitter and exhausting. The solo career that went nowhere. Getting a humiliating DUI, blood alcohol level of 0.21, on the eve of his twenty-second birthday, and deciding to get clean. Rehab not taking for a year or so. Meeting Umsa. Spending six months in Nepal. Getting clarity. And finally, staying sober.

He told her about making friends with real musicians, talented people who worked hard and wanted to start families. Making amends with the members of Boyz Unbridled, all going through the same confusing stages of reimagining, rebranding. Taking some small indie roles, realizing how fun it was to be on a movie set as part of a team. Meeting

Greg at a group skiing weekend in Montana, bonding over nights spent on the slopes and under the stars, deciding to help this sweet, genuine guy get a movie made: a funny, harmless movie, a script Greg had written called *Funderland*.

"This film is my second chance," Tristan said. "To be more than just the kid from Boyz Unbridled."

"I know what you mean," Krista said. "It feels like a second chance for me too."

"I'm really glad we're working on this together, Lenks." Tristan squeezed her knee. "It feels right."

Krista smiled. A wave of warmth enveloped her, filling her with love for her costar, and Greg, and everyone outside the trailer working so hard on making this movie the best it could be. "Yeah," she said, not without a touch of surprise. "It really does."

55

"Sounds like someone has a crush." From her position in front of the mirror, Evie smirked at her roommate, who was sprawled out on Evie's bed, leafing through an old copy of *Salty*.

"Actually, I don't. We're just friends." Krista sounded oddly, atypically genuine.

"Yeah, right. That is not Krista Kumar's vibe." Evie arched an eyebrow, then tweezered a stray hair from it.

"It is today." Krista flipped a page. "I just like being around him. Plus nothing could happen, even if I wanted it to. We can't get attached, Eve. You know that, right?"

"Of course," Evie said. "Velma and I are . . . casual."

This was a total and complete lie.

Ever since Velma dropped Evie home after the engagement party, an emotional valve had been released. They'd been texting each other nonstop. Literally: Evie had spent all weekend at home, connected to her phone. And not just frothy flirtatious banter, at which, Evie had to admit, Velma was just as good as she was. This afternoon, their epic chain of correspondence included everything from fantasy holiday destinations to thoughts on children. They even named their future kids, Thing 1 and Thing 2; a joke, of course, but still . . . Evie had never thought seriously about kids. Which was why it was so odd she spent an entire thirty-minute shower imagining raising them with Velma. Everything from baby's first steps to tearful pride at graduation.

Trouble was, in these fantasies, she was Chloe. Evie Selby, it seemed, had no place in her future.

Krista rolled onto her tummy to examine Evie's outfit: a bell-shaped blue dress that made her eyes look as big as Betty Boop's. "You look so Instagram right now. I take it this is for her benefit."

Evie studied herself in the mirror. "Does my chin look pointy to you?"

"What?"

Evie pressed it with her fingers, turning her head to see a different angle. "I feel like it's pointier."

Krista sat up. "I thought my eyes looked different too. The second time. And Willow mentioned she thought that maybe food tasted different when she turned back."

The girls exchanged a look of unease. Krista jostled Evie away from the mirror. "See?" she said, her nose at the glass. "Different, right? Not as green."

"I swear it's pointier." Evie elbowed Krista out of the way. "I really don't like this."

"Well, we still don't have a lot of answers about it."

Evie meant her chin, but this was true too. "Right."

"Not even Penny knew what it was," Krista added.

"Probably the souls of girls who died of anorexia," Evie muttered. "They'd have had pretty pointy chins by then." Evie met her gaze in the mirror. Chloe looked back at her, eyebrows furrowed in concern. She didn't look as pretty like that, face all screwed up. Channeling her inner yogi, Evie let out a breath, relaxing her expression into an unblemished canvas. There. Better. Pointy chin or not, Chloe was definitely prettier when she wasn't emotional. She watched Chloe's beautiful wide mouth speak confidently. "I am invincible. I am Chloe fucking Fontaine."

Krista was staring at her with a dumbfounded expression.

"What?" Evie asked, suddenly self-conscious.

"Maybe this should be our last go." Krista spoke slowly, as if Evie wasn't to be alarmed. "You think that, right?"

Evie met Chloe's gaze in the mirror. Her big blue eyes looked startled, scared even, almost as if she was pleading her case to stay. Evie couldn't look at herself when she nodded an agreement. But she couldn't look at Krista either.

The last time Evie had been to Jay Street, she hadn't been allowed to enter the gorgeous redbrick building Velma called home. Now the doorman at the front desk was expecting her. Velma lived in PH2, one of two penthouses on the top floor. When the elevator doors slid open into an innocuous hallway, Evie was accosted by a biting smell.

Burning toast?

The front door was ajar. "Hello? Velma?" Evie stepped into a large, airy loft. A number of thick, ribbed black columns ran up to a huge expanse of white molded ceiling, easily fifteen feet high. Evie glimpsed several oversized bookshelves and a wall of huge rectangular windows, curved at the top. The lovely hardwood floor was dotted with bright rugs and standing lamps. On one wall hung an enormous photograph of a woman's milky white throat and the curve of her chin, bloodred lips turned up in a sly smile. It was a little messier than she'd imagined, and maybe even a little smaller, but more or less what she'd assumed Velma's home would be like.

What Evie wasn't expecting was the sight of Velma trying to beat back the small but enthusiastic fire that was leaping about a stainless steel stovetop. She was doing battle with a kitchen towel that had just caught alight, forcing Velma to chuck it into the sink.

"Shit, *shit*!" Velma threw Evie a panicked look. "There's a fire extinguisher. In the closet—"

Evie dashed down the hallway Velma had flung a finger at. The first door she yanked open revealed towels and sheets. The second housed winter jackets, board games, and, yes, a small fire extinguisher. Evie grabbed it and raced back to the kitchen.

"I've never used one!" Evie cried.

"Neither have I!" Velma unhooked the long black nozzle and aimed the cylindrical end at the fire. Evie squeezed the two metal levers on the top together. Nothing happened.

"Why isn't it working?" Velma pumped the metal levers too, her fingers mashing into Evie's.

Evie grabbed the nozzle from Velma and peered into the end of it, just as Velma yanked at a silver ring on the top and squeezed the levers. A powerful blast of white hit Evie in the face. She screamed and stumbled back.

"Are you okay?" yelled Velma.

Evie pawed at her face, gasping, "Fire! Just get the fire!"

Velma aimed at the stove. Seconds later, the fire was out.

The two women stood in the silent kitchen, panting. It was only now that Evie realized Velma wasn't dressed for dinner. She was wearing old sweats and a tank top, with no makeup, and her hair pulled back into a messy bun.

In the reflection of the long glass windows that separated the apartment from the balcony outside, Evie saw that her carefully constructed look was completely ruined. Everything was sprayed with white powder and dark smudges.

"Jesus, are you okay?" Velma dropped the fire extinguisher and strode toward her, face alert with concern.

Evie's eyes were watering. "I feel like I just got punched in the face by a snowman."

Velma laughed. She came to rest both hands on Evie's shoulders. "I'm so sorry. I was frying some onions and got distracted. Completely lost track of time." Velma met Evie's eyes with soft sincerity. "I'm really, really sorry, Chloe."

"That's okay," Evie whispered. She flicked her eyes to the kitchen, which, apart from a pan full of blackened onions, was devoid of any other ingredients. "Is it weird to ask what the plan is? I'm kind of starving."

Velma grinned. "Not weird at all. Let's see . . . How do you feel about Thai takeout?"

Thirty minutes later, Velma and Evie were sitting cross-legged around Velma's large, square coffee table, digging into a sprawling Asian feast. While Velma ordered food, Evie took a shower. Although she was disappointed to destroy the supervixen effect of two hours of date prep, she did enjoy getting undressed in a place as intimate as Velma's bathroom. It was full of expensive products she could never afford and thick, white towels she could never keep clean. In the waterfall shower, Evie lathered her body with lavender soap and wondered how long it would be before she and Velma would be showering together.

Velma had loaned her clothes to wear: an oversized white button-down and a pair of black leggings. Evie strolled out in just the shirt. Velma's slow smile of approval made her tingle with pleasure.

Now Evie accepted the wine Velma offered and they tipped their glasses in a toast. "You're making me break all my own rules," Velma chided. "Dinner on the floor is strictly a solo activity in this apartment."

Evie glowed. She loved feeling like Velma was making exceptions for her. That was how you treated a girlfriend. "What were you going to make?" Evie asked, helping herself to some pad thai. "Before the Great Fire of Five Minutes Ago?"

Velma stabbed a piece of chicken with her chopstick and frowned. "I guess a pasta . . . thing."

Evie arched an eyebrow. "Not exactly Nigella Lawson, are you?"

"I wouldn't mind her cooking for me," Velma said. "But no. Shamefully inadequate in that arena. My mother wasn't much of a cook either," she added, popping a water chestnut into her mouth. "Guess it rubbed off."

"Where did you grow up?" Evie knew the answer to this already.

"North Carolina."

"Very white bread," Evie suggested, and Velma nodded. "And when did you know you were gay?"

Velma smiled and swallowed a mouthful of food. "I feel like I'm on your show again."

Evie shook her head emphatically. "No, off the record."

Velma knitted her eyebrows in faux-suspicion.

"Seriously." Evie laughed. "I just really love origin stories. C'mon."

"Okay." Velma dabbed her mouth with a paper napkin. "I remember being in about sixth grade, and feeling like there was something about me that was different, but I didn't know what it was. My girlfriends were starting to talk about which boys they liked, and I didn't have those feelings for them, so I just pretended I did. I think I thought that's what everyone was doing, just pretending. And one day, this girl in my class, Prue Wilfred-Scott, came to school and said she'd seen one of our teachers, Mr. Sullivan, out on the weekend holding hands *with a man.*"

Evie gasped, affecting shock.

"Exactly." Velma chuckled. "It was very scandalous, and confusing. I'd just never heard of that; I didn't really know what it meant, how it was possible. And then one of the boys said Mr. Sullivan was gay, that's what being gay was. And I remember thinking, I'm like that. I'm gay, for girls." Velma met Evie's eyes unemotionally. "It was a horrible realization. The kids were talking about Mr. Sullivan like he was sick. Diseased. I knew immediately it was true for me, and at the same time that I'd never be able to tell anyone or act on it for the rest of my life."

"God, that's so awful," Evie said.

"Mm. Not exactly a Call-me-Charlie-type awakening, unfortunately." Velma tipped her head to the side. "Do you really want to hear about all this? It's not very romantic—"

"No, I do," Evie said, surprising herself with how insistent her tone was. "I really do."

Velma swallowed some more wine. For a moment, Evie was worried she'd overstepped the line, that Velma was about make some weird excuse about having an early start. But instead, Velma cleared her throat and kept talking. "When I was fifteen, I woke up one morning and thought, 'It's never going to get any better than this, it's just going to get worse.' So I went into the bathroom, found every kind of pill I could, and swallowed them all."

"Oh my god," Evie said.

"My mother found me passed out on the bathroom floor, called an ambulance, took me to the hospital. I was there for a few days. And that's where I met Ann Jackson." Velma smiled ironically. "If there's one thing my mother knew about, it was therapists. Thank god for Ann Jackson. That woman saved my life. I started seeing her three times a week, and within the first month, she got me to admit I was gay. I'd never said the words out loud before, and the relief!" Velma groaned. "It really was like this huge weight lifted from my shoulders. It was a turning point. Within a year, I told my parents, which went a lot better than expected. They agreed to let me switch schools, so I did junior and senior year at this very liberal artsy-fartsy high school where half the guys were gay. My homeroom teacher was a tranny. I told everyone I was a dyke on my first day, and no one batted an eyelid. Started seeing my first girlfriend, took her to prom. And so"—Velma lifted her palms up—"here we are." Her forehead creased in alarm. "Chloe, are you crying?"

Evie brushed at her eyes furiously. "No, no, no, I just . . ."

Velma scooted closer and handed her a napkin. "Here."

Evie took it and blew her nose. "Sorry," she said, feeling her face start to redden. "Such an overreaction. It's just . . . fuck, I can't bear to think of you being so unhappy."

Velma studied Evie's face. "God, you're so sweet." She said it as if she was only just now figuring it out.

Evie stared back at Velma. Her voice was as soft as the rain. "I just think it's so sad that some people think two women loving each other is horrible, when it's the most beautiful thing in the whole world."

Velma's expression was serious as she held Evie's chin between her thumb and forefinger. Then she moved her head toward Evie and gently kissed her lips.

Evie closed her eyes and kissed her back. She felt grateful. Grateful Velma was alive. Grateful the world was changing. And grateful for the Pretty, the special key, the secret handshake that allowed her to be here, in this nice apartment, drinking this nice wine, being kissed by this nice woman.

Their kissing began to change. From sweet and tender to driving, more urgent. Evie opened her mouth wider and felt Velma do the same. Velma's hands wound into her still damp hair, cupping her head hard. Evie groaned, low in her throat.

Velma broke away, eyes bright, breath ragged. "Bedroom?"

Evie nodded without hesitation.

They tumbled onto Velma's king-sized bed as one, legs tangled, mouths wet and searching. Velma ripped Evie's shirt open. Buttons flew like bullets. Evie laughed, which turned to a gasp as Velma's lips found her nipples, sucking, circling, playing. Chloe's pink, perfect nipples, standing to attention in the middle of Chloe's peppy, perfect breasts. Watching Velma touch them was like watching a kind of porn that could only exist in her wildest, wettest imagination.

She pulled Velma's top off over her head, kissing her breasts, her throat, her neck, her lips. She pressed her chest to Velma's, hungry for the sensation of two women together, two soft, luscious, writhing women letting their fantasies take over.

Velma's fingertips grazed the outside of Evie's underwear. Her body snapped involuntarily. Velma grinned, lit only by a lamp on the bedside table. Her hair had come loose from its messy bun, falling around her face in tendrils. Velma slid Evie's underwear down, scooped it to her nose, and inhaled deeply. "You smell so good."

Even the sound of her voice made Evie whimper. She fidgeted, wanting Velma to touch her clit, but almost fearful of the sensations she knew she'd conjure.

Velma positioned Evie so she was lying on the pile of pillows at the top of the bed. She kissed her mouth, slowly, then whispered, "Can I go down on you?"

Evie nodded.

"Can I put my fingers inside you?"

Evie nodded again, and whispered, "Find my G-spot," assuming Velma would be well versed in such a move.

Velma began to move down between Evie's legs.

"Wait." Evie pulled Velma back up. Her breath came unevenly. "Tell me I'm beautiful."

Velma paused, surprised, before obeying. "You're beautiful, Chloe."

Evie shook her head a little. "Differently."

Velma murmured the words directly into her ear. "You'd end wars. You'd make angels weep. You're all I ever think about."

Evie sighed, dreamy, hot, and happy. "Make me come."

And Velma most certainly did.

Three times.

56

She had to press the buzzer three times before Mark answered, sounding disoriented. "Willow?"

The night had its hands around her, pressing every part of her, its darkness violating her. She felt like her blood was running black. "It's Caroline."

Nothing. She pressed the buzzer again, the skin under her fingernail turning white. *Let me in. Get me out.*

"Caroline, I can't let you up. I'm sorry."

The night showed her its teeth, everything too loud, too hot, too dangerous. Her voice was a whimper. "Mark . . . please."

"No, Caroline, I—"

"Please."

When she arrived at his door, Mark was standing behind his armchair, arms crossed. All the lights were on. "Hey," she said softly.

He spoke without moving. "Hey."

She waited, hoping to be asked in. When the invitation didn't come, Willow crossed the threshold herself. She was carrying a large duffel bag.

"So." Mark rocked back on his heels. "What's up?"

Willow let the duffel bag fall from her fingers. "Have you ever been to Paris?"

"Paris? No."

Willow moved Caroline's body forward like a puppet, each limb dumb and heavy. "I spent a summer in Paris. Or maybe it was fall by then, I can't remember." She sat on the edge of Mark's sofa. "I remember the smell of fireworks over the Seine—there were fireworks every night. Explosions lighting up the sky." She hugged her arms around herself. "I love fireworks. I would walk the banks of the river by myself, you see, just following the patterns of the fireworks reflected in the water. One night I was down there, alone, and I came across a group of men drinking by the river." She looked directly at Mark. "There are a lot of Africans in Paris. Did you know that?"

"What is this, Caroline? What's going on?"

"They were drinking," Willow continued as if he hadn't spoken. "And laughing. They invited me to sit with them. They were drinking out of a bottle in a paper bag. They gave me some." Her eyes were far off. "It tasted like fireworks. They wanted to know where I was from. I said I was an American. They told me I was very beautiful. In French, you say, *très jolie. Très jolie fille.*" Willow paused, then said, "They suggested I might like to take my clothes off."

Mark gripped the edge of the armchair.

"It was a very warm night, no chance of catching cold." Willow's voice was wistful. "I thought, why not? Together we removed my clothes, until I was naked. We burned my dress in the fire. They had a small fire. Once I was naked—"

"Caroline, I can't sleep with you again—"

"Once I was naked, the men lifted me up and carried me to the water. They were so careful with me; I remember how careful they were. They brought me all the way down to the water. Soon it was deep enough to let me go, to let me float. I floated naked, in the Seine, while the fireworks exploded overhead." Willow closed her eyes. Tears slipped down her cheeks. Her voice was barely a whisper. "I want to be back there. In the river. But I can never go back." Her thoughts were a shattered mirror reflecting back a broken picture, a picture she couldn't see clearly no matter how hard she tried. It was exhausting. Everything was just so exhausting. "I can never go back." Her head dropped into her hands, and she began to weep.

After a moment's hesitation, Mark walked to the front door and quietly pulled it shut.

57.

Evie woke early, momentarily disoriented by the strange sheets, the smell of lavender. Pale yellow light filtered through gauzy white curtains, beyond which was the vague outline of the city. Reality whooshed in. The fire. The Thai food. The sex.

I had sex with Velma Wolff.

She stretched, feeling warm and decadent, tangled up in gray silky sheets. She couldn't shake the smile from her lips. It was more than a carnal conquest. They'd connected. Really connected. And Velma was here, right next to Evie, mere inches away. This, this moment of being in bed with someone as majestic as mountains, as alluring as moonlight: this was everything. *The answer to a question I've always wanted to ask.*

Evie rubbed at her eyes, wanting to clear them of blurry sleep, to see every contour, every pore, of the woman next to her.

Her vision stayed blurry.

She had changed back.

She was Evie Selby again.

Fear banged into her veins, hard as a hammer blow. *Please no. Please please please no.* She clutched at her hair, her cheeks, her plump upper arms in silent horror.

It was true.

She was a different person.

The sickness came a split second later, two Mack trucks slamming into each other in midair. It took every scrap of willpower to cry out silently, contorting her body in a way that wouldn't rustle the covers. Pain seared her insides and her mind was racing, trying to work out how this had happened. It was Wednesday. It was Wednesday and she'd taken the Pretty on Thursday and it had been seven whole days for Krista not six and oh god her stomach hurt and oh god she was Regular again what the fuck what the fucking *fuck*?

She slid her eyes to Velma. *Don't look at me. Do. Not. Look.*

Escape.

Now.

Evie inched the edge of the covers up. Velma sucked in a breath, snuffly deep and throaty. Evie froze. Every inch of skin was boiling with anticipation, with hot horror, with pain. But Velma settled and so Evie continued her inch-by-inch escape. She slipped out of the bed, falling into a crouch with another silent cry. A few seconds to catch her breath. Then a hunchback shuffle-run for the door.

In the living room, Evie zipped up her crumpled blue dress with numb fingers, heart rate still galloping recklessly. She should just leave, never come back. That was too close a call.

Way too close a call.

When Velma opened her front door, her face shifted into surprise. "Hello."

"Morning, sleepyhead." Evie brushed past her.

Velma followed her back into the living room, which was now blasted with morning light. "I thought you'd done a runner on me."

"Don't be silly. I woke early, thought I'd get breakfast. Coffee and croissants?" She held them up. Her grin felt crazed and her stomach was still unsettled, but she was here. She had to be.

Velma slipped her hands into her pajama pockets and cocked her head to one side. "Well. Aren't you full of surprises. You went out dressed like that?" she asked, nodding at the dress Evie had left wearing, and had no excuse not to return in.

"Sure," Evie said, affecting the petulance of a child star. "Why not?"

Velma chuckled. "Go sit outside. I'll put these on a plate. Might even have a dash of whiskey for that coffee, if that's your poison."

You're my poison.

Velma took the pastries and coffee, pausing to drop a kiss on Evie's lips. She pulled away with an odd smile. Evie's heart stopped—had she tasted the vomit? Had Evie forgotten something, slipped up? "Peppermint."

Evie went to rush a reason—gum, breath mints, toothpaste (all true)—before she realized Velma didn't care: she was already heading for the kitchen.

She'd done it.

She'd fooled her.

Outside on the balcony, the sky was royal blue and thirsty. Evie took a seat at the little table and chairs, grabbing the newspaper. For the first time since waking, she could finally catch her breath. And it was only now, with the sun on her skin, the scent of coffee in the air, that Evie realized what she'd just done.

Retaking the Pretty hadn't been a dilemma or a hard choice. It was a matter of course. It was the only option. The fact she'd just told Krista it would be her last go not even twenty-four hours ago hadn't even crossed her mind.

Because I will never not want this, Evie realized. *The woman. The sex. The view. I want this to be mine.*

And then, suddenly, as dangerous as an unsheathed knife, the next thought.

What if I don't stop?

58.

Willow woke to the familiar sound of traffic bleeding in from the open window. Next to her, Mark slept soundlessly.

Their relationship was over, of course. He had proven himself untrustworthy, and that seemed inevitable. But it was a bitter victory. Because underneath it all, underneath the feeling of Mark's hands on Caroline's body, she sensed his good. She hadn't planned this. She hadn't planned any of it. It had just happened this way, *Caroline* had just happened this way, and there was nothing she could do about it. *It was all already done*, Willow thought. *All already doomed.*

She rolled over, and then she felt it.

A cramp.

A painful punch to the gut.

All sleepiness evaporated. She knew this feeling.

She drew a breath, fast and sharp. No. No, it couldn't be. But one look at her chest, at the two sexless lumps that had replaced Caroline's lush, full breasts, confirmed it.

Willow was back.

How was that possible? Her mind tried grabbing at days—had it been a week? Had the fact she'd been staying up, working all night and not sleeping, prolonged the transformation back? It didn't matter. She didn't even know where the Pretty was. Evie's? Fuck, fuck, *fuck*.

She eased out of the bed, snatched her small pile of clothes, and hurried to the bathroom. Less than a minute and she could be out of— The floorboards next to Mark's bed creaked. Footsteps. He was up, he was already up!

He couldn't find her in his bathroom, how could she possibly explain that? Or where Caroline had gone? She was trapped. In a panic, she tore off her underwear—*Caroline's underwear*—and shoved her clothes behind the toilet.

The footsteps drew closer. He was heading for the bathroom. She hadn't locked the door. Her hand flew toward it just as he twisted the knob from the other side, pulling it open.

Mark's eyes met Willow's. Naked Willow, standing, impossibly, in the middle of his bathroom. His eyes bugged wide. He inhaled hard in shock. "Fuck!" He stumbled back a step. "Fuck, what are you doing here?"

Willow whipped around to grab a towel, turning away to allow herself to reel, to panic. She pulled the towel around her with trembling hands. When she looked up, Mark was scanning the living room, openly desperate.

He's looking for Caroline.

"Surprise." Willow tried hard to smile. "Hi, baby." She squeezed past him, brushing his cheek with dry lips.

"Wh-what?" Mark followed her, eyes wild, as she went into the living room. "How did you get in?"

"My key, silly." Willow's attempt at playful sounded downright crazed. "Thought I'd crawl into bed with you, and . . . surprise you."

Mark's eyes flew down to the duffel bag Willow had left by the door. Without wanting to, she followed his gaze. For a long moment, they both stared silently, intensely, at the bag.

"Planning a trip?" Willow asked brightly. "Don't forget to take me with you."

Mark walked quickly to the kitchen, checking, Willow was sure, that the towheaded Caroline wasn't pressed into its far corners. When he returned, he looked visibly calmer. "Um, yes," he replied. He pounded both fists lightly on the edge of the armchair. "Business trip. I've been trying to tell you. I've been trying to get through to you all week." His tone became accusatory.

"Oh really?" Willow's eyes hardened. "Have you?"

She stalked into the bedroom.

"What are you doing? Where are your clothes? What—" His voice finally cracked. "Fuck, why are you here?"

She didn't bother replying. She dressed in a pair of his jeans, a T-shirt, and flip-flops, all a few sizes too big. Mark watched from the bedroom doorway, fists clenched. When Willow pushed past him, heading back into the living room, he followed her. "What, so that's it?"

"What do you want from me?"

Mark stood, opening and shutting his mouth a few times. Then he raked both hands through his hair and rubbed his eyes. He looked terrible.

"I want you to go," he said. "I just want you to go."

The words hit her with a force she wasn't expecting. She nodded, triumphant and devastated. Her parting blow tasted like metal. "I'm not sure what's worse: you disappointing me, or me thinking you wouldn't."

59.

When the elevator doors to her apartment slid open, Willow felt like she was walking into a lie. The high ceilings, the colorful artworks, and the unearthly quiet all felt foreign and strange.

A new bouquet of flowers sat on the carved white entry table. The gerberas, sunflowers, and pale pink roses were all slightly wilted, as if they'd already been there for a few days. There was a small white envelope with her name on it. She tore it open.

All my love, Mark.

His name struck her in the chest, a sharp and efficient blow. She placed one hand on the vase and neatly knocked it off the table. It shattered spectacularly, bursting apart like a supernova. The sound echoed musically, bouncing off the walls.

Footsteps hurried toward her. Her father appeared from the kitchen. His eyes moved to take in the broken glass, the scattered flowers, and his unmoving, unrepentant daughter, standing silently with icicles in her eyes.

"So," he said. "We're back to this again, are we?" He took off his reading glasses and began wiping them on the edge of his shirt. "If you want my attention, Willow, you can just ask for it."

As if that would work, Willow thought sourly. *Besides, where's the fun in that?*

Her flip-flops crunched over the shards. "Aren't you going to tell me to be careful of the glass, Daddy?"

"You're twenty-one, Willow. I'm sure you're old enough to take care of yourself."

She smirked darkly. "I'm twenty-two."

In the kitchen, she pulled a bottle of white wine from the fridge. Matteo watched impassively as she filled a glass all the way to the rim. "Cheers," she said. She lifted it to her lips and began drinking steadily. After three sips, Matteo interrupted her in a strained voice. "Willow, stop. I can't . . ."

She paused, her throat burning pleasantly. "Can't what?"

"I can't watch you do that."

"Oh *god*." She slammed the glass down so hard she was surprised it didn't shatter. "Don't try and start now."

"Start what?"

She slit her eyes at him. "Trying to be a good father."

Matteo thumped the kitchen counter in anger. "I was home for every one of your birthdays, Willow, every one! I was home for Christmas, home for Thanksgiving. Do you know what I sacrificed for that? How many films I had to turn down because of you?"

"You're my father, of course you had to be there for my birthdays!" Willow cried. "That's your *job*—"

"No, my job was being a filmmaker," Matteo said. "A job that was significantly compromised—" His hand flew to his mouth and jaw, as if something awful—the truth—had just crawled out of it.

Willow reeled, swaying back a few inches. She snapped back, her voice a hiss. "Maybe you should've thought more about your precious career before you decided to breed."

The words jettisoned out of him. "It wasn't a decision I made."

Willow felt like he'd just struck her across the face. Her vision swam. For a long moment, neither said a word.

Matteo stumbled forward a few steps, his voice thick now, and pleading. "Willow. I love you. I've always loved you. I'm sorry. Please forgive me. I lost my temper, I'm sorry."

But Willow wasn't listening to him. A memory was forming, finally, a complete picture allowing itself to be seen. "That's why," she whispered. "That's why I'm . . . Because you . . ." Willow focused on her father. "I must've been six, or maybe seven, so it must've been in the old apartment on Seventy-Fifth. I remember standing in the doorway and seeing you. You were with that makeup artist you always worked with. The blond one. The pretty one. I remember her name." She looked at him evenly. "Caroline."

Matteo raised a shaking, gnarled hand to his forehead and pressed it between his eyes.

And now Willow felt as if the memory was lifting her and taking from her and intruding into her all at once, many fingers, many hands, showing her what she knew to be true. "And I remember thinking you were hurting her, because you both looked like you were in pain. I know now, of course, that you were"—Willow drew in a shaky breath— "fucking her. In our kitchen. In Mom's kitchen. And I know she wasn't the last and I'm guessing she wasn't the first. And after you both noticed me standing there, you told me if I didn't tell Mom you'd buy me a present, so I didn't, and you did. You kept your promise." Her words dripped sarcasm. "Like a good father would."

Tears glided down Willow's cheeks, and her heart, her heart was shattering into a thousand pieces of fiery light, carried away by dark rushing water. "You have no idea, *no idea*, how much you've poisoned me."

60

"Hey." Krista rapped on Tristan's trailer door. "Morning, T-Bird."

"What's up, L.P." He patted a spot on the sofa next to him. "Damian just dropped off a new call sheet for today. We're doing scene sixty-one."

"Which one's that?" Krista flipped through her script. "Oh." She looked up at Tristan, suddenly speechless.

Tristan found the page too. "Ah," he said, his tone changing. "The kissing scene."

Of course, Krista knew they had a kissing scene. Last week she'd been relishing the prospect. But now it felt weird. Tristan was her friend. Friends don't kiss. Krista wasn't sure where to look. "Do you still want to run lines?" she asked.

Tristan shook his head a tiny bit. "Of course. Some of the older kids had to do kissing scenes in *Heartache*; they're not romantic. Or, you know, sexy . . ." His voice drifted off, but the word *sexy* hung in the air.

Krista felt a weird thrill spark out from her chest. She got to her feet quickly and trained her eyes on the script. "Let's take it from my line, 'I've never had a more fun summer.' "

"Okay." Tristan stood opposite her.

She took a moment to connect to her character's spirit animal, a baby unicorn. Then she said, "I've never had a more fun summer, Zach."

Tristan returned her gaze. "Me neither. When Arj and I started working here, I didn't think there was anything, or anyone, here for me. But now I think, maybe I was wrong."

He took a step toward her and placed a hand on her forearm. A *zing* of energy shot up her arm, so unexpected she yelped.

"What?" Tristan broke character.

"Nothing." Krista rubbed her arm. "I just feel a little parched."

"Me too." Tristan sprang for the sink, filling two glasses of water. They drank them all in one go without making eye contact.

"From the top?" Tristan asked.

Krista nodded, trying to clear her head. *Professional. Professional. Professional.* "I've never had a more fun summer, Zach."

"Me neither. When Arj and I started working here, I didn't think there was anything, or anyone, here for me. But now I think, maybe I was wrong."

This time, she absorbed his touch easily. "What do you mean?"

"I mean, you're here for me. Aren't you?"

Krista stepped forward, closing the distance between them. Now they were only inches apart. Her heart was racing. "Yes, Zach. I am."

Tristan swallowed, unmoving.

Krista raised her eyebrows and whispered, "This is the part when you kiss me."

"Right." Tristan looked as if he was in pain, his voice a whisper too. "Just feels weird."

"I know," she said. They were practically in each other's arms.

"You're my friend," he said. His fingers pressed into her arms, as if exploring her skin.

"I know."

"And friends don't . . ."

"Kiss." The word was as soft as lamb's wool.

They locked eyes.

Tristan dropped his mouth to Krista's, and suddenly he was kissing her. Like he fucking *meant* it. Krista was so stunned that it took a hot second before instinct kicked in and she started kissing him back. She pulled him close, her hands wanting to be in his hair, around his neck, on his chest, all at once. They tumbled onto the sofa, all lips, and hands, and heavy hot breath. After what had to be a full minute, Tristan pulled back from Krista, in a series of soft, slow pecks.

He opened his eyes. Started back.

Without a word, he got to his feet and left the trailer.

Krista was left alone, one hand brushing her lips in stunned, dumb-founded amazement.

What?

The?

Fuck?

61.

"Morning, Kelly!" Evie sang out as she swept into his office.

"Chloe-with-a-C." Kelly looked up from his computer. "You're in a good mood."

"It's seventy-two degrees in New York City and I have the best job in the whole world, what's not to like?" Evie chirruped. "This is for you. Double macchiato, extra froth." She placed the cup on Kelly's desk. "*And a raspberry and white chocolate muffin. Your favorite.*"

Kelly narrowed his eyes. "What do you want, Chloe?"

Evie pressed her hand into her chest in exaggerated shock. "I am outraged you'd think I'd stoop so low as to *bribe* you. But now that you mention it, I did have an idea I wanted to discuss with you. Have you heard of the Arzners?"

"The awards show for chicks?"

Ignoring the word *chicks*, Evie beamed enthusiastically. "Exactly! *'Named after one of Hollywood's first female directors, the Arzners bring Hollywood's best and brightest together to celebrate the stunning contribution women make every year to the arts.'*" Evie quoted the website verbatim. "*Extra Salt* could do a live stream of the red carpet. An extraspecial *Extra Salt* event."

Kelly frowned. "I don't hate it," he admitted. "It's probably a fit. But I'd never get you press passes. We're not big enough, mate. We're just a web series."

"I thought of that. You remember Cupcake Girl?"

Kelly snorted. "How could I forget?"

"I kind of know her. Lenka. We went to college together."

"You know her?" Kelly sounded annoyed. "Then why'd you talk me out of featuring her?"

Evie remembered making a passionate case for Dildo of the Week after Krista went viral, in order to minimize Lenka Penka's exposure. "I didn't think she'd remember me. But she did! She's shooting a movie with Tristan McKell. Strings were pulled. And . . ." Evie held up a handful of lanyards, all emblazoned with the word Press. "Ta-da."

"Wow." Kelly sat back in his seat, stunned. "When's the ceremony?"

"Carpet starts at 4 p.m. next Tuesday. Marcello can be there, and Gemma and Rose are waiting for your approval to start sourcing a dress." Evie tried not to look smug. "So . . . that's a yes?"

"Yeah," Kelly replied. "Sure."

Evie backed toward the door. "Thanks, Kelly! You won't regret this!" Her mind was racing. It worked!

She passed Marcello, stationed outside Kelly's office, surreptitiously eavesdropping, eyes gleaming. "Phase one is complete," he said, offering a fist.

Evie bumped it, returning his grin. "Time for phase two."

62.

"Lenka, sweetie." Ora waggled a tube of lipstick at her. "Stop chewing your lips, you keep eating the lipstick off!"

Krista glanced up at the head makeup artist guiltily. "Sorry, Ora."

"What's got your goat, huh?"

The kissing scene. They were shooting it this afternoon. What if Tristan couldn't go through with it? She couldn't bear being the reason for him screwing up a second time. Plus she knew Gillian was itching, just *itching*, for an excuse to fire her again and she absolutely had to pay Evie back for the bills: she'd promised.

He was just being so *weird*. They'd ended up next to each other in the lunch line. At first he could barely look at her, then he laughed too hard at a lame joke she'd made. It was almost like he was nervous around her.

Greg wanted the kissing scene to take place in the "golden hour," the short window of warm, late-afternoon light before the sun set. The crew darted around, busy as ants before a storm. Tristan wasn't anywhere to be seen.

"Okay, everyone, first positions," Min called. "We're losing light, so we're shooting the rehearsal."

Someone asked Krista to close her eyes so they could powder her face. When she opened them, Tristan was standing in front of her. His hair was set into full boy-band glory, while his eyes looked as soulful as a sad puppy. He looked like an album cover.

"Hi," she said.

"Hi." He smiled back timidly, sending a flurry of butterflies whirling through her.

"Remember," she whispered. "Rawr."

He nodded, obviously recalling the lion-centric sexual chemistry they'd created in his trailer. But pulling off the scene didn't feel as important to Krista as making sure things were okay with Tristan. Both outcomes felt tenuous.

The crew calls began, then Greg called, "Action."

Krista gazed up at Tristan. "I've never had a more fun summer, Zach," she said truthfully.

Tristan took Krista's hands. They were damp with sweat. "Me neither. When Arj and I started working here, I didn't think there was anything, or anyone, here for me." He rubbed his thumb over hers. The effect almost made her swoon. "But now I think, maybe I was wrong."

Krista shook her head. "What do you mean?"

Tristan searched her eyes with his. "I mean, you're here for me. Aren't you?"

Krista moved toward Tristan, instinctively wanting to be closer. "Yes, Zach," she whispered throatily. "I am."

And in this moment they really were just two kids who found love one summer, two people whose hearts had connected, whose souls had intertwined. Even though this wasn't the first time Tristan's mouth had met hers, in this moment, it was. All the nerves, and excitement, and the wonder of true love found its way to both of them as their lips met. Sweetly. Passionately. In a way that felt like forever.

"Cut!" called Greg. He sounded amazed. "Fuck, that was awesome!" A few of the crew members even started clapping. "Uh, guys?" Greg called. "I said *cut*."

Tristan and Krista had not stopped kissing. Tristan cupped the back of Krista's head, and she responded in turn by crushing herself against him, oblivious of her surroundings. When they did break apart, a full minute later, they both started laughing. Tristan touched his lips to

Krista's forehead. She wrapped her arms around his iron-strong waist and squeezed, feeling simultaneously protective and protected.

Two things immediately became obvious.

Krista had just nailed her most important scene. And Lenka Penka and Tristan McKell were officially a thing.

63

Over the next week, Evie alternated between preparing for the Arzners and becoming increasingly besotted with Velma Wolff.

One night they stayed in and watched old episodes of *The L Word*. Evie teased Velma for liking Jenny, the precocious self-obsessed femme who could make someone's funeral all about her, while Evie confessed her attraction to Marina, the sexy, shark-eyed European who alternated carnal conquests with running a successful small business. They only made it to the first sex scene before ending up in bed.

Later that week, they went to the opening of a play that one of Velma's friends had written. The show was quite good—an absurdist drama about a scorpion who gave relationship advice in between managing a Wendy's—but what Evie really liked was the after-party. Photographers requested pictures, and Evie found herself arm in arm with Velma, both smirking like they had secrets. She was becoming one of the women in Velma's Google search. But she knew she was more than that.

Velma didn't look at her like they were just flirting. Like Evie was just someone she enjoyed having sex with. She *really* looked at her. As if she could see past Chloe's pretty mask and into the fissures of Evie's soul.

Being apart was unbelievably stressful. When Velma didn't reply immediately to texts, anxiety would build in Evie's chest like a nightmarish storm, chipping at her sanity and kidnapping her concentration. When they weren't together, Evie lost all sense of certainty: Velma was too distant, she mustn't be into it. Evie found herself staring intently at the bottle of Pretty, calculating how much was left. Even with the three of them all using it, they'd barely skimmed the surface. But it wouldn't last forever. Even though she knew Krista wouldn't approve, she'd made a note of Penny's address: 500 Park. Was it possible to get more? They really shouldn't be taking it for so long that it would ever come up. But what if things with Velma got more serious?

Every metaphor for love being a drug now made sense. Being apart from Velma was like going cold turkey: an exercise in physical and emotional pain.

This anxiety would evaporate as soon as Evie got her hit of Velma's presence. Her lupine eyes and her gap-toothed smile were an elixir that cured every ailment, fizzing scars away to leave unblemished skin. Whether Velma wanted it or not, she could tell they were falling for each other. The loft was starting to feel less fantastic, more familiar. The front door lock was dodgy (Velma kept forgetting to tell the super), which meant Evie could open it without a key. Every time she pushed the door open, it felt more and more like she was coming home.

On the weekend, Velma suggested they see the writer Chess Hudsen do a reading at Word Nerd, a cute bookstore in the East Village. Evie asked if the two had ever been involved, having seen pictures of them together online. "Briefly," Velma replied. "But we worked out we're better as friends." This struck Evie as being incredibly adult. She'd cross state lines to avoid her college girlfriend, a drama-thick love affair that had ended with light stalking and heavy drinking.

There was a line out the door by the time they arrived, but Velma bypassed everyone waiting, to be greeted enthusiastically by the guy with the clipboard. Inside, they had reserved seats, right at the front. Multiple people asked Velma for a picture, shy and excited. Evie wondered if this would ever get annoying, being the girlfriend of a literary superstar. Perhaps, she conceded, one day. For now, it just made her feel special.

After the reading, Chess, Velma, Evie, and a handful of others went to a cozy Italian restaurant for a late supper. Over plates of buffalo mozzarella and handmade gnocchi, the conversation drifted from publishing politics to the New York theater scene to a playful argument over who was the bigger brat, Chess or Velma. Velma kept her hand on Evie's knee, generating both a low buzz of desire between her legs and a warm, comforting glow of belonging to someone, part of a team. Red wine flowed freely. The more Evie drank, the more she felt convinced of the night's wonder. Here she was, Evie Selby, the girl no one asked to prom, the girl who lost her virginity only three short years ago, with a table of artists and thinkers and professionals in their prime, in New York City.

Their sex was insistent, urgent, and dramatic, recalling Rachmaninoff in size and scope. Evie shouted her orgasms. She did not moan or whimper: she screamed until her throat was sore. One morning she lost her voice. But despite the regularity, Evie could never get close enough to Velma. And not just because Velma refused to let her penetrate her, preferring exclusively clitoral orgasms. She just wanted more: more of her past, more of her attention. More intimacy. Velma came with her eyes closed, while Evie's were wide open, searching, demanding to meet her lover's. She evaded sleep with questions, reaching out to tug a lock of Velma's hair and ask something like, "Do you think you're a good writer?"

A sex-weary Velma smiled at Evie with tired indulgence. "I think other people think I'm good," she replied. "And I've learned to appreciate what other people think."

"Why?"

"Because it's a lot better than listening to what I think."

Evie nodded in understanding.

"But that doesn't mean I like all my books." Velma suppressed a yawn.

"What do you mean?"

"*Underskin* was terrible. Even for a debut."

Evie lit up with surprise. "No, it wasn't!"

"It was."

"It's a cult book."

"And cults are not exactly known for their good judgment. Except when it comes to inventive ways to kill people."

Evie raised her eyebrows. She simply could not accept this about the novel that sparked a literary love affair. "It was universally adored."

"It was not," Velma refuted, rearranging her pillows. "That's simply not possible. The universe has seven billion people. I hate to break it to you," she added, "but some people don't like the Beatles."

Evie affected mock horror. "No."

"They hate Joni Mitchell."

"Stop."

"They think *Ghostbusters* is stupid."

Evie narrowed her eyes. "I would kill them if I had the means."

Velma chuckled. Evie snuggled closer, wanting to lay her head on Velma's chest, but not wanting to lose sight of her face. "Okay. I get what you're saying. There are probably some terrible reviews, somewhere—"

"There's lots," Velma countered. "If you look for them. I don't look for them. Not anymore. This is what I've learned about all that: you see what you want to see." Velma's gaze moved around Evie's face in a way that felt more intimate than a kiss. "You really are exquisite, Chloe." She yawned, her words thick and exhausted. "You're poetry."

The experience of becoming Evie Selby in Velma's bed had not left her unscathed. A stash of Tums, bleach, and paper towels was quietly hidden in the main and guest bathrooms. She'd even brought over a pair of old glasses to hide in the bedside table. Pausing at the bedroom doorway, Evie checked that Velma was sufficiently distracted with their dinner order. "Indian or Japanese?" Velma called, without looking up.

Evie wrinkled her nose. "If I eat another blue crab hand roll, I'm going to turn into one."

"Vindaloos it is."

Evie smiled and pulled the bedroom door shut. Quickly, she crossed to her side of the bed, removing the old glasses from her pocket. They weren't as thick or striking as the frames she wore now. She'd worn these freshman year. Holding them reminded her of bad cafeteria food that always smelled like chicken fingers, cramped quarters with Krista, and thrilling collective meetings that ran late into the night. The world was revealing itself to her back then, and she was hungry for it, hungry to make a change and leave her mark.

Back then, she could never, ever have been convinced of her current situation: hiding a pair of glasses to avoid another stupid mistake. Because Evie Selby tried hard not to make stupid mistakes.

The thought of losing herself—her clever, careful, rational self—gripped her. Who was this entitled idiot, this girl who rolled her eyes at too much sushi? Had this girl lost touch with her ideals, her standards, the essence of her being?

Because she'd certainly lost touch with her friends.

Willow.

Where was Willow?

Evie tightened her grip, only then remembering she still held her glasses. She hid them in the bedside table drawer and she sank down onto the edge of the mattress.

After their fight about the photos, Willow had stopped staying at the apartment or picking up Evie's calls. But to be honest, Evie had stopped making them. Taking on the problem of Willow forced her to become Evie Selby again, when really, she was far more comfortable being Chloe Fontaine.

Shame and guilt overwhelmed her, as if Willow were a dinner date she'd forgotten and only just remembered, three hours too late. Quietly, she tiptoed to the doorway and edged open the door. Velma's head was bent to her phone, oblivious. Evie pulled the door shut again and crept into the bathroom off Velma's bedroom, locking the door behind her. Something about having to call Willow—as Evie, while still Chloe—made her feel particularly exposed. She dialed Willow's number. Voicemail.

"Willow, it's Evie. I'm sorry I haven't been in touch. Can you just let me know you're okay? Otherwise I'll assume you're dead and call the police." She meant it as a joke, but it probably didn't come across that way.

An hour later, as Evie sat with her legs braided with Velma's on the sectional, she received a text: not dead. preparing for my show. Evie checked the Wythe Gallery website. Caroline's tear-streaked face filled the screen. The show name screamed at her in neon-yellow caps: BEAUTY IS A WITCH. Evie's stomach kicked with anxiety. "Jesus Christ."

Velma looked up from her notebook. "What?"

After a second's hesitation, Evie turned her phone around. "Catchy title, no?"

"It's Shakespeare," Velma said. "*Much Ado*, I believe." She squinted, conjuring up the words. "'*Let every eye negotiate for itself, And trust no agent; for beauty is a witch, Against whose charms faith melteth in blood.*'"

Evie smiled. "Impressive."

Velma gave a tiny shrug, reading the website on Evie's phone. "Willow Alice Hendriksen. That's Matteo Hendriksen's daughter, right?"

Evie nodded. "She's a . . . friend." Willow's show left a bad taste in her mouth. "I need to make a call."

On the balcony, Evie wrapped her arms around herself as she found the number. The air was fresh tonight. Below her, the sweep of the city glittered back at her.

Her city.

Her New York.

"Hello?" The male voice that answered sounded surprised.

"Mark, hi, it's Evie."

There was a pause. "Yeah, I have your number in my phone."

"How are you?"

His reply was uncharacteristically clipped. "Fine."

"Have you spoken to Willow lately? I've been staying at my—" Evie almost said *girlfriend's*, but stopped herself just in time. "Friend's house, so I don't know if she's been at the apartment."

Another long pause. Then, in a colorless voice, Mark said, "Willow and I broke up."

Evie almost dropped the phone. "What?"

"We broke up."

Willow and Mark broke up? *Willow and Mark?* "Oh shit. But . . . why? What happened?"

"That's my business, Evie."

Evie rubbed her face, distressed. "Mark, I'm worried about her. It's a pretty weird time for us all right now."

"What do you mean?"

Evie glanced at her reflection in the glass balcony doors. She was wearing Velma's robe, Evie's underwear, and Chloe's skin. "Just your twenties, I guess," she replied faintly. "They're kind of a wild ride."

There was muffled noise on the other end of the line, like Mark was covering up the speaker. Then his voice reappeared, crisp and efficient. "I have to go."

"Wait! Mark . . . what's going on? You don't sound like . . . you."

Mark huffed out a breath, irritated. "I'm still me. Willow's still Willow. It just didn't work out."

"But—" Evie wasn't sure, but she thought she heard a female voice.

"I have to go," he repeated. "I'm with someone."

Evie's mouth dropped open. "Another girl?"

"Good-bye, Evie." The line went dead.

Evie stared at the phone as if it had just gained sentience. What was going on? Mark wasn't a dick. Mark marched in Take Back the Night rallies and actually listened to her feminist rants. If Mark and Willow couldn't make it, who could?

When she came back inside, Velma told her she looked troubled. Evie regarded her, curled on the couch like a feline, her blond hair tousled and golden.

"I feel troubled," Evie said in a small voice.

Velma's lips curved into a smile, lazy as smoke. The sight softened the anxiety in Evie's throat. "Baby," Velma said. "Come here."

Evie curled into Velma's open arms, pressing her forehead onto her lover's. Velma's face kaleidoscoped into three, four different versions of herself, refusing to settle into a single image.

64.

Being Tristan McKell's unconfirmed, alleged love toy had its ups and downs.

The downside was: paparazzi.

Legit paparazzi.

Krista had been leaving her apartment building in South Williamsburg, predawn, precoffee, when a swarm descended on her, flashes popping like broken strobe lights. She'd stumbled back, dazed and confused, swatting at them like flies before Eduardo hustled her into the car. It wasn't until he said the word, in his soft Mexican accent, that she understood what had just happened.

At first, she was excited. Paparazzi! Like in the movies, like in the magazines!

Then the article came out.

Bizarrely, it wasn't something Lana or Greg or even Cameron had warned her about. She'd simply picked up one of the gossip mags in the hair and makeup trailer and there she was. On the front freakin' cover. Face blotchy, eyes half open, under a bright red headline that screamed with all the subtlety of a freight train: "Stars Without Makeup!"

When Ora asked her what was wrong, she couldn't even answer. She just held it up.

Her makeup artist clucked sympathetically. "That's not very nice, is it?"

"It certainly is *not*." Krista stared at the picture mournfully. "It was 5 a.m.! It was 5 fucking a.m. and I was on my way here. To hair and makeup!"

Ora patted her on the shoulder. "That's when you know you've made it, pet. When the rag mags take a swipe at you."

Krista threw the magazine into the trash, feeling horrible. It seemed like an awfully high price to pay. On top of that, it just seemed *mean*.

The upside was she was getting a lot of oral sex.

A lot.

Whenever she and Tristan weren't on set, his nose was between her legs in the twin bed in Tristan's trailer. At first, this was more than enough. Scurrying off to go at it in between setups, lazing around in a Sunday-morning kind of way when in reality it was a weekday afternoon: all very satisfying. Plus, Evie had been right about Tristan. The kid really was the king of cunnilingus. It felt like he could unlock his lower jaw like a serpent. Tongue: velvet. Stamina: superhuman.

But after a week of oral and nothing but oral, it was actually getting frustrating. She wanted *all* of Tristan. But every time her fingers started heading south he'd pull them up or wriggle away. Tristan didn't want to have sex with her. As in, pee-in-the-vee sex. Eventually, she just had to ask. "T?"

Tristan lifted his head, wiping his mouth. "Yeah, babe?"

"Are you a virgin?"

She was hoping for surprised laughter or vehement denial. But instead, Tristan glanced at the closed trailer door. "We probably need to get to set—"

"We have an hour." She gave him her best *you're not getting out of this* face.

Tristan drew in a deep breath. Unconsciously, Krista did the same. In a quiet, confessional voice, Tristan said, "I'm not a virgin, Lenks. But . . . there is something."

A flash flood of worst-case scenarios: STD, married, could only do it dressed like an adult baby. "What is it?"

Tristan ran both hands through his hair. All color had drained from his face. "Okay. I'm ready." He leveled his gaze at her. "I like you, Lenka. I think we have a connection. A connection that goes beyond the physical. Don't you agree?"

Krista pressed her lips together, wholly unsure of where this was going. "Mm-hmm."

"I don't believe that love can only be experienced by a man and a woman. It can be a man and a man, or a woman and a woman."

"Well, duh." Krista squinted at him. "Are you saying you want a threesome? 'Cause I've totally done that, like, a million times—"

"No, what I'm saying is, couples don't necessarily need a . . ." He paused, frowning.

"A what?"

He cocked his head at her. "You know how blind people have a great sense of smell?"

"Tristan!" Krista exclaimed. "Just tell me what the fuck you're trying to tell me!"

"Okay!" He took both of Krista's hands in his and squeezed them. "Lenka. I have . . . a micropenis."

Krista blinked. "Cool," she said. "What's that?"

Tristan looked genuinely surprised. "A micropenis. You've never heard of a micropenis?"

Krista shook her head. "Nope." Relief was edging its way into her veins. He wasn't married, didn't have an STD, and didn't want to get into a diaper and have her bottle-feed him. All of this was good.

"A micropenis."

"Okay."

"Do you know what I mean?"

"No."

"Micro," he repeated. "Penis. Micropenis. Almost a million guys in the US have one."

"Oh!" The strange term finally registered something. "You mean, like . . . you have a small dick?"

Tristan nodded. "Not just small. Very small." He studied Krista anxiously.

"That's okay," Krista ventured. "I like a big dick as much as the next girl, but once I fucked this Korean basketball player who wasn't packing much. I mean, he had girth, you know, but not length. Wasn't even four inches, and it still felt pretty good."

"That's not exactly—I'm not exactly like that guy."

"I know," Krista said. "You're not Korean."

"That's not what I—"

"Tris!" Krista cut him off. "Dude. I'm kind of done with talking." She leaned toward him and gently kissed his lips. "Sometimes, talking kills the vibe." She kissed him again, letting her lips linger. "When what we should really be doing is talking with our clothes off. Do you know what I mean?"

Tristan nodded as Krista kissed him again.

"So maybe we should just get naked and see what happens," she whispered.

"Okay," Tristan said uncertainly.

Krista flipped the light switch, sending the small bedroom into near blackness. "Better?"

"Yeah."

So the guy wasn't packing an anaconda. So they wouldn't be able to use his penis to jump rope with. It could've been worse. In seconds she had his T-shirt off over his head. Her fingers ran over his stomach, and she gasped. His abs were *perfect*. Christmas morning perfect.

Krista pulled off her top and shoved his hands onto her chest. On feeling her breasts, enormous in a push-up bra worn exactly for this occasion, Tristan let out a moan.

Of their own accord, her hands began undoing his belt buckle. This time, he let her. Soon only boxer briefs stood between him and nakedness. Glorious, wonderful nakedness. She hooked her fingers around his underwear.

"Wait," Tristan said. "Are you sure you're ready?"

"Dude," she breathed, "I was born ready." In two seconds flat, his boxers were around his ankles.

This was it. Her fingers moved over the light hair of his thigh, through the coarse pubic hair around his cock . . . and past it, to the top of his other thigh. She dove back in, groping through his pubic hair, not finding anything more than a small bump. Tristan groaned. "Yeah," he panted. "That's it."

Krista pulled back and uneasily flipped on the light.

Tristan's naked form became fully illuminated. His perfect six-pack. His muscular thighs. And . . . his complete lack of a penis. Nothing but the small bump she'd been touching. Krista's jaw loosened, the truth landing like a grenade. *That was it.* That was his penis. His micropenis. It was the size of a button mushroom.

"Babe?" he asked. "Are you okay?"

A voice inside her was telling her to calm down, to not hurt Tristan's feelings, but that voice was being drowned out by a wild whirling, a terrific crashing. Panic welled inside her, hot and insistent. "I, uh, didn't expect it to be so small."

"Compared to some, it's actually on the larger side."

"Compared to what?" Krista's voice cracked. "Baby mice?"

"Lenka." Tristan sat up. Krista jerked away, but Tristan took her hands, his voice stern. "Listen to me. We all have things that aren't perfect about us. But this is what a relationship is—showing each other the things that make us imperfect."

Krista was trying to look at him, but her eyes keep drifting down to the absence between his legs.

"I can still make you come," he said. "With my hands. With my tongue. With a vibrator. So can we at least give it a try?" He fixed his soulful gaze on her. "Please?"

Krista swallowed. "Sure." She nodded, unsure who in the room she was trying to convince.

"Good." He cupped the back of her neck and brought her head toward his. He kissed her gently, again and again, until her shoulders relaxed. His hands raised to fondle her breasts, and in response she pushed her chest toward him automatically, her body moving with muscle memory, with desire.

Once again, her hands drifted down.

She touched the tiny lump.

Tristan moaned. "Oh, Lenka."

Button mushroom.

"Lenka."

Baby mice.

"Lenka—"

"I can't!" Krista pulled away. "I just—Tris, I can't."

Tristan rolled onto his back and let out a frustrated groan. All the lust, all the excitement that had been building up inside her deflated, leaving a painful empty hollow. The illusion, the magic, had disappeared, like the lights being switched on at the end of a middle school disco, revealing the space to be nothing but a school hall.

Krista drew her knees up to her chest. "You must think I'm so superficial."

Tristan took a moment to answer. "You have expectations. All beautiful women do."

Krista shook her head. "But I'm not even . . ." She was a hypocrite. Krista Kumar wasn't perfect. And here she was rejecting Tristan McKell, beautiful, sweet Tristan McKell over one tiny thing.

One seriously tiny thing.

"I'm going to go." She fumbled for her clothes and started pulling them back on.

"Lenka, wait."

"You deserve someone so much better than me." She jammed her shoes on. "I'm sorry, Tristan."

"Lenka!" Tristan swung his feet onto the floor. "Wait. Let's just talk—"

"I'm sorry!" Krista pulled the trailer door open, stumbling on her undone laces. She flew straight into a sea of bodies, tripping over someone, landing on her hands and knees.

"Lenka!"

Around her, a collective intake of breath. A sudden freezing of motion.

Damian was herding a crowd of thirty or so extras past Tristan's trailer. Kids, she remembered, for a crowd scene later that afternoon. Krista had landed among them, knocking a young boy over as she fell.

But that wasn't why everyone was staring.

Tristan stood in his open trailer doorway. Paralyzed. Naked. With his lack of a penis on full display.

Krista saw the girl who moved first. The extra couldn't have been more than ten, her hair in two pigtails. Her jaw was unhinged, but her hand moved like lightning. Krista didn't even have time to turn her head before she heard the solitary click of an iPhone camera.

65.

For most *Salty* readers, the idea of walking a red carpet was a glittery wet dream. The attention, the glory, the dress that was worth the GDP of a small country. Evie Selby did not share this dream. Her experience with red-carpet fashion was limited to what she'd copyedited: "Oops! Ten Red-Carpet Mistakes A-Listers Are Still Making" (nasty) or "Chatting Snap: How to Pose for Paparazzi" (ridiculous). Which was why, on exiting the SUV that was transporting her, Rich, Marcello, and the camera guy, Adrian, to the press entry for the Arzners, her first instinct was to tell the driver to turn around and take them all back to Brooklyn.

The scene before them was chaotic, buzzing with fresh, nervous energy. Prom night on steroids. Dozens of people were scurrying about, some speaking into earpieces, some barking orders into cell phones. Evie's fellow reporters were recognizable as the only ones in designer gowns. The effect was vaguely unnerving. It reminded Evie of the time she'd arrived at a fancy dress party dressed as a shrimp, only to discover the only other person in costume was a drunk guy wearing a barrel-sized jar of mayonnaise. He'd followed her all night, glassy-eyed and beer-breathed, repeating, "Shrimp cocktail? Hey? Shrimp cocktail?"

Evie negotiated the crowds to an area hung with banners announcing itself as Press Check-In, flashing the lanyards Tristan friggin' McKell had helped them procure. The woman who crossed their names off handed Evie a press release emblazoned with Revlon's logo, and told them they'd find *Extra Salt*'s allocated spot in the Print, Radio, and Online section, past the photographers and TV crews. Evie was so riddled with nerves she had to have this information repeated several times. The woman flashed her an encouraging smile. "You'll be fine. You look gorgeous," she added, as if this alone was success enough.

Gemma and Rose had procured for Chloe a floor-length cream silk gown, which they'd assured her was understated but classy, with just the right hint of sex appeal. Evie felt like she was wearing a nightie. But at the end of the day, it didn't really matter. All she needed the dress to do was pass as normal red-carpet attire.

Velma will be able to see me in this dress, she thought, before realizing it was the first time she'd thought about Velma all afternoon. She was so in the zone that separation was actually bearable, but only just.

They flashed their passes at several sets of security. And then, there it was.

The pathway of the privileged.

The most auspicious flooring of them all.

The carpet.

Evie felt both over- and underwhelmed. After all, it was just a temporary structure, not more than a hundred feet of red, leading toward an auditorium where the ceremony would be taking place. It was hardly the Eiffel Tower or the Taj Mahal. But at the same time, Evie's heart leaped about her chest like a bouncy ball. She was really here. This was really happening.

They found their spot on the sidelines, demarcated with a paper printout. Behind them, rows of fans stood craning their necks for the first sniff of celeb. Organizers milled about, seemingly oblivious to the growing crowd. While Rich helped Adrian set up the best angles, Marcello dabbed at Evie's sticky forehead. "Are you ready?" he asked.

She nodded, trying to appear confident. "Take these." She pushed her index cards of notes into his hands. "I can't have them on camera." She also didn't want Rich to see them.

Marcello slipped them into the pocket of his electric-blue blazer. Today, the fedora matched the chains around his neck: gold. "You look the part," he murmured. "No one suspects a thing. Just relax, and do everything like we planned."

"Right." Evie wet her dry lips. "Just like we planned."

Marcello gave her a wink and melted off.

"Kelly wants you to wear this." Rich handed her a small silver earpiece.

She heard Kelly's tinny voice. "G'day, love. Hear me okay?"

"Loud and clear."

"Great. Just wanted to remind you about the Trifecta of Terrific."

"The what?"

"Dress, love, role," Kelly said. "Dress: what they're wearing, who the designer is. Love: how's their love life, what's up with their kids or when are they going to have them. And role: plugging their next movie. Short, sharp sound bites."

Inwardly, Evie rolled her eyes. Outwardly, she nodded efficiently. "Got it."

"I'll be feeding you who to speak to, what to say—"

"I've already done my questions."

"Mate, it's your first time doing a live stream. I'm here to help."

"But—"

"Chloe, I'm the producer. You hear it, you say it."

Evie bit the inside of her cheek. "Absolutely, Kelly. No problem."

"All right. I'll be back when it starts."

Minutes passed, the tension rising every second. Rich got Evie to run practice openings into a fat cordless microphone with a hot pink clip-on attachment that read *Extra Salt* on all four sides, and offered suggestions for interview topics Evie nodded at but ignored. It was all treading water. There was no denying what the main event was. At exactly 4 p.m., a roar swept the now-sizable crowd. Evie spun around. Coming around the corner, surrounded by a clutch of regularly dressed handlers, was the actress Olivia Wilde.

"Showtime." Kelly was back in her ear.

Adrian shouldered the camera. "All set?" Rich called.

Evie raised the microphone to her lips. She flashed on seeing Velma Wolff for the first time, in the elevator in the Heimert Schwartz building. How afraid she'd been then, how insecure. Seeing Olivia, in a glittery frock that'd make the Milky Way feel underdressed, threatened to unleash that familiar wave of nerves.

But she didn't let the wave break.

"All set," she said. The light on the camera switched to red. Rolling.

Evie took a deep breath and flashed a confident smile straight down the lens. "Hi, I'm Chloe Fontaine, coming at you live from the red carpet for the Arzners, the annual awards show that celebrates women in film and television." She took a few steps toward the red rope that separated the reporters from the carpet. From the corner of her eye, she saw Rich give her an encouraging smile. "While there's a lot to celebrate, we still have a long way to go. So tonight, *Extra Salt* gets up close and personal with your favorite celebs to ask them: How can we change Hollywood to make it more sassy, less sexist?"

Rich's smile wavered. His expression morphed to confused. "Ah, Chloe?" she heard Kelly say. "What the fuck was that?"

Olivia's people were herding her down the line of reporters. Evie jostled into position, trying to angle her body toward the camera, keep her smile fixed in place, and remember Olivia's questions. Adrian's camera followed her obediently. After a few odd seconds of dead air, the actress was right in front of her. "H-hello," Evie said, raising her voice to be heard above the screaming crowd. "Good afternoon."

Olivia cocked an eyebrow. Evie felt a spike of embarrassment. "Good afternoon to you."

"Right, she's got a kid," Kelly said. "Ask her about work-life balance."

Evie's words came in a garbled, skittish rush. "Chloe from *Extra Salt* this is a great event celebrating women in film and television but we still don't have enough good roles for women how do you think we can change that?"

"What the— No!" Kelly shouted in her ear. "Jesus F. Christ, Chloe, I said work-life balance—"

In one smooth motion, Evie plucked the silver earpiece out of her ear. Olivia blinked, taken aback. "I'm sorry, could you repeat that?"

Evie repeated her question, trying not to sound like a speed freak. "I'm interested in how you think we can change gender inequality in Hollywood."

Olivia bit back a smile.

Oh god, Evie thought, *I've done something wrong.*

"Wow, I've never been asked about gender inequality on the carpet before." Olivia met Evie's eyes evenly. "Look, that's a great question. It's really hard to get stories that are about women made, stories that aren't just about women being obsessed with or supporting men. We've got a lock on those films, seriously."

"How can we change that?" Evie asked.

"It's really important for women to write, direct, and produce more movies," Olivia replied. "Men need to step up and support women behind the camera. We need to think about affirmative action, we need to think about mentorships."

"Right," Evie said, thinking aloud. "What if every male director working today was mentoring a female director?"

"I think the world would be a better place," Olivia replied. "Look, we all benefit from a society that actively pursues equality. It makes the world culturally richer." A woman wearing a headset touched the actress' arm, indicating it was time to move on.

"Thank you so much, have a great night," Evie said.

Olivia smiled at Evie, and gave her arm a squeeze. "Thank you." As she moved off camera, she shot Evie a look over her shoulder, and gave her a quick thumbs-up.

Evie was too stunned to respond. She was panting, insides swirling, heart racing. It was only then that she realized it had worked. Olivia Wilde had answered her questions: not stupid questions about designer dresses, but actual questions about things that mattered.

Someone nudged her. It was Adrian. She was still on camera. She snapped to attention. "Olivia Wilde offering some sage advice to the boys' club in La-La Land. C'mon, people, let's demand more stories by the double-X set." Behind Adrian, she could see Rich. He was shaking his head, bewildered. As she watched, she saw him answer his phone. Kelly, for sure.

A rise of cheers alerted her back to the carpet. Evie made out a tiny blonde dripping with diamonds making her way up the line of reporters. It was Juici, a plasticky pop star who'd starred in a cheesy rom-com. Evie tried to make subtle *move along* gestures, but Juici was shepherded in front of her.

"Hi!" Juici gushed, waving at the hysterical fans. Everything about her was fake: tits, teeth, tan.

"Looking very sparkly," Evie said, one eye over Juici's shoulder.

"Thanks." Juici blew a kiss at the camera. "Diamonds are a girl's best friend."

"Not if they're blood diamonds," Evie told her. "Then they're more like oppressed people's worst enemy."

Behind the camera, Rich made a cutting motion across his throat, the phone glued to his ear. They'd have to get through to Jan to pull the plug on her, and she was at a screening. From the corner of her eye she saw Juici get shuffled away, looking confused.

Evie caught sight of the next actress. She didn't need to fake enthusiasm—or nerves—when addressing the camera. "She's one of the biggest young stars on the scene, but her attitude has always been so refreshingly down to earth. Jennifer Lawrence, what's your opinion on Hollywood beauty standards?"

"They suck," Jennifer replied, before laughing. "Oh, want to know why men don't look good with makeup? Someone just told me this."

"Why?"

"Because they haven't been told they look bad without it," Jennifer replied cockily.

"Ooh, I like that," Evie said. "That's good. But I do notice you're wearing makeup now."

The actress made a face. "Yeah. I am. They held me down."

"You were powerless?"

"Yeah, they forced me." She laughed.

"Well, I think there is way too much emphasis put on how women look in Hollywood," Evie said, switching her attention between Jennifer and the camera. "I think unrealistic beauty standards, perpetuated by Photoshop and mandatory makeup, have to stop."

"Hell yeah, sister!" The starlet pumped a fist.

"So I challenge you, Jennifer Lawrence, to follow my lead, and go makeup-free for the Arzners."

Jennifer glanced around. "What, really?"

"Abso-totally. I have my main man Marcello right here." Marcello appeared by Evie's side bearing wipes, makeup remover, and Q-tips. "I'm game if you are."

A small crowd had gathered around the pair. Marcello held up his wipes like a magician.

"All right, you're on," Jennifer said. "Let's do it!"

"Screw makeup!"

"We don't need it!"

Working quickly, Marcello began removing every trace of mascara, blush, and lipstick from both women's faces. The crowd around them was swelling. Fans pointed excitedly, caught up in the spectacle. As Evie waited for Marcello to finish Jennifer, she saw Rich. He was on the phone, nodding grimly. All color had drained from his face. As Marcello removed the final scrap of Jennifer's makeup, and the crowd of people around them began clapping, Rich strode over to Adrian.

Seconds later, the red light on the camera went dead.

Extra Salt was off the air.

66.

Kelly's face was the color of an heirloom tomato. "What the hell was that? What the *hell* was that? What the hell . . . *was that?*"

"You could also try, '*What* the hell was that?'" Evie replied. "If you're aiming for all possible emphases."

"Don't be cute with me, Chloe!" Kelly railed. "Not now. I am so sick to death of you being cute with me!"

The pair was in Jan's office; Jan was absent. Evie didn't notice the awards or the view or the signed photographs on the walls. She was riding high, ecstatic with success. The red-carpet takeover had worked.

Kelly paced the hardwood floors, considerably less happy. "Dress, love, role!" he shouted. "Dress, love, role, is that so fucking hard to—"

His tirade was interrupted. Jan. She slammed the door behind her. Apprehension shot through Evie's veins.

"Sit," Jan ordered them both.

They did.

Jan swung her computer screen to face them both. It was the You-Tube video of the Arzners. Jan tapped at something in the background. "Can you read that?"

"Yes," Evie muttered.

"What," Jan continued icily, "is it?"

Evie winced. "It's a Revlon logo."

"Exactly," Jan hissed. "Because Revlon sponsors the Arzners. And what is Revlon?"

"Do you mean, like, metaphorically?" Evie asked.

"They're a makeup company," Kelly answered.

"And not just any makeup company," Jan continued, her voice sound-ing almost manic. "The biggest makeup company in America. They don't just advertise with *Salty*, they advertise with twenty-five of our titles. Or should I say, *advertised*." Her voice was a tight hiss. "*Past tense*. Funnily enough, the world's biggest makeup company didn't take too kindly to the message of 'Don't wear makeup,' because, you know"—and now Jan started shouting—"they're a fucking makeup company!"

Kelly groaned and dropped his head into his hands.

"Don't you have something to say?" Jan asked Evie.

Evie almost laughed. "Do you expect me to say I'm sorry? Because I'm not. I don't give a shit if your capitalist empire crumbles around you because I did something constructive for women." Evie stood up. "You know the video's gone viral, right? You should be thanking me."

"Oh my god," snorted Kelly.

"Don't you walk out on me, Chloe," Jan said. "Don't you dare walk out on me."

"Watch me," Evie said, eyes glittering. Every cell in her body was vi-brating, phoenix-strong, a fountain of light. She pulled Jan's door open, sucked in a deep breath. "I. Quit."

A wild-eyed Ella-Mae shoved Evie out of the way, hurtling into Jan's office. At the end of an outstretched arm, an iPhone. Her voice was a strangled, banshee shriek. "Tristan McKell has a micropenis!"

67.

Tristan's micropenis broke the internet.

It had taken the extra who snapped the picture 3.5 seconds to post it to Twitter, a decision she, and her parents, came to regret only because its asking fee would have been seven figures. It was the tweet that was heard around the world. Within four minutes, it was one of the most retweeted pictures in history, momentarily collapsing the site's servers. By day's end, Tristan's people released a statement confirming the picture was real, a move equally lauded and laughed at. Production on *Funderland* ground to a halt. This time, Krista didn't bother giving Gillian the satisfaction. She just packed up her stuff and took a car home. For the past few days, she'd been a prisoner in her own apartment. Paparazzi swarmed across the street like giant cockroaches. They'd even found the fire escape. Her phone would not stop ringing—Cameron, Gillian, Lana Lockhart, even Greg. The only person she wanted to hear from, Tristan, wasn't returning her texts and calls. The feeling that clung to her like a persistent black mist was unfamiliar, and refused to dissipate no matter how much whiskey she drank or pot she smoked. Eventually, she named it. Regret. And not just because she was fired (again) from *Funderland*. She had really hurt Tristan, she legit couldn't be with him, all because he had a tiny dick and most guys didn't. It was almost impossible to believe that puppy-dog-pretty Tristan McKell suffered from the same sort of ideals, or maybe standards, that she did. And while dick size and prettiness weren't totally the same thing—after all,

Tristan hadn't suffered from any prejudice until now—a relationship existed between the two. Didn't it? Krista wasn't totally sure, but what she did know was: She felt like crap about it all.

So when she'd turned back to being Regular, she didn't feel like she deserved to take the Pretty again. Penance. Plus, she really needed a day or two where she could leave her apartment without being hassled by a million flashing cameras. Krista Kumar, she who absorbed attention like a sponge, was officially over it. Could someone please turn the spotlight the fuck off?

She tried to let the whole thing go and think of Tristan like any one of the past boys she'd hit and quit. After all, he wouldn't even recognize her as Krista Kumar. But she couldn't let it go. She needed to apologize. In person. Which was why she found herself anxiously hunched at one of the three tiny tables at Dr. Wei's Magic Juice Bar in Connecticut, at 6 a.m. It had taken three hours to get there.

At 6:15 a.m., the door swung open and Tristan came in.

Krista felt like a string that'd just been plucked. Every part of her—heart, stomach, pussy—thrummed at the sight of him. His confusing status of former lover and current celebrity mashed into an odd feeling of tender longing and fan-girl excitement. He ordered a green tea and kale smoothie.

"Just the one?" asked the old Chinese guy behind the counter who might or might not have been Dr. Wei.

"Just the one," Tristan repeated. He took a seat, glancing at Krista perfunctorily.

She sat bolt upright. "Hey."

He gave her a mild nod. "Hey," he said, pulling out his phone.

Krista drummed her hands on the plastic tabletop. "I hear you're working on a new movie." Her voice sounded a little too urgent. "*Funderland.*"

He flicked a gaze at her. "Yeah." He looked back at his phone: a polite rebuttal.

Krista said, "That must be . . . hard—"

"Green tea and kale smoothie?" the guy behind the counter called.

Tristan got up, handed over some money, told the guy to keep the change. Krista rose too, mind now whirring. *Say something! Talk to him!*

Without looking back at her, Tristan headed for the door.

"I know Lenka Penka!"

Tristan paused. He spun, eyebrows furrowed. "What?"

"I know her." Krista took a step forward, nervously jamming her hands into her jacket pockets. "She told me you'd be here."

Tristan regarded her with an expression that recalled the first time they'd talked in his trailer: suspicious yet intrigued. "How do you know Lenka?"

"College. We were on a competitive eating team together." Krista was better at detecting lies than telling them. "She's really sorry, Tristan. She's really, really sorry."

She was half expecting Tristan to roll his eyes, tell her to get lost, tell her Lenka Penka ruined his life and he'd have nothing to do with her ever again. But instead, the former pop star just seemed to soften. "Is she?"

Krista nodded. "Yeah."

Tristan's eyes grew distant. "I miss her. She was fun." Krista stared at him forlornly, painfully aware of the chasm between them. She wanted to say she was sorry for rejecting Tristan for his body, and how angry she was that she felt that way in the first place, how frustrating it had been not to be able to turn her expectations off. And she felt like he wanted to tell her that Lenka was more than just fun. But they were strangers to each other: strangers for whom intimacy and truth were not permitted. Tristan blinked, seeming to reorient himself in the here and now. He said, "I should go."

Krista followed him outside. A pristine black town car idled by the curb, its door open invitingly. She could almost feel the butter-soft black leather seats under her thighs, hear the crystal-clear sound system, taste the free snacks. She'd be getting a series of subways back to Brooklyn. Her best-case scenario would be not getting sneezed on by a stranger.

Tristan paused by the open door. For a second, Krista thought he was going to ask her to get in. "I never got your name."

"Krista."

"Huh." He smiled. "Krista and Tristan. We should be on a kids' show."

She sighed, wistful. "Or fall in love."

"What?"

"Nothing." Krista shook her head, reddening. It was over. "Good luck on the movie. I hope the new Dream Girl means as much to you as Lenka did."

Tristan smiled. A sweet, boyish, serene smile. "That would truly be a blessing. Bye, Krista."

The town car rumbled away quietly down the empty street. She didn't start walking until it had disappeared.

68.

While Krista was avoiding the internet, Evie was basking in it. Clips from her interviews at the Arzners had been picked up by both feminist and pop culture sites around the world. Thoughtful opinion pieces were written on red-carpet interviews. Vicious debates sprang up about "mandatory makeup." Revlon released three statements. Trolls went nuts. She had as many detractors as she had supporters, equally passionate if not equally articulate.

It was like tossing a match into a house soaked in kerosene and watching it explode. She surprised herself by how much she enjoyed the controversy. The idea of being a public commentator, and suffering the inevitable sexist backlash any woman with an opinion seemed to endure, had always frightened her. That was why *Something Snarky* had to be anonymous. Chloe's lovely mask made a public persona possible. But plenty of people still hated her. To some she was a hypocrite, to others she was a hero. There was literally no way, Evie was realizing, to please everyone.

After all, it wasn't as if everyone was pleasing her.

Evie was dreading Willow's opening with an apprehension usually reserved for socializing with her workmates. She had to go. Willow was family. Which was why it was okay to feel several emotions simultaneously: love, annoyance, and worry. "I'd forgotten how she can just . . . disappear," Evie muttered, tucking the hem of a gold tank top into some skimpy black hot pants. "She's like a human hermit crab."

"Can we not talk about things disappearing?" Krista sucked on a cigarette, blew smoke out Evie's window. "Or anything, like, tiny?"

Evie spun away from the mirror, grinning. "Tell me again what it was like."

"No." Krista stubbed out the cigarette. "Let's just go."

Gray clouds the size of stadiums rolled overhead. The air was thick with humidity, inspiring a light sheen of sweat. Even though it was only 7 p.m., it was almost dark.

Krista looked up at the sky doubtfully. "Do you think it's going to rain?"

Evie laughed and pulled her close. "It's going to storm."

They hurried down Wythe toward the gallery, hoping to beat the downpour. Evie let Krista's chatter about The Fallout of the Micropenis wash over her, only half listening. After the opening, she was spending the night at Velma's. Their first summer storm. She pictured them lying in bed together, listening to the rain pour down over a misty city. They'd open a bottle of the good wine, the dusty French ones Velma kept in the back of her pantry, and drink it from generously sized glasses. They'd giggle, and kiss, and sink deeper, exquisitely deeper, into this wonderful drowning, this dopey paradise.

She was also looking forward to an in-person compliment from Velma about the Arzners. She'd been expecting Velma to text about it. She didn't. Evie reasoned someone like Velma Wolff must be too highbrow to have seen it. So she sent her the YouTube link. Hours later, Velma texted back. Just three words.

You're so cool.

It was an elegant response: understated and casually flirtatious, but Evie felt disappointed. Maybe Velma was just so cool herself that she could never be impressed by anyone. Or maybe this was her version of going game-show-contestant crazy. Evie wasn't sure who had to change: her or Velma. Did she have to adjust her expectations, or just make them known?

"Whoa." Krista's voice pulled her from her reverie. "Looks kinda . . . packed."

At Willow's last opening, a sum total of five people had been out front. Now, easily a hundred billowed from the entrance. If art was the thinking person's sport, this was game night.

"Someone got popular." Evie exchanged a glance with Krista. "Here goes nothing."

Inside was just as crowded, the humidity milkshake-thick. Krista said something about needing a drink and disappeared. People were practically shouting, clutching cups of champagne with black or orange or blue fingernails. Evie pushed past women with undercuts and men with ironic mustaches. She felt a few stares of recognition, and someone she didn't know warbled, "Chloe, you're brill."

But Evie wasn't concentrating on the well-dressed throng. She was concentrating on the artwork.

Giant photographs of Caroline in various stages of distress filled the gallery's white walls. Her sea-green eyes were rendered silvery-black in the prints, bloodshot, brimming with tears. In some, her face had fallen into her hands. In others, her mouth was open in a silent cry.

It was a hall of horrors. A shrine of sadness. Evie's blood began to curdle. Something was horribly, horribly wrong with Willow.

The crowd parted momentarily, revealing a photograph on the far wall. This picture was the largest, ten feet high, six feet wide. Evie pushed her way toward it.

In it was Willow herself, not Caroline. She was completely naked, floating in water, arms spread wide, eyes open but sightless. Dozens of hands from unseen owners were holding her afloat, their fingers white, black, and brown against her pale skin. Evie read the placard. *Rebirth*. The woman in the photograph looked dead.

"Jesus," Evie muttered. "We are in the bell jar."

"Willow!"

It was Meredith, gesturing toward a stunning blond woman in a long black dress and bloodred heels. It took Evie a full five seconds to recognize Willow. She came to stand arm in arm with Meredith, posing with a glassy-eyed smile for pictures being taken by three different people. Her lips were painted scarlet, her eyes rimmed with black. Willow never wore makeup. The long dark dress clung to her frame, accentuating her thinness, which seemed unnatural. She looked beautiful. In the worst possible way.

Evie took a few dazed steps toward her. Willow caught her eye. She whispered something to Meredith, then drifted over. The two women stood in front of each other, silent and uneasy. Someone squeezed Willow's arm, breathing, "Congratulations." She ignored them.

Evie wrapped her arms around herself. "I thought you hated high heels. Too painful."

Willow's gaze dropped dully to her shoes. "I really can't feel my feet right now." A small, sad smile twisted her mouth.

"Is that supposed to be funny? Because it's not."

"Oh god, Evie." Willow sighed. "Just don't."

Evie whipped her eyes around the room, checking for Velma, wishing Willow hadn't used her real name. She stepped closer, and lowered her voice. "Don't what? Care?"

"Exactly," Willow said sourly. "Why start now?"

"What's that supposed to mean?" Evie exclaimed at the same time Velma appeared at her side, brushing her cheek with a kiss and saying, "Hey, you." Velma glanced at Willow, missing the tension. "Hi, I'm Velma. Willow, right?" She extended her hand. Willow shook it limply, her eyes not leaving Evie's. "Congratulations," Velma added. "Your work is incredible."

"Incredibly disturbing," Evie muttered.

"Why is it so hard for you to accept that I'm a good artist? That I have a voice, I have something to say?"

"What is it you're saying, Will? That it's so cool to see women suffering? In pain? I hope you invited Lars von Trier," she added. "This is so far up his alley he's basically living on this street."

"Hey, Chloe." Velma slid a hand across Evie's back. "Easy."

"Yeah, *Chloe*," Willow said. "Easy."

Evie bristled. She doubted Willow would blow Chloe's cover. But she really wouldn't put anything past Willow right now. "Can you get me a drink?" Evie asked Velma.

Velma ticked her eyes from Willow, back to Evie, hesitated, then nodded, disappearing in the direction of the bar.

The crowd was swelling, feeling as if it was pushing in closer. It would be all too easy to record their conversation and turn it into click bait: *Chloe Fontaine rips into Willow Hendriksen's hot new show!* Evie spoke in a low hiss. "I don't know what's more disturbing: the fact you're hiding something from me or your newfound love of hipster sexism."

Willow looked at Evie for a long beat, her eyes cold. "It's not hipster sexism. It's what I'm going through. I'm sorry if that doesn't conform to your worldview."

"What are you going through?"

Willow huffed air and shot her gaze to the ceiling.

Evie tried to speak calmly. "Willow, talk to me, please. I'm your friend, I care about you."

The sentiment seemed to land. Willow stopped darting her eyes around angrily, and instead let them settle on Evie. When she spoke, it sounded less accusatory, more resigned. "I'm just having some realizations."

"About what?"

"How the world really works. What people are capable of. What I'm capable of."

Evie exhaled, her throat tight. "What does that mean?"

Willow stared at Evie, as if Evie was either dumb or naïve or maybe as if she was trying to protect Evie, and it was at this moment Evie noticed Mark, standing a few feet behind them. He was looking at the walls like he was afraid of them.

"Mark!" Evie breathed. Maybe he could help.

"Oh my god." Willow looked dumbfounded. "How did he find out about this?"

Evie stared at Willow. "I invited him. He told me you guys broke up, but . . . Whatever's going on, you can fix it, right?"

"You invited him?" Willow gaped at Evie.

"Why is that so crazy?"

"Because I've been *sleeping* with Mark."

Evie blinked, her confusion growing. "Good. I'm glad you guys are—"

"No." Willow's lips were bone dry. "*Caroline* has been sleeping with Mark."

He was behind them both, face aghast.

"Mark." Evie grabbed his arm. "Mark, I . . . I . . ." But she couldn't form a sentence. Her mind whirred viciously. Willow had been sleeping with . . . Mark. As Caroline.

Mark stared at Evie in confusion. "I'm sorry, who are you?"

She was Chloe. Not Evie.

Willow had frozen, as if suspended in a block of ice.

"I don't know who I am," Evie said hoarsely. "I don't know who anyone is anymore."

69

The clouds unleashed and the heavy rain sent everyone outside scurrying in. The crowd in the gallery swelled until it was barely possible to move. Still, the mood remained electric. Dream-pop blared, champagne flowed, and the damp air smelled like weed.

Evie's desire for Velma—for her attention, her distraction, her comfort—transcended simple want into naked need. It took Evie ten minutes to find her, crushed into a corner with someone. "Hey." Evie clutched Velma's shoulder. "There you are."

"Hi." Velma smiled at her. "Chloe, this is Annie." She waved the tip of a beer bottle at a woman Evie instantly assumed was a model. Auburn hair in a short pixie cut, huge green eyes, a spray of cute freckles over a tiny nose. Closer to Velma's age than Chloe's. Velma's hand rested casually on Annie's forearm. Jealousy gripped Evie so quickly and unexpectedly that she almost choked. "Hi." Evie had to force the word out.

"Hi, Chloe." Annie's voice was a too-cute purr. "So nice to meet you."

Velma slipped her hand off Annie's forearm far too slowly in Evie's opinion. "Is everything okay with Willow?" Velma asked.

"Yeah," Evie lied. "Fine. How do you guys know each other?"

The pair exchanged an amused look. "Velma broke into my apartment." Annie giggled.

"I did not!" Velma said. "Tom broke the lock, if you recall, I just . . ."

"Yes," Annie prompted.

"I . . . broke into her apartment," Velma admitted. "You were supposed to leave keys!"

"I did, Tom lost them!" Annie said. "Remember what he told my landlord? *'I've never lost anything—'*"

"*'—except my virginity!'*" Velma finished, and the pair dissolved into giggles. Once again, Velma's hand found its way to Annie's arm.

"What a . . . hilarious story," Evie said, unable to drag her eyes off Velma's fingers.

Annie gasped. "Do you remember him at karaoke?"

Velma's eyes lit at the memory, and she began singing, "*Hold me closer, Tony Danza—*"

"Tom sounds like my kind of guy." Evie addressed Annie. "Is he your boyfriend, or . . ."

The pair fell silent. "Actually, Chloe," Velma said, "Tom passed away last summer, in a tragic polo accident."

"Oh god," Evie said. "I'm so sorry, I had no idea—"

The pair burst out laughing. "I'm kidding!" Velma spluttered. "I'm kidding. He's married, he lives in Phoenix."

"Right." Evie was officially pissed. "What a fucking relief."

"Sorry, kid." Velma wiped a tear away. "Couldn't help myself."

"I think self-control is one of the most important human qualities there is," Evie said. "That's what stops men from being rapists and murderers, isn't it? Self-control."

The statement fell in the middle of the trio like an anvil. Annie glanced at her half-full beer bottle. "I'm just going to . . . use the bathroom."

After she was out of earshot, Evie fixed Velma with a hooded stare. "Why don't we get out of here?"

Velma glanced around the busy gallery. "What, now?"

Evie nodded. She put her hands around Velma's neck, pulling herself close. "Just the two of us, listening to the storm . . . What do you say?"

Velma made a small noise of pleasure. "Actually, Annie suggested we all grab a drink at this little tapas bar across the road."

"Oh really? Annie suggested that?" Jealousy was flowing so freely through Evie's veins that she had to physically repress the urge to hiss the other woman's name. She moved her lips an inch from Velma's ear. "But Annie isn't the one licking your pussy right now, is she?"

Velma's cheeks colored.

"I just really want to get out of here," Evie whispered. "Please?"

Velma met Evie's eyes. Telltale arousal quivered around her mouth. Her eyes were dark, liquid moons.

Evie knew she'd won.

While Velma ducked away to call her driver, Evie found Krista pressed under the gallery's awning, watching the rain bucket down. "I'm leaving with Velma."

"Eager for her beaver, huh?" Krista brushed droplets of water off her arms. "Did you talk to Willow?"

"I fought with Willow. Does that count?"

"Oh, did you do that thing where you get angry at someone because you're worried about them?"

Evie frowned, wanting to deny this, but at the same time feeling it might actually be true. She gazed out at the sheets of water slamming onto Wythe Avenue, roaring like a stadium crowd. "Maybe," she murmured.

Krista edged back from the rivulets of water that had begun pouring from the roof. "Maybe I'm smarter than you think I am."

Evie glanced at Krista, surprised. "I don't— I think you're smart."

"Do you?"

"Yes! You got into law school, for fuck's sake."

Krista crinkled her nose. "You think I'm a hot mess, though. Right?"

Evie glanced at her, half smiling, unsure. She poked Krista's shoulder. "I thought you liked being a hot mess."

Krista stared out at the rain, silent, and Evie had the unusual sensation of wondering what Krista—she who wore her heart on her sleeve, she who had no filter—was thinking about. After a long moment, Krista said, "Have you turned back yet this week?"

"No, not yet." After a second's hesitation, Evie dug into her purse and sheepishly pulled out the small purple bottle with the smeared black lettering. "I borrowed this. And I know I had a hissy fit when you took it, but—"

"Dude, it's cool," Krista interrupted. "I don't want it right now. What's your plan?"

"I'm going to set an alarm—Velma always sleeps through it—and take it in the guest bathroom." If all went according to plan, Velma wouldn't even know she'd been up. If not, there was always the excuse of food poisoning.

"Pretty risky," Krista said. Evie couldn't tell if she was impressed or concerned.

"I've got it under control."

"I really don't know if you do, Evie."

Evie felt a sharp twinge of irritation, but because Krista sounded concerned, not patronizing, the only response she could manage was a shrug.

Krista glanced back at the rain, and sighed. "Guess I'm just going to make a run for it."

"Where are you going?"

"Home. I need some me time."

Evie tried to hide her surprise. Krista had never initiated me time before in her life. Evie pulled her umbrella from her bag. "Use this. We're taking Velma's car."

"Thanks, dude." She circled her arms up around Chloe's slender neck. "Have fun," she said. "And be careful."

Evie hugged her back. "I can't believe you're the one saying that to me."

Krista opened the umbrella. "Well, you're breaking all your own rules for her. But you must be aware of that." Then she scampered off, up Wythe Avenue, disappearing almost instantly, swallowed up by the storm.

Evie gazed at the violet liquid in the tiny glass bottle. Krista was right: she was breaking her own rules. Staying at Velma's place was extraordinarily risky. But the idea of Chloe not spending the night curled up in Velma's arms was more than unpleasant. It was impossible.

The gallery doors opened, spilling music, laughter, shouted conversation. Two boys stumbled out, squealing, "Holy fuck, it's *pouring*!" One of them shoved the other into the rain, but his sneakers skidded on the wet concrete and he tripped, knocking into Evie.

It happened so fast.

One minute she was holding the Pretty.

The next, she wasn't.

The little purple bottle pitched out of her fingers, arcing toward the street. It landed in the swollen gutter, splashing soundlessly.

"Sorry!" laughed the boy before the pair made a run for it.

Evie lurched forward, into the downpour, stumbling after the Pretty as it was swept along in the wash of gray water. She didn't even make it two steps before it disappeared down a grate in the city street. "No," she exhaled. "No, no, no." She fell to her knees in front of the grate, already soaked through, hoping desperately to see the bottle caught on the ledge, still within reach. Nothing. Just water, endless water, disappearing down, underneath the city.

She was numb as she returned to the awning, hair plastered to her skull, water dripping from her clothes, her elbows, her chin.

The Pretty was gone.

"Oh my god," Velma said, laughing. "What happened?"

Evie stared at her, face aghast.

"Don't worry." Velma wiped away water from Evie's cheeks with her thumbs. "We'll get you dry at home."

Evie just kept staring. The Pretty was gone. Chloe was gone: her sister, her better half. It was over. Everything with Velma was over.

"Chloe," Velma tried again. "Baby. Are you ready to go?"

"I can't go with you." The words were a horrible whisper, not her voice, not her truth. "I can't ever see you again."

"What?"

"It's just . . . It's over." Evie's stomach was sour and her heart . . . something was squeezing her heart hard, cruelly cold.

"What's over?" Velma frowned slightly.

"Me. You." Evie stared at her miserably, her voice becoming a whimper. "Us."

The door to the gallery widened once again, people from the opening talking, laughing, seeing the rain, retreating back inside. It was all just background noise, all disposable.

"Are you serious?" Velma's forehead creased in confusion.

"This isn't what I want to do."

"Then don't do it." Velma's voice rose, somewhere between annoyance and concern. "Is this about Annie?" She huffed a sigh. "I'm sorry, I'm a flirt, always will be. But let's not end the night like this."

"I don't want to." Every word was a stab, painful in her chest. "I really, really like you. I like you so much."

"I like you too, Chloe. Okay? I like you too."

Evie closed her eyes, hot tears spilling down already damp cheeks. "Have you ever felt like you can't show yourself—your real self—to someone?"

Velma's voice was soft, somber, kind against her ear. "Hasn't everyone?"

"I feel like that now—" Evie started, but her words were cut off as Velma's mouth found hers. One kiss. Then another. And then they were making out, passionately, desperately, and Evie clung to Velma, not wanting the kiss to end, because she knew, she absolutely knew, it had to be the last one. When Velma finally pulled back, Evie opened her eyes slowly. She gazed at the woman in her arms, at her moist lips and concerned eyes.

"Good-bye, Velma Wolff," Evie said before spinning to run, as fast as she could, into the rain-washed Brooklyn street.

70.

She was barely conscious of leading him into Meredith's office, of the din from the party quieting as she pulled the door shut.

He knows, he knows, he knows.

Willow reached for the bag she'd stuffed under Meredith's desk, willing there to be a few Valium left. Her fingers were numb. As she fumbled for the pills, a paperback fell out. *Lacan and the Shadow Self.* Mark's eyes snapped to Willow's. "That was the book— Why do you have her book? Are you— Was this a setup?"

"I don't know," Willow whispered, unable to look at him. "I don't know what this is."

"But how do you— Why did—" Mark shook his head, unable to make anything fall into place. "That morning, when you were in my bathroom. You knew—you knew that Caroline had"—he took a deep breath—"spent the night. You knew that."

Willow nodded.

"Why didn't you say anything? Where is she?" Mark's voice was agitated. "Don't tell me she's here."

"She's here." Willow started to cry softly. "But also . . . not."

"Will." Mark stood across from her. "Just tell me what's going on. Please."

"Okay," she whispered. She inhaled, feeling sick. "You better sit down."

He did. His expression morphed from anger to fear.

Willow drew in a long, shaky breath. "It started about a month ago. Krista. Someone gave something to Krista."

"Someone gave Krista what?"

How could she possibly explain it? "Chaos. Beauty. The truth."

She told him everything. Mark sat listening, eyes glazed, fingers pressed into both temples. At first, he couldn't believe her. She was joking, she was high, she was trying to take him for a fool. But when Willow began recounting exact exchanges he'd shared with Caroline, when she explained she'd turned back to being Willow the morning he found her in his bathroom, when she told him it was Evie who'd grabbed his arm just now in the gallery, he'd started, finally, to accept it.

He shook his head, words sounding dumb and foreign. "Why did you take it?"

Willow shrugged morosely.

"No, really." He sat up. "Why? You're already beautiful."

"I'm an acquired taste," Willow said bitterly, quoting Mark's own words from one of their first nights at Lenny's.

Mark winced. He was silent for a few moments, studying her sadly. "I'm never going to know you," he said. "You're never going to let me."

Willow dropped her head, hair spilling around her like a wall. Not denying it.

Mark stood up, shouldering his bag. "You know what hurts the most?" His jaw was set, his chest tight. He looked like he was trying hard not to cry. "That you never even thought about what would happen when I saw the photographs." His voice cracked, but he forced the words to keep coming, one by one. "It never even crossed your mind."

71.

Evie burst into the apartment, choking in gasps of air, drenched from head to toe. "I lost the Pretty! Someone pushed me, and I dropped it, and it's *gone*."

Krista ran to get a towel. Evie collapsed on the couch, soaking everything she touched. "I broke up with Velma." Evie's gaze was wide, wild, unhinged. "I couldn't even tell her why." She began sobbing, her chest shaking violently.

"Babe. Oh, babe." Krista wrapped Evie in the towel, holding her as she wept. "Oh, Evie. It's okay."

"How is it okay?" Evie wailed. "I think . . . Oh god . . . I think I was falling in love with her." Evie grabbed the corner of the towel and pressed her face into it, crying harder.

"Evie. Eve. Hey. Look at me." Krista tipped Evie's face up so her best friend met her gaze, sorrowful and snotty. "Do you really like her? Like, for real?"

"Yes," Evie whispered.

Krista pressed her lips together resolutely. "Then you have to show her."

"Show her what?"

Krista raised her eyebrows. "You have to show her the real you."

Evie stared at her sullenly and huffed out a breath. "Don't be stupid."

"I'm not."

"She would never go for the real me!" Spelling it out for Krista added insult to injury. "Chloe Fontaine could be a model. She has a

pretty-person job, she hosts a show, for chrissakes. Evie Selby is . . ."
Short? Fat? Plain?

"Evie Selby is fucking awesome." Krista's voice shot up a register,
so vehement that Evie jumped. "Evie Selby is funny as shit and cool as
hell. Evie Selby was the one interviewing those celebs at the Arzners.
Evie Selby is the one who wants to change things. She's brave, and
she's smart, and she looks after me." She met Evie's stunned expression
meaningfully. "Evie Selby is the best friend I have."

Evie's hand pressed into her chest. It took her a few moments to find
her voice. "You're my best friend too, Kris."

Krista took Evie's hand and squeezed it. "If she likes Chloe, then she
likes you. You're the one always saying women shouldn't be judged by
their appearance. So don't judge yourself." Her voice was compassionate. Her voice was sure. "Let her see the real you, Eve."

72.

Velma's foyer was strangely empty when Evie dashed inside. Lightning flashed overhead. A second later, thunder boomed. The storm was right overhead, as exuberant as a parade. But Evie wasn't afraid. She whisked past the artworks and standing lamps, trying to quiet a pulse that insisted on being loud. She punched the elevator button and stepped into the mirrored square cube.

Her cheeks were flushed, eyes bright, heart racing.

How would Velma take it? Would she think she was crazy? Or would it be the start of . . . everything?

She wanted to be the girl Krista saw. Brave. Smart. Cool as hell. Someone who put things on the line, someone who knew her worth. Someone worth loving.

She was someone worth loving. And, oh, it was romantic. As the elevator doors slid open, her feet couldn't move fast enough to Velma's door. She would take it all back, she would fall into Velma's arms, and tell her she loved her.

Ella Fitzgerald's "At Last" drifted from inside, summoning a smile. Their song.

Almost as if Velma already knew.

She pushed the familiar front door open, into her loft, her life, her love—

And froze.

Evie Elizabeth Selby had experienced her fair share of surprises over the last month. The fact a tiny bottle of purple liquid could inexplicably and illogically alter the physical appearance of her and her two best friends. The fact Willow's boyfriend had been cheating on her with her Pretty self. The fact Tristan McKell had a micropenis. But nothing could have prepared her for the sight presented to her now. Velma, splayed on the sofa, shirt unbuttoned, hair mussed, mouth open in shock, having jerked up and away from Annie's exposed neck.

Air drained out of Evie's lungs. "Oh my god."

Annie shot up, hands whipping to cover her breasts. "Oh my god."

"Chloe." Velma's eyes bugged. She struggled to pull herself away from the petite redhead. "What are you— How did you—"

Evie stared at Annie, who was fumbling desperately for her shirt in between shooting incredulous looks at Velma. "I took a car," she said faintly. Outside, lightning flashed. Only Velma and Annie jumped when the thunder cracked, loud as a gunshot.

"How could you?" Evie whispered. "I thought—"

Velma finished buttoning up her shirt and got up to walk toward her. "Baby, don't freak out—"

"Don't." Evie raised her palm. Then, in a dark and ugly voice she didn't even know she had, she turned on Annie. "What the *fuck* are you doing with my girlfriend?"

"Girlfriend?" Annie repeated.

"Chloe." Velma caught her gaze, held it. "I'm not . . ." She sipped in a breath, her face contorted. "I'm not your girlfriend."

"What?" Evie's head started to whir loudly.

"I'm not your girlfriend," Velma repeated in a voice that seemed both kind and cold.

"But—" Velma's tongue in her mouth, Velma's hand on her knee under a restaurant table, Velma whispering in her ear that she was irresistible. "But—"

Annie was staring at her with a look Evie could only just now name. Pity.

Thunder boomed again, flickering the lights.

Evie backed up a step. "I'm going to go."

"Don't go." Velma held a hand out.

"Don't!" Evie's voice cracked. "Don't even—"

The room plunged into darkness. Annie let out a small cry. The lights in the buildings visible from the balcony had disappeared. The city was gone, in its place a blank and terrifying nothing. Velma and Annie were only lit by a few candles on the coffee table, their faces jagged with shadows.

"I'm going." Evie's words disappeared into darkness.

"You can't," Velma said.

"I'm *going*—"

"It's a blackout," Velma said tightly. "You won't be able to get a taxi, or the subway. It's too dangerous to leave."

"Oh god." Velma was right. Evie's hand flew to her mouth, and she had to bite her fist to keep from crying. "Oh *god*." She turned and raced blindly for the bathroom.

A single scented candle lit the guest bathroom. Lavender. Velma's smell.

She buried her face in a white fluffy towel and began to weep. She'd have given anything, literally anything in the world, to be at home in her own apartment, where the candles were shitty Ikea candles that only lasted one night and didn't smell like anything. Where there was one bathroom for two people, but that other person was someone who cared about her. Back home, in her own skin, her familiar body, with a face that needed glasses but was undeniably, irrevocably, *hers*.

She wanted Evie Selby back.

Part Four:
Blush

73.

Evie woke with a cry, catapulted from a nightmare that had already vanished. Somewhere, a phone alarm chimed with calm persistence. The world was pale.

Blurry.

Painful.

She was cramping.

Chloe was gone. Evie had returned.

Soft, gentle snoring sounded near her. Someone was asleep, just a fuzzy blob on the floor.

Moving with the swiftness of a thief, Evie reached under her pillow for her phone, silencing the now-pointless warning to retake the Pretty. The bedside table drawer still hid the old pair of glasses she'd stored there, in case of emergency. Which this had become.

The world shifted into sharp relief.

It was early. The sky, glimpsed through Velma's floor-to-ceiling windows, looked unrehearsed, oyster white. Velma slept with one arm thrown over her face, as if to block out a horrible sight. The horrible sight of last night.

Evie had stayed in the guest bathroom, praying for the lights to flicker back on so she could leave and never come back. They didn't. At one stage she heard Annie's voice, almost shouting. "If it walks like a duck, V. If it walks like a fucking duck!"

Later she had curled up on the bathroom floor, trying unsuccessfully to find a comfortable way to lie on the tiled floor, when there came a tentative knock. "Chloe?"

Evie stiffened. If she had to suffer the added humiliation of Velma seeing her lying on a bathroom floor, she'd definitely dissolve into tears again.

"Annie's asleep on the couch. I'm going to be on my bedroom floor. The bed is all yours." The sound of footsteps receding.

She hadn't wanted to accept Velma's offer. But when the candle burned down, leaving her in a horrific grip of claustrophobic blackness, she did.

Velma was just a dark figure on the floor, a lump under a throw blanket. Outside the rain was starting to ease. Evie stood in the doorway, equidistant from the actual bed and Velma's makeshift one below it. It would be so easy to slip in with her. To find that warm, safe space in Velma's nook, the place that smelled like lavender and felt like home.

She got into bed, facing away from the woman she thought she'd fallen in love with.

After a minute, Velma's voice sounded, quiet in the darkness. "I'm sorry to have disappointed you."

The words sucker-punched her, inspiring a bright bloom of anger, a flash flood of responses:

Disappoint me? You fucking lied to me!

Your arrogance is what's truly disappointing.

You don't deserve me, Velma. You. Don't. Deserve. Me.

But then a final thought, a feeling that was only just starting to make itself understood.

I've disappointed myself.

When she started to cry, she made it sure it was silent, so Velma wouldn't hear.

Now, Evie eased out of Velma's bed and made her way to the door. She threw one last look around the master bedroom that was never hers to begin with. The gray silky sheets. The mounds of pillows in matching pillowcases. The beautiful bedside lamps. A lovely, stylish facade.

Velma wasn't snoring.

She was awake.

Evie could tell.

And even as she stood there, in a now-ill-fitting outfit, with a face she couldn't explain, she almost wanted Velma to look over. To try and stop the departing Chloe.

She didn't.

Like a coward, Velma was waiting for her to leave.

And that made it so much easier.

The living room was empty. Blankets and pillows lay askew on the couch. Annie hadn't even left a note. And although Evie was expecting to feel devastated, she didn't. The expansive, manicured loft felt like a set, unreal in its perfection, and ultimately, temporary. The movie was over, the lights were back on, and she was getting up, readying to leave the cinema and return to real life: imperfect, strange, wonderful real life.

Jay Street was littered with leaves and small branches, a quiet scene of past chaos. Water galloped in the gutters.

Her phone was dead. Comfort from Krista would have to wait. First, the subway of shame: sad, solo travel in last night's clothes. But when Evie reached the Franklin Street stop, she found red tape had been strung along the entrance: Subway Closed Due to Flooding.

It was a sneering *fuck you* from a city for whom affection seemed masochistic. For a moment, she wavered on the edge of tears.

But then she drew in a resolute breath. If she could survive Velma Wolff, she could survive New York.

She would walk home.

At first Evie felt self-conscious of the way her stomach bulged over the satin hot pants' tiny waistband, the way her arms seemed heavy and thick in the sleeveless gold top. But none of the other early risers even gave her a second look. Not because she didn't matter, Evie realized. Because in New York, everything was permissible. No one cared what you wore, how you looked. Only *you* cared about those things. And if they didn't worry you, then they didn't matter.

She crossed Canal Street, went north up Wooster, then east along Broome. She increased her speed, legs moving forward in long strides. Cool, fresh air, damp with yesterday's rain, pulled in and out of her lungs.

As she strode forward, her bitterness toward Velma began to soften. Not into forgiveness; she certainly wasn't there yet. It just began to taste a little less acidic. Velma had lied to her, or at least, was happy for Evie to believe that Velma cared about Chloe in a way that felt committed. And that was wrong. That was selfish and self-serving. But maybe it took two to tango. Had she misread things, maybe even deliberately? Had she suspected Velma wasn't to be trusted, and gone with it anyway?

She wouldn't see Velma again, and not just because Chloe was gone. But somehow, even now, she couldn't regret it completely. It was an experience. A lesson. Life—painful, confusing life—was made up of her mistakes, her choices. There was something oddly liberating about that.

She made it to the Williamsburg Bridge and began heading toward Brooklyn. Below her, the silvery East River moved restlessly, snaking south toward the sea.

What a strange adventure she'd just had. Hosting *Extra Salt*. Rich and Kelly. Marcello. Morgan Freeman. Telling Gemma and Rose she would only wear an old gray T-shirt. Claiming she loved Velma on meeting her. Everything that happened at the Arzners. It was ridiculous and unbelievable and *funny*.

Soon she was back in South Williamsburg, only fifteen minutes from home, her small, messy, cozy home with small, messy, cozy Krista. She passed hipsters in ripped jeans and T-shirt dresses holding iced coffees, looking sleepy. Her people. Her neighborhood. She came across a tatty stoop sale, in the process of being set up. Amid plastic jewelry and yellowed paperbacks, she spotted a small dream catcher, white string threaded with green beads and speckled feathers. It was the sort of thing her mom would love. She paid three dollars for it and wrapped it carefully to slip into her pocket.

In a coffee-shop window, she paused to take in her reflection. Evie

Selby looked back at her. Short black hair, black-rimmed glasses, and tattooed print decorating her forearm.

Her body was back.

And she felt *good* about it.

It was her face and her body—the ones that'd been there for the beginning of her life and she'd be damned if they weren't there for the rest. Changing herself to become "beautiful," in a way that was painful and unnatural, was never going to make her happy. Owning her face, unapologetically, or—even more revolutionarily—happily was the bravest thing she could possibly do.

She laughed out loud, almost delirious, speaking to the girl in the shop window. "I am happy to see you."

And she really meant it.

74.

When Evie opened her apartment door, Krista and Mark were standing in the middle of the living room with an odd sort of alertness. On seeing her, they deflated. She was not who they were expecting.

"Hey, guys—" Evie began, before Krista cried, "Willow's missing!"

"What?" Evie closed the door behind her.

"Willow's missing." Krista hurried forward to hug her, jumpy with nerves.

"Um, okay," Evie said. "Willow's kind of been MIA all month, so—" She glanced at Mark.

"He knows everything," Krista said, answering the question in Evie's head. "Chloe, Lenka, Caroline. He knows everything."

"Have you called her dad?" Evie asked Mark.

He nodded. He looked strung out, like he hadn't slept. "She didn't stay there, or here, last night."

Evie dropped her bag on the sofa, refusing to give in to the panic that was written so clearly over Krista's face. "She could be anywhere," Evie said. "Friend's place, hotel. Have you tried calling her?"

Mark gave her a withering look.

Krista addressed Mark. "Show her the text."

Mark cut his eyes grimly at Evie. A small flare of worry fizzled in her stomach. "What text?"

Mark held out his phone. A text, from Willow, sent to Mark just before 3 a.m. i can't do this anymore. see you on the other side, my love.

Evie read it again. And again. It refused to change.

"What do you think it means?" Krista asked.

Mark took the phone back from Evie.

"Evie?" Krista's voice quivered. "What do you think it means?"

Evie pictured Willow in the Wythe Gallery, smiling sadly, telling Evie she couldn't feel her feet. *"It's what I'm going through,"* she'd said. And how had Evie responded? With an accusation. With the opposite of empathy.

"Oh god," Evie breathed. "I've been so stupid." Her eyes hurtled to Mark's. "You don't think she'd— I mean, she wouldn't actually—"

She couldn't finish the sentence.

"It's become apparent to me," Mark said, forming words with evident difficulty, "that I have no idea what Willow is capable of."

"My phone!" Evie all but shouted. "It's dead." They all winced at the word, and Evie had to let a punch of fear pass before continuing in the calmest voice she could muster. "Maybe she's texted me."

Evie ran to her room, inserted the charger. They watched, hovering, hopeful, as the black rectangle blinked awake.

"C'mon," Evie muttered. "C'mon, c'mon, c'mon." *Please, Willow,* she prayed silently. *Please don't have done anything stupid.*

There were no messages.

When she called, it went straight to Willow's voicemail. Usually, Evie would end the call before the voicemail ended: Willow rarely checked messages. This time she let it play. "Hi." Willow's voice sounded floaty, almost shy. "It's Willow. I'm not here." A long beep.

"Will, it's Evie." She reeled, totally lost, fighting the thought that she was speaking into the ether: a voicemail that would never, could never, be checked. "We're all worried about you. Please call me. I'm sorry. God, Willow." Evie sucked in a breath, her chest shuddering. "Please just come home."

She dropped the phone onto her bed. Krista sank next to her, her small hands reaching over to squeeze Evie's. Evie squeezed back, drawing strength. Then she was on her feet. "Mark, why don't you start calling everyone, just literally everyone she could be with: family, friends, fuck, old boyfriends, I don't know."

"Okay." Mark nodded efficiently.

"Kris, you call hotels. McCarren Hotel, the Wythe—anything around here. Then the downtown ones: Lower East Side, the Village. Maybe she got a room after the opening." Evie glanced at Krista, expecting her to whine something about how many hotels there were in New York City.

"Got it," Krista said. "What are you going to do?"

Evie tried to keep her line of sight steady, but it began wavering, shimmering like heat. Both hands had clenched into fists. "I'm going to start calling hospitals."

For the next four hours, they worked feverishly on an endless cycle of calling numbers, waiting on hold, reaching a dead end. The storm had flooded lower Manhattan and parts of Brooklyn. NPR was reporting at least three deaths: a couple swept away in Battery Park City, a man hit by a tree branch in Red Hook. Every now and then, Evie was struck by the thought they were overreacting. How silly! How paranoid! Willow was unreliable, that was her deal, she was obviously fine, they were wasting their time. This wasn't how this was all supposed to end.

Then she'd remembered the text, sent at the height of the storm.

see you on the other side, my love.

And she realized that she had no idea how any of this could end. No idea of the power of the Pretty.

And she'd call the next number.

She was on hold, spacing out to a memory of Willow telling her that Virginia Woolf's death, drowning with pockets full of rocks, was "such an elegant way to go" when Mark burst into her room.

Evie took one look at his face and reeled back. Something snapped inside her, a knife thrust under her ribs. The sound she made wasn't a word. It was just fear.

"No!" he said. "It's not—I just got hold of Meredith. Something's happened at the gallery."

"Something's happened? What do you mean something's happened?"

"I couldn't make out what she was saying." Mark pulled Evie upright. "She was crying."

"Why was she crying?"

"I don't know!" Mark shouted. "She's not picking up, let's go, let's go!"

They were collectively heaving and red-faced when the gallery came into view. Last night hundreds of people had spilled out from the entrance. Now the street was empty. Except for the water. A moat had gathered around its entrance, stretching out for twenty feet.

"Be careful," Mark panted as they waded across the street.

The doors to the gallery were open.

Meredith stood alone, beneath Willow's *Rebirth* photograph, in ankle-deep water the color of smoke. The gallery was flooded. Watermarks lined the walls, staining every photograph. A few were even floating, like empty life rafts.

Meredith looked up. It took her a few seconds to focus on the three figures in the doorway. "Gone," she whispered.

They were struck dumb, before all speaking at once. "What's gone?"

"Where's Willow?"

"All gone." Meredith waved one limp hand around the exhibition. "My insurance . . . It doesn't cover floods."

"She's talking about the gallery," Evie said.

"Meredith!" Mark reached the curator, clamping a hand on each shoulder, forcing her to meet his gaze. "Have you spoken to Willow since the opening?"

Meredith looked up at him, eyes watery, bloodshot. "Willow?" she asked. "No. Oh dear." She sighed. "She'll take this especially hard."

Mark and Evie exchanged a glance. *Another dead end*, Evie thought, before wishing she hadn't.

Dead.

End.

Mark said, "Let's go."

Evie glanced again around the flooded space. One of the photographs passed her, floating amid junk-food wrappers and cigarette butts, relegated now to garbage.

She took a step forward and stopped.

A few feet in front of her, beneath the gray water, something purple winked at her.

She sucked in a breath.

Impossible.

She sloshed forward a few steps, peering through the water.

A small, purple bottle was resting on the gallery floor. Evie shot her hand down, achieving what she'd failed to do last night.

She grabbed the Pretty.

It was intact, dripping wet, now lying innocently in the palm of her hand. Her mind whirred frantically.

It had gone down the gutter, she had seen it.

The gutters that had flooded.

The gutters that had vomited their insides onto the street, flooding the gallery. Quickly, before Meredith wondered what she was staring at, she slipped the Pretty back into her pocket and sloshed forward.

Krista and Mark stood on the street corner, tipping water out of their shoes silently.

The return to the apartment would be unbearably tense . . .

"Evie?" A voice spoke her name, so low and lyrical that it almost sounded unreal.

Willow stood on the other edge of the water, looking like a ghost in her long black dress.

"Willow!" Evie started running toward her, hearing Krista and Mark cry out too, their feet smacking the concrete as all three of them raced for her. "Willow!"

Evie threw her arms around the girl in violent relief, squeezing until Willow let out a cry. Evie felt like laughing and crying, and when she pulled back she realized she was doing both.

"Willow!" Krista screeched like a chimpanzee, leaping onto them, and the three rocked, almost toppling.

"You're alive, thank god you're alive," Evie kept gasping. She held Willow by her shoulders, only now realizing how ruined her dress was.

"Dude, where are your shoes?" Krista stared at Willow's scratched, red bare feet.

Willow shook her head, eyes brimming, trying to smile. "I've always hated high heels."

"We've been looking for you all day," Evie babbled. "We thought you were— Where were you?"

Willow's eyes turned inward, and she shivered slightly. When she met Evie's gaze, her voice sounded fortified. "Somewhere I'm not going again."

Evie had one hand on Willow, one hand on Krista, and as she stood there, still panting, still trying to tame her breath, she realized each of them was clinging on to the other two. All three of them were wet and muddy and flushed. And for the first time since it all started, they were all Regular. Reborn, once again, having survived the storm.

Willow's gaze shifted over the girls' shoulders.

Mark was standing behind their trio. His face was white.

Evie threaded her fingers into Krista's, "We'll wait on the corner for you."

Evie tugged Krista away, leaving Mark and Willow to face each other.

For several long moments, they both just stood there. *I ruined it*, Willow thought. *I had it, and then I burned it down.*

"You scared me, Will," Mark said. "You really fucking scared me."

Willow bit down slowly on her bottom lip. He was such a good person, and she'd poisoned him. "I know."

Mark took a step forward, unsure. "Sometimes I think loving you makes me sick, you know? That there's something wrong with me."

In a voice that didn't ask for pity, that was simply stating the truth, she said, "I am sick."

Mark nodded, continuously, before drawing in a breath and blowing it out. His shoulders relaxed. The tension started to visibly drain from his body. He was looking at her as though he seemed to really see her. As if he knew her better than she knew herself. He said, "Then maybe we can be sick together."

And then he held out his hand.

75

Evie was waiting for the lights to change when the construction workers began catcalling her.

"Hey, sexy! Give us a smile!"

"C'mon, honey! One little smile."

Evie stared straight ahead, hoping her nonreaction would be enough to make them stop.

"Oh, come on, love!"

"Smile for the man!"

Her fingernails bit into her palm. The men wolf-whistled, laughing.

"C'mon, baby! Hey! Hey—"

"Jesus Christ, shut the fuck up!" Evie whirled on them. "I am trying to make the world a better place for your *daughters*. So they won't be harassed in the street by jerks like you! So the least you can do is show me some goddamn respect!"

The two men looked completely taken aback. They were both in their forties, slightly overweight, wearing scruffy orange safety vests. "Calm down, honey."

"Yeah, it's a compliment."

"No, it's not!" Evie snapped. "Your attention is unwanted by me, I have given you *no* signs that I want it, I do not encourage it, and deep down, you *know* it makes me uncomfortable." A few people stopped to watch them. "I am a human being, like you. I have problems, like you. So just do me a fucking solid, and *shut the fuck up*." And now she stepped toward the pair, enunciating clearly. "Stop yelling at women in the street. We don't like it." She waved her hands to indicate the small crowd of New Yorkers watching. "*No one likes it.*"

The group broke into scattered applause. The two men shifted, embarrassed. Evie gave them one final glare and crossed the street.

When Evie strolled into the *Salty* offices, there was a stranger sitting at her desk. A freelancer, whom Ella-Mae had hired.

"I didn't know you'd be back today," the girl said apologetically. "No one told me—"

"Evie!" Ella-Mae stood behind them both, holding a stack of glossy page proofs. A strange expression of surprise, relief, and distaste colored her face. "You're back." Around them, girls clicked past in perfectly pressed blouses and matching shades of lipstick. Ella-Mae cocked her head at Evie. "You look . . . different."

Evie regarded her coolly. "Different how?"

"Just . . . different. Did you change your hair?"

"No."

"Oh." Ella-Mae hesitated for just a moment before handing Evie the printouts. "You can start on these. And I'll need that final copy on the spa feature by noon."

"The what feature?"

"The spa feature," Ella-Mae repeated. "It was due last week."

"Oh, the day-spa thing!" Evie remembered, starting to laugh. "The Arab Spring mix-up." It seemed like a lifetime ago.

"It better be good, because I do not have time to rewrite it today, I'm totally swamped." Ella-Mae wiped an invisible piece of hair away from her face delicately. "And I'm going to need you to type up my notes from the Real Girl feature about the girl who ate nothing but lipstick for a year—"

Evie handed the page proofs back. "First, you can type up your own notes, Ella-Mae. That's actually your job and it's ridiculous I've been doing it for so long. Second, I'm not going to do the spa feature."

Ella-Mae blinked in icy shock. "Why not?"

Evie shrugged, speaking matter-of-factly. "I've got better things to do."

"So." Jan tented her fingers. "What did you want to discuss?"

At first, her boss had been concerned about her absence. When Evie failed to produce a life-or-death situation to have caused said absence, this became annoyance, bordering heavily on suspicion. But justifying her disappearance wasn't why Evie was there. Instead, she'd told Jan she needed to take advantage of the you-can-talk-to-me-about-anything policy. "I've been thinking," Evie said. "About *Salty*. And it being empowering for women."

"Yes?"

"I can't agree. I've thought a lot about it, and I can't agree."

The editor-in-chief's British accent made her response sound neat and formal. "Why not?"

Evie counted her reasons off on her fingers. "One: way too much focus on pleasing dudes. Way. Too. Much. And as someone who is"—Evie drew in a half breath—"bisexual with a chance of gay, it's just not for me."

Jan's tone was unreadable. "Fair enough."

"Two: you can have all the 'you go, girl!' rhetoric you want, but at the end of the day, *Salty*'s ethos is rooted in materialism. You want to be happy? Treat yourself to a new purse. Sexy? Long-lash mascara. Clever? New eyeglass frames. And this shouldn't be surprising, because *Salty* is in the pockets of its advertisers. And that's not just bad for the meager earnings most of our readers make. Studies prove people who pursue wealth and material possessions tend to be less satisfied, more unhappy. We think buying things will make us feel better, but it won't." Evie lifted her palms up. "Consumerism is a drug. Magazines are enablers."

Jan looked amused, as if Evie were a pet who'd learned a new trick. "I don't know if I'd go that far."

"I would," Evie said. "And this brings me to point three. Why are readers so susceptible to buying all the sh—stuff in these pages? Because they don't look like this." Evie picked up a copy of the new issue that had come out while she'd been away. On the cover, Selena Gomez puckered candy-pink lips into a kiss, one finger curled around an aggressively glossy tendril of hair. "Or this." She flipped it open to a random page: three laughing girls in bikinis by a pool. Stomachs as hard as shields. Chewing-gum-commercial smiles. "Or this." Another page: a beautifully sad girl staring out a window, hands clasped gently around a cup of tea. "*Salty* is still insanely prescriptive when it comes to body image and pretty faces. It's clear skin, big tits, white is right, look like a preteen, fuck like a porn star. And sure, our readers know these images are Photoshopped, they know these girls are models. But I don't think we acknowledge just how easy it is to internalize these messages. That *this* is pretty. And regular people are ugly."

Jan's expression had hardened a little. "That's certainly a unique perspective."

"I don't think it is unique."

"Regardless, I think I've heard—"

"No, please. I really need to get this off my chest." Evie leaned forward intently. "I think a lot of women view themselves as unattractive when they're not. They're just regular. But this is what I can't stop thinking about." She leveled her gaze at Jan. "One in three women on this planet is beaten, abused, or raped. One in *three*. That's over a billion women."

"I'm aware of the statistics." Jan's voice was becoming progressively steelier.

Evie picked up the new issue, reading the cover lines. "'*MEOW! Meet Your Inner Bad Girl!*' '*Is Facebook KILLING Your Sex Life?*'" Evie dropped the magazine. "Is this helping? Is this addressing that? I know we run the odd anti–sexual harassment story, but in the scheme of things, I don't think it is helping."

"All right, Evie. No need to make a fool of yourself—"

"*Salty* pretends feminism is over: we won, so now we can be fuck-puppets with no consequences—"

"Evie, I said, *enough*."

"But that's just not true!" It was only now Evie realized her heart was racing, her insides bubbling with adrenaline. Jan was telling her to stop but she couldn't. "I can't devote my energy to it anymore. I respect myself too much. I quit."

Jan sat rigidly in her chair. Her expression had become so sharp she looked like she could cut something. "After that little speech, I can't say I'm sorry to see you go." Evie could hear the metal in her voice. "And don't even ask about a letter of recommendation. Or a job anywhere in this building."

Evie absorbed the blow without flinching, her body still fizzing with the thrill of unfiltered honesty. She nodded, bloodlessly, like they'd just settled a particularly dull business transaction. The office was deathly silent as she got to her feet. But at the doorway, she paused. Evie Selby would usually escape quickly and quietly after something so caustic. But Chloe had taught her just how to push the envelope when it came to getting what you want. "I have one last question. In the auditions for *Extra Salt*, the day before you met my roommate, why didn't you ask me?"

"Ask you what?"

"To audition. We'd just seen Tiffany or Brittany or someone, and you asked if I knew anyone. Why didn't you give me the chance to audition?" Evie braced herself. Part of her didn't want to hear this. But another part of her had to know.

Jan narrowed her eyes, and for a second Evie thought she'd refuse to answer. But to her surprise, Jan said, "I seem to recall that I did. I asked if you knew anyone. You said you didn't."

Evie blinked in surprise, playing back the memory. Jan asking her if she knew anyone they should get in. Evie saying they should audition her roommate.

"If you want something," Jan continued, "you have to speak up." She arched an eyebrow at Evie meaningfully. "The world doesn't owe you any favors. But it will bend to your will."

Evie nodded. "Okay. Thanks."

"Now kindly get the fuck out of my office." Jan's smile was predatory. "I have a magazine to run."

76.

The grounds of Columbia University were distinguished but relaxed, like an elder statesman at a tea party. The fall term had yet to commence, so only a handful of students dotted the tidy campus. Willow rarely came this far uptown. Everything seemed raw and hard and bright, but she was making an effort to relax, to stay calm, to breathe. A girl wearing baggy overalls and a messy topknot directed her to the Cinema Studies Department.

To say Claire looked shocked when Willow tapped nervously on her office door was an understatement of gigantic proportions. The pencil that'd been lodged between her lips clattered onto her desk. "Willow!"

"Sorry." Willow hung limply in the doorway. "Hope I'm not interrupting."

"No! No, I was just, uh, preparing my lecture notes. Come in, please."

The office was tiny, walled up by floor-to-ceiling bookshelves. There wasn't really room for the three potted plants that crowded the space, but they were there anyway. Claire swiped a chair free of a stack of notes and an empty sushi box. "Have a seat."

Willow sat, positioning her small backpack under the chair. The script she'd been rehearsing on the subway vanished. Maybe this was a mistake.

"It's good to see you." Claire licked her lips, eyes darting. "Can I get you something? There's a coffee machine in the hall—"

"No, thanks." Willow met Claire's concerned, confused gaze. "I just wanted to say I'm sorry."

Claire's face twitched in surprise. "Oh, Willow. You don't have to—"

"No, I do," Willow said. "I've been really unfair. My dad and you . . . I think you're good for him. I know you're good for him," she corrected herself. "You make him happy. And, I guess he makes you happy too."

Claire's cheeks colored pink. "Yes, he does. I love your dad, Willow."

Willow nodded, her hair falling into her eyes until she tucked it behind her ears. "I know." She shifted in her chair, trying to sound confident. Mature. "I'm moving out."

"Oh. Oh, that's . . . uh . . ."

"Good." Willow supplied for her, smiling. "That's good. I mean, I'm twenty-two. It's time."

"Can you afford it?"

Willow nodded. She'd sold a staggering forty-eight prints at her opening. Even though the flood had ruined her exhibition, she could still print pictures from the computer files. The combined total would be enough to find a decent studio somewhere in Manhattan, for at least a year. But this news wasn't the real reason she'd come. "Have you spoken to my dad?"

Claire gave a small, sympathetic sigh. "I have. He told me about your argument."

"Does he hate me?"

"Hate you? No. I think he's worried more that you hate him."

Willow hugged her arms around herself. "I don't hate him."

The window in Claire's office looked over a small leafy courtyard where a few students sat reading in the late-afternoon sunlight, sipping iced coffees. It was calm here. Peaceful. Willow wondered if Columbia had a photography program, and how hard it would be to get in. "What are you doing tomorrow night?" Willow asked.

"Tomorrow night? Nothing."

"I was thinking, maybe we could get some food. You, me, and Dad."

Claire's face lifted. *She has a nice face*, Willow thought. You could tell she was smart. "I'd really like that, Willow. Yes."

"I'll make a reservation somewhere." Willow stood quickly, wanting to leave before she changed her mind. "I should let you get back to work." She shouldered her backpack, turning to leave, surprised to realize it was almost reluctantly that she did so. "Does it ever get any easier?"

"Does what get any easier?"

Willow shrugged, tracing the doorframe with a fingertip. "Just . . . everything." Life. The world. Other people.

Claire tapped her pencil against her desk, a *rat-tat-tat* of firing synapses. "I don't know if it gets easier. But I think you get better at dealing with it."

Willow hoped this was true. It had to be. "See you back at the apartment."

The hallway was empty when she walked down it. But strangely, she didn't feel alone.

77.

Greetings Snarksters,

I'm baaaack. Lock up your daughters.

~~I'm sure you're wondering where~~ I bet you never even noticed that I've been MIA for the past month or so. And I'd love to tell you that was because I contracted some supercool rare disease or they finally discovered that I am the Lindbergh baby, but the truth is . . . I was Having A Grand Adventure. Here's what I learned:

1. Love lifts you up where we belong, but it can also break you into teeny, tiny pieces, and then you need your best friend and a bunch of wine to put you back together again.
2. People listen to you if you're confident.
3. Standing up for what you believe is supercalifragi— You get it.
4. The world will bend to your will, if you tell it to.
5. My soul is not a piece of coal. It is a jackalope.

That's all for now. I'll post something proper soon.

Your friend and savior,

Madame Snark

Evie posted it and switched off her phone.

She was sitting in the front of Frankie's Gin Joint, a local bar she'd only ever been to at night. Dappled afternoon light patterned the worn wooden bench that faced the street. She was the only person there. On the stool next to her was a plastic crate containing all her work crap. Drinking a beer on a Monday afternoon felt downright indulgent. Almost reckless. Definitely free.

In front of her sat a small white box, just a few inches wide. It had been sent up from the studio for Chloe Fontaine, left on Evie's desk to pass on to her "roommate." Evie was a little nervous opening it, afraid of what parting shot Kelly might take at her.

Nestled on a bed of white satin was a card printed with neat cursive.

For when you're feeling beautiful.
—MARCELLO

Underneath the card was a weighty gold tube. Lipstick. She smiled. It was the perfect shade of red.

Her phone chimed. A text. From Velma.

I'm sure you don't want to see or hear from me right now, and that's understandable. I just want to say I'm sorry. I never planned to hurt you. I should have been clearer from the beginning that I'm not in the position to be in a relationship right now.

Please know you are delightful, and I'm glad for the time we spent together. And if you'd ever like to get a no-strings-attached drink, you have my number.

A few seconds later, she texted again.

P.S. I forgot to tell you: I spent a few hours reading your sister's blog last week. She's a great writer. I have a friend, Mia, who's interested in it. Here's her cell. Tell her I sent you.

Each time Evie read the messages, a new emotion washed through her. At first, hurt. The sharp sting of rejection, the slow pang of sadness.

Then dark amusement: the nerve of suggesting a "no-strings-attached drink"!

And finally, curiosity.

Who was Mia?

Ordinarily, Evie would use Mia's cell number to Google stalk her, playing detective until she found a last name, read everything she could about her, develop a series of anxieties about the phone call that would have to be workshopped in depth with Krista, before making the call three days later with two separate plans of attack.

But today, she just tapped on the number. A woman's voice answered on the third ring. "This is Mia."

"Mia, hi, my name's Evie Selby. Velma Wolff passed your number on to me. She mentioned you were interested in my blog, *Something Snarky*."

"Evie! I'm glad you called. Yes, Velma turned me on to you." Mia sounded efficient and warm at the same time. "I'm a fan. Very funny, very feisty. Lots of potential."

Evie warmed with pleasure. As her blog was anonymous, she rarely received a compliment about it. "Thanks."

"My partners and I are launching a new website that focuses on female op-eds. Smart, fresh, opinionated. We're looking to work with a dozen writers from a range of backgrounds who all have a unique perspective on everything from what's happening in the White House to what white privilege looks like today. It's a paid gig, livable wage. And we'd love to make you one of our signature columnists."

Evie blinked. "Okay."

"We want each writer to build up their own following, have their own brand, but united under our umbrella," Mia continued. "And we want a combination of written pieces and video content."

The clumsy, bewildered excitement that'd been growing in Evie's chest stopped short. "Wait, what?"

"Video content," Mia repeated. "I know *Something Snarky* is anonymous, but if you work for us, you can't be. We want Evie Selby unmasked."

"But . . . you don't even know what I look like."

Mia let out a confused half laugh. "That really doesn't matter. So what do you say? Like I said, I'm a fan. I'd love to email you a contract and have it back by the end of the day."

Evie closed her eyes. Her heart was hammering. Her palms were sticky with sweat. It was everything she wanted, suddenly, on the other end of the phone with a woman who sounded like she had a mortgage and was vaguely important. How could it be that easy? It couldn't be as good as it seemed. Could it?

But beyond the suspicious nature of serendipity: being on the internet, a public person? People would hate her, just like they hated Chloe Fontaine.

"Evie? Are you still there?"

"Yes, give me a minute. I'm just trying to think."

"Okay. But I don't have all day."

Evie sat back in her chair, and for a second Chloe's brazen yet proper sort of posture came back to her in a feline sweep of confidence.

Chloe didn't really care about the haters: not really. She was too busy getting shit done. And, Evie had to admit, she was quite fond of her supporters. It was fun seeing so many smart, funny people reblog and tweet about her red-carpet stunt at the Arzners.

Well, maybe I'll do it for those kinds of people, Evie thought. That seemed like a pretty good audience. Hell, she could even reintroduce Chloe's presence on the net. After all, Chloe was her roommate or her sister (depending on who you asked). She'd always be there to help.

"No."

"No?"

"I won't sign a contract without first coming in to meet you and the team. I need a clear understanding of what kind of creative control I have and how much exposure I'll get. And I'll want to negotiate my wage and benefits."

Mia was silent. Evie felt very still as she waited for her to respond, as if the world were holding its breath. Mia chuckled. "Evie, I have a feeling we're going to get along just fine. I'll get my assistant to set a lunch up for us. I'm sure we can work out a package that suits us both." She clicked off.

Evie stared at her phone in disbelief. Just like that. Just. Like. That. Five minutes ago she had been unemployed. But now, maybe things had changed. Maybe that phone call was a door that led places she'd never dreamed of, to a future she could be excited about . . .

"Can I get you another?" A waitress had her hand on Evie's empty glass.

Evie felt a bang of recognition, a quick flick of adrenaline. It was Quinn.

"Oh!" Quinn's eyes widened. "Hi."

"Hi," Evie said. "I guess you remember me."

Quinn smiled charmingly, a blush coloring her cheeks. "Didn't you lie to me about working for the *New York Times*?"

Evie made a face, and nodded. "Really gunning to be your worst first date of 2016. Am I in the lead?"

"Mmm." Quinn waved her hand around as if to say *so-so*. "I've been on some pretty bad ones, so—"

"I have a lot of competition, got it," Evie said, and they both laughed. "How are you?" Evie asked, noticing as she did how pretty Quinn's eyes were: a light caramel brown. "How's the music thing going?"

"It's going," Quinn said. "I get out there. I sing my songs." She pretended to play a guitar. "People talk during most of it, but I think I'm getting through to them."

"Is that your invisible guitar?" Evie asked, pointing at where Quinn had just been miming one.

"Oh this? Yup, that's it." Quinn nodded, mock-serious. "Not so great with the sound, but so easy to transport." She mimed throwing it behind the bar. Evie giggled, remembering Quinn was funny, as well as cute. "What about you? How's *Salty*?"

She remembered, Evie thought in surprise. "Actually, I just quit."

"No shit."

"Yup. Officially fun-employed."

"That explains the day-drinking," Quinn suggested, and Evie nodded. "I'm going to get you another beer, on the house."

She took Evie's empty glass. Evie watched her pull another beer, realizing as Quinn returned with it that she'd been watching her do so with a weird smile on her face the whole time. It wasn't just that Quinn was really cute. It was the fact Quinn had a weird smile on her face too.

"There you go," Quinn said. "One 'Good work on not working' beer."

"Thanks." Evie took a sip without tasting it.

Quinn tapped her palms together, looking unsure whether to keep hanging around.

Evie definitely wanted her to. "Look, I'm just going to say this," she said. "I'm really sorry for lying to you. I was in a not-great place. But I've had a very . . . transformative month. And I don't think I need to"—Evie cocked her head, searching for the right phrase—"disguise myself anymore."

"What happened in your transformative month?"

"I kind of got my heart broken," Evie said. "A little bit."

"That sucks." Quinn made an empathetic face.

"Yes, and no. It was one of those 'what not to do' scenarios."

"I've been in a few of those."

"But it's over now," Evie said. "And . . . I'm excited for what might come next."

"Cool." They stared at each other until they both realized they were staring at each other, and looked away, exhaling embarrassed laughter.

"I better let you get back to your day-drinking," Quinn said, seeming reluctant. "It was great seeing you again—"

"Can I take you out?" Evie blurted. "Or . . . however the kids are saying it these days. Take you on a date? No more lies. Scout's honor."

Quinn ducked her gaze to her hands. When she looked up again, she was grinning goofily. "I'd like that."

"If you give me your number, I will call you," Evie said. "That way I don't have to message you through the app."

"Oh, good idea." Quinn dug out a pen from her pocket and flipped a beer coaster. Her pen poised above it.

"Second thoughts?" Evie teased.

Quinn shook her head, and started scribbling. "No. I just forgot my cell number for a minute." She handed the coaster to Evie. "There you go."

"Thank you. And thanks for the beer."

Quinn nodded, twisting a few strands of hair around her fingertip. "So I'll . . . see you later."

"Definitely." Evie nodded. "Without a doubt."

Quinn gave Evie one final smile before turning back in the direction of the bar.

Evie picked up Marcello's gold lipstick and rolled it between her fingers. She would wear it on her first date with Quinn. Not because she had to. Because she wanted to. Because Quinn made Evie feel like she'd just been given a book that she'd always wanted to read.

Evie's gaze dropped to the coaster. Next to her name and number, Quinn had drawn a tiny heart.

78.

Evie, Willow, and Krista sat side by side on the couch, silently regarding the only thing on the coffee table.

The Pretty.

"How's everything going with Mark?" Evie asked Willow tentatively.

Willow was silent for a minute. "We're taking it one day at a time. He's still pretty freaked out by everything. But . . . I'm going to fight for him."

It was such an unusual thing for Willow to say that Evie and Krista traded a glance. "That's great, Will." Evie reached over to squeeze her hand. "That's really great."

Their attention returned, inevitably, to the Pretty.

"Would you do it again?" Evie asked. "Knowing what you know now?"

Willow shuddered. "No way. Taking that was the biggest mistake I've ever made."

"At least you'll keep New York's legions of therapists employed for a few decades," Evie offered, and Willow smiled. "And maybe you shouldn't just talk to them," Evie added. "Maybe you should talk to us more too."

Apprehension flitted around Willow's face, but then she nodded, resolute. "Okay. I will."

Evie turned to her roommate. "What about you, Kris?"

Krista took an uncharacteristically long moment to answer. "It was good for me," she said finally. "In the way prison might be. Oh, check it out!" She held up her phone. On the screen was a banking app. Krista tapped at the most recent deposit. From Creative Professionals United:

$9,315. "A partial payment from *Funderland*! So I can pay our bills and get ahead with rent. I know it's not everything, but it's a start, right?"

"Definitely," Evie told her. "Nailed it, Kris. I'm really proud of you."

Evie noticed a package at Krista's feet, addressed to Lenka Penka. "What's this?" She fished around into the bubble wrap and pulled out a gold trophy, shaped like a bald little man. Krista handed her a small card. It read, *No hard feelings.—T.*

"Oh, is this from Tristan?" Evie asked, impressed. Then she remembered what exactly this trophy had been used for. She dropped it hastily back into the box, wiping her hand on the couch. "That's nice of him."

"Yeah, I know. He sent it to Cameron. Which kind of gave me an idea." Krista glanced at the girls. "Maybe I'll try becoming an agent."

"An acting agent?" Willow asked, and Krista nodded.

"Really?" Evie said. "That's cool."

"Right?" Krista sat up. "I'm a people person, and I love doing contracts and negotiations and shit. I don't think I want to be an actor, but I like them. I get them. It would get my parents off my back. Maybe I can even use Lenka to help set up a few meetings."

"That actually seems like a really good idea, Kris," Evie said, trying not to sound surprised.

"What about you, Evie?" Willow asked. "Would you do it all again?"

Evie regarded the purple bottle sitting innocently on the coffee table. "I don't know," she said. "Maybe . . . yes? In a weird way, I think it helped. I think it helped me feel better about myself," she said. "But at the same time . . . I just really want to think less about my face right now. You know?"

Willow and Krista both nodded.

"Given that," Evie said, "there's just one more thing we need to do."

The three girls stood in the bathroom. Evie unscrewed the bottle slowly, ceremoniously. She met Willow's, then Krista's gaze in the mirror. *One drop. One week.* "Ready?"

Willow nodded, certain.

Krista followed suit.

Evie turned the bottle over. The brilliant purple liquid spilled out, running in a lilac stream to gurgle down the sink. It only took a few seconds before the Pretty was finally, absolutely gone.

They stared at the empty bottle, each girl lost in the memory of where it had taken them.

Krista broke their respective reveries with a loud sigh. "Oh well." She smacked her lips together. "Do you guys feel like pizza?"

In the living room, Krista workshopped pizza toppings while Willow decided on a playlist. Evie opened a bottle of sauvignon blanc in the kitchen and filled two glasses and one coffee mug. *Note to self: buy fancy wineglasses with first paycheck.*

The evening was muggy—summer was lingering in Brooklyn like a bad houseguest. Cold air billowed out from the freezer when she yanked it open. Evie was expecting to find the ice cube tray empty: the Krista Kumar special.

It was full.

Wonder of wonders, Krista had filled it. Evie felt a deep swell of affection for the former Lenka Penka.

It was only after she cracked out some cubes and plopped them into the glasses that she remembered the photograph. She'd printed it out at a pharmacy on her way home. She stuck it onto the fridge with a cartoon fish magnet. The glossy image, and the moment it captured, flooded her with warmth.

In it, the three girls were in the middle of someone's loft in Bushwick, just before they realized they'd drunk entirely too much tequila. Krista and Willow were both laughing at something Evie had evidently just said. Evie had a dry smirk on her face. Willow's and Krista's mouths were both open, eyes squinty.

They didn't have the wow factor of their Pretty selves. But comparing the beauty of Chloe and Lenka and Caroline to the beauty of Evie Selby and Krista Kumar and Willow Hendriksen was like comparing strawberry-flavored bubble gum to actual strawberries. All the things being Chloe promised her—sexual sophistication, charm, a voice that demanded to be heard, self-respect—Evie Selby could have. She was sure of it. They might not be their ideal, cookie-cutter, fantastical selves anymore. But they could be themselves. And they could try to be compassionate and clever and curious about everything, especially when it came to each other. And especially when it came to being a woman in this world. That sounded beautiful.

Honey-colored light glowed through the kitchen window. But the storybook summer evenings would soon be coming to an end. Evie could almost feel a shift in the weather.

She should call her mom.

But only after a glass of wine. After all, they were celebrating.

Acknowledgments

What a pleasure to be able to acknowledge the endlessly enthusiastic and superbly sharp-eyed Megan Reid, my wonderful editor at Emily Bestler Books. Working with you and the warm, wise Emily B., as well as Hillary Tisman, Kathryn Santora, Matthew Rossiter, Lara Jones, Albert Tang, and Judith Curr's entire team at Atria/Simon & Schuster is a dream come true. I'll be forever grateful that you all fell in love with my Regulars as much as I did.

I owe so much to everyone at Sanford J. Greenburger Associates, especially my intrepid, patient, in-all-ways-kickass agent, Chelsea Lindman, and rights director Stefanie Diaz. I am so thankful for your belief in me: we did it! Let's go get a cheese plate.

Sarah Cypher: *you* are my secret weapon. I worked with Sarah, who runs The Threepenny Editor, on two drafts prior to submission, and her brilliant editorial feedback transformed *The Regulars* from a rambling hot mess into a coherent hot mess. Authors—hire this brain before you submit, trust me!

Thanks to my exceptional beta readers: Alexandra Collier, Peter Neale, Sarah Oakes, Alecia Simmonds, and Nora Tennessen. These trusted friends are all accomplished creatives in their own right—Google them.

I raise my smoothie to Jason Richman and Johnny Pariseau at UTA:

thanks for falling for *The Regulars* and pitching it as a "feminist fairy tale" (I'm claiming that idea as my own: all good authors are just talented thieves). Thanks also to Addison Duffy for important enthusiasm.

Kisses for my awesome early blurbers: Brenda Bowen, Caroline Kepnes, Elisabeth Egan, Maggie Grace, Sara Shepard, and Scott Westerfeld; for Claire Elizabeth Terry and Juliet Blake for the Rocaberti Writers' Retreat scholarship in a fourteenth-century Spanish castle; and for Ms. Allen for Year 12 English. (Gosford High, what's up?!)

Thanks to everyone who answered my research questions about everything from film sets to law school jargon. I am always wowed by how generous friends and strangers alike are with their knowledge.

Shout-out to the team at the New York Writers' Room and to Justen Ahren at the Martha's Vineyard Writers Residency for providing calming writer-centric places to create.

Mum and Dad, I love you so much. Thank you for always letting me read at the dinner table, on family holidays, in my countless baths, etc. William and Louise, the fact we both created a plucky young heroine in the same year named Evie is cause for so much celebration!

My friends in Sydney, New York, and LA are all outstanding humans with golden hearts and oversized brains: thanks for the giggles, dummies.

And finally, I acknowledge my partner in life, crime, and love: Lindsay. My sweet girl, you inspire me every day with your endless love for everyone around you. You are the kindest, quirkiest, most fun person I know. You gave me a heart, and it will always be yours. Thank you for loving me.

BANYAN TREE
~ VABBINFARU ~

WIN A HOLIDAY OF A LIFETIME AT BANYAN TREE VABBINFARU IN THE MALDIVES!

Included in the prize:

- A seven night stay at Banyan Tree Vabbinfaru in a Beachfront Pool villa for two people
- Full board basis, incl. soft drinks, excl. alcohol
- Return transfers from Male to Banyan Tree Vabbinfaru
- Two × return economy flights from London to Male up to a value of £700 per person
- Trip to be taken between 1 November 2017 and 30 April 2018 Blackout dates include 27 December 2017 – 5 January 2018